I0747041

THE ANGELIC ANNIVERSARY SHOW

A GAME OF LOST SOULS

BOOK TWELVE

LISA SILVERTHORNE

AWARD-WINNING BESTSELLING AUTHOR

LISA SILVERTHORNE

THE ANGELIC ANNIVERSARY SHOW

A GAME OF 12 LOST SOULS

A supervillain in chains.
Emboldened archangel treachery.
A Heavenly tribunal convenes.

Will Jack and Talia lose everything?
As the Maker decides Lucifer's fate.
And theirs.

As their first wedding anniversary approaches and ratings on the show plummet, Talia and Jack are summoned to testify at Lucifer's tribunal. But when a group of archangels openly protests their forbidden relationship–and Jack's angel powers–Talia and Jack find themselves on trial.

But the erratic behavior of the Archangel of Wrath prosecuting the case causes chaos as disgruntled archangels grows bolder, threatening to seize power and unleash a forever war between Heaven and Hell as a new villain rises in the shadows of judgment and whispers of Armageddon echo across the Heavens.

THE ANGELIC ANNIVERSARY SHOW

Copyright © 2025 by Lisa Silverthorne

Published by ElusiveBlueFiction.com

2709 N Hayden Island Dr

STE 354914

Portland OR 97217

United States of America

Cover Design, Book Layout, and Character Renders by Lost Souls Studio

Cover Imagery by Benny Productions, Brusheezy, Creative Market, Deposit Photos, HWWO Stock

Elusive Blue Fiction Logo designed by Samantha Romage

Printed and bound by IngramSpark.

Australia: Ingram Content Group AU Pty Ltd, Melbourne, Victoria. *US:* Lightning Source LLC, La Vergne, Tennessee / Allentown, Pennsylvania / Jackson, Tennessee, United States. *UK:* Lightning Source UK Ltd, Milton Keynes, United Kingdom. *Europe:* Lightning Source UK Ltd, with facilities in Germany, France, and Spain.

The EU GPSR Authorized EU Representative is:

Lightning Source UK Ltd, 1-3 Deltic Avenue, Rooksley, Milton Keynes, MK13 8LW, United Kingdom (email: info@lightningsource.co.uk) Lightning Source UK Ltd, with facilities in Germany, France, and Spain.

All rights reserved.

This work, or parts of this work, may not be reproduced in any form without prior written permission from the publisher, except brief quotations for review purposes.

This is a work of fiction. Any resemblance to actual persons, places, or events is merely coincidental.

ISBN: 978-1-955197-72-4 (Hardcover)

ISBN: 978-1-955197-71-7 (Trade paperback)

Novels by Lisa Silverthorne

Standalones:

ISABEL'S TEARS

LANDFALL

PACIFIC BLUE TATTOO

A Game of Lost Souls series:

THE CINDERELLA HOUR

THE PRINCE CHARMING HOUR

THE EVER AFTER HOUR

THE FALLEN HEARTS SEASON

THE RISING SPIRITS SEASON

THE ETERNAL SOULS SEASON

THE ROYAL WEDDING HOUR

THE HEAVENLY HONEYMOON HOUR

THE DIVINE NEWLYWEDS SHOW

THE CELESTIAL COUPLES SHOW

THE ENOCHIAN APOCALYPSE SHOW

THE ANGELIC ANNIVERSARY SHOW

Curse and Crown series:

THORN & BLADE

STORM & STEEL

The Spiral series:

BETWEEN

REPRISE

AVENGE

The Resurrectionist Papers

GRAVE RECKONING

Short Story Collections

THE SOUND OF ANGELS

THE MAGIC OF ORDINARY THINGS

TIMELESS

WINTER'S EMBRACE

Science Fiction Writing as L.S. Silverthorne

Standalones:

REDISCOVERY

Experiencing True Purple series:

RECOMBINANT, Book 1

HELIX, Book 2

SPLICE, Book 3

FORTHCOMING!

A Game of Lost Souls series:

The Perdition Picture Show, Book Thirteen (Series End)

Curse and Crown series:

Flame & Dagger, Book Three

Frost & Foil, Book Four

Curse & Crown, Book Five (Series End)

The Spiral series:

Ruin, Book 4

Descent, Book 5 (Series End)

The Resurrectionist Papers:

Corpses Delicti

Stiffed Again

Cease and Deceased

SCIENCE FICTION WRITING AS L.S. SILVERTHORNE

Experiencing True Purple series:

Cipher, Book 4

Renascence, Book 5 (Series End)

1

JACK NEVER DREAMED THAT HE, TALIA, AND HIS FRIENDS COULD SHUT down the apocalypse payloads of all seven Hell Princes. Or reach Heaven's Throne room in time to confront Lucifer and stop him from killing the Maker. Jack never expected to survive the King of Hell's all-out assault on Heaven and Creation—much less take Lucifer prisoner. At full power.

Jack even lived to see his twenty-seventh birthday. With Talia still beside him.

But that deep, burning dread still roiled in his gut like bad gas station pizza.

This wasn't over yet. Not by a long shot.

He'd actually stood in the presence of the most supreme being in the universe. Now, he felt like three-day-old Sesame Chicken, microwaved too many times.

Fridge light burned against the set trailer's dim lighting as he stared into the stainless-steel abyss, the chill reminding him he'd survived the apocalypse and was still alive—and hungry.

He scowled at his mostly empty fridge, staring at the old red and white cardboard container marked Sesame Chicken—the only thing in there besides two bottles of local microbrew and six cans of Coke

Zero. Gianni and Banks had given him the beer. Ironically called Lucifer's Rage and Apocalypse Ale. Dudes both had wicked senses of humor. But after dealing with Lucifer for so long and his Hell Princes, Jack found nothing funny about the apocalypse or the King of Hell.

Nothing at all.

Even though he and Talia defeated that douchebag, Jack knew that by bringing Lucifer down, he may have doomed his marriage to Talia. Every angel and demon in Creation knew about their relationship now, reminding the Maker of their ongoing forbidden relationship.

The fridge alarm startled him, screeching like the entire world would burn unless he closed that door. Growling, he slammed the door shut. He'd just watched the entire world seconds from burning and it sure as hell didn't look anything like warm beer and an open fridge door.

Saving the world was a thankless job—especially for a soon-to-be out-of-work actor who'd married an angel of death despite their forbidden relationship. Along the way, angels, archangels, seraphim— even the Maker and their Scribe—let them stay together. Unofficially sanctioning their relationship. Allowing it to deepen and grow. Now that all of Heaven and Hell knew, the Maker suddenly wanted to address it. Before all of Heaven.

Nothing good could come out of that, but he had to hold onto a flicker of hope anyway.

Talia was the one thing he couldn't lose. And he had nothing else to give.

Now that his show was in trouble, he'd probably lost all the ground he'd gained with his mother, too. She'd have nothing to do with him now that the popularity of his show was waning. Without his fame—and fortune—he'd be uninvited from family holiday dinners again.

He smiled. A small price to pay for stopping the apocalypse.

He opened the lacquered grey kitchen cabinets one by one, finding them all empty, not even some stale goldfish crackers or a bag of microwave popcorn left. It's not like the apocalypse had left him any time to get some groceries delivered.

God, he was starving after his early morning set call and filming all the last-minute shots leading up to the finale of *The Celestial Couples Show*. So much of the show had been interrupted by the apocalypse. The rest of the cast knew. They'd helped him make up excuses and back up his reschedule requests for his and Talia's couple's spots.

Images faded into focus on the large television screen mounted on the trailer wall beside the taupe couch. He cringed. Dailies.

Of Rachel's latest onscreen meltdown.

He sighed, beginning to pace at the muffled voices growing louder, his stomach rumbling.

Since he and his Hollywood squad had neutralized the final Hell Prince's payload, the skies had returned to normal and the world had gone a little crazy for a few months. Shooting schedules at the studio got postponed. Whole episodes got delayed until after the new year when the show resumed filming in February.

Over the past couple of months, he and Talia had done enough onscreen home renovation to make his head spin. So had Gianni and Izzy, Banks and Morgan. And Rachel and Eric. Much of that time, though, Talia had been absent from filming. At times, Jack had to remind himself that she still existed, to remember that they were still together by watching videos on his phone. Replaying moments in his head with her. Remembering when they'd been inseparable. When the only place she'd wanted to be was at his side.

"Ow!" Rachel's raspy alto voice echoed through the dimly lit trailer as he continued to stream the dailies on the television screen.

But he couldn't watch what came next as Rachel incited an entire on-set meltdown—with the entire cast. It was the worst one to date and he just couldn't stomach watching it unfold.

He looked away, but the voices still transported him back to this morning's on-set brawl.

"Dammit! Not another one!" Rachel's angry voice was louder, sharper this time.

Hearing the start of her onscreen explosion cut through him like broken glass, especially when he knew what came next. It hurt to watch his hit show—and the cast—coming apart at the seams.

"Let me see, babe." Eric Saunders' calm, patient baritone voice was soothing against the sharp grate of Rachel's tired, raging voice.

A pause.

He winced. Waiting for it. Dude, don't turn around. Don't watch this disaster start again.

"You're okay," said Eric finally in his comforting, smooth voice. "Nothing a manicure can't fix."

"That's the third nail I've broken this week!" Rachel shouted, her shrill voice scraping down's Jack's spine. "I didn't sign on for this. Why can't my stunt double break her nails?"

Stunt double? No one had a stunt double on this show. She was delusional—as always.

"Stunt double?" Izzy's voice was sharp with annoyance, but quiet enough that only the mics picked it up. "Is she serious? Wish they'd replaced her with a stunt double."

Izzy was so over Rachel Daniels. She'd had enough for a lifetime.

He couldn't help it. He turned around. Watching it all unfold again. This time from the objective view of the lens and not from his own point of view. Maybe it wasn't that bad?

He sighed. Like the apocalypse hadn't been *that bad*.

"I don't need a manicure! I need reconstructive hand surgery! This is ridiculous!"

"Don't say it, Izzy," Jack said with a groan. "Please don't say it."

Like his wish for a different outcome would change anything. Yeah, he still had seraphim powers and Talia's rare powers were still mirrored in him. But even if he used them all right at this moment, and somehow changed the outcome of this daily, he couldn't change them all.

Couldn't change the inevitable.

Besides, he'd drained all of his power in the Maker's Throne room when the Rod of Creation absorbed it all, neutralizing the blast and his powers. Drained every last drop. Berith said it would take him some time to regenerate and replenish it all.

He might have just enough juice left to change these dailies, but using them might draw Lucifer's scattered demon army (and the Hell

Princes) back to the studio for another shot at the title. At him. That might include Lare Dumont, Kesien's former death angel squad, and maybe even Archangel Samael.

He couldn't risk that—not for this. It wouldn't change tomorrow's dailies. The day after's dailies. Or the inevitable. Besides, he'd never used his powers for his own gain and he wouldn't start now.

Izzy's commanding alto, evening news anchor voice filled the trailer. Jack pulled in a breath, teeth gritted.

"Can't handle a little hard work for once, Rachel?" Her tone was icy, dripping with frustration. "Don't you have people to do the work for you?"

Jack cringed as onscreen, Rachel screeched out an exasperated shout and lunged at Izzy. They tumbled to the set's dusty maple hardwood and rolled across the sun-drenched living room floor, the set empty of furniture, walls theatre-screen white. He could almost smell the sawdust and the freshly opened cans of paint surrounding a stack of lumber as Rachel and Eric struggled to finish framing in a wall that had been taken down to its studs.

Izzy, in tan coveralls, and Rachel, in pink coveralls, rolled across the hardwood floor, kicking up plumes of sawdust. Rachel tried to hit Izzy who dodged her fists' wild flailing. Jack had faced her in a cage fight down in Hell. Izzy was in over her head. Even with those broken fingernails.

Almost on cue, Jack watched as he entered the frame and threw himself between the two of them. Holding Rachel back. Gianni grabbed hold of Izzy, peach-colored paint daubing his face. He wore tan coveralls like Izzy, a pale blue T-shirt, and dark blue sneakers.

"Stop it!" Gianni shouted.

Jack groaned. Like that's ever stopped a fight?

"Izzy, enough!" Gianni snapped, grabbing his wife around the waist, and hauling her back from Rachel.

And then Eric had Jack around the throat, dragging him back from Rachel who exploded across the set. Lunging at Izzy again.

Banks and Morgan, dressed in sunny yellow coveralls, stepped in front of Rachel who veered left.

Jack wanted to cover his face, to stop watching Eric choke the life out of him onscreen. But he couldn't. He couldn't stop watching as Rachel knocked over five cans of paint that spilled an angry river of turquoise, peach, old gold, glass bottle green, and cornflower blue across the brand-new, just installed maple hardwood floor.

Hardwood flooring that he and Talia had spent an entire evening installing. Board by board. No angel powers or archangel intervention. He couldn't move off the trailer couch for two days afterward.

"Way to help out, Banks!" Gianni shouted, keeping himself between Rachel and Izzy as the paint oozed around his feet.

"Like that was my fault?" Banks replied, stepping over the river of paint. His spiky brown hair and gently lined face were stippled cornflower blue and old gold. "She's too fast."

"Izzy started this, not Mark," Morgan said with a glare at Gianni, her thick brown bangs spattered pale green, hands on her hips. "So, don't be mad at him."

God, it hurt to watch this.

"You're still within reach of a throat punch, Morgan Boyer Banks," Izzy growled, glaring as she faced off with Rachel.

Poor Gianni was sandwiched between Rachel and Izzy as they lunged at each other now. His black hair was disheveled, those warm brown eyes fearful, his Cary Grant poise eroding quickly as Banks and Morgan tried to step over the widening river of paint. To hold back Rachel.

"A…little—help here," said Jack onscreen in a tight voice, gasping, still trying to shove body builder Eric Saunders off him.

Rachel's fiancé outweighed him by a good forty pounds.

Finally, Jack slid out of Eric's headlock and dropped him to the paint-covered hardwood with a punch to the kidney.

In the trailer, Jack held his hands over his face, but he splayed his fingers, unable to look away, watching himself leap across the overturned cans of paint as Rachel did a pivot turn and slipped past Banks. And Gianni.

Tackling Izzy to the hardwood.

Eric lumbered up from the floor and like Hell's linebacker, he slammed between Morgan and Banks.

Paint cans skittered across the floor as Eric surfed through the rainbow of wet paint. Drenching Gianni and Jack as he leaped at Rachel.

Hauling her backward.

Bowling over Jack like a wobbling headpin. And then Izzy.

But Eric slipped, Rachel still in his arms. And the two of them faceplanted into the river of paint.

And then Gianni was in Eric's face as he scrambled to his feet, landing punches. Leaving Rachel and Izzy covered in paint and back at each other's throats again.

Covered in four shades of trending awful turquoise and peach paint, Jack got to his feet, wiping turquoise and gold off his chin and neck.

"Is this how we're rollin' now?" Jack shouted onscreen and everyone froze, surprised at his outburst. "Brawling? At each other's throats now?"

Jack couldn't stand it anymore and turned his back to the television as his voice crackled through the trailer.

"A few months ago, we were unstoppable! We took down the freakin' apocalypse together! Now, we can't even paint a wall without going for each other's jugulars! If this is how this season's gonna end, I'm out."

The sound of his angry footfalls reverberated through the empty living room stage as he stormed off set.

The memory of that moment echoed through his trailer with a heaviness that still sat on Jack's chest.

Those reno moments should have been all laughs slapstick with the smell of pepperoni and onion pizza waiting for them offstage. Back when they'd eat meals together and hang out to watch the dailies. Now, everyone was back to hating each other again, watching the dailies in their trailers, and judging each other like a bunch of angry film critics. Like that first season on *The Cinderella Hour*.

Herb didn't even try to stop it—or send Jennifer or Steve in to stop it. They were all there. Behind the lights and cameras, filming it in brooding silence. None of them said a word or moved in to wrangle the talent while the crew cleaned up the set. He groaned. They'd just given up. Herb was so jaded that he just kept the cameras rolling, hoping for a spark—anything they could edit in, some lightning strike that might keep this show alive for one more season.

Jack stepped into his trailer's kitchen so he couldn't see the screen.

Herb didn't even bother cutting the action. Not once. No, he just let the cameras capture it all, Jennifer and Steve looking pale and frustrated. Like the camera and set crews.

Still seated in his director's chair behind the two main cameras, Herb just shook his head until finally, Rhonda, one of the camera operators, stopped filming.

"That's it," said Rhonda, shaking her head. "I'm done."

"I'm done, too, Herb," said Roy, his jeans, work boots, and sleeveless blue T-shirt dusted with sawdust as he slid the camera off his shoulder and walked off with the sound still recording.

Rhonda, dressed in a red tank top, Doc Martens, and jeans shorts, let a smaller camera slide off her left shoulder as she handed it to Steve. The lens fell onto its side, capturing Rhonda walking beside Roy, his short dark hair greyer. Her blond curly hair was wrapped into a black bandana.

That left one camera still rolling.

None of this was about breaking fingernails. Arguments. Or renovations.

Jack remembered back in the fall when everything had been at stake. He and his costars had been so good together. Unstoppable during the apocalypse. They'd been the best friends he'd ever had, but now that Lucifer's threat was contained, everyone seemed like they'd forgotten what had almost been lost.

Focusing on their own little apocalypse here on set instead. The death of their hit television show.

The show had drastically fallen in the ratings.

And Jack knew what happened next.

All the pandering and posturing on set, the fights, his agent taking longer and longer to return his calls. He'd been here before. Herb's director chair had been vacant for long periods of time, leaving the episodes' completions to Jennifer and Steve. Gianni and Banks spending a ton of time on their phones. Being late to set calls. Absent for several takes.

Avoiding each other—and Jack.

Even the craft services food tables on set had gotten sparse—cheaper. Emptier.

He knew all the signs. Everyone else was in denial. Refusing to accept what came next.

The show had run its course. It was May. Sweeps week. This finale would be their last as a cast. As a series.

And with Heaven's tribunal about to start, it might be the end of Jack's marriage, too. He sucked in a pained breath.

The end of his relationship with Talia.

As the television went dark, Jack sat down on his angelically reconstructed taupe couch that filled the small sitting area in his and Talia's set trailer. Talia's squad of death angels had gotten much better at putting this stuff back together. But the cushions didn't sit quite as high and the furniture squeaked a little when he got up.

The maple wood floors were still a little singed—a few boards out of place. Okay, more than a few boards. No one here at Four Acre Studios would even notice—including director, Herb Rutherford. They'd never know about all the times he'd fought demons inside this brand-new luxury trailer.

Jack smirked. But he would. And it. Was. Awesome!

The trailer's high-end taupe and grey finishes had lost quite a bit of their shine and luster. The L-shaped kitchen's taupe quartz countertop was a little dull, concealing cracks that skittered across the almost indestructible countertop. Almost. Didn't say anything about being demon-tested. Or archangel-approved.

He studied the shiny grey European lacquered cabinets, tilting his head, squinting as he noticed that even now, they still hung a little off center.

He glanced over at the large flat screen television, dark now, mounted on the wall that separated the bedroom from the living space. Yeah, even the television hung at a slight angle. Okay, a little more than slight. A good twelve degrees.

Traces of sulfur still tanged the air, mixed with the chemical stink of new flooring and new cabinets. Along with a touch of ozone and last night's chicken barbacoa street tacos he'd brought back from a food truck because he couldn't stomach re-re-warmed Sesame Chicken again. Or eating alone in the dimly lit trailer, watching some history show about mysteries of the world. Boy, could he tell this host a story or two. Dude would never believe him though. He'd be like that aliens dude only with wild blond hair, holding out his hands, babbling...angels.

The trailer lights sputtered a moment, went dark, and then flickered back on again like a bad, straight-to-DVD horror movie.

Demons? Again? Why didn't this damned fridge make itself useful and screech its alarm when demons were near the trailer instead of its door being open? Warning of demons instead of warm beer. Or, hell... why not both? Now, that was his kind of smart appliance.

Muriel said there were still some electrical issues with the trailer to work out. That was death angel code for Azrael needed to come down and zap everything back the way it was again. Maybe Herb could bring Azrael in to save the show? At least reno hell would be more interesting than just tired, scripted couples' fights and ridiculous faux arguments about nothing. Until they were really fighting about nothing.

Jack rose from the couch and began to pace through the dark, silent trailer.

Who was he kidding?

Nothing could save the show this time. But after what he'd been through during the apocalypse, he was okay with that. He had much bigger problems than wrangling another season of reality television. Like testifying about his relationship with an angel of death before a celestial tribunal—and the Maker. Like saving his marriage. And testifying as a witness for the Heavenly prosecution against The Devil.

No pressure there.

Ever since his birthday, Talia had been acting more and more distant.

She had been spending more and more time in Heaven, dealing with the aftermath of Lucifer's assault. And Lucifer's capture. That added up to about half of every week. But after months of increasingly longer absences, Jack couldn't help but take it personally. Like she was avoiding him. Distancing herself from him. Her husband of almost a year.

Like she knew what was about to happen.

He could have flown up to the lower Heavens and found her, but one of them had to keep the show going. Looking back now, he knew that was just an excuse. He was just as much to blame. He should have ignored his insecurities and gone after her, even if it was just for a moment to tell her that he loved her.

The nights were the worst. Sleeping alone. Wondering if she was even thinking about him up there in Eolowen? Did she know how bad he ached all over when she was away from him? Or how much he hurt when he crawled into that king-size bed alone. Without her beside him?

Now that the apocalypse was over and Lucifer was in custody, was she rethinking her life with him? Was it regret? Or Heaven recalling her to her crossing over souls duties? Maybe she was ready to move on from all of the bad memories she'd gathered from humanity. Bad experiences that all began with him.

Or did she know something he didn't?

She said she was just busy with the rebuilding of High House and the aftermath of losing so many seraphim and angels. With Lucifer's impending trial. With what came next for the death angel guard now that the apocalypse was over.

Jack believed most of it, but he couldn't help feeling the contradictions, too. Her turmoil. And the feeling that she was avoiding him.

When she fell out of the sky during the Sixth flight battle above Earth and had been a breath away from oblivion, her light extinguished, he'd brought her back somehow. And together, with

Azrael and her squad, they'd faced Lucifer, knowing they had almost no chance of winning.

And somehow, they defeated Lucifer. Saved the Maker.

He knew now that's what he had to do with Talia. Fly up there and fight for her, tell her how much he loved her.

But after they defeated Lucifer, he and Talia stood together in front of the Maker, flaunting their forbidden romance to the supreme being who'd declared it forbidden—but had let it alone all this time. Until it became an issue that all of Heaven and Hell knew about it.

Now that Lucifer's tribunal was about to start, Jack knew that he and Talia's relationship would also be on trial.

He winced, remembering how he'd stood in front of the Maker as a living, breathing human with angel wings (that he shouldn't have) spread wide and halo (that wasn't really his) spinning bright. Did it look like he'd been mocking angels? He was a recovering coke addict. A human with seraphim powers and the rarest angel abilities—not an angel. How arrogant that must have looked to all those angels.

It must have supremely pissed off the Maker (and Heaven) and every angel he'd ever encountered when they saw what Jack was…and what he'd become.

Ever since they'd taken Lucifer into custody, Jack had been waiting for the other shoe to drop. Waiting for his own trial.

Waiting for the Maker to separate him and Talia. Or outright smite him for being this abomination of human and angel.

And here on Earth, in his little world, the show's ratings were tanking.

He'd felt it since they started back filming again. Knowing it was the beginning of the end. He'd been preparing for this moment since he'd climbed back on top again. Because, no matter how high that rollercoaster cart climbed, it always dropped before returning to the station.

He could handle the end of his television show. But how did he prepare to lose the love of his life? The woman he couldn't live without? He could lose everything else and survive.

But not Talia.

Were these prolonged absences Talia's way of showing him mercy? Hoping if she was gone long enough, he wouldn't hurt so much when Heaven—and the Maker—returned him to his completely human state again. And life.

Without wings and a halo. Without angel powers. Without his wife?

He was nothing without Talia.

And he was prepared to fight to stay with her at Lucifer's tribunal. Even if the Maker smited him out of existence, he'd still fight for her to his last breath. And if it became his last breath, at least he'd know that he'd given it everything he was, everything he had.

Wherever Talia was right now, he hoped she knew that. Knew that he'd give it all up to stay with her. Everything he had. Everything he was.

If he managed to survive the Maker and this tribunal with his current life intact, his and Talia's first anniversary was coming up. First anniversary as husband and wife. Requiring an amazing first anniversary gift. But what did a dude like him give to his angel of death wife? She had no use for anything a human could give her and she could smite anyone she wanted.

He needed to give her something special. Something that meant a great deal to him. At the party they were having for their anniversary. They'd already sent out invitations inviting all their closest friends-angels, humans, and a demon or two.

The trailer began to shake, warm gold light seeping into the corners and drifting outward until Jack felt like he'd stepped outside without his sunglasses.

He closed his eyes and grabbed hold of the wall, waiting for whatever angel had come to visit him materialized. Unannounced.

That wasn't ominous at all.

"Muriel? That you?" he called out. "You come back with an angel reno crew for this trailer? It really could use an archangel's touch."

Hell, it could use a miracle. Like his shithole studio apartment he was leaving behind this season. He really wanted to win the beach house that he and Talia had been renovating this season. But he'd already bought it ahead of the show's outcome. For him and Talia. Their move-in date was the week of their first anniversary—and the party. They'd live here in the set trailer until then. At least Talia knew this much.

To his surprise, Pravuil, God's Scribe, materialized in front of the couch, dressed in his flowing white robes, crisp white wings tall and unfurled at his shoulders, white-gold halo brighter than set lights. His short white hair was windblown, gold eyes intense.

Jack's face felt hot as the force of Pravuil's entrance sent a burst of warm air rolling past him. Air that smelled like new-fallen rain, sunlight, and jasmine—and a trace of ozone. He bit his lip. Almost like Talia's scent after returning from Eolowen. God, he missed his wife.

"Pravuil!" Jack cried. "How you been?"

Pravuil, angel-tall at six and a half feet, ran his fingers through his thick, shaggy white hair, gold eyes stern—almost hard—as he glared around the trailer in his grumpy eagle-eyed archangel way.

"Jack?"

He sounded surprised. Concerned. That made Jack immediately nervous.

"Something wrong?" Jack asked as he moved in front of God's Scribe.

Was Talia all right?

"Wasn't expecting you to be alone," said Pravuil.

Jack shrugged. Was that good or bad? He could never read the gruff but caring archangel. Then he realized what the Scribe meant. Pravuil hadn't come here to talk to him. He'd come to see Talia. Who wasn't here.

"You're looking for Tal, aren't you?" said Jack as he leaned against the kitchen countertop, his stomach rumbling.

Now, he was worried sick. He hadn't heard from her in weeks.

Pravuil's gold eyes narrowed as he looked Jack up and down a moment and then gazed around the trailer.

"I am," he said finally. "She's not here?"

Jack couldn't hold in his pain as he shook his head and shoved his hands into his jeans pockets, his pale blond hair looking a little a disheveled in the grey lacquer cabinets' reflection.

Pravuil's brow furrowed. "You and Talia have a fight?"

"I wish," said Jack in a quiet voice.

"Why would you wish that, Jack?" Pravuil asked, those hawkish gold eyes intense, studying him with a surprised glint.

Jack shrugged and moved toward the refrigerator behind him, hands still in his jeans pockets.

"At least there'd be some passion behind it. Some emotion. A little heat."

Pravuil gave him that dog look, cocking his head to the side in confusion. He had no idea what Jack meant. Dude was an angel after all. Emotions confused him—especially the most painful ones. Like love. Attraction. Jack sighed. And passion…especially passion.

"Sorry, Jack—I'm not following you." Pravuil glanced toward the ceiling. "I need Muriel here to translate the Jackspeak."

Jack paused in front of the fridge, bowing his head as pain twisted his chest.

"Tal spends most of her time up in Heaven these days. I was just about to ask you if you'd seen my wife."

Jack leaned against the refrigerator doors and stared at Prevail, unable to keep the ache out of his face or stinging his pale green eyes that looked so haggard in the dented appliance's dull chrome sheen.

"Have you seen her, Pravuil?" he asked in a tight, small voice that threatened to crack.

Pravuil stepped toward him, white robes trailing like clouds behind him.

"Don't need Muriel to translate that," said Pravuil in a quiet voice as he scrutinized Jack, his brow furrowing. "That's pain I hear."

Jack nodded.

"Yes, Jack—I've seen her," said Pravuil, the gruffness softening into a gentler tone. "She's so worried about this tribunal that it's making her sick."

Jack's eyes widened and he lurched toward the Maker's Scribe.

"Talia's sick? I need to find her, I—"

Why didn't just fly up to Heaven? Right now! But that might put him front and center on the archangels' and the Maker's radars right now. And according to Azrael, that was the last place he needed to be.

Pravuil gently but firmly gripped Jack's shoulders. "Jack, listen to me. She's not physically sick, but she's worried about what will happen when you and she testify. In future, I'll be more careful with my words."

Jack let a relieved sigh slip through his gritted teeth as he sank back against the refrigerator doors.

"Jack, she's preparing to fight for you when the subject of your relationship comes up with the Maker. And trust me, it will. There has never been an angel with a human soul before. Or a human with wings and a halo—and seraphim powers. It's all over Heaven now. The Maker has to address it once and for all."

His eyes stung at Pravuil's words. She was preparing to fight for him!

"But she's been avoiding me for weeks, Pravuil," he said in a heavy tone.

Pravuil lowered his voice. "Jack...there are angels who don't approve of yours and Talia's relationship. And they are furious that you—a human—have received seraphim powers. And rare angel gifts. Gifts coveted by nearly every angel in Heaven. And they're furious that these powers are being wielded by a human."

"Wait a minute," said Jack, anger burning at his temples. "I never asked for any of these powers. Well, I asked to keep them that one time—so I could defeat Lucifer. But I've never used these powers for anything but saving my world. And the angels."

"I know that, Jack," said Pravuil, waving him off. "Every angel of death in Heaven and several of the archangels knows that, too. They've fought beside you. They know better. But there are some... lesser angels—putzes who still believe Raziel's lies. They want to see you stripped of these powers and those powers returned to the angels."

"They want the powers for themselves, you mean."

"Greed isn't a uniquely human emotion, Jack."

From Pravuil's restrained tone, Jack knew the Scribe wasn't telling him everything.

"All right…spill it, Pravuil," he snapped, sliding his hands out of his pockets. "What else?"

Pravuil stared down at his feet and Jack stiffened. This wasn't going to be good.

"Some of the archangels…agree with—Samael."

"What?" Jack roared.

Pravuil's gaze snapped back to Jack and Jack saw disgust. Whatever it was, Pravuil didn't agree. At all.

"Some of them are just stodgy purists, Jack," Pravuil began as he paced from the kitchen to the sofa. "Misguided fools. They don't believe angels and humans should ever mix—much less love and marry. They don't believe in love—one of our seven tenets."

"Humans and angels should never mix? Or hell, save the Maker together, either," Jack snapped. "Or the world."

A snarky smile lit Pravuil's face. "That's the Jack Casey I know. You were starting to scare me a little, Jack."

Jack shuddered as the rush of emotions swelled inside him—quickly wrecking him. Like Talia's continued absence.

"Sorry, Scribe," he said in a quiet voice and leaned back against the fridge again. "I'm just going out of my mind without her. It's been so long…"

Pravuil laid his hand on Jack's shoulder a moment, squeezing.

"I know time is such a tidal force to humans. It passes so quickly—or slowly—and it all carries so much weight. Angels forget how painful that can feel to humanity."

He paused as Jack turned toward the fridge and opened it, its thin gold light paling against Pravuil's warm angelic glow.

"She's not avoiding you, Jack. And you know she still loves you. She's doing everything she can to keep the two of you together when you stand before this tribunal. Hasn't been one of these in millennia. Biggest shindig since The Fall."

Jack whirled around.

"Did you just call Lucifer's trial a shindig?" he said, chuckling.

Pravuil shook his head, pointing a finger at Jack. "I did. You humans are a bad influence, you know that, Jack."

"Lucifer being tried and possibly thrown into the Lake of Fire," Jack said with a snicker. "And you call that a shindig?"

He broke up laughing as Pravuil's face turned red.

"Okay, yes, it's a very big deal. And it's not a shindig, all right. Having the Maker presiding over the trial of the millennia in the brand-new High House Cloud Chamber…well…it has me a little nervous, okay, smart guy?"

Jack laughed harder as he reached into the fridge and pulled out the two bottles of microbrew.

"Well, let's toast a big yee-hah to having this shindig over soon," he said and held out the two bottles. "What's your poison, cowboy? Er, Pravuil? Lucifer's Rage or Apocalypse Ale?"

Pravuil squinted at both bottles and gave Jack that familiar look of disdain, one white eyebrow raised.

"You're serious?"

Grinning, Jack nodded.

"Fine. I'll have the Apocalypse Ale. Humans…always so glib."

Jack handed him the bottle and twisted off the cap on his Lucifer's Rage ale. "Angels. No sense of humor."

He took a big swig of Lucifer's Rage, the cold, yeasty beer easing some of his warring emotions. It was good. Locally brewed. He just hoped he would be as good as this Hefeweizen at quelling Lucifer's rage at his trial. And the Maker's at seeing a human walking around with wings and seraphim powers.

Pravuil threw a massive book on the kitchen counter.

"Where'd that come from?" Jack asked, squinting as he took a long pull off his ale.

Had the Scribe pulled it out of thin air? Or those archangel robes of his?

"You don't want to know," Pravuil snapped. "It's been my life's work since we captured Lucifer. Now, before that trial, I want you to go over the events in the Throne room as they were documented by the Throne angels." He patted the heavy dark blue book. "In here."

"What are you, my public defender? I'm not the one on trial here, Pravuil."

Pravuil slapped his hand against the book.

"Jack Casey, don't think for one moment that you're not on trial, too. Because those problem archangels know you're walking around with seraphim powers in addition to that halo and wings. And mirroring Talia's rare powers. Powers they want. They're going to spin everything to make you look reckless and unable to control those powers, hoping to get them stripped from you. So they can get the powers for themselves."

Jack rubbed his hand over his face and took another long drink of ale. Were they going to try to tie him as an accessory to Lucifer?

"And for the record, Jack," said Pravuil, an angry edge to his voice. "I'm a judge not a solicitor."

"A judge?" Jack frowned.

"Yes, a judge. So, get used to it. And this is the last time we'll speak before the tribunal. That clear?"

Wow, Pravuil would be passing sentence on Lucifer. He shuddered. And maybe on his and Talia's relationship? At least he knew Pravuil would be fair. And was in both his and Talia's corners.

"Crystal, Pravuil."

"That a yes?"

"That's a yes."

"Humans," he said with a groan. "Never say what you mean."

Pravuil froze, his gaze jerking around the room. Like he'd seen something move.

"What's wrong?" Jack whispered.

The Scribe's eyes narrowed. "Demons. Sniffing around your trailer. They must have followed me." He pointed at the book again. "You! Open that book and start studying while I ward your trailer and eliminate a few demons."

Jack motioned toward the taupe couch. "Sure we can't invite 'em in? I'll put on a little AC/DC, call up a couple of murder marbles, and have ourselves a little shindig."

Claws raked along the side of the trailer.

Jack turned.

As six demons leaped through the walls at him and Pravuil.

"There's too many!" the Scribe shouted.

Jack smirked and held out his bottle of ale as he called up a sparkling gold murder marble in his left palm.

"Pravuil…hold my beer."

2

Talia floated on a warm updraft above the newly erected High House spire that climbed high into the cottony billow of Constable clouds skittering across the vibrant Parrish blue skies, the air sweet with traces of jasmine and honeysuckle. Heaven's beauty was returning—almost erasing the memory of the carnage that had happened here.

Almost.

The memory of the hard-packed rubble and the black, smoking stone spires remained, their tops torn away like someone had lopped them off with a scythe.

Her dove grey wings gently beat against the air currents in an even rhythm, Muriel on her right and Azrael on her left as cherubim floated in eagle forms above the spire's new golden dome and lowered a golden dove finial onto the rooftop. With a burst of angelic fire, the cherubim anchored the dove finial in place.

It glowed white and gold, sparkling with sunlight and angel light that quickly cooled, shimmering a sunny rich hue that radiated whorls of gold and blue and violet light against the clouds floating past. An ethereal melody, like a chorus of wind chimes, floated at the edge of her hearing, the layers of harmonies and melody familiar and soothing. She hadn't heard music in the lower Heavens for so long that she'd almost forgotten what it sounded like. She'd always hated harp music, but even the sharp thrum of harp strings would have eased her anxiety.

For the events to come.

"High House is at last complete," said Azrael, grinning, arms spread, his flowing charcoal grey locks were more silver-white now around his shoulders.

The apocalypse had changed him. Especially the battle in the Maker's Throne room.

His hair was lighter now. Charcoal grey (what happened to archangels of death's hair) had given way to a silvery archangel white. Even his red-gold halo had lightened to a lustrous white gold. An archangel's eyes turned gold, the color growing more intense with their bravery and good deeds. Azrael's should have been liquid gold and hair pure white by now, but he was an archangel of death. Dealing with death kept his eyes charcoal grey instead of archangel gold, but the weight of it all—an archangel's responsibilities—had caused his hair to lighten.

Angels of death were different from other angels, regardless of their status. Their hair turned darker with experience as the rest of their form turned pale from dealing with constant mortality. But the grey color of their eyes grew more intense, almost silvery. Jack had been telling Talia for months—on the rare occasions she got to spend time with him—that her eyes were so light and vibrant.

Thankfully, all of this interaction with angels hadn't changed Jack's eyes. They were still that irresistible, intense pale green she'd fallen hard for, his light blond hair as bright as the Southern California sun. Had Jack realized that her hair had darkened since the apocalypse? They hadn't been together enough lately for him to have even noticed.

Most of that was her fault.

She was doing her best to keep all attention—especially the Maker's—off Jack. Hoping her distance would protect him. She couldn't take it if something happened to him. All she wanted was to drop through these clouds and follow the airstream right back to

Burbank, California. Where Jack waited for her in the studio lot's set trailer. Alone. If she knew her husband, he was probably wondering what he had done to make her avoid him like this.

She only wanted to return to him. To hold and kiss him and make love to him. Show him that he was still the love of her life. That she hadn't forgotten him.

Now, in the aftermath of the apocalypse, Azrael had the weight of Creation, Heaven, and Hell on him. And the Maker's tribunal. So many angels had been lost during the Sixth flight. The Enochian Apocalypse. The worst loss of angels since Lucifer's fall. And with only one seraph left after Lucifer blew up High House, Heaven was short on angelic presences. Only the Maker could create angels—or bring the ones lost back again. If there had been even a trace of light left, she and Berith could have brought those angels back again with resurrect. But without that light, only the Maker could recover them from oblivion.

Talia had no idea how the Maker would address the loss of so many angels. Or the fate of the few humans who helped foil the Hell Prince payloads. They wouldn't be summoned to Lucifer's trial, but she wondered if the Maker would allow them to remember the apocalypse—and their roles in it.

"Let's hope no one else tries to bring it down," said Muriel, a wariness in her voice.

Like she expected Lucifer's army to attack again. Or Archangel Samael, who was still on the run and taunting Heaven with his treachery.

"It's more beautiful than ever, isn't it?" Azrael said, his face aglow in the wash of angelic light surrounding the new spire.

He ignored Muriel's comment, but Talia felt the same way. She worried how long it would be until another demon attack. Would they regroup and attack Heaven again—trying to free Lucifer? Or would Samael return to finish what he'd begun at the grand hall of Eolowen?

"I will never forget the image of High House in smoking ruins, Azrael," said Talia.

"Can't say it was my favorite place after they almost reeducated me," said Muriel with a shrug. "But seeing it destroyed was awful. Hope I never see that again."

"Me either," said Azrael as he watched the cherubim in eagle form fly in formation around the Cloud Chamber and then blink through the clouds toward the square below.

"How will all of Heaven get to see this tribunal, sir?" Muriel asked. "Since it'll be held in the Cloud Chamber. So that Seraphina can sit in attendance. And face Lucifer."

Azrael pointed toward the curved white platforms being erected in the square below.

"Those platforms will float around the spire as the tribunal is projected from the Cloud Chamber onto the spire walls of High House. The platforms will encircle the spire and allow every angel left in Heaven the chance to witness Lucifer's fate."

"Why even give him a trial?" Muriel demanded, her brow furrowing, velvety black hair floating around her shoulders, her eyes a bright grey. "It's not like the evidence isn't overwhelming."

"Every angel has the right to face their accusers and the accusations against them," said Azrael. "Even Lucifer."

"I guess it will be a short tribunal, then, won't it?" Talia offered.

How could it not be?

Lucifer had done so much harm to Heaven and the Maker's Creation. And to humanity—especially Jack as his latest obsession. Would Jack have to face Lucifer like this, too? Or would the Maker allow Azrael—or her—to face Lucifer on Jack's behalf? But she knew the answer to that question. Jack had already been called before the Maker. And now that the Maker realized the totality of what Jack had become—and her—they had no choice but to rule on Jack's fate. And the fate of this forbidden romance. Hers and Jack's marriage.

She remembered a time when the Maker let them remain together. But that had been before the realization that Jack's wings and halo couldn't be removed. Before Jack had absorbed the rarest of angel powers. And seraphim powers. It was a good thing he still had those powers after Lucifer erased most of the seraphim from existence. But now that all of Heaven—and its angels—knew about Jack's incredible powers—and their marriage—Talia knew the Maker would rule on it.

On Jack.

And she was terrified for her husband.

Could those powers be extracted from him at all now? Without killing him? Or destroying his soul? His existence? Could the Maker just take them back again? And what about her relationship with Jack? Would the Maker separate them now? Erase her memory of Jack? Or Jack's memory of her? Rewind time to before they had ever met?

She couldn't take seeing that blank look on his face. That *do I know you* look she'd seen on his face before, but never directed at her. Not even the first day they met beneath the hot, sweltering set lights of Studio 22. He had been so scorching hot that day. Temptation personified—and he took her breath away (and still did). Resisting him had been impossible. Not showing her attraction required Heavenly intervention. Even now.

She and Jack went through something similar together when Lucifer took control of her through a rare angel power (cast by a fallen angel). The moment she no longer recognized Jack had broken him and he nearly died when he challenged Lucifer after arming all his seraphim powers to ignite. Fortunately, Berith found a way to save Talia's memories while the seraph found a way to save Jack.

Talia knew Jack couldn't go through that a second time. It would destroy him.

She planned to throw herself on the tribunal's mercy—the Maker's mercy—and beg for Jack's life. His soul. And she would offer up her wings, her halo, and her rare angel powers to stay with him. She loved being an angel and she loved crossing over souls to a new journey. The thing she hated for so long had become a sacred privilege now.

But she refused to give up her human soul. It was her one chance to spend a human lifetime at Jack's side. And ascend beside him to a place where most angels could not follow.

It felt like a lifetime ago since she'd been forced into that first wager with Lucifer and sent to Earth in human form to save two souls. Even now, those two souls were still in jeopardy.

And she would still do everything in her power to save them both.

Or be smited out of existence alongside Jack if it came to that. Either way, she refused to exist without him.

"Talia? Did you hear me?"

Azrael's commanding voice shook her out of her panic.

"No," she said, forcing a sense of calm back into her body as cool air flowed through her angelic form—through her wings. "What did you say, Azrael?"

He looked concerned as he reached out and brushed his thumb across her chin.

"Talia, you are so troubled," he said in a quiet voice. "What can I do?"

She bit her lip to keep it from quivering and then stared into Azrael's charcoal grey eyes. They could be fierce and deadly, but right now, they were soft and misty. Muriel reached out and squeezed Talia's arm.

"Archangel," she began as a burst of wind rushed over them from one of the platforms below rising into the air on the wings of her squad: Kesien, Deemah, and Anahera.

She watched as they circled around the newest, highest spire in the lower Heavens, reconstructed at least fifty feet taller than the old spire, and released the platform into a light-filled tract that wrapped around the spire. It moved slowly, like a cloud on a windless day, and floated along the trail of light.

"Talia, what is it?" Azrael replied, shifting his body in front of her to block the wind.

"What will happen to Jack?" she asked in a tight, pained voice, her grey eyes welling with crystalline tears.

"Happen to Jack?" he asked, frowning. "What do you mean?"

"Now that the Maker realizes Jack's walking around with seraphim powers and rare angel gifts...along with a halo and wings...I mean, what if the Maker decides to..."

She couldn't finish the sentence. She couldn't say the words and give them any sort of breath or life. She wouldn't put them out there.

Muriel's supportive touch tightened into a protective one.

A look of surprise touched Azrael's eyes, his face turning pale.

"I can't say it," she said, beginning to shake as tears slid down her cheeks. "I'm sorry, archangel—I just can't say the words out loud."

She wanted Azrael to allay her fears. To tell her that the Maker would never destroy Jack or dismantle him. That the Maker would never erase Jack's memory of any and all his celestial encounters. Of her. That the Maker would never reset Jack's life back onto its original course—before Lucifer changed everything with those damned wagers. To disguise the Phoenix Shift he was engineering. But she knew this had never happened before—with a human. How could Azrael reassure her when Heaven had never dealt with this before?

Azrael didn't say a word, his expression a mix of compassion and worry. A chill shuddered through her body right down to her wingtips.

"You're afraid the Maker will erase Jack from existence, too," said Muriel, glancing from Azrael to Talia. "Aren't you, sir?"

The worried look furrowed Azrael's brow and darkened his eyes. And it terrified Talia.

"Tell me that won't happen, Azrael," she said, pleading. "Please. Tell me that won't happen."

Azrael pulled in a deep breath and bowed his head a moment.

"Talia…I don't presume to know what the Maker will do," he said, holding her by the shoulders. "This is the first time something like this has happened with a human, one of the Maker's chosen. Regardless, I want to believe…with all my heart…that the Maker won't reward Jack with oblivion. Or by erasing his memory. Or taking away the only thing his heart aches for. And you've got to believe that, too. With all your heart."

She tried to speak a hundred things at once and put a voice and words to her pain, but all that came out was a squeak. And more tears.

Azrael wrapped her in his arms, holding her in a fatherly embrace.

"We have to believe that Jack's incredible and extensive service to Heaven and Earth speaks for itself. And that the Maker's mercy will shine on him, too. After all, Jack Casey never asked for any of this."

Talia felt Muriel's hand on her neck, rubbing.

"And the Maker's knows what's already in Jack's heart. And yours. Believe in that, Talia."

Muriel was right. The Maker knew everything, being omnipotent and omniscient. She had to believe in what was in her heart and Jack's. And the fact that their two hearts were forever entwined.

Nodding, she let go of Azrael, floating back from him as her squad lifted a second white platform up from the square and released it into the tract of light encircling the spire. It floated at a comfortable distance from the first platform.

"You and Muriel are right," she said, wiping away her tears. "I have to believe in what's in my heart and in Jack's. That the Maker will see our unbreakable bond. And know that we belong together."

"If it comes down to it," said Azrael in a quiet voice. "Pravuil has a long list of angels lined up to speak on yours and Jack's behalf, Talia. But please understand that Lucifer is the one on trial here. Not you. And certainly not Jack. But because of the uproar about yours and Jack's relationship—your marriage—among the angels, the Maker has no choice but to rule on it...once and for all."

Azrael was right. The pettiness among some of the surviving archangels had brought the issue to flashpoint. And since she and Jack were asked to testify at Lucifer's trial, putting their marriage on trial was unavoidable.

"Thank you, Azrael," she said. "I understand. And I appreciate Pravuil's efforts on Jack's and my behalf. And yours. Because I know you're helping him, too."

The archangel blushed, making Talia smile. He always worked behind the scenes to right wrongs. He shunned the spotlight, but she needed to thank him anyway.

"Thank you, sir," she said.

"Always, Talia," he said. "I will do everything I can for you and Jack, you know that."

Talia nodded and hugged Azrael. "You always do. Thank you."

A shadow passed over the spire.

Talia froze.

Azrael's gaze shot upward as a squad of cherubim rose from the square and shot toward the long shadow darkening the streets of the lower Heavens.

In moments, Kesien, Anahera, and Deemah formed a circle around Azrael. Talia and Muriel slid into the V formation, turning toward the dark cloud floating above them.

Like a storm cloud, the dark, frantic wings flitted across the lower Heavens and passed over the High House spire.

Talia's stomach dropped. Knowing what had made that shadow.

Demons. Lots of them.

Three shrill tones echoed across the Heavens, alerting the angels to the sudden demonic presence. And floating at the swarm of demons' helm was Archangel Samael. Surrounded by Kesien's former squad members. Along with Laren Dumont, Jack's former costar who had done lots of terrible things—especially to Jack.

Talia wanted to capture all of them, but she longed to try Archangel Samael alongside Lucifer.

Cherubim took defensive positions around High House, joined by Talia and her squad and the rest of the angels of death assigned to the spire. They fanned out into a staggered formation, allowing them to react faster to an enemy-positioned attack from above or below.

The large force of demons writhed overhead, black wings beating the air. Infuriated, Talia held position between Muriel and Azrael, waiting for the moment to engage these vermin.

Lare Dumont floated at Archangel Samael's right shoulder, his black leathery bat wings shiny in the sunlight, in continuous motion as they circled High House twice, the threat clear.

Would they dare attack the tribunal? Or High House and try to break Lucifer free of his captivity?

"Azrael!" Samael shouted, a defiant grin on his face. "Still fighting the good fight, I see. And failing miserably."

"Well, you are the expert on failing miserably, Samael," said Azrael, sounding relaxed. "I'll bet the Maker can smite you from here. The guard and I would appreciate some fireworks to kick off Lucifer's trial."

Archangel Samael's smile faded as he flew his demon army in a wide, slow arc around the spire. Just out of cherubim—and angel of death—reach. As a show of force.

"Tell the Maker we aren't here for Lucifer."

"Like any of us cares!" Talia shouted. "And it won't stop us from knocking you right out of the sky."

Azrael tossed Holy fire into the air above Samael's head, a warning shot that startled Samael, the fire crackling as it burned across the sky in a burst of red flames.

"Then why are you here, traitor?" Azrael demanded. "Planning a holiday at the Lake of Fire? Lord Kushiel would be happy to arrange a time share for you and the other traitors. Save us all some time."

Talia smiled. The archangel had been around Jack too long. And it made her ache for her husband even more.

"We're as curious about Lucifer's fate as you are," said Samael. "We just came to witness the trial."

"You gave up that right when you turned traitor and assaulted and betrayed Heaven," Muriel shouted.

"Angels, engage. Smite them out of our skies with blade or shield, "Azrael ordered. "Holy fire begins in three." He smiled. "Targeting you first, Archangel Samael—unless you'd refer to surrender."

Samael's smile broadened into a wolfish grin. "I never give up, Azrael. Surely, you know that by now."

"Well, I assure you, Samael," Azrael said, eyes narrowing. "We've given up on you."

"You'll learn of Lucifer's fate soon enough," Talia called out to the fallen archangel. "Because I promise you, you'll be sharing it."

"That's big talk for an angel on trial," Samael called out to her. "Heard your forbidden romance is about to get smited by the Maker. Including your human boyfriend."

"Husband!" Talia shouted as the sky above the demons darkened. "He's not on trial. He's testifying—something he'll happily do at your trial, too. To make sure you burn just like Lucifer."

Samael circled overhead, shaking his long mane of dark hair, that stupid archangel smile he'd perfected plastered across his long face.

"Careful, little angel of death. That sounds like vengeance and pride talking."

"No, that's violence and retribution talking, Samael," Talia said as her eyes flashed with Holy fire. "And some old-fashioned angel of death justice."

She held up her hand and rained lightning down on Samael and his demons.

Azrael chuckled. "Looking forward to your next visit, traitor! When you're in chains."

A bolt of Holy fire slammed into one of Samael's wings, setting the sparse black feathers on fire. When he began to lose altitude, a pair of demons grabbed him and quickly shuffled him off, disappearing into a distant cloud bank that hung over the Garden and the Haunted Woods.

Kesien, gritting his teeth, raised his sword. Deemah was right beside him, shield aloft as together, they started after Samael, but Azrael grabbed hold of their wings, tugging them backward.

"Let him go," Azrael ordered. "Samael's practically begging you to follow. There's too many of them. It's a trap."

Kesien fumed. "But, sir, I—"

Azrael was still glaring at them. "Stand down, Kesien. You, too, Deemah."

Grudgingly, they gave in. Kesien's gaze shot toward the distant clouds, like he planned to follow them the moment Azrael let him go. Talia understood. Kesien needed justice for his lost guard of death angels, that Samael had either sacrificed or destroyed. Like Heaven needed justice for Lucifer's crimes. But she worried what else this tribunal would draw to Heaven once it began.

"Don't worry, Kesien," said Azrael, releasing them. "As soon as Lucifer's trial is over, I plan to go after that monster, Samael. He won't escape his crimes against Heaven."

That seemed to satisfy the six-foot-seven angel of death, his black hair windblown, grey eyes so bright, charcoal grey wings spread wide, and halo spinning wildly. Talia knew that Kesien still felt responsible for not stopping Samael's betrayal. He and Deemah were obsessed with capturing the archangel of death and the traitorous former members of their squad.

That trial would have to wait until Lucifer had been dealt with by the Maker.

"Where are they keeping Lucifer?" Talia asked, still watching the clouds.

Azrael's eyes narrowed. "That smug monster is in a newly constructed cell in High House. Right below the Cloud Chamber where a squadron of cherubim can stand guard over him. In a cell built just to contain him."

"The demons, sir," said Muriel, staring at the gold High House dome. "They're planning to try and spring Lucifer, aren't they?"

A curious grin touched Azrael's face, his gaze still on the sky.

"I sure hope they'll try," he said. "So we can slam Samael into a cell right beside Lucifer—along with Kesien's and Deemah's three rogue squad members."

And Lare Dumont who had once again chosen the wrong side. Talia studied the spire, wondering if Lucifer had been plotting an escape with Archangel Samael since he'd arrived in his cell.

A lot of demons had flown through the skies above High House, way too many for some casual flyby of Heaven. No, this was a coordinated show of force by Hell's demons. Had Lucifer summoned them? Would they soon attack and destroy this newly built spire?

The thought filled her with trepidation. And she worried about that other shoe dropping, as Jack called it.

"Has Lucifer said anything?" she asked.

Azrael shook his head. "Nothing. Not a word to Pravuil. Or me. Or even the Maker. Pravuil thinks he's resigned himself to his fate." The archangel cast another glance toward the sky. "But after seeing this display of might...I'm not so convinced."

Resigned to his fate? Talia pulled in a breath. Of being erased from existence?

"The Lake of Fire?" Talia asked.

Azrael turned back to her, looking grim. "Most likely. The Maker's firstborn angel. They won't prolong suffering, not even Lucifer's. He'll get off easily with a quick incineration. Not what he deserves, but unlike Lucifer, this is about justice not vengeance."

Talia worried what would happen to her and Jack. And she worried that Jack would pay the ultimate price for their relationship.

"When does the tribunal begin?" Talia asked.

"As soon as all the pieces are in place," said Azrael, motioning toward the platforms below. "For now, there are a lot more viewing platforms to place around the spire for the angels. There are witnesses to gather. The seat of judgment and five judges to assemble. Pravuil said in about five human days. So, you'll need to get Jack up here by then, Talia."

Less than a week? That wasn't long.

"Who will sit in judgment of Lucifer in the Cloud Chamber courtroom?" Talia asked.

Azrael's gaze was intense. "The Maker. Pravuil. Archangel Sarathiel. Archangel Kushiel. And Archangel of Death Sidriel."

Muriel turned around with a sharp snap of her wings, staring at Azrael.

"Sidriel?" she cried. "Why not you? You are the most senior Archangel of Death."

Azrael patted Muriel's shoulder. "I'm much too close to the situation, Muriel. Of all the remaining archangels of death, Pravuil felt that Sidriel was the most objective choice. And I agree. I can't be impartial. This whole mess began with my pridefulness in accepting Lucifer's first wager to save Talia from falling."

"Azrael...I'm so sorry I caused all of this—"

He was beside Talia again, a hand on her cheek.

"Talia. You were vulnerable. You were suffering. You needed help instead of sending you out to crossover more souls. I should have recognized that sooner. But you didn't cause this. And honestly, neither did I."

A heavy sigh slid through his teeth.

"You're right, sir," said Talia, pressing her hand against his. "Lucifer caused this whole mess."

Azrael let his hand slide free of her cheek as he motioned toward the new High House spire.

"It will all be known to Heaven soon. And Lucifer will finally face responsibility for the destruction he's caused. So, prepare yourselves."

Kesien glanced around the skies and over at the spire. "Sir, where is the Scribe? I haven't seen him since yesterday."

Azrael cast an uneasy glance at Talia and she wondered what that look meant.

"He said something about gathering witnesses and disappeared," said Azrael. "With the Maker here in the lower Heavens, I doubt he's gone long."

Five days until Lucifer's trial started.

Somehow, she had to break free from these preparations and return to Jack. She had no idea what chaos her absence on the show had already caused. It felt like a lifetime since she'd seen Jack. She'd tried her best to stay away. To keep any demonic–and angelic— attention off him, but her resolve was quickly melting. She ached to see him.

And she needed to explain why she'd been gone so long. She hoped he would forgive her. That he still loved her.

But the tribunal would interrupt their reunion. Jack had no idea that the trial started in less than a human week. And from there, she had no idea what would happen to either of them. And more than anything, she wanted to stand beside her husband as his wife at their first anniversary party with all their friends present. At the beach house that Jack loved.

She would trust her heart. And hold onto Jack with everything she had.

Another shadow blocked the sun. She glanced up.

Three black-winged angels of death with rusty halos hovered above her, swords raised. Flanked by a terror of leathery-winged demons. Four of them surrounding three angel traitors those black wings displaying their corruption to all of Heaven.

A feral growl escaped from Kesien's clenched teeth, his grey eyes murderous. Deemah had a hungry smile on her face.

"Reptev," Kesien snarled.

Deemah flew beside him, sword drawn and shield out, her dangerous smile brightening.

"And Lix and Pharzus. Retribution time."

Azrael sang out deep baritone orders as more demons appeared above them.

But Talia was already in motion behind Kesien, Muriel on her right as Deemah blinked beside Kesien.

Talia and her squad shot upward through the clouds toward the demons. And her traitorous former colleagues.

3

THE NEXT MORNING, AFTER PRAVUIL'S UNANNOUNCED VISIT, JACK showered, shaved, and dressed in blue work coveralls, a grey T-shirt underneath. His wings felt all bunched up inside the coveralls and no matter how he shifted them, he couldn't quite get comfortable. At least no one could see them.

He'd been up most of the night, unable to sleep, and left his trailer half-awake for the early set call. Dreading the aftermath of yesterday's on-set meltdown. Crew had walked off set. Actors weren't speaking to each other. And the studio set had been trashed beneath a river of paint. Jack had no idea what awaited him at this morning's set call once he got out of the makeup chair.

But he expected to be sitting around all day, waiting for the set to get cleaned up and reassembled. More waiting than usual thanks to this latest meltdown.

The spring air was cool, the wind sharp, blowing dust and paper around the edges of the squat grey buildings of Four Acre Studios. Even the studio grass had turned bright green after a day or two of rain that smelled like asphalt, eucalyptus, and car exhaust. The sky was still a softer blue than normal, fragile as the world struggled to shake off the apocalypse's aftermath that almost no one realized had happened. And most people didn't even know about it. Thought it was Santa Ana winds, CMEs…even chemtrails.

Probably better explanations than the real one.

As he stepped down the two steps out of his trailer, a muffled voice somewhere off to his left carried on the wind. From Gianni's and Izzy's trailer beside him.

He paused on the pavement and listened.

"Of course, I've seen the ratings," said the calm, poised, and familiar baritone voice. "And we're all worried."

He peered around the corner of his trailer.

A tall man stood between his and Gianni's trailer, dressed in tan coveralls, pressed and wrinkle-free, a crisp white dress shirt and Windsor-knotted red tie underneath. He was poised and confident, phone pressed to his ear. In those coveralls, he looked like he was modeling them in an ad for *Vogue*. Like he'd just stepped out of the 1946 film, *Notorious* starring Cary Grant.

Armand Gianni.

Jack could almost smell the whiffs of jasmine and vanilla from his Clive Christian cologne that carried on the wind. Hints of Heaven. He sighed. Reminding him of his absent angel of death wife.

"And you're sure?" Gianni asked, one arm folded against his chest as he looked down, pacing, his warm brown eyes so intense, so worried, all his focus on that phone. "And there's no chance of a boost during the finale? Or sweeps week?"

Was he talking to his agent?

Jack's stomach dropped. The bad news was spreading fast. From here, it would grow like cancer. There was no stopping it now. By his first wedding anniversary, his hit show would be cancelled—if not sooner. The ride was over. He sighed, his chest tightening. It had been nothing short of meteoric. But short. And his heart ached at what came next.

The goodbyes. He hated goodbyes.

Armand Gianni was the best friend he'd ever had and it twisted his gut to think that by fall, they would all move on to other shows. The beginning of the end of his and Gianni's friendship, marked by occasionally running into each other and polite small talk about doing lunch until Gianni would just become another name in his phone contacts. One he never called or hung out with anymore.

Just another friend he'd lost.

And he didn't want that to happen. Not with Gianni. And not with Banks either.

"Well, I'll definitely keep the offer on my radar and I thank you for considering me for such an incredible role. Yes. Right…Nan Connelly, my agent, will be in touch soon. Thanks, Evan."

Jack froze. Evan?

Was he talking to Evan Bellows? About a role?

Jack had had quite a few calls, but none from his former *SanFran Confidential* director. Things were so very different from the last time he spoke to Evan. When he'd turned the dude down about returning to the show. But now that things were turning in the other direction, with Jack's star falling again, Evan had evidently forgotten he knew Jack. Guess it was more payback from before and Jack couldn't say he hadn't earned it.

But casting his best friend and rubbing it in his face? So very Hollywood.

When he looked up, Gianni was staring at him, looking a little panicked.

"Uh…hi, Jack."

"Hey, Gianni," he said, scrutinizing him, anger warming his gut.

A few awkward moments of silence passed between them, something Jack had never felt before. He'd always been able to talk to Gianni about anything—even when they were rivals. But now, there was this secret between them. Not one like his wings or Lucifer— things that defied explanation and required…time to explain. No, this was a secret much closer to home. To his heart.

The job.

Right now, he felt like he'd traveled a million miles away from his best friend. Only to find a knife in his back.

"Was just talking to…"

"So, when were you going to tell me? When the billboards showed up all over L.A.?"

"Billboards? Jack, what are you talking about?"

Gianni's intense gaze enveloped him, staring searchingly. For the right words to say? To let him down easy because he was leaving the show early? That he'd snatched Jack's former show out from under him. Which excuse was it? All three maybe?

Jack wouldn't let him off easily. He said nothing, instead maintaining a cold stare at his once-best friend, waiting for him to come clean about that phone call. To not lock him out and to be straight with him.

Gianni's voice trailed off into silence as he held out his phone, a pained look deepening on his handsome, tanned face.

"Never thought I'd see my best friend stab me in the back over ratings," Jack said finally, hurt by Gianni's betrayal.

He'd expected it from anyone else, but not from Armand Gianni.

Jack turned away and stormed off toward Studio 22, but Gianni chased him down, grabbing his arm and spinning him around.

"Jack, wait!" Gianni said in an anxious voice. "Listen to me."

He glared at Gianni, pulling away. "Forget it! I've already heard enough, dude."

"Okay, yes," Gianni said, sounding exasperated. "That was Evan Bellows. Your former director. He's considering me for a role in one of his productions."

"Davy Pierson or Drummond Turillo?" He glared at Gianni. "Or hell, maybe both? Crossing Paths not able to match what he's paying?"

"Jack, listen—please," said Gianni, sounding contrite but insistent.

"I've heard all I need to hear. Break a leg, dude. It's your big primetime break. Your chance to be one of the spoiled, rich, primetime stars you've hated for so long. Like me. I can almost smell the sulfur."

Jack turned away, but Gianni spun him around again.

"Jack! Dammit, listen to me. He hasn't made any official offers yet, okay? We're just talking."

Jack sighed. Was he overreacting? With Talia still gone,

yesterday's huge on-set meltdown, and Lucifer's tribunal soon to start, he was feeling like he had a target painted on his forehead again.

"And you know as well as I do how far the show's ratings have fallen."

"Yeah," said Jack, staring at the old blue, paint-spattered Vans he wore. "I know it's over." Finally, he looked up, unable to hold back a smirk. "But it was a great ride, wasn't it? Ending with the apocalypse. Can't say that's not the perfect ending, y'know?"

Gianni returned his smile.

"It was a great ride, wasn't it? I met the love of my life here. Fought demons—with a sword." His gaze fixed on Jack again. "And I met my best friend. A friendship I wouldn't jeopardize for a damned part on SanFran Confidential, Jack. I know how this must look to you, but I'd never stab you in the back like that."

Jack nodded, still feeling doubt.

"But if it comes down to taking a role," Gianni said, his big brown eyes so intense. "I would have talked to you first. I know what that show did to you. It almost destroyed you and I would never be a part of repeating that harm. After everything we've been through together, you have to know that."

He hung his head. He did.

"Sorry, dude...I overreacted."

Gianni poked Jack's shoulder with his fist. "Not your fault. I'd have felt the same way if I'd heard that name on this set. With everything falling apart and Talia still gone, I get it. Still friends?"

"Yeah. Of course."

Gianni smiled as he put his phone in his front coveralls pocket. "So, how about those dailies?"

Jack rolled his eyes. "Holy hell...what a dumpster fire. And Herb just kept the cameras rolling. Didn't say a word of—y'know... direction? I thought Eric Saunders was either going to break my neck or I'd drown in that river of paint."

Gianni laughed. "Don't think I'll ever get all the paint out of my hair."

"Me either," said Jack, running his fingers through his light blond bangs, but his mind was already racing ahead to Rachel.

He'd worked with her a long time and even at the height of the flake use on the *SanFran Confidential* set—and her gaslighting—he'd never seen her melt down like that.

"I've never seen Rachel like that before. And her fiancé is never going to get it through his head that I'm not trying to get back with her. I'm married. To the only woman I'll ever want. And I'd rather fight Lucifer in Heaven all over again than do reality competition shows with Rachel Daniels."

Gianni's eyes got wide. "When are they putting him on trial?"

"Soon," said Jack. "I'm trying not to think about that since they'll be looking at me, too." He sighed. "And my relationship with Talia."

"Why?" Gianni asked, frowning.

"Because angel and human relationships are forbidden," he replied, the words heavy on his lips. "They've always been forbidden. But I didn't even know she was an angel until I'd forever lost my heart to her. And I'm not taking it back. Ever."

Talia knew a relationship with humans was forbidden. It's not like she'd planned this. But they gave her a human soul and then acted surprised when she used it. After she fell in love. As a human.

Besides, he'd lost his heart to her after that first meeting under the hot stage lights. Long before he knew she was an angel.

It was Lucifer's fault. He knew sparks would fly when they met. He'd been counting on it to accomplish his grand plan to get his wings and power back.

For so long, everything in Heaven seemed fine with their relationship. Until Jack started changing. Mirroring Talia's rare angel powers. Getting wings and a halo. Absorbing the seraphim powers. Pravuil told him the tribunal was a powerplay by a bunch of insecure angels. Regardless of the outcome, Jack would do what he had to do to stay with Talia—the love of his life.

"But why now, Jack?" Gianni asked. "Lucifer's in chains and the apocalypse has been aborted."

"It's a power grab by these douchebag archangels who want these powers for themselves. Like they're going to carve them out of my skin when Heaven takes back my wings and divvies up these powers like they'd robbed a vending machine. They're even willing to take me and Talia apart to get them. So, either way, the Maker has to weigh in about this."

Gianni looked worried now.

"Don't worry, dude," he said with a chuckle. "They'll have to smite me to break us up."

Gianni winced. "And that's exactly what I'm worried about, Jack." He thumped Jack on the back. "Come on. Let's go see if the set's been cleared yet."

"Not unless they called in Azrael to throw his archangel mojo at it," said Jack as he walked along the back alley toward the sidewalk and patches of bright green grass framing the building.

He and Gianni veered between Studio 18 and Studio 20 and came out at the entrance to Studio 22, still shadowed by the sun's early morning light. The shade felt ten degrees cooler as Gianni opened the door and entered, the set's cozy lightning still warming the space. Jack was a step behind him. The air smelled like old paint, sawdust, and warm stage lights.

Inside, as stage lights pooled in dramatic gold rivulets against the dark, matte charcoal living room paint covering the walls and floors, trendy for this year according to the studio's interior designers, Jack felt the stillness.

The silence.

He'd never walked into this building when the show was in production and saw it empty and quiet before. Except when Lucifer froze time.

This wasn't good.

He glanced at Gianni who looked apprehensive as he gazed around the studio. No sounds of a saw in motion or a hammer pounding nails. No thump and scrape of boxes or furniture or measured sweep of a broom. No people and carts moving through the building. Not even the tap of a single footstep.

"Where is the set crew?" Gianni asked in a half-whisper, glancing around.

All four back offices were dark. Not a makeup artist in sight. No director. No camera crew. Not even a script supervisor or a Craft Services table being setup with breakfast sandwiches and those little mini quiches everyone binge-ate and denied it later.

"Anyone here?" Jack shouted.

Silence.

"They filming on location today?" Jack replied, gazing at Gianni. "At one of the reno houses and got the call sheets mixed up?"

"They already cut those scenes, remember, Jack?" said Gianni. "For budget reasons. Everything was to be filmed here. At Studio 22. This building should be packed with people."

He pulled out his phone. Checked for texts and emails. Nothing. Gianni checked his phone, too.

"Izzy's set call isn't for another hour," said Gianni as he followed Jack through the empty studio.

"Let's check the sound stage," said Jack, motioning him toward a dimly lit hallway that wound through the long, narrow building. To the back where the massive sound stage had been setup yesterday to look like the living room of one of the reno houses.

Since the audience had never seen footage of the actual houses, only still images, the set stage had become one more example of Hollywood magic—including the sound. Okay, it was more duct tape and an old fog machine at this point, but it was close enough to look like the real thing.

Jack moved toward the set that was only one half of a house's living room with fake windows equipped with high resolution screens displaying images of the outdoors behind them. As Jack approached, set lights illuminated the river of dried multi-colored technicolor paint sludge that still covered the maple hardwood floors that had once matched one of the reno houses.

"It's just like we left it yesterday," Gianni said with a moan, his brow furrowed, his mouth gaping as he surveyed the damage.

"Yeah, still meltdown city." Jack sighed. "No way we're filming anything here today."

Footsteps ticked behind them.

He turned.

Jennifer Collins approached. In torn, faded jeans, lavender Converse high tops, and a baggy lavender sweater. Her rich brown hair, pulled back in a loose ponytail, was a little windblown, wisps of hair framing her face. She wore a pair of tortoiseshell glasses that slid down her nose. She had no phone or clipboard in her hand. And she looked a little lost. A little scared.

"Jennifer?" Jack replied, squinting as he moved toward her. "What's up with the empty studio? And the hell spawn set?"

"Where's the crew? The cameras?" Gianni asked, hands on his hips. "And the makeup artists? Jack and I both had seven fifteen set calls."

Her eyes got glassy, her lips pressing together as she bit her lip.

"Herb called me at six this morning and told me to stop all production. All filming. I'm supposed to tell you that there's a technical delay and to go back to your trailers and wait for an update."

She was shaking.

"But," said Jack, gently taking her by the shoulders. "We all know that's not what's going on."

"This isn't about Rachel's meltdown yesterday, is it?" said Gianni.

She shook her head, tears rushing down her cheeks.

Jack put his arms around her and held her while she cried.

"Oh, Jack, Armand..." she said as she let go of Jack. "It's terrible news."

Jack knew what she was going to say.

"What news?" Gianni asked.

Jennifer glanced at Gianni and then him, more tears slipping down her face. "The show's been cancelled."

Cancelled. The fate of so many television shows. Eventually. Jack had just hoped this one would last longer. And end on its own terms.

But fairy tales were ethereal—even the ones found on cheesy, low budget reality television. And this one had already been to the ball, saw the clock strike twelve, and then matched its glass slipper to its princess. Its crown to its prince charming. All that was left was rolling credits and showing the happy couple take a sunset carriage ride toward their happily ever after.

"We had a good run," said Jack, a little choked up. "Gonna miss the people who made it special. And all those stupid little couple's challenges."

"Me too, Jack," said Gianni in a soft voice.

"What happens to the finale?" Jack asked finally, the sadness winding its way through his chest like heartburn.

"They're going to piece together a special episode called the Angelic Anniversary Show."

"Each couple's greatest hits," said Jack, nodding.

Jennifer wiped her eyes with the back of her hand. "They plan to film some final couples' interviews in your trailers to finish out the episode and air it to commemorate your three first wedding anniversaries. Go out on a high note."

Gianni frowned. "Are they just going to leave the reno challenge hanging? Unfinished. And not crown a winner?"

"No," said Jennifer, fidgeting as she glanced from the set to Jack and then Gianni. "They are going to combine all the footage, link it with some voiceovers, and crown one of the couples the winner. They've already got the voting website ready to launch. They'll open the viewer voting at the end of the special for all the fans and then film a short on-location scene with the winning couple."

So that was really it then. No closing party. Not even a parting breakfast burrito. Ironic that Talia, an angel of death, wouldn't even be here to see the show take its last breath. Or cross it over to the place where all Hollywood shows ended up. Syndication if they went to Heaven. Obscurity if they went to Hell.

"Keys to your trailers are due back to the studio by next Monday."

Jack wanted to be surprised, but all he felt was jaded. And more than a little lost. Right now, he didn't even have a place to stay. He closed in two days on the beach house, when he'd give up his shithole studio apartment, his things (what little he had) were already in storage until the move-in date the week of their anniversary and party. He'd expected to live here in his studio trailer until then. Guess he needed to contact Phil and start evaluating any offers still on the table. News about the show being canceled would travel fast though. Was it already on *TMZ*? Regardless, he hoped something viable still remained once the bad news broke.

Jennifer reached out and hugged Gianni and then Jack. A long hug this time.

"Jack, Armand, it's been my privilege to work with both of you." Jennifer fidgeted again, like she was lost without that ubiquitous clipboard. "And Jack, no matter how this show ends, know that you're still on top. Don't let anyone bring you down from those heights. Because of you, we all got a taste of being number one. We'll never forget you for saving this show—and bringing us along for the ride."

Jack chuckled and laid his hand against her flushed cheek.

"Thank you, Jennifer. Thank the crew for me. And thank Herb for giving someone like me, someone who'd fallen almost as far as I could fall, the chance to climb back up again. You guys brought me along for the ride and I'll never forget this show for giving me my life back."

Smiling, she squeezed his hand and then reached out and touched Gianni's cheek.

"I'll be in touch in a day or two to shoot the remaining couples' interviews and let the winners know about filming the final scene at the winning location. Take care, you two."

"You too, Jennifer," said Jack. "And if you need anything—anything at all—you've got my number."

"Mine too, Jennifer," Gianni added.

Her smile turned into a brief grin. "Thank you, both."

Jack heard her sob as she turned away from the empty, dark studio set. He turned to Gianni.

"Well, that's it then," said Jack. "It's over. No more Cinderella Hour."

"Izzy still has her evening anchor position and for now, I've still got Crossing Paths."

Jack shook his head. "That wasn't very convincing, dude."

"I know," Gianni said with a sigh. "Jack, I don't think I can go back. Not now. If you're okay with it, I'm going to call Evan back."

Jack's phone rang. He held up his hand and answered the call. It was Banks.

"Dude!" Jack replied, putting him on speaker. "Where are you? Gianni and are on set and—"

"Jack?" Banks sounded devastated. "Jennifer Collins just called me. Told me and Morgan not to come to the set. The show's been cancelled, hasn't it?"

"Like another over-budget remake of Dracula."

"Damn! What am I going to do now?"

Banks was older than him and Gianni and had the most to lose with this cancellation.

"Got anything in the works?" Gianni asked.

"Just a call from…uh…"

His voice trailed off.

Jack's eyes narrowed. That didn't sound ominous or anything. Had Bellows called Banks, too? Offering him a part on *SanFran Confidential?*

Another slap in the face.

"Bellows called you, too, didn't he?" said Gianni.

A pause.

"Sorry, Jack. I was going to tell you about it. He called me yesterday."

Jack bristled. "So, he offer you the part of Drum? To Gianni's Davy?"

"Jack, I thought we were past this," said Gianni, a little annoyed now.

"That was before I knew he'd called all my costars and offered them parts while I lose everything again."

Gianni stared at him, arms crossed. "So, you're telling me there's no big offer on your plate? Not one you're considering?"

Jack shoved his hands into his coveralls pockets and began to pace.

"You think any of those offers are gonna stick now that the news is out about the show being cancelled?"

Gianni winced and shook his head. "Probably not."

"Great. Guess I'm right back where I started. When this show first began."

"Jack, where's Talia?" Banks asked. "Does she know yet?"

"Since I haven't seen her in a couple of weeks, I wouldn't know. And I'm about to close on the beach house we renovated for the show. Damn. It's all coming down around me again. And I haven't even testified at Lucifer's trial yet. Maybe if I'm lucky, the Maker will smite me out of existence. Put me out of my misery."

"Don't say that, Jack," said Gianni.

"So, you haven't heard from Bellows, Jack?"

"Not a word. Of course, why would I?" he said, still pacing. "It's not like he didn't already offer me everything and I said no."

"Guess you don't know about Rachel then. Do you?"

Jack froze, holding out his phone, frowning.

"What about Rachel?"

"Banks…" Gianni hissed.

His gaze snapped to Gianni.

"Bellows offered Rachel her old job back on SanFran Confidential," said Banks, his voice echoing through the quiet set.

Jack's stomach dropped, his heart smashing against his rib cage.

So, just like that, she was back on the old show. After what she'd done to him.

"And both of you knew about this?"

Gianni bowed his head, pain and shame in his pinched features.

"And you didn't bother to clue me into it. Any of it. Wow…thanks, dudes."

"Jack, please just listen," said Gianni as Jack backed away.

"Forget it. Enjoy your new roles. Tell Evan to shove it for me."

He cleared Banks' call and stormed off the set, Gianni shouting at him as he veered into the dark hallway that led to the front of the building. And outside.

He needed air. With all these betrayals, he couldn't breathe.

As soon as he hit the pavement, he broke into a run, but collided with someone moving through the bright sunlight toward the studio entrance.

Jack hit pavement and rolled into the grass. Dizzy and blinded by the sun, his eyes watering, Jack stared up at the tall, lanky figure with stringy, shoulder length dark hair.

And red eyes.

"Where you going, Casey, in such a hurry?"

Lare Dumont.

"Lare." He glared at his former costar-turned-demon. "Figured you'd show up sooner or later. Perfectly timed entrance, dude. Like it was scripted or something."

"Hey, I still got it," said Lare with a curt bow and dropped down on his haunches beside Jack, a dangerous smile on his long, lean face. "And thanks for setting off the apocalypse, Jack. And opening the door to Hell for me."

Jack shook his head. "And I see you've done so much with your chance to fix things."

Lare laughed, those red eyes sparkling. "Fix things? Why would I want to fix what ain't broke? And now, I get to kick your ass—it's a gift from Heaven."

Like all the signs came together and the stars aligned to set the apocalypse in motion. Just so Lare Dumont could escape his cage in Hell to come back to Earth and kick his ass.

Only Lare Dumont would be arrogant enough to think the apocalypse had been about him. Douchebag.

Lare grabbed Jack by the nape and jerked his head up.

"With Lucifer gone and Samael on Hell's throne, I've got the chance at power you've never dreamed of."

"Like these seraphim powers I'm rockin'?" Jack asked. "Or the rare angel powers? Any one of these powers could crush your demon ass, Lare. Including my wings."

Jack freed his wings from his coveralls that tore between his shoulder blades, but Lare fell on top of him, stopping him from unfurling them.

"Not this time, Jack," Lare said with a laugh, holding his wings closed as he dragged Jack across the grass.

Around the side of the building. And into the shadowed alley between buildings.

Guess they were doing this here. And right now.

Lare pinned Jack against the pavement and leaned over top of him, leering, those red eyes bright in the half-dark of the alley.

"See, we're about to strip away those powers and these wings from your sorry ass." He grabbed Jack by the front of his coveralls. "And then you're mine."

"And here I didn't get you anything for Valentine's Day this year."

Jack twisted his shoulder, getting in a punch to Lare's gut. Knocking his demonic former costar off him and onto the pavement.

"All I've got to give is a gut punch," Jack said with a smirk. "Because I care."

Lare doubled over.

"And until you and your demon dudes actually take my powers," Jack said, pressing something into Lare's open hand. "Here's a burst of those powers for you. A free sample." He patted Lare's hand and closed it into a fist. "Don't use it all at once."

He pointed his finger and blinked past Lare out of the alley, back into the sunlight as Lare looked down.

At the gold murder marble shuddering in his palm.

"Jack!" Lare screamed.

The murder marble exploded. Knocking Lare into the air. Halfway across the roof of Studio 22.

"Never gets old," Jack said with a chuckle.

But the shadows that passed over the sun made him shudder and look up.

More demons. Headed his way. Dropping out of the sky.

Right on top of him. Slamming him against the pavement with a sickening crack.

4

down on the crush of black-winged demons zipping past the High
House spire.

Muriel was beside her, sword slicing through leathery black wings
and black feathers, shield bashing fiery red, demonic heads.

More demons plunged out of the crisp Parrish blue sky and landed
on the white-stoned square below. Startling the cherubim still
working on platforms for the tribunal. They sprang into action.

Kesien and Deemah engaged the demons as their former squad
members, now corrupted angels, dropped out of the clouds around
them.

Swords flashed in front of the corrupted angels' flame-red eyes as
they taunted Kesien. Deemah got their attention, shield in motion as
she shield-bashed the leader, Reptev, slamming her shield against his
head. Where a gold halo had once been, the light was dull and
rusty now.

As his former squad members struggled against the blows, Kesien
knocked them out of the sky with a roundhouse swing of his shield.

Reptev, Lix, and Pharzus plummeted toward the shimmery white
square below, but more of those red, leathery winged demons

appeared around them. Catching the three corrupted angels before they slammed into the ground. Or into the awaiting custody of cherubim, now in eagle forms.

Azrael summoned his fiery archangel sword. It guttered white and blue with Holy fire as the archangel swung it wide and cut down demon after demon. Below, in the square, cherubim launched into the air, joining the fight.

"Cherubim, stay at your posts!" Azrael's voice thundered across the Heavens. "Protect the Cloud Chamber. I repeat, do not leave your post."

The cherubim immediately gathered as a force in human form and surrounded the entrance to High House. The rest, in eagle form, lifted on the updrafts and shot around the spire, stretching their wings wide until they formed a line of angels from the square to the dome. In front of the warded portal.

This attack was a demonic diversion, Talia realized. A misdirection to keep the angels occupied. And away from something else.

Was this Lucifer's doing?

Was he about to escape and wage war against Heaven and the Creation again?

Her and Jack?

"Death angels!" Talia called out. "All squads surround the Cloud Chamber. Now! Defensive formation"

The rest of the guard blinked into the air around the High House spire and positioned themselves around the dome alongside the cherubim. Around the Cloud Chamber. Where Lucifer was being held.

Every time Talia dropped a demon, two more rolled out of the clouds above her and attacked. Until she summoned a rolling burst of Holy fire that incinerated more than two dozen demons.

Only when a handful of demons remained did Reptev, Lix, and Pharzus blink away from High House. Leaving Kesien furious and throwing Holy fire into the clouds until Azrael pulled him back into formation. The rest of Talia's squad quickly took positions around

Kesien. In a moment, Talia joined them in formation as they floated at attention in front of Azrael.

"As of right now, all of you are on permanent assignment to High House until this tribunal concludes," Azrael ordered, wings spread wide. "Defend it at all costs. Acknowledge your orders."

Talia cringed. She needed to go to Jack. Not be one of dozens of guards around High House. Not with her rare angel powers. And his.

Muriel and Anahera spoke up. "Acknowledged."

Deemah followed with a quick, "Acknowledged, sir."

"Kesien, Talia," Azrael barked, charcoal grey eyes flashing with lightning. "Acknowledge your orders."

Talia tried to stare Azrael down, tell him she had to go to Jack, but Azrael's gaze was like granite. He wasn't going to let her out of his sight. But why wasn't he concerned for Jack's safety? He probably figured Jack's seraphim powers—and his wings—would get him out of any danger. But what about Armand and Izzy? Mark and Morgan? And the cast and crew of their reality television show. Where she should have been filming alongside Jack. With no angels to fill in, poor Jack had to be using every excuse in his human toolbox to account for her absence.

"Acknowledged," she said finally.

What could she do? She smiled. Sneak away when Azrael returned his attention to those spire viewing platforms.

"Kesien?" Azrael said in a threatening tone, arms folded against his soft white robes.

A defeated sigh rolled off Kesien's tongue. "All right," he snapped, brushing a black curl out of his eyes. "Acknowledged."

Azrael pointed toward the spire. "To your posts. Now! Leave them and I'll have your wings. Now, go."

If he noticed her missing.

Still, Talia didn't want to get any of her squad mates in trouble.

Grudgingly, she flew off toward the spire and took up a defensive position around the dome—the Cloud Chamber—alongside Muriel and Kesien who took their places on either side of her. Deemah and Anahera flew into place beside Kesien.

Now, she couldn't slip down to Earth and check on Jack without getting her squad mates in trouble.

She was worried. If she'd faced some demon attacks outside the newly reconstructed High House here in Heaven, what was Jack facing down on Earth?

As she floated beside the dome, trying to come up with a way to get back to Jack, Pravuil, the Maker's Scribe appeared beside Azrael.

"Azrael!" Pravuil shouted, in a gruff, urgent tone. "A word please."

They spoke in notes and sounds that she could barely hear. They weren't angelic tones from the melodic Enochian tongue. No, they were short, clipped, rudimentary sounds that she couldn't interpret. Some sort of archangel code?

"You sure about this, Pravuil?" Azrael replied, looking incredulous.

"Of course, I'm sure."

Pravuil looked short-tempered and anxious, nodding his head in an exaggerated gesture.

"Be quick about it then," said Azrael as he pivoted on an updraft. "As you can see, it's not a good time."

"Maybe not, but it's imperative."

Azrael nodded toward High House and Pravuil blinked across the sky, landing in front of Talia. Startling her as he laid his hand on her arm.

"All right, Talia," he said in his gruff, impatient Scribe way. "We need to talk about this tribunal."

She frowned. "When?"

He gripped her arm. "Now."

With a wave of his hand, she and Pravuil disappeared in a burst of white light. A heartbeat later, they appeared inside a small square office within the High House spire. Beside the Cloud Chamber.

White walls glowed with ethereal light, the floor covered with puffy, white alabaster clouds. Pravuil didn't say a word as he flew along the four walls, casting a warm gold light along each one. Across the hazy ceiling. Over the cloud floor.

He was warding the room. Making sure no one heard their conversation.

Then he blinked across the space, gripping her arms. Looking apprehensive.

"All right, Talia, we need to talk about this trial." He sighed. "And Jack."

A cold wind brushed across her heart.

"What about Jack?" she demanded.

"There are archangels out there who want his angel powers torn out of his body and given to *deserving* celestials."

Talia gaped at him. Had the surviving archangels grown that petty? And ridiculous enough to think they could steal those seraphim powers? If anything, those powers would return to Seraphina, not be divvied up like loot.

"Yes, that's right, Talia," Pravuil continued, not moving, his presence intimidating. "Powers torn out of his body and passed out to the archangels who survived the Sixth Flight."

So, Lucifer still had co-conspirators in Heaven. And a demon army still fighting for him. They had boldly attacked Heaven—again— hiding their numbers. That meant they didn't have enough demons for a head-on assault. Yet. For now, they had enough to launch these familiar hit-and-run tactics. Archangel Samael had used them against Azrael and Eolowen for quite a while—before he overtly joined Lucifer and assaulted Heaven.

Samael had already shown his leering face, leaving no doubt who commanded these demons.

Would they keep attacking? With the entirety of Lucifer's remaining but scattered army eventually showing up? To break Lucifer out of prison during the tribunal? With Samael leading the charge?

But the Maker would be presiding over this tribunal. Not even Samael was bold—or stupid—enough to launch a direct attack on the Maker. Besides, the Maker would never allow such a traitorous act to happen during Lucifer's trial. At least she didn't think so. Regardless, the totality of Lucifer's remaining army—even scattered—was no match for the Maker of All Things.

But would the Maker act to prevent this treacherous act against Jack from happening?

Prevent them from killing Jack right in front of her and taking his angel powers? Justified because of her forbidden relationship with a human.

"While you were at the spire," Pravuil continued. "I flew down to Earth to check on him."

She gasped.

Pravuil cast a withering glare at her. "You're welcome."

"Scribe, thank you. I'm not ungrateful. I'm just…surprised that you'd go all the way down to Earth just to check on Jack."

Pravuil's face was a mask of anger. "Well, someone needed to make sure he was okay and not running for his life from a horde of demons. He's fine by the way."

She felt the tension drain from her body, her wings going slack as she stared at the archangel. God's Scribe.

"I misrepresented myself to him," he continued and then sighed. "All right, I out and out lied to him. Told him I was looking for you, but I knew where you were the whole time. I just needed to make sure he was all right. Gave him some trial materials to study. To keep his mind off you being gone so long. And to keep him distracted with that book until you returned."

"I know he's beginning to despair," said Talia, knowing Jack would be blaming himself for anything going wrong.

Worrying about her. Aching to hold her. She only wanted him back in her arms.

"Now that Azrael's assigned me to the spire, I can't leave Heaven. Pravuil, how do I get back down to him?"

She tried to keep her voice objective, but her anxious tone bled through.

"With all these demon attacks, I'm afraid you're stuck here, Talia."

Talia gripped the Scribe's arm.

"But Scribe…there are more than enough death angels to contain these demon attacks. They wouldn't miss me for a couple of days."

They didn't need her rare angel powers to combat today's demon attack, but she fought alongside her squad anyway.

Pravuil shook his head, clicking his tongue. "Talia, I wasn't talking about the attacks in Heaven."

"What?" She froze. "What do you mean?"

He pointed toward the cloud floor. "I'm talking about the demon attacks down on Earth. Jack's alone down there."

Her breath caught in the back of her throat. "Jack was attacked by demons?"

Pravuil nodded, hands behind his back as he floated through the room. "Twice. Lare Dumont was behind the second attack."

Talia couldn't hold back her shock and horror. Pravuil rushed back over to her.

"Relax…Jack is fine for now."

"How can I relax?" she demanded, pulling away, her wings twitching and a dull ache beginning to thrum through her halo. "He's all alone and—"

"And he's got seraphim powers. He'll be fine, Talia. For a little while."

Talia turned back to the Scribe. "Then we bring Jack back here. To Heaven. Where I can protect him. Where the guard can watch over him until the tribunal begins."

The Scribe turned away, hands still behind his back. "Talia, these angels who oppose yours and Jack's union are the same archangels that have demanded he be barred from Heaven until called to the tribunal. And the Maker's ruling."

"Barred?" she cried. "Why?"

"Because living humans aren't allowed in Heaven. They're trying to force all the rules into play."

"Why?" Talia asked.

"To make a case that breaking them leads to angels falling." Pravuil glared at the walls. "To set a precedence, make an example of Jack. All to grab his power. And get him thrown out of Heaven for good. Or incinerated. Like Lucifer."

"What would throwing him out of Heaven accomplish?" Talia

asked. She didn't understand what they gained by this pettiness. "Much less incinerating him?"

"Throwing him out of Heaven gets him out of the Maker's line of sight," Pravuil explained matter-of-factly, but she felt the tension behind his words. "And away from any sort of angelic protection. So, they can ambush him and take his powers when no one's looking."

Her heart began to hammer against her rib cage.

"But incinerate him? With all those powers they covet?"

"That's an easy one," said Pravuil with a wave of his hand. "They incinerate Jack in the Lake of Fire, nothing remains but those rare powers—and the seraphim powers. Those powers would all float to the top of the Lake of Fire where a warded archangel could blink what remained across that inferno and back into angelic hands. To be absorbed by other angels."

Jack was in terrible danger.

"But Talia, it's not just Jack they're after."

She stared at him wide-eyed. "What do you mean?"

"If that chamber into the Lake of Fire is opened by the wrong hands, they'll try to incinerate you, too. To harvest your rare angel gifts." He sighed. "But I'm also concerned for Seraphina. If they lured her into that chamber and incinerated her, they could also steal her powers. Any and all angel powers they wanted to take."

"All of this to help Lucifer escape?" she demanded.

"Not escape—that's not the worst part, Talia," said Pravuil as he floated beside her. "They're after Lucifer's power, too. His legendary Lightbringer powers—if they can get at them."

The Lightbringer powers! The thought of these traitors acquiring the strongest angelic powers in existence terrified her.

"But Lucifer hasn't been the Lightbringer in millennia, Pravuil."

"Or ever," said the Scribe as he landed, leaning against the warded walls.

"Ever?" Talia frowned. "But he was the Lightbringer. The Maker's most favored firstborn angel."

"In title only. It was the Maker's most bitter disappointment. Lucifer never ascended to those powers because of his petty jealousies and insecurities, leading to him staging a rebellion. But these traitors could still harvest his current powers and possibly the Lightbringer's dormant powers. But those powers would have to be awakened in order to be used. Or they could hold the Heavens and the Maker hostage with those powers."

Archangels. Plotting to steal the wealth of rare angel and seraphim powers left in Heaven. To finish what Lucifer started. For their own selfish gain.

Somehow, she had to identify these traitors and stop them. Before they took control of everything. Before the Maker ruled on Lucifer's fate.

Pravuil frowned. "Unfortunately, these greedy putzes are at it again, Talia," he said, sounding weary. "Somehow, we need to stop them."

"We'll do our best," said Talia. "I need to get back to my post now."

And find a way to sneak down to Earth and protect her husband.

Pravuil opened a portal through one of the glowing walls and they flew through it. Into the room beside the Cloud Chamber entrance that was above them. Two huge, white double doors without windows stood before them, closed and locked. In an alcove to the right stood four holding cells that gleamed crystalline white with seraphim wards.

Talia paused, staring at the pure white light of the holding cells.

Lucifer stood in the doorway of the first cell, leaning against the doorframe. The corners of his mouth quirked with amusement, curly blond hair disheveled, his eyes a delicate, fragile blue. His black general's coat looked torn and frayed, gold buttons and gold flourishes missing. His black wings were bound against his back, blood red halo dull against the warding light, the thin white scar across his forehead barely visible. He looked defeated, but something amused him.

And that deadly smile unnerved her.

"Hello, dear Talia," he said in that charming, energized British accent.

"Lucifer," she said in a breathless voice, casting a nervous glance at Pravuil.

Who looked as unnerved as she felt.

"Lovely air show the guard's putting on," he said, a dangerous glint burning behind the serene blue of his eyes. "Oh, wait—those are mine, aren't they?"

"And we'll put all of them down like we always do," Pravuil shouted, pointing a finger at him. "Until you burn in the Lake of Fire."

The smile left Lucifer's face but not that deadly twinkle in his eyes.

"Not very objective for a tribunal judge, are we, dear Pravuil. But there's always a third act. We'll see who's left onstage this time. After that final match is lit. Heaven can be so fickle, you know. Especially its Maker. My father."

Lucifer nearly spat out those last words, a red glow burning behind his blue eyes.

"Careful these winged hypocrites don't turn on you, old boy. Especially with so much power to snatch up. Temptation's too great. As the King of temptation, I would know."

He laughed, the sound raking across her wings.

"Oh, and Talia," he said, turning back toward her. "Might want to pop off down to Earth. Now."

She frowned. Had he ordered his demons to do something to Jack?

He nodded. Like he knew exactly what she'd been thinking.

"What did you do?" she demanded, rushing at the cell door, but Pravuil yanked her backward.

Lucifer laid a hand against his torn black general's coat. "Me? Nothing. A bit tied up at the moment. But I feel Lare Dumont up to no good—now that the bellend has wings and escaped Hell. And Jack's running out of viable air. Better hurry before that trailer burns up and kills him."

"Lucifer!" Pravuil shouted. "You'll pay for this!"

Lucifer held up his shackled hands. "Don't shoot the messenger, old boy. Believe me, I'd like nothing better than to see him burn. But my fight is with dear ol' Da and the ol' homestead. Not Jack. Thought maybe you'd want to save him. I'd hate for you to lose a key witness at my trial and all. Pravuil. How ever will you see me burn without Jack's testimony?"

Talia backed away as Pravuil closed his eyes a moment. Probing. Checking on Jack with his archangel powers as she called up omnificence, focusing it downward toward Earth. Toward California. Burbank. Four Acre Studios. And finally, Studio 22. Where their set trailers stood nearby.

Before she even reached toward the images and sounds in her head, she saw the trailer burning. Out of control.

"Pravuil!" she cried.

"By the Maker!" Pravuil shouted.

"I told you he was dying down there," Lucifer replied and sat down on the narrow bunk bed in his cell. "Bloody arrogant archangels. Although, I do love a good soap opera as much as a good barbecue. Watching them fight for these angel powers is even better than the first season of Game of Thrones."

Pravuil grabbed hold of Talia and blinked them through the walls of the spire. They shot across the Parrish blue skies like an asteroid, hurtling through the Constable clouds until they dropped into a free fall toward Earth.

And Jack.

5

marbles did their job. Again.

Jack tried to stretch his wings, but the sharp pain in his right one made him ache to curl into a ball and scream. Pain radiated in waves along the wingtip and up into his right shoulder. The wing hung at an unnatural angle—well, unnatural for being an ethereal angel's wing attached to his human body.

It was broken.

Dammit! He couldn't fly with a broken wing.

He tried to fold his wings against his back, but the right one was like a broken windshield wiper that wouldn't fold back into the well of the windshield anymore. And it throbbed as he turned and stagger-ran toward his trailer. He held the wing immobile as best he could, both steps up to the trailer door radiating more pain.

More shadows passed across the sun, blunting its warm gold light.

Too many demons. He couldn't fight them all. Not like this.

Now that Lucifer wasn't running the show anymore, these Hell creatures didn't have a real leader. And Jack doubted they saw Archangel Samael as a worthy replacement, especially with all those fallen angels in Hell. Demons didn't care about the rules anymore. Not killing humans had just become a polite request at best.

Another wave of pain knocked him to his knees as he fumbled his trailer key out of his pocket and shoved it into the lock. Opening the door.

A demon swooped low, trying to carry him off.

He rolled inside, stifling a shout when his broken wing hit the maple hardwood floor. And slammed the door closed.

Shaking, he crawled across the floor to the couch. Pulling himself up on his knees.

As the trailer door creaked open. And the first shadow filled the trailer doorway.

Black leathery wings blocked out the sun, blood red eyes burning through the shadowy space, drapes closed across all the windows. Only thin streams of sunlight poured in through the small kitchen window as the demon moved toward him.

Smoke rose behind it, coalescing into four more demons. Five. Six.

Wincing, Jack held out his hands, calling up murder marbles.

Like rabid dogs, the demons leaped at him, claws and teeth tearing.

Jack rolled the murder marbles between them and crouched, covering his face.

The explosion sent a spray of red and black from the couch to the door. It settled like a fine mist around the threshold as it mingled with the dust motes.

And still more smoke churned up the steps and flowed into the trailer. Solidifying into more demons.

If he used his seraphim powers inside here, he'd obliterate the whole trailer. Gianni's trailer beside it. And Banks' trailer on the other side. Not to mention the surrounding buildings and about fifty feet of concrete and dirt beneath where the trailers stood. And anyone unfortunate enough to be walking past.

And he'd probably obliterate his friends in those trailers and himself, too, being at ground zero and all. Inside the seraphim blast.

Jack tossed out a white burst of warding light that wrapped around his body.

The demons rushed him, bouncing off the ward as they swarmed like frenzied wasps trying to break through to him.

"Ja-ack? Where'd you go-o?"

Lare's gleeful taunting singsong echoed from somewhere beyond the demon swarm.

"Fun's just getting started. Can't wait for you to run out of juice for that ward, so I can tear you apart and watch you bleed out near Studio 18."

Where they filmed *SanFran Confidential*.

In a few moments, sweat broke out across Jack's face, his body shaking as he tried to maintain the seraphim ward. Why couldn't he have just flown out of here? So no one else got hurt.

But his broken wing wasn't taking him anywhere this time.

The white glow of the ward began to flicker.

Already? He had more juice than that!

But then he realized that every time one of these demons threw itself at the ward, it drained a bit of power from it. From him. With a demon swarm, he wouldn't be able to keep the ward at full power for long. Not alone anyway.

He had maybe ten minutes before they broke through. If that.

He threw down three more murder marbles. Spraying the trailer with another coat of red demon primer.

And still they came at him. In waves he'd never seen before. Frenzied. Frantic. Unstoppable.

Carefully, he focused down his seraphim energies to a three-foot swath in front of him.

He held his breath.

And let it go.

The burst rolled through the swarm of demons. Setting them—and the trailer—alight.

The blowback of seraphim energy sent Lare and any remaining demons through the walls, propelling them in all directions. Like a sonic boom.

The front wall caught fire. And then the wall to the right of the sofa.

Shit. Azrael was going to kill him if he had to put this trailer back together one more time.

Before Jack could release the ward, fire chewed up the wall. And blocked his only way out of the trailer, a wall of flame roiling where the door had once been.

As his ward fell, smoke built throughout the trailer.

Jack dropped low, struggling against the broken wing as he crawled through the smoke toward the bedroom. Toward the one window he could crawl out and escape from this growing inferno.

More flames flowed up the walls and across the ceiling—growling, crackling, chewing through the trailer with horrific speed. The heat stung his face and skin, getting hotter.

He crawled toward the bedroom's far wall and pulled himself to his feet, leaning as pain radiated through his shoulder in throbbing waves into his chest as he struggled to unlock the window. It was high up the wall and he had to work by feel to open the lock.

As the smoke grew dark and acrid, drifting like an apparition through the long, narrow trailer, shapes moved through the smoke.

His stomach dropped, heart racing. Those shapes weren't shadows. They were demons.

A lot of demons.

The window clicked as the lock disengaged.

As the couch ignited in a burst of flames, dozens and dozens of red eyes peered through the smoke.

Heading down the long, narrow hallway toward him.

Channeling more seraphim power, Jack threw another white ward up between him and the growing mob of demons.

Across the bedroom door.

Using his left shoulder, he lifted the stubborn window with all his might. And it screeched open.

Black smoke poured out of it, into the air, and floated into the sunlight.

He had to get out this window fast.

Before demons blocked it.

He looked up as the light disappeared.

His seraphim ward! Already engulfed by demons.

He tossed another across the threshold, knowing it wouldn't last but a couple of minutes at most.

Taking a deep breath of clean air from the open window, Jack pulled his body up onto the narrow window ledge.

But a rush of black smoke flowed in through the open window.

Knocking him to the floor.

The roar of flames intensified. The fire had reached the bedroom, flames devouring the roof and the walls, burning the floors as it bumped against his seraphim ward.

The screech of a new horde of demons was shrill and tore along his spine as the fire roared around him.

And with a heave of smoke and flames, the seraphim ward fell to the overwhelming force of demons.

Jack stumbled back against the wall, coughing and struggling to breathe as the swarm flowed into the bedroom.

Lare Dumont moved behind it, the smoke like a cloak around his body, those red eyes so intense.

"End of the line, Jack," he said with a smile.

Jack filled both hands with murder marbles, feeling the drain of his power beginning. The weakness that made every step like slogging through quicksand. He didn't have much power after the apocalypse, so it wouldn't take long to drain his angel powers—and his stamina. Murder marbles were his last shot at taking down Lare and his demons.

But afterward, he wouldn't have the energy to even get to the window, much less lifting himself up and out that window.

Maybe firefighters would get to him in time, but he knew better.

Not even an alarm had been raised across the studio.

"Forgive me, Talia," he whispered, the ache in his chest profound.

When his soul left his body, he'd never see her again.

Lare was right.

Ride was over.

The whine of murder marbles was shrill and frantic in his ears as he flung them into the approaching wave of dark smoke.

An overwhelming force of demons.

He couldn't fight them all. Not here. They knew he wouldn't risk harming anyone else by using his seraphim powers. So, they'd waited patiently to get him alone. Corner him. And swarm him.

He'd just spite all of them and die before they could take any of his powers.

"Gonna enjoy tearing each one of those rare powers out of your hide, Jack."

Lare's voice carried above the roar of flames.

"Almost as much as I'm going to enjoy watching these demons turn you into coleslaw."

Coleslaw. He'd give this little bitch coleslaw. With all the hot sauce he could muster.

As the swarm of red eyes descended, Jack flung the murder marbles onto the hardwood in front of him.

One after another, the murder marbles exploded as demons passed over them.

The first blast slammed Jack against the wall. He covered his head with his good wing, waiting for each successive blast to fire.

Demon after demon screeched and disintegrated as the entire bedroom went up in flames.

But too many demons were still standing. Eyes burning stoplight red. Floating toward him.

Until something big dropped through the bedroom window.

Snarling. Growling.

In the roil of smoke and rumble of flames, Jack saw the ruddy glow of ten red eyes and five long, leathery snouts. With knife-like teeth. Feral growls vibrated around him.

He froze. Hellhounds.

Shit. He was so dead.

From somewhere in the inferno of smoke and flames, Lare Dumont laughed.

"Demons weren't the only things to escape Hell, Jack. Time to say goodbye."

Hot, fetid breath hit him in the face like opening a door into a firestorm as red hellhound eyes surrounded him.

He held his breath, panic rising. Hoping they'd quickly tear him apart instead of playing with their food.

6

Jack wheezed, thick black smoke tightening around his lungs. He coughed and sputtered. Fighting to breathe, he waited for razor-sharp teeth to tear him apart.

Until something hot and wet slapped against his face.

He gasped for air and froze as something began a steady staccato beat against the hot hardwood floor. And his leg. Something long, whiplike, and spiky.

A tail?

The smoke fanned away until he was staring into the gaping mouths of a two-headed hellhound.

"Orthy?" he sputtered between coughs.

The two-headed hellhound whined and nudged Jack's chest with its snouts, tail thumping wildly against the floor.

In front of Orthy stood his brother, Cerberus. Cerby growled with all three mouths, red eyes burning through the smoke and flames. Daring the demons to come at him.

"Good boy, Cerby," said Jack.

Cerby's tail thumped wildly against the floor and he whined, but it quickly rumbled into a fierce growl as Orthrus took hold of Jack's arm and leg with both mouths.

Pulling him onto Cerby's back, the larger of the two hellhounds.

Cerby backed up toward the window, allowing Orthy to climb onto his shoulders. The smaller hellhound grabbed hold of Jack's arm and leg with both snouts and leaped.

Carrying Jack out through the high bedroom window.

Into the cool, clear morning air.

The heavy weight of the gritty, acrid smoke began to lift from his lungs and chest as Cerby's fierce howls echoed through the trailer. Blowing out the fire. It went out fast, like a candle in an open window.

Smoke poured out the trailer's bedroom window as the horde of demons tried to escape the guardian of the Gates of Hell. And his little brother, Orthy who jumped back inside to route the demons. They had apparently left Hell when the gates were opened. Like Lare Dumont and a shit ton of demons. Along with Kesien's traitor angel dudes from his former squad.

Jack panted, lying on the ground, struggling to breathe, his broken wing throbbing when Orthy and Cerby returned, licking his face and pawing at his chest as they stood guard. Trying to make sure he was okay.

"Good boys," said Jack between coughs.

He gave them scratches behind their leathery ears and petted them until he couldn't move his arms anymore. The hellhounds ate up the attention until Jack collapsed against the pavement, unable to move another muscle. Orthrus and Cerberus laid their heads on his legs and chest. Keeping watch over him.

"Jack!"

Growls rumbled against his body as Cerby and Orthy lifted their five snouts, teeth bared, bodies tensing as Gianni's voice pierced the solitude of his exhaustion.

"Oh God—he can't be in there! Jack!"

"Move, Banks!" Gianni again. "Jack? Jack! Dear God—JACK!"

Gianni sounded frantic.

Wood cracked as the sound of Gianni kicking in the trailer door made Jack open his eyes.

The hellhounds began to growl, but Jack stroked their furry necks.

"Easy boys, they're bros." He gathered as much breath as he could. "Gianni—behind the trailer."

Footsteps pounded along the pavement.

"Jack? Where are you? Jack!" Gianni.

"Keep talking, Jack." Banks. "We'll find you."

Gianni turned the corner of the burned trailer and found Jack on the ground, but he froze.

"What. The Holy Hell. Are those?" Gianni demanded, pointing at the hellhounds, his mouth gaping.

"Hellhounds," said Jack, "Long story."

"For real, Jack?" Banks said, sounding intrigued.

Jack nodded. "The three-headed one is Cerberus, Guardian of the Gates of Hell. Orthy here is his little brother."

Orthrus started wagging his tail again, slowly poking one of his snouts toward Gianni.

Grinning, Banks gently reached out and gave Orthy a scritch.

"What a good boy you are," said Banks and Orthy's tail wagged faster.

At last, Gianni laid his hand on Orthy's other head, scratching him behind the ears. When Orthy licked his hand with his other snout, Gianni smiled.

"You are a good boy," said Gianni.

"They saved me from the demons, Gianni," said Jack. "Pulled me out of the fire."

Gianni's eyes widened. "You were attacked by demons? But the apocalypse is over."

Jack nodded. "Lare Dumont was leading them. He had wings and everything." Jack winced and tried to sit up. Couldn't.

Gianni knelt beside him and helped Jack sit up, anchoring his right wing. His angel power to hide them had been drained in the onslaught, something he hadn't experienced in a long while.

"I can see from here that your wing's broken."

"They were everywhere, Gianni," said Jack. "Never seen so many. But I couldn't use my seraphim powers or risk killing lots of people on the lot. I started lobbing murder marbles and throwing out wards.

But they just swarmed the wards until they exhausted the power and brought them down. I've never seen it so bad before."

Banks moved to Jack's other side as the two hellhounds took up defensive positions around them, watching for more demons.

"The bottle's been uncorked," said Banks.

Gianni nodded. "Once that gate opened, it let all those demons run free. Gonna be hell to round all of them up again."

"And without Lucifer at the helm," Jack said, wincing, "they have no one telling them what to do. Samael wants it all to burn, so he's not going to give them any orders from Hell's throne either."

"How does it get fixed then?" Banks asked, glancing up as shadows brushed across the sun.

"Wish I knew. Maybe the Maker will take care of them after Lucifer's trial?"

Gianni looked worried. "Let's hope so. Because people are going to die if the totality of Hell's demons—or even a large contingent—are running free with no one holding their reins."

Orthy began to growl. Cerberus bared his teeth, throaty growls rumbling from all three snouts.

"What is it, Orthy?" Jack asked as Orthy stared at nothing. "Cerby, what do you see?"

Both hellhounds seemed fixed on something that Jack couldn't see.

"Gianni, you and Banks might want to get out of here."

"No way am I leaving you to face more demons alone," said Gianni.

"What Gianni said," said Banks, standing tall and stiff behind the hellhounds. "We're your buddies."

"Dudes who fight in the apocalypse together are friends for life, Jack." Gianni sighed. "And we may have talked to your former boss, but Jack, we would never agree to anything unless you were cool with it first."

Jack smiled. He said dudes.

"You'd really give up the lead in SanFran Confidential for our friendship?"

"No," Banks said with a chuckle. "Are you crazy, Jack? But we'd talk to you first before we said hell yes."

Jack couldn't help but laugh.

"Seriously, Jack," said Gianni. "Banks and I already talked about this before we took Evan's calls. We agreed that you had to be okay with this or we would say no."

"As much as it hurts," said Banks.

"Sorry I doubted you dudes," said Jack as Gianni hauled him to his feet.

"It's okay, Jack," said Gianni. "You went through hell on that set. Reacting like you did was understandable. I was going to give you some time to cool down before smacking you upside the head with the facts."

The sound of wings whispered through the quiet.

Jack looked up and saw Talia rushing toward him.

When Orthy and Cerby saw Pravuil behind Talia, they dissolved into smoke and faded into the shadows.

"Be safe, little dudes," Jack called to them as Talia threw her arms around him.

He held her tighter than he'd meant to, but the feel of her body against his was the most comforting sensation he'd felt in a long time. She was all sunlight and wind and rain. She was his beating heart and his fevered breath. She was the entire pulse of his life force thrumming beneath his skin. And he never wanted to let her go again.

"Tal," he said, fighting not to let his smoke-raw voice break.

"Oh, Jack—what happened! Are you hurt? The trailer's... destroyed."

She kissed him with a burst of heat and passion that radiated against his skin like an electrical storm.

He smashed his mouth against hers and frantically kissed her, pressing his body against hers, aching to move closer into her angelic presence.

"Demons," he said as she pulled back, waiting to hear what had happened. "Where have you been?"

"In Heaven, Jack," she said, her brow furrowed. "You know where I was."

"You've been avoiding me," he said in a quiet but hurt voice. "What did I do?"

She laid her hands against his flushed face, pain in her crystalline grey eyes that sparkled with sunlight and angelic energy.

"Oh, Jack, you haven't done anything. Preparing for Lucifer's tribunal has been so difficult."

Even now, he felt her pulling away from him. Emotionally. Physically.

"You're so distant," he said in a quiet voice, trying not to let Gianni or Banks hear him. "Like you're trying to push me away."

"Push you away?"

He nodded. "You don't think the Maker's going to let us stay together, do you? That's why you're keeping your distance, isn't it? So, it won't hurt so much?"

Anger bloomed in those grey eyes, flashing like a lightning storm.

"Jack Casey, you stop that right now," she said, her tone sharp. "Yes, I'm worried. And yes, I've been keeping my distance. Because I didn't want you to get hurt." She held him at arm's length, wincing when her gaze settled on his broken wing. "Like this."

"I get why Lare's trying to end me," said Jack. "That's nothing new. But why do you need to stay away to keep me safe?" His gaze narrowed. "What's going on, Talia?"

She glanced around and lowered her voice so only he could hear her. "Jack, they're trying to take your powers."

"Which powers?" he asked.

"All of them," she said with a sigh. "And they're willing to do anything for them."

A strange sense of calm settled against his chest and spread a chill along his arms and legs. It wasn't about him then…the reason she'd been so distant.

"And how could they take these powers when the seraphim couldn't take them back?"

"By destroying your body and soul in the Lake of Fire. And then taking the angelic power essences that survived."

Damn. That was harsh. "And just who are these fine upstanding angels trying to steal my seraphim powers?"

"Archangels, Jack," said Talia, holding him tight again.

"Loyal to Lucifer until the very end, aren't these traitors? Even with the Maker in the house?"

She shook her head. "Actually, Lucifer is the one who warned me that you were in danger."

Jack stared at her a moment, frowning. "Lucifer? Why would he do that? He hates me."

"I'm not sure what new game he's playing, Jack, but Pravuil and I are here because of his warning."

"Probably trying to make sure he still gets the pleasure of killing me himself," Jack muttered.

Pravuil reached out and laid his hand on Jack's right wing. A wash of white light surged across the feathers and sinews until Jack heard a crackle. In the warmth of the bright light, his wing knitted its broken bones back together.

"There, Jack," said Pravuil, stepping back. "Good as new—at least for now."

Jack flexed the wing, letting it unfurl and then close a couple of times. "Thanks, Scribe. Appreciate it."

Talia gripped his right hand and brought it to her lips, gently kissing his fingers.

"Better?"

"It's a start," said Jack with a smirk, but his face fell when he realized the hot mess that was his and Talia's trailer.

There would be no sexy time in that hell zone.

"Pravuil," said Jack, nodding at his trailer. "Think you could archangel this slag back the way it was?"

Pravuil looked it up and down, shaking his head. "I can try. But this might be a project for Azrael."

"Appreciate the attempt, dude."

Pravuil blinked toward the trailer's only door and laid his hands on it until he'd reclaimed the door from oblivion. Sighing, he opened the new door and went inside, slamming it.

"Guess that's gonna take a while," said Jack as Talia slid her arms around his waist.

"So, how's the show going?" she asked. "We're due for our couple's interview and…"

Jack couldn't keep that everything's all right smile on his face. Her voice trailed off as he looked away, a storm of emotions roiling through him.

"It's been cancelled, Talia," said Gianni in a soft voice. "We just got the news."

"Cancelled?" She turned toward Jack, but he couldn't look her in the eye.

This show brought them together. Kept them together. Protected them. Saved them both in ways he couldn't even voice.

And now, it was over?

Was it only the first of many devastating changes about to happen? He was afraid it was the first shoe to drop and he couldn't survive the second shoe being forever separated from Talia—by Heaven.

Even the thought sent a wave of pain through his chest that burned all the way into his feet.

"Oh, Jack," she said, holding him tight again. "I'm so sorry."

Her tone bothered him. Like it was only happening to him and not her. Like she was fine with it. Because it no longer affected her.

"You sound like it doesn't affect you, Tal," he said, pulling away from her embrace.

Her eyes widened. "Jack! Of course it affects me."

"Sounded like that sympathy was only for me." He sighed. "It was our show. Talia, what's happened to us? Are we the next cancellation?"

"Jack Casey!" she cried, looking terrified. "You and I are not being cancelled."

"Are you sure?" he asked in a soft voice.

She moved toward him, sliding her arms around him again. She kissed him hard on the lips until he felt his heart beating into his feet.

"You're my husband," said Talia, brushing his hair out of his eyes.

"And I made a vow to love you forever—not that I needed a promise to love you. No matter what happens at Lucifer's trial, you and I are a couple. Intertwined. Inseparable. Married. Got it, Jackson Seeger Casey?"

He smiled when she used his full name. She had no idea how much he'd needed her to say those words right now.

"Got it," he said and held her closer. "Mrs. Casey. No matter what."

At last, the tension left her face and she nodded, laying her face against his shoulder, holding him tight again.

In a moment, Pravuil blinked out of the trailer, looking puzzled, holding the book he'd brought Jack and something between thumb and forefinger. He held it out as Jack let go of Talia.

"What the hell happened in there, Jack?" Pravuil demanded, eyes bright gold.

Talia squinted at what he held out. A large tooth.

"That's a hellhound's tooth," said Talia, gaze narrowing as she summoned a white angel ward between her hands.

Jack laid his hand against hers until the white light dissipated.

"For once," said Jack. "They were on our side."

"They?" Talia cried, her eyes widening as she glanced at Pravuil and then at Jack.

"Orthy and Cerby were here," he said. "Protected me from Lare's swarm of demons." He had to tell her about his seraphim ward. "And Tal, there were so many demons that they drained my seraphim ward in minutes. That's never happened to me before."

Pravuil grumbled under his breath. "The Maker has already summoned Abaddon to Heaven. Intending to send him down here to Earth to recapture as much of the demon hordes as he can. And get them back behind the Gates of Hell. Including Orthrus and Cerberus."

That made Jack sad. Those two hellhounds were trained to guard. Without a gate to guard, they were dangerous running free here on Earth. But still, the thought of them stuck with that douchebag Samael or Lare Dumont made his blood boil. Or just stuck in Hell— with no one to pet them or play ball with them.

"Isn't there anywhere they could go instead of Hell?" Jack asked. "They're not demons. They're good boys just doing their jobs."

Pravuil clapped Jack on the shoulder. "I wish, Jack, but we both know the danger they pose outside of Hell."

"But why Hell?" Jack asked. "They don't deserve that place. Why not Heaven? Or at least Purgatory."

Pravuil shrugged. "They were created to guard Hell's Gate. If that position was no longer needed, then only the Maker could decide to send them elsewhere."

That gave Jack some hope. He'd ask the Maker when he testified. He'd try to get better digs for the loyal hellhound brothers.

"All dogs go to Heaven," said Jack. "That should include Orthy and Cerby."

"Talk to the Maker, Jack. Maybe they will reward the hellhounds with something celestial to guard?"

"I will. Thanks, Pravuil."

"How's the trailer?" Talia asked.

Pravuil shook his head. "See for yourself."

Talia gave Jack a worried look and blinked into the trailer. In moments, she returned, looking pale.

"Oh, Jack—it's a mess."

"Gonna take Azrael to put it back together," said Pravuil. "I got rid of the smoke and some of the damage, but right now, it can't even be properly warded. I'm afraid you can't stay there until Azrael gives it some attention."

"And let me guess," said Jack. "The archangel's dance card is full until October?"

"More like October a decade from now," Pravuil said and unfurled his wings. "Lucifer's trial's been delayed a little. It now starts in four angel days." He shifted his gaze to Talia. "Bring him to Eolowen until the trial. Those demons don't want him testifying any more than the archangels do."

Jack frowned. "Uh, what archangels?"

"The archangels that want your powers, Jack," said Pravuil, his tone grim. "We need to get you somewhere safe."

Jack turned around toward Gianni and Banks. "Looks like I'll be away for a few days, dudes. When I return, I'll be on the sidelines, watching you two on my old show. Hope you dudes don't forget me."

Gianni pulled him into a hug. "Be safe, Jack. Nothing's going to happen with your old show until you get back. And I will never forget my best friend."

Banks hugged him next. "Me either. We sure as hell aren't going to steal your old show out from under you. When you're back here on set—or at the studio—we'll decide what happens next."

"Appreciate that, Gianni. Banks. Hope I still exist to talk about this —me and Talia."

Talia hugged Gianni and then Banks.

"Watchers are stationed around the area," she said. "They'll make sure you, Mark, Morgan, and Izzy are safe, Armand. And the studio. Jack and I will be back soon. Together. To talk about what happens next. And to celebrate our first anniversary together."

"The party," said Gianni. "Izzy and I got the invitation. We'll be there."

"So will Morgan and I," said Banks. "No matter what happens here."

"Be safe, Jack!" Gianni called as he and Banks stepped back.

Jack gently unfurled his wings and nodded to Pravuil. The Scribe slid one arm into Talia's and one into Jack's. With a deep breath, he blinked them into the air, shooting like a bullet across the sky. Up through the Heavens. Until the bright white stones of Eolowen's terrace materialized beneath them.

An empty terrace. Not one angel trained or sparred at the grand hall.

"Where is everyone?" Jack asked as Pravuil shot across the lower Heavens' Parrish blue sky.

Toward High House.

"Finalizing preparations for Lucifer's trial," Talia said and pointed at the tall spire that sparkled against the crisp blue sky, clouds scuttling past. "And guarding High House."

"The new spire is up!" Jack cried.

Talia nodded. "We're finishing the addition of some viewing platforms, so every angel in the lower Heavens can watch the tribunal in the new, secured Cloud Chamber. Archangels and other special guests can watch it from the courtroom gallery."

Jack remembered how Lucifer had used a rare angel power to control Oseira, one of the cherubim guard to cause a deadly explosion of Holy fire. Destroying the spire and erasing two seraph from existence.

Jack wondered if the Maker could—or would—bring back those angels. He didn't know how angels were created though. Maybe that wasn't possible? Or only possible through the Maker?

Guess he'd find that out—and more—and soon.

"So, four angel days 'til the tribunal?" Jack said to Talia who glanced up at the sky.

"Three now, Jack," she said.

Jack couldn't tell how angels tracked time up here. The sun never set. It never got dark, even though Talia said the light waned in the late afternoon and what they called evening. But it was too subtle for his human eyes. He'd let Talia tell him when it was time for this tribunal to start.

"Jack Casey!"

Berith descended from the sky and landed beside him, her rose-gold halo bright as she folded her wings against her back.

"Berith!" He threw his arms around her and hugged her tightly.

"Good to see you," she said and then frowned. "Jack, your face! What happened?"

"Demons, uh…cancelled my set trailer. Again."

"He broke one of his wings, Berith," said Talia. "Pravuil healed it enough to fly, but those demons will return. We thought it best to bring him here, out of their reach until the tribunal begins."

Berith nodded. "Good plan. Come on, Jack," she said, motioning him toward the billowing white curtains that led into the round room off the terrace. "Let's get some healing light on those injuries."

He'd already spent a lot of time in this room. But he worried that this might be the last time he ever stepped foot in Eolowen.

"I'll be there in a moment, Jack," said Talia, her gaze on the horizon.

On the new spire.

"I need to make sure my squad gets the rest of those viewing platforms in place."

Jack frowned. She was already leaving him again.

"How long will that take?" he asked finally.

She slid her arms around his waist and kissed him. "Not long. I'll bring you some mana cakes when I return."

His eyes lit up. "Mana cakes?"

She nodded and kissed him again.

"Hurry back, babe," he said. "I—"

She blinked into the air and shot across the clouds toward the spire.

"Love you," he said to the rush of air she left in her wake.

He sighed. Didn't even get all three words out.

A moment later, a patrol of cherubim in angel form flew low over Eolowen. Like they did when Lucifer was about to march on Heaven after getting his wings and halo back. And during the apocalypse. Jack just hoped Lucifer didn't have a third assault planned. The sight of the cherubim patrols made him uneasy.

"Come on, Jack," said Berith, sliding her arm around his waist. "Let's get you healed."

"Thanks, Berith. It's great to see you again."

She was like the mother he'd always wanted.

She hugged him. "You, too, Jack."

He cast a longing look across the Heavens, the ache in his chest deepening. Talia's absence hollowed the pit of his stomach as he followed Berith into the round room. And he hoped Talia wouldn't be gone long. In angel or human time.

7

WHEN TALIA RETURNED TO EOLOWEN, SHE BROUGHT JACK TWO MANA cakes. A white bed had been brought into the airy, terrace room. He hurried toward her, pulling her into his arms, and kissing her. She held out the mana cakes and his eyes lit up.

"Thanks, Tal."

She handed him the cakes.

Jack kissed her again, a long passionate kiss that left her weak in the knees. He sprawled across the bed on his stomach, eyes half-closed, his healing wing drooping against the white sheets as he brought the first cake to his mouth.

She sat down on the edge of the bed and ran her fingers through his light blond hair.

"After you've eaten, promise me you'll get some sleep, Jack," she said.

"I'm fine," he said. "It's just been a long day."

Jack always forgot that she knew when he was lying, but she ignored it this time, knowing how much stress her husband of almost a year had been under. He never told big lies, just little ones to keep her from worrying. She was an angel of death, a soldier in Azrael's guard, something else Jack always forgot. He didn't treat her like she was made of glass because he thought she was so delicate that only a man could protect her. He protected her because his heart was made of glass and the thought of losing her broke him.

And she loved him for that.

Berith motioned her out of the room and onto the terrace, still empty of angels of death who worked tirelessly to secure the new spire ahead of the tribunal.

Talia rubbed Jack's shoulder and rose from the bed, following Berith out to the terrace as Jack took a big bite of that first mana cake.

"What's the matter, Berith?" Talia asked, concerned by Berith's anxious expression as she kept glancing back at Jack.

"Talia, he's done nothing but pace since you left." Berith cast another worried look over her shoulder. "What's going on between you two? You both seem like you're worlds apart—not together."

Talia bowed her head. "I've been away," she said. "Much longer than I'd intended."

"I was afraid of that," said Berith, crossing her arms against her white and gold armor. "I haven't seen him look this lost and forlorn since Lucifer took control of you and spirited you away."

Berith was right.

Talia had been away so long trying to protect Jack from the archangels' treachery that she'd made him think she no longer cared about their relationship. Why hadn't she just gone to him? Even for an hour. To keep him from losing hope. He'd done his best to hide it, but not even his seraphim powers could hide his pain from her. Pain she had caused.

"This is all my fault, Berith," she said finally, singing her words in the angelic tongue so Jack couldn't hear. "I was away too long without even a word to him. He thought I wasn't coming back this time."

Jack seemed content devouring a mana cake, blue Vans kicked off beside the bed, his ash-dusted, paint-encrusted blue coveralls torn where his wings had burst through the back. His wings were folded loosely against his shoulders, making him look less tense and anxious.

"Why would he think that?" Berith asked.

"Because, despite what he says," said Talia. "The damage Rachel and Lare inflicted on him has never healed. Deep down, he still believes her gaslighting and insults, that he isn't worth loving. And when he thought I wasn't coming back, he started reconnecting those dots on those old messages. Because he thought he wasn't worthy."

Berith's face pinched. "Jack…"

"He's always anxious whenever I'm away, but this is a whole new level of uncertainty. And I caused it."

"What's he worried about?" Berith asked. "The tribunal?"

"Us," she said, wincing, that word heavy on her lips. "He's convinced that the Maker will separate us. And he's convinced that I've grown tired of us and want out."

"You? Tired of Jack Casey?" Berith laughed. "How could he ever think that?"

"He's under a lot of stress, Berith. His show just got cancelled."

Berith's eyes grew wide, brows lifting. "What? Not his hit TV show! Where you and Jack met?"

Talia nodded. "After six seasons, it's over. I heard him and his costars talking about how they were offered parts on Jack's old hit show. But not Jack. He's taking that hard, too. With that awful demon attack on top of it—and the tribunal looming—it's too much."

"That's a lot to deal with—even for Jack," said Berith, her gaze softening. "Especially with some entitled archangels trying to steal his powers."

Talia's wings twitched, anger burning through her wing feathers. Every time she thought about those opportunistic monsters, she wanted to spit fire.

These archangels were egotistical and greedy. They thought angels were better than humans and sought Jack's powers to rise in the angel hierarchy. Jack had never used his powers for personal gain. Ever.

"Not just steal them, Berith," said Talia, the edge in her voice sharpening. "They intend to pass those powers around their cadre of arrogant archangels. As if the Maker would allow that."

Berith propped her hands on her hips, her expression darkening as she gazed from Jack to the distant spires.

"Not directly anyway. Do they think they can just reach inside Jack's chest and yank out those powers?"

"No, they plan to extract Jack's powers by throwing him into the Lake of Fire."

"The Lake of Fire?" Berith's eyes widened. "But only the Maker and Lord Kushiel have the keys to that door. Or know where the Lake is located!"

That gave her hope that the archangels' plan was unlikely to succeed. Talia gritted her teeth, hands clenching into fists.

"I swear, Berith, if they touch one blond hair on Jack's head, I'll smite every one of them out of existence."

Berith laid her hands on Talia's forearms, healing light warming her angelic form with waves of pale gold calm. Soothing her anger. Quelling her fury as Berith's expression sharpened, her mouth flattening into a taut line. She was worried about Jack now, too.

"No archangel knows where the door to the Lake of Fire resides, Talia," said Berith, her tone reassuring. "And even if they did find it, they couldn't unlock the door without the key which has to be assembled. Besides, if Heaven knew how to reclaim those powers without harming Jack, Seraphina would have already taken them back. And his wings and halo, returning Jack to a completely human state."

Berith was right. If it were that easy to take Jack's powers, Heaven would have already reclaimed them. Taking his wings and halo would turn Jack into a fallen angel and ban him from Heaven. Forever. And right now, no one in Heaven knew how to do that either.

The thought of that made Talia shudder.

But she couldn't help wondering what all of these celestially born things were doing to Jack's body—and his humanness. He'd already stopped aging. Had those powers and the wings and halo made him immortal? Or something halfway between human and angel? No one in Heaven could answer that question.

"And I doubt that Lord Kushiel would willingly give up that key to these power-hungry embarrassments," said Talia.

Berith nodded, putting her hands on her hips. "So, these cowards plan to not-so-subtly condemn yours and Jack's relationship during the tribunal. Complain to the Maker like spoiled children. If they can get your marriage dissolved, then they will be emboldened enough to try and throw Jack into the Lake of Fire as an abomination."

Talia felt the cold air rush through her wings, her heart aching.

"Abomination," she said, a growl in her voice. "I've heard enough of their petty accusations. The whispers. The archangels' snide comments. Jack is still human, with a human soul. He poses no danger to anyone—except maybe himself. Surely, the Maker already knows that."

But Jack had stopped aging. No one in Heaven understood why. Even she didn't know if he was angel or human anymore.

Berith turned toward the sun that hung low over the Heavens. It would sink lower, projecting warm golden light across the lower Heavens until it rose on the other side of the sky again. Dimming but never really going dark. The time after the celestial golden hours (that lasted longer than on Earth) was considered evening in Heaven.

"I never get tired of Heaven's golden hours," said Berith with a wistful smile, closing her eyes and lifting her face into the warm, almost liquid gold radiance drenching the streets and buildings. "Okay, let's talk history."

"History?" Talia said with a frown.

Like Azrael, Berith had been around since the Beginning. She knew Heaven's and the Creation's histories. The lore. The precedents behind decisions and outcomes.

"In the past," said Berith as she turned back to Talia. "If Heaven discovered a Cambion, the half demon half human was either destroyed or sent to the Middling. There have been a handful. Nephilim, half angel half humans were sent to High House for evaluation whenever they were discovered. A handful, like Campions, have been found. If Heaven discovered a Nephion's existence, angels would hunt down a rare half angel half demon and evaluate it in High House. I don't think Heaven has ever seen a Nephron though."

The angel light inside Talia dimmed for a moment, turning cold and searing. Right now, as far as she knew, Heaven didn't see Jack as a Nephilim—much less a Nephion. Were these archangels trying to get Jack declared such an abomination, demanding he be destroyed alongside Lucifer. Where they planned to scavenge his angel powers from the Lake of Fire, something no angel had ever before tested.

She knew that such celestial beings and their power were light itself, the first and strongest of the Maker's powers. If one of these creatures was hit with the Lake of Fire's flames (fueled by this light), then only the purest part of that light would remain: any celestial powers the being once carried. This light would float on top of the Lake and wouldn't burn. Light that contained both the power and the creature's essence. Anything else (like the demonic side of these hybrids) would burn away.

Nothing made of darkness could survive those purging flames.

Using her rare resurrect power, she could only bring back angels— creatures of the light. Humans in their physical form only had the potential for light—the soul they carried. But it didn't become light until it floated free of the human form. If a Nephion or Nephilim were thrown into those waters, only its angelic half' (its light) would remain, its demonic half purged.

Resurrect couldn't bring these hybrid forms back from oblivion either, because only half its form was pure light. The demon side, made of darkness, would burn away.

Talia shifted her wings, glancing painfully at the new High House spire. Where the Maker currently resided under a seraph and cherubim guard of angels. Death angels and archangels flanked them. Archangels couldn't fight such a force, so they planned to use the tribunal against Jack and force the Maker to rule on his existence.

Once and for all time.

Or ambush him. Dead or alive, they didn't care as long as Jack ended up in the Lake of Fire where they could gather the light that remained. Because those powers would float on top of the lake, waiting to be pulled free from the light.

But Jack wasn't any of those hybrids. He was all human, even if Heaven had never seen anything like him before. Even Talia with her human soul and rare powers…that didn't make her a hybrid—just rare like Jack. But her powers came from light and they would survive the Lake of Fire (while she and Jack perished).

The archangels' angelic outrage over Jack's power and her human soul barely hid their greed as they plotted to steal Jack's powers. Her powers. And even Lucifer's—like they had some sort of right to them.

Somehow, she had to reveal their twisted plot. Before another war erupted in the Heavens. A Civil War that would dwarf Lucifer's Rebellion—especially if these archangels got hold of some rare angel powers.

But only the Maker could stop this before it started.

She'd gladly give up thee powers to ensure that her marriage survived the tribunal. With her and Jack free to live as husband and wife. And celebrate their first anniversary together.

She still needed the perfect gift for her worried husband who loved her more than his own life. She'd keep looking for the perfect gift for him to open at their beach house party.

"But Berith, everyone knows that Jack isn't a Nephal or a Nephion. And so do these corrupted archangels. Now, he might look like a Nephilim, half angel half human with those wings, but I assure you, he is all human."

Berith shrugged. "Technically true, but even if he was one of these hybrids, there are still precedents for handling Cambions, Nephals, and Nephilim. Because of the danger they posed to humanity. That's the case these few but loud archangels will try to make against Jack. That he should be treated like these other hybrids—because he's dangerous."

"Jack? Dangerous? To himself maybe. That's absurd!"

To even suggest that infuriated Talia.

"Most of Heaven—including the Maker—knows Jack isn't dangerous, Talia," said Berith. "But the argument is that he'll accidentally hurt or kill an innocent with his powers—like these other dangerous hybrids."

"That's not going to happen," Talia snapped. "Besides, he never asked for these powers."

Berith motioned toward the crossroads. "Neither did the hybrids. Talia…the majority of Heaven is on Jack's side—like me. Regardless, these few but loud archangels will insist Jack's dangerous and should be destroyed. And we need to be prepared to counter their arguments."

The pit of Talia's stomach plummeted. Only the Maker could rule on that. Now that Lucifer was in custody, would the Maker backpedal on that decision? Leave it to the five tribunal judges instead. Would the Maker order hers and Jack's marriage dissolved? Jack destroyed? And her human soul taken?

Her eyes stung with tears. If that happened, she had no way to protect Jack.

"They can't destroy him," she said in a small, tight voice as tears threaded down her cheeks. "Not my Jack…"

Berith gripped Talia's hands. "Talia, the Maker knows the hearts of these archangels. And what Jack's done for the world and for Heaven. What he's given to save it."

She nodded, her gaze shifting to Jack who bit into his second mana cake, his eyes closing to slits.

"I have to trust that."

Berith squeezed Talia's hands gently. "I still remember when Jack prayed to the Maker in the Haunted Woods after he'd set all his seraphim powers to overload," said Berith.

Even now, that moment still hurt. "You'd just restored my memory and we were rushing to stop Jack from challenging Lucifer after he thought he'd lost me."

Berith nodded, a smile lifting the corners of her mouth. "Exactly. Remember what the Maker said about Jack's prayer?"

Her eyes got misty, her heart squeezing. "Selfless down to the very last word."

"It moved the Maker deeply. And Jack's done nothing but show his selfless devotion to saving his world and Heaven."

Berith let go of Talia's hands and put her arm around Talia's shoulder, hugging her.

Talia felt more tears slipping down her cheeks. "In the Throne room, Jack put himself between Lucifer and the Maker, taking the blow from the Rod of Creation. To save the Maker. Knowing I would lose him."

"If the Maker had been killed, it would have been the end of all things anyway," said Berith, rubbing Talia's shoulder. "So, Jack knew he had nothing to lose by taking that blow. He didn't know that when both those forces collided, they would neutralize each other."

Berith was right. Jack had proven whose side he supported. And he'd offered his life more than once to protect Heaven. And Talia. These archangels weren't fooling anyone but themselves.

"None of us knew that," said Talia.

"Least of all Jack," said Berith with a nod.

Talia wiped away her tears. "You're right. I have to hold onto that. I just wish I could get Jack to understand though."

"Good luck," said Berith with a smile. "He's a worrier. And he'll worry his way through the tribunal until it ends."

"That's my Jack," said Talia, hugging Berith. "Will you watch over him while the squad and I complete work at High House? He'll probably pace the entire time I'm gone, still convinced he's losing me; but I have to do my job."

Berith let her go. "I'll do my best. But if you could blink back even for a minute or two, please do it. Otherwise, he won't eat or sleep."

She had a point. That was also her Jack.

"If I bring him more mana cakes, he'll eat."

Berith nodded, motioning toward the round room.

Talia blinked to the entrance and hurried inside where Jack now paced after finishing both mana cakes.

"Talia!" he cried, rushing toward her.

His arms slid around her shoulders, pulling her against him, making everything feel warm and safe as she sank into his embrace. She'd missed his touch, the heat of his arms, his warm cedary scent.

"I've missed you so much, Jack," she whispered against his ear.

He closed his eyes, pressing his face against hers, his heart racing, his breath quickening.

He was always so affectionate, especially after she'd been gone for a while. He understood that she had ethereal duties requiring her to be away from him and he never complained. Even though it broke his heart every time she left him. He had no idea how quickly she raced back to him the very first moment she could. How she blinked across the air currents the whole way, pushing her angelic body as fast as her powers—and wings—allowed. That's what made this absence so difficult.

She loved being an angel of death. She loved shepherding humans on their final journey home. But all of that paled to having a human soul and returning to her new husband. It was a moment she lived for and she hoped that someday soon she wouldn't have to leave him so often. If he got to keep his wings, he could come with her once this was all settled. She just wanted to spend all her time with him. Home had always been Eolowen...until she met Jack Casey.

Now, home would forever be in Jack's arms.

She studied his handsome face and luminous green eyes. By now, it was apparent, as their first anniversary as husband and wife approached, that Jack Casey had truly stopped aging. Was he becoming a Nephilim? Or something that both Heaven and Earth had no name for (and considered an abomination)? Was he immortal now? Like her? She never wanted to lose this man. Or be without him.

"I'm so glad you're here with me, Jack," she said and kissed him hard on the lips.

At last, he opened his smoldering light green eyes as that familiar, sexy smirk curled the corners of his mouth.

"I'd follow you anywhere, babe," he said in a quiet voice. "Especially since I'm kind of homeless at the moment."

She frowned. "Homeless? Oh...the trailer."

He nodded. "With our move-in date approaching at the beach house, I had to terminate my apartment lease. Big loss there."

"I won't miss its small size or its...lack of amenities," said Talia with a wry smile. "But I have some wonderful memories of that place—being there with you."

He stroked her hair, the light brightening in those sexy pale green eyes that still took her breath away.

"Me, too," he said, his voice deepening. "Some incredible nights holding you in my arms in that creaky Murphy bed."

She remembered waking out of her separation fever after she fell from Heaven, feeling safe and warm in Jack's arms as he held her tight underneath the covers, sleeping soundly against her. His sexy blond hair tousled and that luscious mouth so close to hers. Even now, that memory burned through her.

Her arms slid around his waist and she pulled him closer.

God, he was still temptation personified. But she wouldn't have him any other way.

"Some of my favorite memories, Jack Casey."

"I was planning to stay in the set trailer until we moved into the beach house, but with the fire and the show being cancelled..."

"There's always the grand hall, Jack," said Talia.

He grinned and twirled her around until they landed on the bed together. She snuggled against him, desire burning flames in those gorgeous green eyes, shadowed from worry and lack of sleep.

He slid his body on top of hers, entwining his fingers in hers, palms pressed against hers as he gently leaned down and kissed her again.

"Welcome home, Mrs. Casey," he whispered against her ear, his hot mouth brushing across her earlobe, sending sparks of desire through her angelic form. "Even though we'd have more privacy in the middle of L.A.'s Union Station than Eolowen's round room."

She laughed. "At least Azrael's overseeing things at High House and won't be pushing Eolowen's communal spaces. Like this one."

"But he could blink in at any moment," said Jack, glancing at the ceiling.

He covered her mouth with his, the weight of his body thrumming against her skin. And she ached to make love to him.

She pulled the crisp white covers over them as she unzipped Jack's soot-covered blue coveralls. Pushing them off his shoulders, past his waist, and down his hips. Until he was down to green boxer briefs and a grey T-shirt.

A torn and bloody grey T-shirt. Claw marks, some of them deep, cut across his chest, down his side, and across his left shoulder.

Demons.

"Jack!" she cried, sitting up, her hands against his chest as she called up gold healing light. "You're hurt."

He glanced down at his bloodied, torn T-shirt and then up at her, that reassuring glint in his eyes, a smirk on his face.

"It's just a few demon scratches, babe," he said. "I'm fine."

Talia shook her head. "No, you're not."

Carefully, she lifted the T-shirt over his head. He winced as the stiff fabric pulled away from the deep gouges across his stomach, chest, and shoulders. Gouges that had bled a lot.

"Berith!" she called.

In a moment, Berith blinked into the room, frowning when she saw all the wounds across Jack's bare chest and stomach.

"Jack, how did this happen?"

He shrugged, staring down at the gashes. "Demons threw me a little Happy Series Cancellation party in my trailer this morning. Burned down my wards. Burned down my walls. And the whole trailer."

"Cancellation party?" said Berith, frowning as she summoned gold light at her fingertips and pressed them to a deep wound across his shoulder. "Oh, the show."

The claw marks were thick and deep.

He winced, sucking in a pained breath.

"Yeah," he said through gritted teeth. "They told us this morning that the show was done. Gotta turn in the key to the trailer on Monday. It's…kind of the—only thing left of the trailer."

"I'm so sorry about your show, Jack," said Berith, letting the gold light wash over his wounds.

He shrugged. "It's the inevitable end for lots of hit shows. It's all good. That show saved me. It's where I met the love of my life." He reached out and gripped Talia's hand. "I think I got a lot more out of it than they got out of me."

"So, what's next?" Berith asked, moving her hands to the next set of claw marks.

Again, he shrugged. "My memoir? Broadway? Shaving commercials? Hopefully, another show. I suck at writing."

Berith cast a quick look at Talia and then back at Jack.

"Any prospects for new roles?" she asked as he winced again and pulled in another pained breath.

"Not at the moment," he said through gritted teeth. "Looks like Gianni and Banks are gonna take over my old show though—Rachel, too. Maybe they can get me a cameo? One I'll actually show up for this time."

Talia's mood darkened. "What? They're bringing Rachel back to that show and not you?"

He nodded, not looking at her.

Berith frowned. "Why would that director be stupid enough to not sign the actor who made that show into a hit?"

Jack laughed. "Because he's worked with that actor before and knows better than to rehire that kind of trouble again. Besides. I turned him down months ago."

Jack's response surprised Talia. Jack knew better than that. Even if he was trouble, he would still bring ratings back to that show.

"Jack, you know that's not true."

He sighed, bowing his head. "Bellows hasn't so much as texted me about SanFran Confidential, Tal, but I've watched Banks and Gianni field several calls from him about the show. Even Rachel's been contracted back into her original role. With no messages from Phil, my agent, I may have to find another line of work now that this show has ended."

Talia climbed off the bed, standing beside it now.

"But you had all those offers," she said, flexing her wings, feeling angry that they'd passed over Jack.

He didn't deserve this.

Jack turned toward her as Berith worked on healing gashes on the other side of his chest.

"I did until the show got cancelled," he said, glancing over Berith's halo at her. "They've probably all dried up now. Now that I'm not in demand anymore."

"But why didn't it cool Armand's and Mark's demand?"

He shrugged. "Wish I knew. Timing maybe? Don't get me wrong, I'm happy for them. But I'm worried that I'll have to sell the beach house now. Or work three jobs 'til I'm eighty."

Another worry he hadn't mentioned until now. Things were unraveling for him and he hadn't expected that. Not in every direction. And so suddenly.

"We'll get through it, Jack," she said and gripped his hand.

He smiled. "As long as you're still with me, Mrs. Casey, I can get through anything."

She leaned over and kissed him as Berith treated the slashes across his stomach.

A rush of wings fluttered across Eolowen's rooftop.

Talia glanced up as her squad of death angels flew over the round room and landed on the terrace, in the grass, and inside the round room.

"Jack!"

Muriel was the first one in the room. She rushed over and hugged Jack, who hugged her back.

"Muriel! Good to see you."

Muriel ruffled his hair. "It's great to see you, Jack."

In another moment, Anahera landed. She rushed over when she saw Jack.

"Jack, you're here!"

He hugged Anahera as Deemah landed and also gave him a hug.

"Good to see you, Anahera. Deemah."

Finally, Kesien landed, a murderous expression on his normally calm face.

"Dude, who got your wings in a bunch?" Jack asked.

"Jack?" he said, turning around, the anger leaving his face.

"Hey, Kesien," he said, extending his hand, but Kesien gave him a big hug.

Jack hugged him back.

"Great to see you, Jack," said Kesien. "Sorry for the black mood. Samael's up to his old tricks again."

"Samael? Seriously?" Jack replied.

Kesien nodded, still scowling.

"Where's Azrael?" Talia asked.

"Finishing up something in the Cloud Chamber," said Muriel. "Glad I'm not with him."

"Why?" Talia asked.

Muriel shivered, wrapping her arms around her waist. "Because. Being near Lucifer gives me the creeps."

"Lucifer's in the Cloud Chamber?" Jack replied, looking apprehensive. "The one he exploded into a bazillion Legos all over Heaven?"

"He's in chains," said Kesien with a growl. "He's not going anywhere. Not an angel in Heaven is going to screw that capture up. Unless they're still working for Samael."

Talia gave them all a strange look. "Say what you want, but Lucifer is the one who alerted me to the demon attack in your trailer, Jack."

"Probably because he's the one who ordered it," Jack replied with a sneer.

Well, she couldn't exactly rule out that possibility. But Jack might be right.

"Regardless, I was surprised that he warned us," she said as Berith finished treating Jack's last wound.

"All right, Jack," said Berith as she held up her hand and a big roll of gauze appeared. "Let's finish this."

Jack made a sour face. "Aw, come on, Berith. Don't mummify me before the tribunal. I may need some speed to get out fast."

"You're human," she said, shaking the gauze at him. "That makes you fragile. And I don't want these demon claw wounds to get infected. We're covering them and that's that."

"Yes, Mother," he replied with a sigh.

The angels of death smiled which annoyed Berith.

"Don't you angels have drills to perform?"

Muriel shook her head. "Not without our vanguard. Welcome home, Jack."

His smile widened into a grin as Muriel ruffled his hair again.

Talia loved how her squad had brightened Jack's mood. And distracted him from thinking about Lucifer's trial.

And right now, Jack needed distractions more than anything.

8

JACK RESTLESSLY PACED THE EDGE OF EOLOWEN'S TERRACE, THE GRAND hall reminding him of an old European basilica with its long nave and towering capitals, white stone brilliant against the vivid blue sky. The sun-drenched grass warmed his bare feet as he unfurled his wings and let them trail in the lower Heavens' cool breezes. Jasmine and rain-scented air washed over his wing feathers, soothing his mood. His mended wing was a little stiff, but it would be fine in a day or two.

Swords clanged against shields, flutter of angel wings whispering across the terrace as the death angel guard drilled behind him.

But he couldn't concentrate on sparring with Talia's squad. His thoughts kept returning to the tribunal and what happened next. Would everything he'd experienced since missing that *SanFran Confidential* cameo disappear like smoke. Including his relationship with Talia? Like none of it ever happened? Would he go back to being to his old, difficult self? Addicted to coke and blaming everyone else for his failed career. Would he even have an acting career after this?

Or would Heaven return him to the end of his life as it had been officially written in his Book of Life and Death—before Talia saved him. All part of cleaning up Lucifer's mess.

To be fair though, Lare and Rachel had been responsible for

getting him addicted to the flake. And getting him fired. But still, it was his life and he'd done little to climb out of his downward spiral.

For two angel days now, he'd rested in Eolowen's round room, healing from the demon attack and watching Talia and her squad train. Letting his seraphim energies replenish. Berith had him all wrapped up with bandages, her magic working on the demons' dark energies that had left him sluggish and slow. He tried to focus, but his thoughts were everywhere at once. Especially on his cancelled show. And the upcoming trial.

Sweet honeysuckle and delicate rose scent floated across Eolowen's meadow from the long white pergola that framed its perimeter, mixing with jasmine and cool rain scent. The pergola burgeoned with jasmine blooms, the vines engulfing the structure alongside climbing pink roses. The sprawling white structure ran alongside a clear blue burbling stream. Wisteria hung in bright purple, grape-like clusters from the top of the pergola, giving the grand hall's white stone a wash of pastel and vivid colors that brightened in the sunlight.

He sat down in the meadow and stretched out in the grass, watching shadows flit across the crisp blue sky above Eolowen. Rushing toward the terrace.

Shadows? He tensed.

A tall, forbidding figure with two pairs of wings spread wide landed in front of him, filling him with dread.

He bolted up from the grass, his heart racing. With the sun in his eyes, he couldn't see the angel clearly, but with all those wings, Jack knew this wasn't a Watcher or an angel of death. This wasn't just an angel. Besides the two sets of wings, he had an air of importance that elevated him somehow. A dark, almost menacing presence that rivaled even a demon Hell prince. Making Jack uneasy.

Jack squinted, trying to cut the glare enough to see the angel's face. The robes. The eyes.

All sounds of sparring halted across Eolowen until only silence whispered on the wind. So, they were wary of this angel, too. It wasn't just him.

Something dark, smoky, and whiplike cut through the air above Jack's head. Snapping like a firecracker and then whipping back again.

What was that about? Trying to get his attention? He glared. Or take his head off.

His thoughts scattered as a golden glow pulsed around the two pairs of wings, piercing gold eyes fixing on him with laser focus.

Some sort of archangel stood in front of him. Bringing back flashbacks of that douchebag Raziel and the Holy fire duel that almost killed Jack.

Not this time, dude. After everything he'd seen and endured, he was so not afraid of these intimidating winged douchebags anymore. Especially these archangels.

"Nice threatening entrance," said Jack, sitting up and crossing his arms. "If you're into pointlessly gothic displays. Or you're Ridley Scott."

The archangel remained silent, halo burning with white fire that crackled in the painful silence. Four large white wings tipped red framed this tall, male angel's long, sculpted face and lean body. His aquiline nose was chiseled and perfect, cheekbones so high Jack would need a ladder to see into this angel's eyes. Even his lips looked full and hewn from marble. His large eyes were a bright rusty gold against a white-gold Eternean breastplate, burnished pauldrons, tall, shiny gold armor boots, and gold greaves that stretched to his elbows.

This archangel looked powerful and messenger god fast—enough to knock Jack all the way into purgatory from here. The archangel gripped a shadowy whip that began to glow white in his right hand, burning with white-gold fire along its long, supple length—that burned away the shadows wrapping it.

Dude looked hella-frightening with all his boujee armor and weapons.

"So," said the deep, commanding almost bass voice, like he'd been wired by a studio set to project his voice in surround sound. His gaze locked onto Jack and didn't stray a millimeter. "This is the chimera?"

Okay, no cap. This was the most intimidating archangel he'd ever seen. Angel even. He knew he had to be careful.

"Chimera? So formal," Jack replied, not looking away. "Really. I prefer Jack," he said.

But he just couldn't stop the smart-ass comment from slipping free. If this archangel could erase him from existence (which looked likely), he was probably contemplating it right about now.

One corner of the archangel's mouth lifted.

Three archangels descended from the crisp blue sky and landed around the badass archangel who carried a whip.

Great, a whole flock of asshalos.

"Didn't know you dudes booked this year's Archangel DouchebagCon at Eolowen. It's still a little early for Comicon this year."

The other archangels glared at him with panicked amber eyes that sparked in Jack's direction. Like they'd just found a turd on one of Heaven's sidewalks.

With his name on it.

And he thought that was just a San Francisco problem.

"That's him, Lord Kushiel!" one of the archangels shouted, pointing, white robes billowing, gold belt gleaming in the sunlight.

This archangel looked brown-skinned, his hair grey and silver, his amber eyes full of hate for Jack.

"That's the one we told you about!" the second archangel shouted. He was pallid with sun-washed red hair tied back into a partial ponytail and hate burning in his brown eyes. "This abomination struts around the Heavens like it was born an angel."

His dull brown eyes brightened as he scurried around the goth archangel like a pet chihuahua that had escaped someone's purse. Pointing at Jack.

"It should be destroyed," the third archangel whined, his skin tanned, his gold eyes hard, an air of arrogance surrounding him. "Before it hurts one of the angels. Or Heaven Forbid, a soul."

"It?" Jack scowled. "Seriously? My pronouns are: he, him, and come at me, bro."

The three archangels shrank back as Jack stood up and took a step toward them.

These archangels were at least six and half feet tall, but the archangel they'd called Lord Kushiel stood nearly seven feet tall. And he was all intimidation, danger, and Heavenly retribution. Wrapped in a gothic façade that would scare even Notre Dame cathedral's darkest rooftop gargoyles, Kushiel was the real chimera here. And he towered over Jack.

This archangel worried and intrigued him. The others? They apparently belonged to Archangel Raziel's little bitch club. And he had no use for them.

"Who is that?" the strange archangel demanded of the other archangels, pointing that whip at Jack. Ruffling his wing feathers.

"It has a name," Jack snapped, glaring at them. "It's Jack. And it only has these wings and powers because the world needed saving with them. And to be clear, it never asked for them. Or wanted them."

The ruddy-haired archangel edged closer, trying to poke Jack. His wide-eyed uncertain stare didn't leave Jack's face, his movements jerky.

Jack turned toward him, glaring.

"Boo!" he shouted, thrusting out his arms.

Shouting, the three archangels skittered back from him. Jack held in a snicker. Bet these three hid in the Archive spire when the Sixth Flight took to the sky, leaving Talia and the others alone to fight demons above Earth.

They shrank back from him, hiding behind Lord Kushiel.

But the strange archangel with the whip didn't move. This Lord Kushiel, a name Jack didn't recognize.

Again, the corner of Lord Kushiel's mouth lifted.

"Chill, dudes," Jack snapped, glaring at the cowering archangels. "I can't hold my seraphim liquor for long and these powers were only meant to defeat the Hell princes. And the apocalypse payloads. I mean, it's not like I'd demand a Holy Fire duel with archangels at fifty paces in the square or anything. Only a douchebag would do something like that." His eyes narrowed. "Oh, wait…"

The other corner of Lord Kushiel's mouth lifted as the whip dropped against his side, its flames guttering.

"So…Jack Casey…"

Again, that almost Vader-like voice (without all the asthma) filled the space around them. Booming. Commanding. So precise with almost a British accent. Not bright and animated like Lucifer's, just formal and distinct—and a little throaty. Raspy.

"*You* are the biggest threat to Heaven since the Lightbringer's Fall?"

His voice was inquisitive, almost a touch of levity to his words despite his intimidating appearance. And tone.

Jack smirked. "You've heard of me. A recovering coke addict and out-of-work actor from L.A. Aren't you terrified?"

The hint of a full-on smile curved across Lord Kushiel's long, lean face.

"The vessel may not intimidate as much as its contents, but I confess, your levity and humility set me at ease." Lord Kushiel cast a withering glare at the three archangels behind him, cowering at his shoulders. They shrank back from him. "I sense no malice or darkness within you. Your soul is still all light, Jack Casey. That is a good thing. That means that even the darkest of events has not defeated you."

"Jack!"

Archangel Azrael's frantic voice echoed from the sky as he set down in the grass between Jack and Lord Kushiel. Talia was right behind him. She landed and blinked to Jack's side. Shielding him.

"Destroy this abomination, Lord Kushiel!" shouted one of the other archangels. "Before it causes irreparable harm to Heaven."

Azrael cast a frightened glance at Jack as he kept his body between Jack and Lord Kushiel. Azrael turned toward to the scary archangel and focused his attention solely on Lord Kushiel, looking the archangel in the eye.

"My Lord, please—forgive him," said Azrael, a tinge of desperation in his tone. "He is human and often speaks first rather than considering his words. What am I saying? He always speaks first. It's Jack we're talking about."

"You're not helping, Azrael," Jack whispered, leaning toward the archangel of death.

If this dude was going to toss Holy fire at him, he wanted to at least see it coming.

"It's a monster!" shouted one of the archangels. "Unnatural. An abomination! Destroy it while you still can."

Jack rolled his eyes as the three archangels began a shrill diatribe against him, shouting and flailing arms and wings as they surrounded Archangel Azrael and Lord Kushiel.

Lord Kushiel turned and snapped his right hand up. Knocking all three archangels backward.

"Raphael, Uziel, Kotabiel—leave. Now." Kushiel's baritone voice was blunt and hard.

They started to object, but with the flick of his right index finger, Lord Kushiel sent them blinking across the sky. Toward the spires.

"Azrael," said Kushiel, his back still to the archangel of death. "You are responsible for this—"

Kushiel paused, turning back around to study Jack a moment, rusty gold eyes narrowing.

"This—human?"

He hadn't said human like it was something on the bottom of his shoe. It was more of a clarification. Like he hadn't been sure if Jack was human or angel. Or a little of both. Jack was surprised that there hadn't been any condescension or malice behind his words.

Azrael nodded. "Please, Lord Kushiel. Jack has never harmed anyone who didn't deserve it."

"Lord Kushiel," said Jack.

The archangel stared at him, unblinking.

Azrael began to sweat, looking nervous as Jack began to speak.

"Look, I never asked for these powers," said Jack. "These wings."

This dude could smite him into oblivion if he wanted to, apparently with a finger twitch, but this archangel was going to hear how he got the powers.

From Jack, not secondhand from those douchebag archangels who wanted him dead and his powers taken.

Lord Kushiel made no move toward him.

Good, still had his patient attention. Jack hoped that would last.

"The powers just started showing up and I had no control over them," said Jack. "And then, I was trapped in a room with a squad of death angels when this eater of hearts demon ordered the celestial tasting menu. Somehow, I summoned a murder marble and shoved it down the thing's gullet until it exploded."

One corner of Lord Kushiel's mouth lifted again.

"A murder marble?"

Azrael looked mortified. "My lord, he's referring to an oblivion sphere. He'd heard about Talia conjuring one, the angel whose powers Jack began mirroring."

"An oblivion sphere?"

Jack nodded. "Whatever."

"Jack," Azrael hissed.

"So, Talia is the angel with whom you…"

Jack hesitated. Was this a trap?

"Archangel, you probably already know, but Talia got stuck in a wager with Lucifer and had to save two souls on Earth. One of those souls was mine. I fell hard for her and I love her more than my own life."

"She is the one you married? In a human ceremony?"

Jack nodded. "Happiest moment of my life."

The other corner of Lord Kushiel's mouth lifted again.

"And you have seraphim powers?"

"I do," Jack said, bowing his head. "Archangel, it was the only way the seraphim could get a message out when that douchebag Raziel trapped them."

Azrael winced.

"And Seraphina had to send me her powers, so we could free the seraphim and cherubim from some powerful wards."

One of Lord Kushiel's pure white eyebrows lifted. "And you still have those powers?"

Jack nodded. "I asked the seraphim to let me keep them—just for a little while. See, Lucifer had assaulted Heaven. And he had Talia, controlling her against her will. Those powers were the only way I could defeat him and break his hold on her."

Lord Kushiel was silent a moment, that fiery whip twitching at his side.

"Yet you still have these powers?"

Jack felt his face flush. "Long story, but after we stopped Lucifer, the seraph appeared suddenly down on Earth, forgetting I was in a room full of angels. Almost burned my eyes out of my head. One of the angels infused a stone with seraph healing light to heal my eyes. And I accidentally pulled those energies out of the stone when I used it on my eyes. Heaven tried everything to put them back in the stone, but nothing worked."

This time, both of Lord Kushiel's eyebrows raised.

"You pulled seraphim energies out of a healing stone?"

Jack sighed. "I don't know how I did it, but I did."

Kushiel pointed at Jack. "And the wings and halo?"

Jack let his wings unfurl. "I lured Lucifer into the Garden and fused the lock, trapping him inside in order to escape Hell. But I couldn't get the other angels out of the Garden in time." He winced. "Including Talia. So, I shoved the others out and fused the lock from the inside, trapping me and Lucifer in the Garden."

"You trapped yourself alongside Lucifer? In the Garden?" Lord Kushiel sounded shocked. And a little appalled.

Jack nodded. "It was the only way to stop him from destroying everything. Of course, he killed me. Talia used resurrect to bring me back again."

Lord Kushiel glanced over at Azrael, seeing Talia behind him.

"Is this true?" Lord Kushiel asked.

Talia nodded. "Yes, my lord, Kushiel, but it wasn't with resurrect. It was through this strange bond that Jack and I share."

"And that bond is—what?" Lord Kushiel asked.

"Love," said Jack.

Lord Kushiel's head whipped around, surprise lifting his features.

"Love you say?"

Jack nodded. "Through that bond, she brought me back. And that's how her rare powers have been mirrored within me."

Lord Kushiel was silent a moment, studying Jack.

"It's Heaven's mantra, after all," Jack added.

"Explain, Jack Casey."

"Love frees all," he said. "That's been Heaven's mantra since I got here, but nobody seems to believe in it. Much less practice it. But I do."

A smile touched Kushiel's stern face. "That pleases me." He pointed at Jack. "And you please me. I sense no malice. No lies. There is a lightness about you, Jack Casey. A selflessness that I've not seen in most humans."

Lord Kushiel turned back to Azrael. "Archangel, he and Talia will be appearing at the tribunal tomorrow. As the Maker has commanded. And I have been tasked with leading tomorrow's proceedings."

Azrael bowed. "It will be done, Lord Kushiel. Thank you."

Lord Kushiel nodded and turned back to Jack, giving Jack a sharp nod. A moment later, Kushiel blinked across the sky toward High House.

Azrael rushed over to Jack as Talia blinked beside him, wrapping him in her arms.

"Oh, Jack! I was terrified," Talia cried, tightening her hold. "Do you know who that was?"

Jack shook his head. He had no clue.

"Lord Kushiel controls the punishment of souls in Hell," said Talia, letting the tension drain from her taut wings. "Or at least he did until Lucifer fell. Abaddon now reports to Lord Kushiel who is both retribution and penance for all of Heaven and Hell. After Lucifer is dealt with, Kushiel will assume control of Hell."

Punishment of souls in Hell? He cringed. He'd just told this dude that he'd been in Hell. Did this archangel think he'd escaped from there? He might need to clarify that statement a little further.

Azrael's knees went slack a moment and he fought to straighten up again. He gripped Jack's shoulder, his eyes wide with fear.

"I was so sure Kushiel would smite you," said Azrael in an exasperated tone.

"Why?" Jack snapped, frowning.

"For flippant looks. Smart comments. Arrogance—I've seen him do it before. He does not suffer arrogance and condescension from angels. Or anyone."

Jack pulled in a nervous breath. "Even if they were directed at douchebag archangels like those three? And not Lord Kushiel?"

At last, Azrael smiled. "Apparently, that's acceptable. Uziel. Raphael. And Kotabiel. They're representing the opposition against you and your powers, Jack."

"There's a shock," Jack replied. "What asshalos! Bet they were part of Raziel's fan club. And Samael's."

"Perhaps. We're still trying to sort that part out."

"Ignorant douchebags are easier to handle that traitor douchebags."

Azrael chuckled. "A very good point, Jack. We need to figure that out before the trial starts tomorrow."

"Wow, is it tomorrow already?"

"Afraid so," said Azrael. "But I think Lord Kushiel has some appreciation for you. And that's good."

Jack squinted. "Why?"

"He is prosecuting Lucifer at tomorrow's tribunal. Lucifer will be judged by him, Pravuil, Sarathiel, archangel of penance and discipline, and finally, archangel of death, Sidriel, who battled Hell with us when we rescued Berith. The Maker is the fifth judge, of course."

Jack's jaw tightened. Kushiel, Sarathiel, Pravuil, Sidriel, and the Maker. Five votes. A vote that could easily turn to support smiting him out of existence, too. After they voted on Lucifer's fate.

"Five votes that could separate me from Talia. And send me to oblivion."

Talia was beside him, arms around his neck, holding him close.

"Sarathiel respects you after that stupid duel with Raziel you were forced to fight," said Talia. "Pravuil thinks the world of you. And Sidriel trusts you, Jack, after you fought beside her and her angels in Hell."

That might be true, but they might still believe that seraphim powers made him too dangerous.

"I'm about to find that out, aren't I?" he said.

Azrael sighed. "Afraid so, Jack. But I promise you, I will fight for you until they smite me."

"Azrael, no!" Jack shouted. "Don't you dare. Even if I'm not here to see it, you have to be here for the rest of us. Making sure souls rise and get back to their families again. You and your guard are the best of the Heavens. Don't sacrifice that for me."

Azrael was speechless. He patted Jack on the back as Talia held Jack closer, tears sliding down her cheeks.

"Besides, I'm not going to count out my chances."

"Why's that?" Talia asked, kissing him on the lips.

He smiled. "I think maybe Kushiel likes me."

Azrael chuckled, making Talia laugh as Jack pulled her into his arms and kissed her.

"Up for some drills, Jack?" Talia asked.

"Me? I'm really rusty."

She shook her head. "Nobody minds. The squad wanted to spar with you. They say drills are much more fun when you're on the field."

Jack chuckled. "They just want to kick my ass because they know I'm rusty."

"And they'll have fun doing it."

"All right," he said and followed her toward the terrace. "Bring it on. I could probably use a few new lessons after those damned demons kicked my ass this week."

"Jack, be careful," said Talia. "You and that wing aren't fully healed yet."

"You heard my wife," he said, turning back to the squad. "Go easy on this poor, out of work actor."

As he walked toward Kesien, Muriel, and Anahera, those three archangels flew low over Eolowen, hurling insults at him before they flew off toward High House.

Talia looked incensed and tossed a murder marble over their heads. Terrified, they fled when the explosion thundered across Eolowen with a burst of gold light.

"I started to throw Holy fire at them," Jack said. "But I decided not to prove their point to Kushiel."

"Let me prove the point of not messing with angels of death instead, Jack."

"Thanks, Mrs. Casey!" he called.

Deemah shook her fist at the archangels as Muriel raised her shield.

"Well, I'm not above giving them a good shield bashing," said Muriel.

"Me either, Muriel," Deemah said as she shook her shield at the retreating archangels.

"I don't think Lord Kushiel appreciated their bullshit," said Jack. "And I have a feeling he's letting them throw out enough rope to hang themselves."

Kesien jerked his gaze toward Jack, looking surprised.

"Lord Kushiel?" he said.

Jack nodded.

"*The* Lord Kushiel? Archangel of Punishment? The Presiding Angel over Hell's Wicked? They brought him out of the field and back to Heaven to preside over Lucifer's trial?"

Jack shrugged and glanced at Azrael. "Archangel, that Lord Kushiel, right? The dude with the whip?"

"A whip of fire?" Kesien cried.

"Yeah," said Jack. "It burned with fire and smoke."

Kesien's face turned white. "Can't believe it. Lord Kushiel...the most feared angel in all the Heavens—besides Lucifer."

Azrael gave him a sharp nod.

Smirking, Jack leaned toward Kesien and lowered his voice. "I think he likes me."

Muriel burst out laughing. "Lord Kushiel? He doesn't like anyone, Jack. You should be afraid. And give Kushiel a wide berth."

Kesien gave him a harried nod. "Be careful, Jack. He could smite you out of existence with that whip."

Jack sighed and kicked at the terrace's white stones with the toe of his blue Vans. Maybe that's why they'd summoned him? To be the executioner.

"Maybe that's why he's here," said Jack.

Everyone fell silent, worried looks spreading across their faces.

"For Lucifer, not me," he said quickly, trying to salvage the mood.

It worked a little, but he saw the worry shadowing their faces. They knew as well as he did that he and Talia were on trial, too.

And that trial started tomorrow.

9

TALIA FLEW BESIDE ARCHANGEL AZRAEL, JACK BETWEEN THEM AS THEY drifted along the air currents that flowed around the newly rebuilt High House spire. The new sparkling white tower stood even taller above the lower Heavens than the old spire. Seeing its familiar tapered silhouette on the skyline calmed some of her anxiety as they approached the Cloud Chamber at its top.

It had been so long since the skies above the lower Heavens looked...well, heavenly. Smoke and haze had persisted across the lower Heavens long after the spire had disintegrated into rubble from the massive Holy fire blast. The murky dove grey smoke persisted after they'd stopped all seven Travelers from unleashing their apocalyptic payloads on the Earth. Only in the last few days had the greyness faded with the returning Parrish blue skies and white Constable clouds.

Even though the skies looked mostly ethereal and pristine again, the pit of her stomach was still heavy with dread. She'd felt it since she'd come face-to-face with Lucifer—and that first wager. And not even seeing the King of Hell in shackles made it go away.

Would her angelic sense of lightness ever return? Had the

darkness and betrayals she'd witnessed since that first wager changed that lightness forever—or destroyed it?

All around the sparkling white tower, cloud tops drifted past, skimming the line of curved white platforms that wrapped around the entire spire like a corkscrew. The perches rested on clouds and began at the square below up to the Cloud Chamber, allowing angels to land and watch an image of the Cloud Chamber reflected off the side of the white spire. Displaying the trial of the millennia.

A view from every angle, giving all of the lower Heavens a peek inside. A secure view of the large, newly constructed courtroom and square platform that stood at the edge of the seraphim's Cloud Chamber. The pyre as Azrael used to call it had been enlarged considerably. It gave the seraphim a lot more space, but the platform wrapped around the edge of the courtroom, allowing the seraphim to float close enough to attend any proceeding in the large courtroom. Without setting anything or anyone on fire.

In that courtroom chamber where Lucifer's trial would be witnessed by all of Heaven.

Within the white marble courtroom, a raised platform-like dais floated above the courtroom floor. The judge's bench where five angels presided in judgment. Below the dais stood a white marble witness stand and a counsel table on either side. Behind the counsel tables was the sprawling gallery that allowed dozens of angels to witness the proceedings in person. The lofty space allowed the cherubim guard to fly above the proceedings, patrolling and setting down wards, protection that hadn't been possible before.

The courtroom stretched to the pyre and the towering edge of the Cloud Chamber's vast open expanse of clouds and blue skies that allowed seraphim to preside and attend. Creating enough distance to protect courtroom angels from the seraphim's full angelic form. Enough expanse for half a dozen seraphim to float free and attend proceedings without burning other angels to ash.

A large gold dome crowned the chamber, warded with much stronger protection for the entire spire. Constructed from tempered Eternean metal created and shaped in Heaven's Forge, the dome and spire had been reinforced to withstand a massive blast of Holy fire—stronger than the one that the cherub, Oseira had been forced by Lucifer to set off. The protective dome prevented another incident from destroying the Cloud Chamber.

As Talia, Azrael, and Jack flew up toward the Eternean dome, Talia saw the empty courtroom projected along the spire's white walls. Angels from across the lower Heavens had already begun gathering on the platforms to see the first images of the Cloud Chamber flashed along the height of High House spire. Some of Puriel's gate staff, Zephana's blacksmiths, and angels from the Heavenly Archive fidgeted on the platform, wings twitching, halos bright as they waited for the trial to commence.

Talia flew closer to the projected images, Jack and Azrael following.

The images showed the courtroom where towering angel statues interspersed with gold ornate braziers stood like sentinels around the perimeter of the marbled chamber, its fourth side open to the Cloud Chamber itself. The statues held gold Eternean bowls low in their large marble hands, the folds of their marble robes sharp and billowing around them, unfurled wings intricately carved down to individual feathers. Nearly two dozen of these stone angelic statues stood in silent witness around the chamber, wings outstretched, heads bowed as they offered large gold bowls filled with brightly glowing stones. Burning with Holy fire.

Each bowl had a word written in the Enochian language. Truth. Justice. Communion. Faith. Penance. Love. Freedom. Written on the wall above the judgment dais, glowing gold Enochian script burned with Holy fire, spelling out *For All*.

"Tal," said Jack, squinting as he pointed at the image displayed on the white stone spire. "What does the writing on those bowls say? And the back wall?"

"Each bowl displays one of seven tenets—in Enochian," said Talia. "Truth. Justice. Communion. Faith. Penance. Love. Freedom." She pointed at the huge symbols above the judgment dais. "The symbols on the wall read, For All."

He nodded, going quiet, looking pensive as Azrael led them up to the round Eternean portal at the top of the spire. Through the dome that gleamed white with seraphim wards.

Cherubim surrounded the entrance and interrupted the ward as the three of them hovered. Azrael entered first, followed by Jack, and then Talia.

Inside, they flew into the spire's vertical gallery, flying up past the bright white holding cells below the Cloud Chamber and up toward the courtroom. The air felt charged, agitated, a hint of ozone sharp against the fragrant scent of sweet amber, lemony pine, rosemary frankincense, and the smoky wood scent of myrrh that burned in the braziers beside each angel statue throughout the room. The fragrant mixture was calming, the blue gold flames softening the memory of those stark white holding cells. Where Lucifer awaited trial.

The memory of Lucifer in chains, standing behind those Eternean metal bars, seared itself into her thoughts. Unnerving her.

All along the vertical gallery in the center of the spire, where humans would have built winding stairs or a lift, angels flew up and down, guarded by the myriad cherubim in their burnished Eternean armor that glimmered with ethereal brilliance. The space was full of cherubim guards, more than she'd seen since the destruction of the first High House spire.

From the bottom of the spire to the top, the cherubim guard floated in silent formations, most in their angelic forms gleaming bright against the angelic fire at the core of the white stone spire. They carried polished swords and golden shields that looked like liquid fire against the white gold of their breastplates. Some appeared in their eagle form as they shot up and down the vertical gallery. Others stationed at the courtroom had shifted into winged lion forms, looking fierce and formidable at the entrance.

With the Maker in attendance for this trial, Seraphina was taking no chances. And with Lord Kushiel also present, the seraph was no doubt ensuring that no demonic assault penetrated these newly built walls. From outside or within these walls.

So many angels had already died defending this spire. The seraph wanted to make sure that never happened again. Phalanxes of angel squads (including a massive contingent of the death angel guard that included Talia's unit) had been assigned to the spire for the trial. They floated in silent formation beside the cherubim, armed with sword and shield in their polished Eternean armor.

Today, Heaven had all its defensive might on display. With the Archive spire and the walkways and parks and streets just as well-protected.

Ready to battle anything that dared get near the Maker. Or close enough to free Lucifer.

Talia wondered if this extra display of force had been coordinated by Lord Kushiel. He had fought alongside the angels in the skies above Earth during the apocalypse's Sixth Flight. The apocalypse had humbled most of the surviving angels—especially Talia.

But the archangels were a different story.

Regardless, none of them had ever battled the number of demons that had assaulted Heaven that day. Whether the angels admitted it or not, all of Heaven knew how close the universe came to losing its Maker during the apocalypse. To an almost unstoppable evil. Even if humanity remained blissfully ignorant.

With this massive display of security and defense, Lord Kushiel wanted to send a message to Hell and its demons. That Heaven would never allow something like Lucifer's assault during the apocalypse to happen again.

Talia felt the angels' uneasiness. They were edgy, their anxiousness vibrating along the air currents and rippling through the clouds as all of Heaven waited for the tribunal to begin, eager to see the cherubim bring Lucifer into the courtroom. In chains.

To at last face Heaven—and the Maker. To face judgment for everything he'd done since The Garden. And the Fall.

Azrael led them past a row of massive angel statues that lined the courtroom's three walls. And past the Cloud Chamber. Toward the two white marble counsel tables that stood below the judgment dais.

Soft, calming scents of jasmine, amber, frankincense, and myrrh trailed through the chamber as Azrael veered toward the courtroom's left side—farthest away from the Cloud Chamber.

Toward the white marble counsel table on the left. A third table, the witness stand, stood on a small raised platform that floated directly beneath the judgment dais. A set of four wooden stairs stood beside the witness stand.

Where witnesses and defendants would face the tribunal judges.

Talia looked up at the judgment dais. It had enough room for five celestial beings to hover behind it and hear testimony. Before pronouncing judgment.

About twenty feet behind the counsel tables stood the cordoned off gallery. The space stretched all the way to the massive, celestial white double doors that opened into the spire's vertical well. Where witnesses and defendants waited to be called before the judgment dais. The gallery also allowed the highest-ranking angels to attend the trial in person.

Talia's eyes narrowed as she watched archangels blinking in and out of the space. Archangels that included Uziel, Raphael, and Kotabiel.

She cringed. They would have to cross the gallery to get to the counsel tables.

It made her heart hurt as Azrael led her and Jack through the packed gallery. Where those arrogant archangels hovered in the crowd. Talia gripped Jack's arm like a vise and kept him wedged between her and Azrael. The archangel leaned in close in a protective stance as he pulled them through the gallery.

Some of the archangels hurled insults at Jack like rotten fruit. Disguised in the beautiful tones of the angel tongue. That Jack couldn't hear. Cowards.

She sang out a response, telling them she hoped they liked the taste of their own rotten fruit. Because they would soon dine on nothing else.

"Enough, Talia!" Azrael hissed and blinked ahead, tugging her and Jack away from the gallery and toward the left counsel table at the front of the courtroom.

Jack looked confused by Azrael's anger, but the archangel didn't bother to explain.

"Did you hear what they called him, Azrael?" she demanded, her gaze fiery. "What they said?"

Jack chuckled. "Whatever they said, I've read much worse in the tabloids. Trust me, Tal."

"We have to rise above this archangel pettiness," said Azrael. "Especially with the Maker present. And Heaven's most powerful punishing angel."

He meant Lord Kushiel, of course. One of a handful of angels considered royalty in Heaven. Like Lady Phanuel, archangel of repentance and hope. And Lord Abaddon the Redeemed.

But only Lord Kushiel was present at this tribunal—and sanctioned by the Maker to mete out punishment.

Talia hoped it was too early for the noticeably absent Lady Phanuel, the avenging angel of repentance, a punishing archangel every bit as fearsome as Lord Kushiel. Thankfully, Lord Abaddon had his hands full with the opened Gates of Hell and the demon incursion. He wouldn't be at the tribunal to punish angels either.

"What's wrong?" Jack asked finally, looking concerned and confused.

"I'll tell you later," Talia whispered.

He leaned in close, his lips brushing across her ear, sending waves of heat through her.

"My place or yours?" His pale green eyes sparkled with mischief, that devilish smirk smoldering hot.

She laughed, a blush warming her cheeks. "How about ours?"

"Much, much better," he said, his voice like hot caramel.

Jack was in the highest court that existed, their forbidden relationship on display to all of Heaven, and he was making sexy jokes against her ear.

She smiled. She loved him for that. It spoke volumes about him whether he knew it or not. To her, it said that he didn't care what any of their detractors thought. That he was unashamed. And he was with her until the absolute end. No matter if it was the Lake of Fire or a beach house on the Southern California coast.

She squeezed his hand.

"I love you, Jack Casey," she whispered.

"I love you, too, Mrs. Casey," he said, gripping her hand. "Now until forever."

The counsel table on the right was empty, a chair behind it. She shuddered. Where Lucifer, shackled and wings fettered, would face his father after the Throne room assault. And be judged.

She, Jack, and Azrael slid behind the counsel table on the left. A moment later, a Watcher landed beside it and placed a chair behind the table.

For Jack.

Her stomach dropped.

"Azrael," she said with a hiss against the archangel's ear. "Why aren't we in the gallery with the other witnesses? Seeing that chair terrifies me."

Azrael frowned. "The chair? Why?"

She motioned toward the other counsel table. "Are they putting Jack on trial alongside Lucifer?"

Jack would be more than their witness. Did they expect to have Jack's counsel throughout the entire trial or did they intend to put him on trial alongside Lucifer?"

Talia reached out and wrapped her arm in Jack's. He seemed overwhelmed, his attention drawn in every direction but the chair. He hadn't paid it much attention, but its presence chilled her angel light right down to her wingtips.

"Talia," said Azrael in a sharp whisper. "You, Jack, and me are key witnesses to almost everything in this trial. Having us in the gallery makes no sense and would waste valuable time moving us back and forth from the gallery to the witness stand."

She sighed. He was right. Was she letting her fears get the best of her? She needed to block out these few but loud archangels trying to somehow incriminate Jack.

Jack nudged her and leaned between her and Azrael.

"All right, where is it?"

Azrael frowned. "Where's what, Jack?"

"The gallows. The guillotine. The stake where they burn heretics."

Azrael pulled back, a horrified look on his face. "There are no instruments of execution in Heaven, Jack," he sputtered. "What are you talking about?"

"I've seen enough legal dramas to know where they place the defendants. And this spot screams defendant. Not witness." He pointed at the witness stand in front, the one below the dais. "That's the witness stand."

Jack's green eyes were bright with apprehension. He wasn't wrong.

"Jack, Lucifer is the only defendant at this tribunal," Azrael snapped, his voice quiet but insistent.

Jack nodded over his shoulder. At the group of archangels gathered at the front of the gallery, glaring at him. Uziel, Raphael, and Kotabiel were in front.

"Not so sure about that, Azrael," Jack continued. "I have no idea what those archangels are crooning over there, but those angel notes are directed at me. And they sound like they want me as dead as Lucifer."

Azrael's gaze turned fiery as he and Talia watched and listened as the three archangels continued their bad behavior at the front of the gallery. Glaring at her and Jack. Hovering as close as they could. Blinking past them. Their words dripped with greed and a self-righteous sense of entitlement. Like these archangels somehow had a right to the seraphim powers that Jack carried.

And hers because was only an angel of death.

"Ignore them and have a seat, Jack," said Azrael as his gaze shot from the gallery to the judgment dais. "You are not on trial here."

"I'll stand if you don't mind," said Jack, looking more and more like a frightened deer in celestial headlights. "Er, float."

Talia reached out and gently caressed Jack's shoulder. A smile rose on his lips, but it quickly faded when Archangel of Death, Sidriel entered the back of the courtroom from the gallery.

Sidriel blinked up to the judgment dais and took her place at the farthest spot to the right. Her charcoal grey wings were spread wide at her shoulders as she hovered in place. She faced the courtroom a moment, her long white archangel hair falling over her left eye, her angel of death eyes a bright grey against her ebony skin. Her eyes were still the silvery grey of her death angel guard. She was young by archangel standards, so her eyes were still a lighter grey.

Off to the right, a writhing flame fluttered red-gold in the distance among the clouds beyond the platform. From the Cloud Chamber.

Seraphina.

The ominous column of flame (a seraph's rawest form) burned against the crisp blue sky and scuttling cloud tops as the only remaining seraph moved toward the platform's edge. Toward the courtroom.

"Gallery's filling up," said Jack in a deadpan voice, his eyes widening at the crush of angels beginning to fill up the spaces. "Gonna be a full house."

He looked worried.

A shudder of nerves trembled through Talia's angel light. Her chest tightened. Jack's face had gone pale and he bit the inside of his cheek as he watched the tribunal beginning to assemble.

On Talia's left, Archangel Sarathiel blinked past the table and up to the judgment dais. He looked a little frail, his short white hair bright against his dark skin, gold eyes eagle sharp as he nodded to Sidriel and took his place on the far-left side of the dais. Sidriel returned his nod.

The center place on the dais was reserved for the Maker.

Pravuil blinked into the chamber and appeared beside Azrael. He nodded at Azrael and gave Talia a hug. He leaned past her and shook Jack's hand.

"Have faith, Talia. Jack."

"Thanks, Scribe," said Jack in an almost defeated voice. "And no matter what happens—thanks for everything, dude."

Pravuil's gold eyes sparkled. Amused at Jack calling him dude.

"Thank you for everything, Jack," he said. "And remember, angels can sense lies. Especially Lord Kushiel."

Jack frowned. "Dude, I don't lie to beings who could crush me with the snap of their fingers. Especially at a trial in Heaven." He sighed. "Well, except Luci anyway."

Pravuil crossed his arms, shaking his head as Azrael gave him that archangel look of his, like a parent who approved of his answer. Talia sighed.

"Lucifer doesn't count," Jack replied, a look of uncertainty shadowing those beautiful green eyes. "Does he?"

"Not when it's a matter of survival," said Talia.

The tension dissipated in Jack's face, the taut line of his mouth relaxing.

"Thought I was dead for a minute there," he said with a relieved sigh.

"Jack," said Pravuil, a hand on the sleeve of Jack's pale green dress shirt. "Don't act during this trial. For once, be Jack Casey. Tell us exactly what you saw, exactly what happened, and you'll be fine."

"Until they start asking about my relationship with Talia," he said, frowning.

He rubbed his hands down his charcoal grey dress pants, his black dress shoes shined to a mirror finish. His blond hair was windblown from the flight, wings tucked tight against his back, but he looked smoking hot, his silver-grey wings folded tight against his shoulders. He'd dimmed his halo, probably hoping it wouldn't stand out against the brightness of the other angels' halos. She hadn't seen him this nervous since their wedding day.

Azrael slid his arm around Jack's shoulder and pulled him close. "Just talk from the heart, Jack," he said. "The Maker knows what's in your heart. And like the Maker, Lord Kushiel will read any discrepancy between your words and your heart."

Talia laid her hand against Jack's chest, gazing into those searing green eyes.

"Jack, this heart of yours is your best feature." Talia chuckled. "Besides these hypnotic green eyes. Talk from your heart like you always do."

"I just hope it's enough," Jack said in a whisper.

He reached out and gripped her hand, their wedding rings clinking together. She squeezed his hand tight for a moment and then let go. She and Jack wouldn't flaunt their forbidden relationship in the courtroom, but they wouldn't hide it either. So, the rings stayed on their fingers and she wouldn't hide her love and affection for him.

"It has to be enough, Jack," said Pravuil. "Because it's the truth."

With a rustle of wings, Pravuil lifted into the air and blinked onto the dais. Taking his place left of center.

Whispers hissed through the gallery as Lord Kushiel entered the chamber. All four of his long, red-tipped wings were extended, his burnished Eternean armor alight against the glow of embers in the braziers as he shot through the center of the room, silencing the crowd. He wore shiny, patterned Eternean sollerets, his quiet but forbidding manner disconcerting.

Lord Kushiel turned, his statuesque presence dwarfing the angel statues lining the walls of the room as he turned toward the judgment dais. And floated up to it, taking his place right of center.

Awaiting the Maker.

Kushiel's presence was heavy. Commanding. Imposing. And he made Talia uneasy. Especially since he held the fate of hers and Jack's relationship in his punishing angel hands.

Conversations slowly filled the silence again as Seraphina's fiery image drew closer to the huge platform's edge. She floated as close to the judgment dais as the Cloud Chamber allowed. About thirty feet away. The burn and glow of her light was intense, but the new courtroom shielded itself from the light and heat of seraphim forms.

The sharp rattle of chains echoed through the courtroom, silencing the room.

Heads turned.

Conversations fled, falling to whispers, until the clank and thump of Eternean chains was the only sound in the room as four cherubim flew in formation through the gallery, leading Lucifer into the courtroom.

His curly blond hair was disheveled, defiant light blue eyes sparkling as he held his head high despite the chains hampering his movements, heavy around his ankles and wrists. His black wings were bound against his shoulders. He stood as tall as Kushiel, his presence mythic. Dangerous. Forbidding, blood red halo spinning wildly.

Talia didn't know if Lucifer was putting on the mask of his lifetime as he sauntered to the defendant's table, head held high. His rebellious expression didn't waver as the four cherubim halted at the right-hand table and surrounded him as they turned him toward the judgment dais. He stared up defiantly.

"Luci looks as insolent as ever," Jack whispered.

"Arrogant to the bitter end," Azrael said with a growl.

Talia saw the righteousness burning in those hard blue eyes. He did not see himself as a defendant. He was still above it all. And in his eyes, he'd done nothing wrong.

"Wonder how much of that is just stupid male bravado," Jack replied.

"We're about to find out," said Azrael as Lord Kushiel turned toward the crowded gallery and lifted his arms into the air.

"Heaven, bow before your Maker."

Lord Kushiel's powerful voice commanded the expanse, rising in layers as the warmest, purest gold light Talia had ever felt enveloped the chamber. Every angel in the chamber knelt and bowed their heads. And so did Jack.

But Lucifer stood with chin held high, eyes narrowed. He crossed his arms against his chest.

And he did not bow.

Jack's face was full of wonder at the Maker's arrival as he gave a deep bow, arms held out, on his right knee. He was feeling the entirety of Creation energy swelling around him. Against him. Within him. For the very first time.

Like Jack, she felt it rush around her—through her in soothing waves.

A force she couldn't explain rushed in and filled the entire space, engulfing it, shaping it.

Commanding it.

And in a burst of white light, the Maker appeared between Pravuil and Lord Kushiel on the judgment dais. A being of pure light.

In that complex, encompassing light, Talia saw stars, planets, galaxies—and time. The forces tangled and intertwined in flashes and pulses of pure energy that was all colors and frequencies at once as the forces surged and expanded through the strange afterglow. The energy became a sheen of colors, soft and ever-changing, ever-rising and falling in the radiance that held all of those energies together. It was the essence that was the Maker in their celestial form.

Controlled so that it didn't burn human and angel eyes away. Controlled like the seraph's—only more so. This was the Maker of All Things. Angelic, human. Ethereal. Demonic. Within the Maker, it was all one. Pure energy and pure light.

Jack looked overcome by the Maker's presence, his face filled with wonder, questions, and pain. Joy and confusion. It took him several moments to recover—even though he had been in the Maker's presence once before. In the Throne room. But until now, he hadn't seen—or felt—the Maker in all their full, unrestrained glory.

When Jack recovered, he turned his gaze toward Lucifer. Studying him. Gauging his reaction.

Talia turned.

Lucifer still stood with head held high. Refusing to bow. Refusing to acquiesce in any way to his father. His Maker. The being who would decide whether Lucifer continued to exist.

Trepidation gleamed in Jack's eyes as he watched the fierce internal struggle between the two powerful beings begin. Like her, he felt it, too.

Lucifer would not repent. He refused to acknowledge any wrongdoing. She was convinced that he would defy his father to the end of his existence. He had resigned himself to his fate and would face it with chin lifted and head held high.

Arrogant until the bitter end, as Azrael said.

Jack seemed perplexed by Lucifer's attitude. Almost surprised. Time would tell if it remained unchanged as Lord Kushiel tore into

Lucifer throughout the trial. Kushiel was ruthless in getting at the truth—even with the King of Hell.

But with Lucifer, even Lord Kushiel had a fight on his hands.

"Now, all, face your Maker and stand witness to these proceedings."

Wings shifted, robes fluttered, voices whispering through the gallery as Kushiel turned his attention to Lucifer.

"Lucifer. The Shining One. The Morning Star. The Lightbringer."

Kushiel's voice was intense as he addressed Lucifer from the judgment dais.

"You forgot King of Hell," Lucifer said in a bitter tone.

Kushiel continued, unaffected.

"You stand accused of the highest of crimes. You face this tribunal for attempting to destroy Creation. And the Maker." Kushiel paused, hands behind his back, red-tipped wings twitching. "How do you plea?"

Lucifer's glare was icy. Deadly.

"Plea? I will never plead a word in this…mockery of justice. In this hypocritical chamber of truth, I plead nothing. I don't plead." A smile touched his lips. "Do your worst, Punisher."

Kushiel paused, watching Lucifer with a wary expression. Finally, he glanced at the Maker.

Talia felt the shift of energy. Acceptance. The Maker would not make their firstborn angel plead innocent or guilty. But it was clear that they would still hold Lucifer accountable.

"Such defiance of the charges won't help your case a bit, Lucifer," said Pravuil as he gestured at Lucifer. "You're on trial nonetheless."

"Help my case?"

Lucifer laid a hand against his tattered black general's coat, that smile turning the blue of his eyes harder. Deadlier.

"Scribe, you speak as though there is more than one possible outcome here today. We both know better, now, don't we? Pravuil. We all know that I have already been tried and sentenced. This spectacle is…" He laughed. "Mere formality. A performance. And one of Father's finest." He shifted his gaze across the room and focused on Jack. "Careful, Jack. You think you know the side you're on, but careful that it doesn't turn on you." He held up his chained wrists. "Now that they have what they want."

Jack looked unnerved.

"Always the victim, aren't you, Lucifer?" Sarathiel shouted, hands behind his back, white wings unfurling, expression fierce. "Your actions put you on trial before the Maker. Remember that. A little humility would go a long way here."

"Humility?" Lucifer's eyes narrowed to slits, his jaw tense, that smile widening. "Oh, come now, dear Sarathiel. We both know that my humility will only extend as far as the door into the Lake of Fire. And my actions were expected, given the circumstances. Regardless, the outcome of this farce is clear and has been clear for millennia. Get it over with already. I tire of these games."

"We will move on to the first incident involving the angel of death," Kushiel replied in his dark, patient tone. "Beginning with…"

Kushiel's gaze was piercing as it settled on Azrael. The archangel of death's wings shifted as he met the Punishing Angel's unblinking gaze. As if resigned to let the whole story unfold for all to hear. Every last detail.

Talia tensed. Jack would hear the entire story from Heaven's side. Whether he was ready to or not. She had no idea how it would affect him, but she knew that parts of it would hurt him. And she hated that most of all.

"Archangel Azrael, angel of death Talia, please approach the dais."

With a nod from Azrael, she and the archangel blinked toward the table below the dais. Azrael looked tense, muscles taut, wings shifting as he faced the Maker and the rest of the tribunal.

"Now then," said Kushiel as he blinked in front of the table, hovering, his unsettling gaze piercing. "Azrael. Tell us how this entire debacle with Lucifer began."

Lucifer rolled his eyes and sighed as he leaned against the table, chains rattling.

"Lord Kushiel, Talia was my best angel of death, but at the time, her performance was suffering."

"In what way?" Kushiel shot back at him.

The Maker's light pulsed with an array of colors above them, but the supreme being remained a silent observer.

Azrael glanced at Talia and swallowed hard. "She kept losing souls instead of shepherding them home."

"Why was that?" Kushiel asked.

"Because they're insufferable and they are their own worst enemies," Lucifer replied. "Every angel in this room knows that. Even Jack."

Timid chuckles echoed from the gallery.

"Order," Pravuil snapped.

"Tell me I'm wrong, Scribe." His gaze shot to the Maker. "Father? Tell me I'm wrong."

"Order!"

"He's not wrong," said Talia. "I had only disdain for humans. Because of it, I was in danger of falling."

"In danger of seeing the truth, dear Talia. That Father's Creations were failures at best. Arrogant embarrassments at worst. It would have been kinder to smite the lot of them."

More quiet chuckles from the gallery.

"I said order!" Pravuil shouted.

"No, he's right."

The gallery went quiet as Jack timidly approached the table.

"Uh, forgive me for butting in, Scribe, Lord Kushiel...uh, judges," said Jack in a quiet voice. "But he's right."

Murmurs rippled through the gallery.

"No, really. We're all kinds of fail. We're arrogant. We're headstrong. We're too ignorant to know when someone's trying to help us. We're all a bunch of toddlers wanting to handle everything ourselves. Until it all goes wrong. It's no wonder that Talia here was exasperated to a point of ending all of us and not looking back."

More whispers.

"But...we have one saving grace," Jack continued. "One quality that not one angel in this room understands. Or has ever felt for that matter." He smiled, glancing at Talia. "Well, except for Talia and the archangel here."

"Explain, Jack Casey," said Kushiel, his tone patient but intense.

Jack glanced up at the judgment dais and then around the chamber, looking apprehensive as he pointed to the angel statues around the room.

"Talia had to read the words to me, but around this uh, courtroom are seven words. I tried to memorize them, but Tal, correct me if I miss one or two. Those words are: Penance, Communion, Justice. Faith. Uh…Truth." Jack counted on his fingers. "Sorry. Freedom. And Love. Now, you dudes have angels overseeing all of these tenets, archangels down to Watchers handling whole initiatives for every single one of those words. Except one."

Azrael flinched when Jack said dude.

"Your point, Jack Casey?" asked Lord Kushiel, beginning to push.

"I've never seen an archangel of love," said Jack. "You have angels of death, angels of punishment—even angels of justice. But not one angel of love. Forgive my ignorance. I don't mean it as arrogance. Maybe I've just never encountered one? Maybe you dudes have a whole department for it and I've never seen it? But this whole thing started because Talia stopped loving her idiot human charges. AmIright?"

The murmurs became a dull roar in the gallery.

"Order!" Pravuil shouted. "Lord Kushiel, you have the floor."

"You are correct, human," said Kushiel, no malice behind the word human. "There is no angel or archangel of love within Heaven. Again, what is your point?"

Jack sighed. "My point is that because none of you angels understands love—because you've never felt it—Talia wanted to smite all her human souls instead of save them. Because of that, the door was wide open for Luci here to step in and propose his wager that looked like it could save her. And at the time, no one realized the dark plan beneath that wager or where it would lead. The Phoenix Shift he'd orchestrated."

"Lord Kushiel, that's true," said Azrael. "Yes, I was prideful and angry when Lucifer offered the wager. But I only had Talia's best interests at heart. I thought that if she experienced the world as one of her humans, through Lucifer's wager, she would learn to care for them again. And the proof would be her saving two souls."

The archangel cast a glare over his shoulder at Lucifer.

"But I was naïve, Lord Kushiel. And I should have known better." He bowed his head. "I should have known that Lucifer was up to no good. But I was just trying to save Talia."

"Lord Kushiel," said Talia, floating closer to Azrael. "Azrael did save me through that wager. Ever since, I have learned—no, I have felt, experienced what these incredible, beautiful humans call love. And I would do anything for the souls I cross over now. My heart goes out to them and I want to make their passing as comforting as possible."

Azrael sighed and rubbed his eyes with thumb and forefinger. "And in the process of sending her to Earth in human form, I accidentally gave her a soul. Completely my error, Lord Kushiel, as I informed the seraphim at the time."

"But that soul connected me to my human charges, Lord Kushiel," said Talia. "Because of it, I felt love for the very first time."

Kushiel blinked right in front of her, his form so intimidating as he leaned on the table toward her, those emotionless gold eyes intense. Filled with judgment? She wanted to shrink away from him, but she had nothing to hide. Especially not her relationship with Jack Casey.

"And did that lead to you undertaking a forbidden relationship with a human?" Kushiel asked.

Excited voices rose behind her in the gallery, almost cheering on Lord Kushiel. But again, she had nothing to hide.

"It led me to love humanity, Lord Kushiel. I tried not to fall in love. I tried to detach myself, but only an angel would believe that such detachment was even possible—now that I had a human soul."

Again, conversations erupted through the gallery.

"Order!" Pravuil shouted. "And you archangels in the gallery better learn some respect or you'll be the next trial held in this chamber."

The voices went quiet.

Kushiel put his hands behind his back as he leaned toward Talia again.

"Please clarify this bold statement you've made," he said, eyebrows pressing into a hard line above his gold eyes. "About angelic detachment."

"Lord Kushiel," Lucifer said in an acidic voice. "You need to shake the feathers out of your ears and adjust that self-righteous halo. Detachment is the angelic way of life and you're rather the poster boy for it. Which makes us nothing like humanity. And perhaps that's been the problem all along? Is that what you're saying, Talia?"

Reluctantly, Talia nodded.

Probably wasn't the best idea to agree with Lucifer, but he was right. That detachment combined with most angels' feelings of superiority were as much the problem as it was with humanity. Both thought they were superior. Love wasn't even on the table.

She felt like the first angel to ever cross that picket line.

"Yes," said Talia. "Humans and angels both think they're superior. Making love between them impossible. Until we met on common ground." She smiled. "A ridiculous human reality television show about being a fairytale princess. That's where I learned to love." She turned toward Jack and laid her hand against his face. "Through Jack Casey."

"The poster boy for human arrogance," he replied with a smirk. "Until Talia Smith changed me. Before that, the only love I'd felt was for my drug dealer's next delivery."

Kushiel was silent for several moments. Finally, he turned toward Jack and then Talia.

"So, the two of you freely admit to engaging in this forbidden relationship since Lucifer's very first wager."

The accusation was sharp. Damning.

Talia cast a glance at the Maker whose light was still a pure, constant white pulse.

"It's not like we tried to hide it," Jack replied.

"We never hid the fact that we were in love, Lord Kushiel," said Talia. "We brought it up the chain. From Azrael to the seraphim. And to the Maker when Lucifer's forces attacked Heaven. Even in the Throne room."

"Lord Kushiel," said Archangel Sidriel, her clear alto voice ringing out through the chamber. "Lucifer is the one on trial here, not Jack and Talia's relationship." She turned, her white hair settling around her shoulders. "May we please refocus on Lucifer's intentional attempts to destroy the Creation. And the Maker. Those are the charges, so let the testimony reflect evidence to support or deny those charges."

A smile touched Azrael's face.

"Archangel Sidriel, you make an excellent point," said Pravuil. "Lord Kushiel, refocus your questioning, please."

Kushiel cast an unsettling glance toward the dais. "As you request. Archangel Azrael, tell us the outcome of this wager and what happened next."

"Yes, Azrael, old boy," Lucifer replied, his tone lighthearted, chains rattling. "Regale us with the outcome of our…first little wager."

Azrael glared at Lucifer.

"Talia saved two souls. Jack Casey's and her own. And won the wager."

Kushiel's wings shifted against his shoulders as he glanced back at Azrael.

"And that was the end of these wagers?"

Azrael sighed. "Not exactly."

Kushiel turned, looking surprised. It was the first emotion Talia had seen on his long, rigid, but attractive face.

"What do you mean, not exactly?"

Azrael stared down at his feet. "Lucifer returned to Eolowen, demanding a second wager. Double or nothing."

Kushiel raised an eyebrow, staring at Azrael for several unnerving moments. "What made you accept a second wager with…Lucifer, the King of Hell?"

"Why indeed, Lord Kushiel," he said, rubbing his face.

Lucifer's laughter rippled through the chamber as Seraphina's light brightened through the chamber, the seraph moving closer.

Talia remembered Lucifer appearing to her backstage at the show's live finale. Informing her that it was now double or nothing. And suddenly, she'd been whisked away, finding herself crossing over two souls on a lonely, dark road in the rain. After she'd crossed over the two souls, and listened to Lucifer's gloating about the new wager, she returned to Eolowen. Only to be sent back to Earth. Back to Jack's reality television show.

At the time, it had been the happiest moment of her existence. She was returning to Jack. But the second wager was to take two souls as an angel of death, rather than save two.

"Explain," Kushiel ordered.

"In order to save Talia's human soul, I broke Heaven's rules of time," said Azrael. "I confessed my sins later to the seraphim when I told them that I had rewound a few moments of time. Allowing an angel of death to deflect the bullet. Just enough that it didn't kill Talia's human soul."

Kushiel's intense eyes narrowed.

"And why did you do this?"

"Talia loved Jack," said Azrael, a pained look on his face. "And it was my fault. Jack was the one thing she wanted more than her own existence. So, in order to give him back to her, I changed those microseconds of time."

"Lord Kushiel," said Jack. "Azrael was the first angel who learned about love. And he recognized it in Talia, that she was in love with me. And his love for Talia made him do what he did."

Kushiel shook his head. "Motive is immaterial to the matter. Azrael, you entered into this second wager for another reason. Speak it, Azrael."

Azrael hung his head. "I did it because Lucifer threatened to tell the Maker what I'd done. I intended to confess my transgressions, but not on Lucifer's timetable. So, I accepted the second wager."

"All of which he told the seraphim," said Talia.

A burst of fiery gold light enveloped the edge of the chamber as Seraphina's song burned through the room, catching Kushiel by surprise.

He turned, staring at the surging seraph fire as Seraphina's words filled Talia's head—and the head of every angel in the chamber. Including Jack's. He grabbed his head, wincing, the sound uncomfortable to humans.

This is a matter of record. Azrael's motives and actions are not on trial here.

"Forgive me, seraph," said Lord Kushiel, bowing toward the seraph. "I only ask to understand the events. I had not intended to put Archangel Azrael on trial. I was aware that the Maker knew all about these events."

At last, the seraph's light dissipated. Along with its heat as she pulled back from the platform's edge. Turning gracefully in the clouds and softening light.

Seraphina did not appreciate Lord Kushiel's line of questioning.

Jack reached out and gripped Talia's hand. She turned to him, losing herself in his pale green gaze. And squeezed his hand.

"Archangel Azrael," Kushiel continued, turning back to Azrael. "What was the result of this second wager?"

Azrael cast a pained glance at Talia. "The second soul Talia had to take was Jack's. She refused. Causing her to lose the wager and her wings. Forcing me to cast her out of Heaven."

"And into my arms!" Jack shouted.

"And still you flaunt this illicit relationship!" shouted one of the archangels from the gallery.

Pandemonium erupted as angels began to argue with archangels.

"Order!" Pravuil shouted.

But none of the angels was listening as a fistfight broke out.

"Oh, I do enjoy a good angelic fistfight."

Lucifer sat back and laughed, chains rattling as the gallery turned into a war zone.

10

Jack watched cherubim flood into the gallery, breaking up fights between archangels and angels. All because he'd said that Talia had fallen from the sky and into his arms?

Seriously?

Even from the start of this trial, Jack felt the polarization among the angels. So many had been on his and Talia's side. But another contingent seemed hell-bent on convicting him and Talia alongside Lucifer. Well, their relationship at any rate.

Was all of it a thinly veiled plot to steal his seraphim powers?

He glanced up at the Maker. He knew nothing about the Maker or this light form that seemed to be what angels had been based off. But the Maker had appeared in human form that day in the Throne room to face Lucifer. Regardless, Jack expected the Maker to be more involved in this trial. Was the Maker even listening? He had no idea and he refused to speculate, but it just seemed odd that the Maker was so hands off after tossing Luci and his followers out of Heaven and into Hell. Pravuil and Kushiel seemed to be in charge of the whole tribunal and this punishing angel had already ruffled Seraphina's feathers. Annoyed some of the judges. And caused fistfights in the gallery.

Jack wanted the Maker to speak. To intervene somehow. To put some boundaries and maybe even a frame on this thing. To keep so many…big personalities in check. Kushiel seemed more interested in convicting his witnesses of crimes than proving Lucifer attempted to destroy Creation—and the Maker. The whole reason for this trial.

Jack knew little about how Heavenly tribunals worked and he had no clue about Kushiel's line of questioning. But he couldn't help feeling like he was slowly being convicted of a crime. Of being a danger to others. Of deliberately hiding his and Talia's relationship despite telling archangels, seraphim, and even the Maker about it. Forbidden despite the Maker tentatively weighing in on them staying together.

That answer had been yes. At the time anyway.

Did punishment rest with Kushiel on that matter? Or was it all on the Maker's plate?

Either way, Jack was worried. And that was an understatement.

Suddenly, Kushiel was in his face.

"Jack Casey! Explain to me how you caught an angel falling from Heaven after her wings were just taken."

Jack held out his arms.

"With both arms," he said. "Like this."

Laughter erupted through the gallery.

Kushiel's expression darkened. His gold eyes turned hard, brow furrowing.

"That was not a literal question. Curb your sarcasm, human."

"I wasn't being sarcastic," Jack replied.

Pissing this dude off was not a good plan, but he'd been called The Punisher for too long. He needed a little focus change if he wanted to understand everything that had happened.

"No?" Kushiel was not happy.

"No. All I know is that I caught her. How? I haven't a clue. Catching someone who had fallen that far would have been going faster than the speed of light. It should have killed both of us. But it didn't."

Kushiel's eyes narrowed and he glared at Jack.

"I wish you would look at this more like a travel log and less like The Punisher."

Azrael gasped as murmurs rippled through the gallery.

"Your human arrogance is beginning to weigh on me, Jack Casey."

"See?" Lucifer replied. "Jack Casey could drive even the Devil to destroy the world. Not guilty."

Laughter rolled through the gallery.

"Dude, I don't mean that as an insult."

"Jack, be careful," Azrael replied.

"I just mean you keep asking questions, looking for the next person—or angel—to punish. So, you're not even hearing the words. You're just rushing ahead to check off names from your list of who to punish. Be objective, but damn, dude, try to see what happened without those red lenses."

Kushiel grabbed Jack by the shirt.

"How dare you tell me how to do my job. Human."

Lucifer let out a peal of laughter. "Oh, this is exquisite."

Jack stared at Kushiel. Dude could crush him, that was true.

"All I'm saying is preside not punish. Until you've heard everything. You've already made up your mind before you have the whole story. I see it in your eyes."

Pravuil had his hand over his eyes. Azrael winced, squirming, looking as terrified as Talia.

Whispers churned through the room as the Maker's gold light began to shift with colors and pulses.

Oh, shit. Jack squirmed. Was that the order to smite him?

Kushiel let go of Jack, whirling around as the lights shifted and changed. And in a moment, the Maker's light turned back to that steady white gold again.

Finally, Kushiel turned around, the anger gone from his face.

"The Maker has reminded me that my arrogance is also showing. Jack Casey should be treated as an equal here at this tribunal and I am treating him like a subordinate. An inferior. He should be free to speak his mind, free of judgment, like the angels. Going forward, I will do my best to allow him the same courtesy as the angels in the room."

"Lord Kushiel," said Jack. "I meant no disrespect. I just see how all the judgments keep flying through this room. I'm just asking you to hear the whole story first. And then decide who or what needs punishing."

Kushiel nodded and no longer looked like he was about to tear Jack apart, molecule by molecule.

"One of you, tell me," said Kushiel, returning to his line of questioning. "When did it become apparent that Lucifer had a plan beyond these wagers?"

"When he showed up at my apartment and tried to drag me and Talia off to Hell."

Kushiel turned around, eyebrow raised. "And you saw him?"

Jack nodded. "Somehow, I was beginning to mirror Talia's angel powers as her wings began to grow back. And the light of her halo began to return. So, I could see the angels and demons that started a brawl inside my place. Totally shot my security deposit." He shook his head. "Had to tell my landlord that someone drove a backhoe through it because he didn't believe me about the shadow panthers and hellhounds. Imagine that."

Laughter rippled through the gallery.

"And then Lucifer showed up to the party. Didn't even bring a bag of chips. Just threats about dragging me and Talia off to Hell. So, we bolted for the isolated beach house where my show was filming." He hung his head. "Had no idea that Luci owned the beach house. And most of my costars. After he tethered my soul, he tried to drag Talia off to Hell, but I made him take me instead."

Kushiel looked confused.

"Take you instead?"

Jack nodded. "I couldn't let him take Talia and torture her for eternity."

Kushiel blinked across to the table where Lucifer sat on top, chains clanking as he sat up straighter to meet Kushiel's glare.

"You dragged a living human off to Hell? And tortured him?"

"I won his soul fair and square in that wager," said Lucifer in a dismissive tone. "It wasn't my fault it was still attached to a functioning body."

"You knew that was against the rules, Lucifer!"

"And your point, Punisher?" Lucifer shouted. "I made sure nothing killed him. I made sure he got food and water. And I kept a close eye on him. But I needed those rare powers he carried. In human form, I expected him to give them up quickly. First, to save Talia. And then to save himself. But he refused to give them up."

Kushiel hit the table with his fist. "Lucifer! You tortured a living human!"

"Only a little," Lucifer replied. "With those damned powers of his, he kept exploding my torture demons. Such an annoyance. It's not like demons grew on trees down there. We don't even have trees."

"Jack Casey," said Kushiel, blinking back to the other table. "Did Lucifer try to torture and kill you down there?"

Jack sighed as he glanced over at Lucifer who was smiling.

"Tell the truth now, Jack," said Lucifer. "Otherwise, Lord Kushiel will blow a vein in his head and mess up Father's new courtroom."

"Oh, he definitely tortured me. But he did bring me food and water the whole time I was there. Had a fallen angel and a demon shadowing me the whole time—protecting me. Healing me. That's how I met Berith."

"See?" Lucifer said, gloating. "I treated Jack like the prisoner of war that he was."

Kushiel whirled around and pointed a finger at the King of Hell. "And out of the goodness of your heart—or its greed—did you let him go? After you got what you wanted?"

"Got what I wanted? Oh, no…Jack Casey here wrecked my entire attack plan. When I brought him with me to Eolowen, to use his powers on the angels, he led me into the Garden and trapped me in there—and himself."

Murmurs echoed through the gallery. Jack wondered how much of this was known by the other angels. They sounded surprised.

"And when you realized what he'd done," said Talia, shifting her wings until she rose above the table, her gaze fiery as she glared at him. "That he'd out-manipulated the master manipulator, you beat him to death in that very same Garden."

Lucifer's mouth twitched and he looked away. "Lost my temper."

"Lord Kushiel," said Talia, her eyes filling with tears, hands shaking as she glanced over at Jack. "Jack took his last breath in my arms in the Garden."

Jack knew how painful those moments in the Garden had been for her. The memory of it still burned through him. The ache in his chest, knowing he would never see her again. That he'd lost her forever.

He bowed his head, eyes stinging.

"I used a rare angel power I had awakened to remove the tether on Jack's soul. So his soul wouldn't be bound to Hell when he took that last breath. But something about our bond returned that last breath to him. And saved him."

The corners of Kushiel's mouth lifted into almost a smile.

"And that's the reason you are still among us, Jack Casey?" he said. "Because of these rare powers?"

Jack shrugged. "My memory was a little fuzzy, but I think so."

"But Lucifer was still trapped in the Garden?"

Jack nodded. "But see, by then, he'd successfully engineered his Phoenix Shift. By freezing time on Earth. So, he was slowly growing back his wings and relighting his halo. The moment they returned, he'd bust out of there and come gunning for me. Because he still needed Talia's rare powers to launch his attack on Heaven."

"So, everything he's done was planned?" Kushiel asked. "In order to assault Heaven?"

"And kill the Maker," Azrael added. "So, to protect Jack, the seraphim got permission to hide him among my angels of death."

Kushiel held out his arms. "And that's how Jack got wings and a halo."

"That's how he became a flying rat," Lucifer replied to chuckles from the gallery. "Who couldn't hide from me for long."

"Lucifer," Pravuil called from the dais. "You're not helping your case with these insults."

"Pravuil, we both know there is no changing my fate," said Lucifer as he avoided looking at the Maker. "So, I might as well enjoy these last fleeting moments while I have them."

Kushiel began to move back and forth between the tables.

"So, Lucifer needed these rare powers to initiate his first attack on Heaven," said Kushiel, summarizing. "And through the traitorous actions of Archangel Raziel and Archangel Samael, he was able to get control of Talia?"

Talia nodded. "Against my will."

"And that led to Lucifer and his army marching on Heaven?"

"Correct, Lord Kushiel," said Azrael. "Talia and Berith used those rare powers to tether Lucifer's soul to Hell. But the powers needed time to work. So, Jack battled Lucifer with the seraphim's powers, waiting for the tether to drag Lucifer back to Hell. The seraphim had been drained of all energy and hadn't recovered from Raziel's sneak attack. They couldn't fight. Leaving Jack the only one in Heaven who had the power to battle Lucifer."

"And he was losing when the seraph came and meddled in everything," Lucifer announced as he leaned back against the table. "And then I got pulled back to Hell."

"And that's when Lucifer had to launch the rest of his plan through other agents," said Azrael.

Kushiel frowned. "Other agents?"

"Lord Abaddon. An archdemonness. Archangel Samael," said Azrael, almost spitting when he said Samael's name.

"And Asmodeus," said Talia. "Until finally, Lucifer lured all of us to Hell to rescue Berith, a redeemed fallen angel who helped Jack escape from Hell."

"She's like a mother to me, so I had to rescue her," said Jack. "But I had no clue that Luci here was luring me to the Gates of Hell. And the stolen Book of Secrets. So, when we were all in proximity, the rare angel power would ignite, popping open the Gates of Hell and freeing

Luci from his tether." He frowned. "And setting the apocalypse in motion."

Talia nodded, laying her hand on Jack's shoulder, squeezing. "All of it was set in motion so Lucifer could reach the Maker's Throne room. So, he could kill the Maker. And then destroy the Creation."

Kushiel blinked across the room, leaning into Lucifer's face.

"Do you deny that you orchestrated this entire plan, Lucifer? From that very first wager to the kidnapping of redeemed angel of death, Berith. In order to face your father, the Maker in the Throne room. To kill the Maker. And end Creation."

Lucifer's face was taut as an angry smile rose on his lips.

"You are quick, Punisher," he said. "Yes. I orchestrated all of it to face my father for the first time since he threw me from the Heavens. To confront him and his blatant favoritism. He chose these miserable meatsacks over his own angels. He threw me away! His firstborn. His Morning Star! Because he preferred his shiny new toys and not his faithful, loyal angels! Who would have extinguished their last flicker of light to protect him. But he threw us away."

The depth of Lucifer's pain ached through the courtroom, silencing the angels in the gallery.

Causing the Maker's light to dim.

Was it detachment? Indifference? Or pain?

Jack wanted to understand what the Maker felt in that moment. Was it even a feeling? Or was it something so deep and complex that Jack had no hope of fully understanding what that dimmed light meant?

Pravuil cast an uneasy look at the Maker.

"All right, this tribunal will take a quick recess."

And with that, the Maker's light vanished from the dais.

Lucifer looked sullen, pain in those watery blue eyes as he lowered his gaze to the floor. Trying to hide his emotions. But it was clear that a deep hurt resonated through this fallen angel. And that hurt had fueled every single one of Lucifer's actions. Jack saw that clearly now.

"That really got to Lucifer," said Jack, whispering in Talia's ear.

Like Azrael, she hadn't taken her gaze off Lucifer.

"I know," she replied. "He's more like the Lucifer we saw in the Throne room right now."

"And what kind of reaction was that from the Maker?" Jack asked.

Talia shook her head, turning toward Azrael. "Archangel, what just happened between Lucifer and the Maker?"

Azrael looked a little uncertain. "I wish I knew, Talia, but I think Lucifer's words affected the Maker in an unexpected way. Pravuil was very quick to call a recess."

"Especially since the Maker just blinked out of the proceedings," Jack added. "That was an emotional response. I'd bet money on it. And it wasn't a pleasant one."

Azrael glanced at him and then Talia. "That's what I'm feeling, too, Jack. Pravuil was protecting the Maker. We'll have to see what happens as Kushiel interrogates Lucifer further and brings in witnesses. Lucifer isn't one to show weakness like that, especially so early in this tribunal. Revealing that kind of pain was dangerous to his case."

"Shows that he has a breaking point," said Jack. "That he isn't made of Eternean like he pretends. So, what happens next?"

Azrael shifted his wings against his shoulders, stretching them as his red-gold halo gleamed. He folded his arms against his chest, studying the emptying chamber, and watched Seraphina linger at the edge of the platform.

Seraphina looked sad, almost forlorn, her light dimming a little.

Jack saw it. And it made him wonder what was going through the seraph's mind right now. What had caused that reaction? It hadn't been the Maker's sudden departure. No, it happened when Kushiel tore into him and Talia.

About their relationship.

"Seraphina is still visibly upset, Azrael," said Talia, motioning toward the Cloud Chamber.

Azrael's gaze shifted to the seraph, studying her for several moments. "Agreed. Seraphina got quite emotional during Lord Kushiel's initial questioning."

"Why?" Jack asked as he cast a questioning glance at Talia. "What do you think set her off?"

Talia smiled. "Lord Kushiel."

Azrael nodded. "Seraphina doesn't approve of Kushiel's callus approach—her angel notes not mine—because she has a soft spot for you and Talia, Jack."

Jack's face brightened. "So, we've got a seraph on our side still? Sweet!"

"Most likely, Kushiel will dismiss for the day and gather a list of witnesses to call tomorrow," said Azrael. "And then, most likely, we'll be called back."

It seemed like over an hour before Pravuil blinked back into the proceedings. Alone. Dude looked anxious. And worried.

Lucifer didn't even look up. He sat cross-legged on top of the table, his wings bound against his shoulders, a sullen look on his face. Like someone had just smited his last demon. The light from his blood-red halo cast sharp shadows across his features, making the dude look threatening despite the shackles. Luci kept his head down as he stared at the floor. And his chains.

"This tribunal will recess until Lord Kushiel has assembled his next list of witnesses to call," Pravuil announced in a gruff, abrupt tone. "You will be sent for by Watchers when you're needed back here." He caught the gaze of one of the cherubim who stood motionless around Lucifer.

"Cherubim, please return the prisoner to his cell until the next session. Dismissed."

Smiling like he was unaffected, Lucifer rose from the table and jumped to the floor, chains clanging as the cherubim closed ranks around him. He held his head high and walked with an amused smirk through the gallery as a cacophony of angel notes created a giant discord.

All of them talked at once as Lucifer passed through the gallery and out of the courtroom.

"Let's get back to Eolowen," said Azrael, motioning Jack and Talia toward him. "Stay close. So, we don't have an altercation with our brothers and sisters in the gallery."

Talia moved in close on Jack's left, Azrael against his right side as they blinked toward the gallery.

"You mean the douchebags trying to steal my angel powers?" Jack asked.

Azrael couldn't hold back a smile.

"Exactly, Jack," he said. "So, stay close."

Talia clutched Jack's left arm. Azrael grabbed hold of his right, blinking past the crowded gallery as the discords got louder.

Jack tried to ignore the angel notes that were normal communication for angels. He understood that they weren't trying to exclude him on purpose. Most of them anyway. Regardless, he could read the room. It felt like Hollywood the day after he was fired from *SanFran Confidential*. For using flake.

With a jolt, Azrael halted suddenly, keeping Jack close. And behind him.

Talia shoved through the crowd and pressed her body against Jack's left side, shielding him.

Suddenly, three archangels blinked in front of them. Blocking their exit.

"Archangels," said Azrael in a distant tone, eyes darkening.

"Why do you speak in meatsack tongue?" one of them asked.

There were too many angels. Jack couldn't tell who was speaking. They were all crowded in front of Azrael. Blocking his path. Like douchebags.

"Because it's polite when one of us can only understand the spoken word."

"Prefer the company of humans do you now? Azrael?" said another angel.

Jack strained to see over the tall, angelic figures flitting around him like angry pigeons.

"To small-minded, greedy douchebag archangels? You bet I do."

Jack snickered. Azrael called them douchebags.

"What is that term you use?" one of the archangels asked and Jack smirked.

"Look it up in the Archive," Azrael snapped. "Now, move."

The archangels crowded closer.

Azrael's grip on Jack's arm was like a vise as he whispered some angel notes that Jack didn't understand.

Without warning, Azrael blinked, dragging Jack along for the ride. Talia was a heartbeat behind him as they shot up through the spire's vertical gallery. And out the Cloud Chamber's warded portal.

———

Once in the sky, Jack spread his wings as Azrael blinked again. And they were hovering over Eolowen and its white stone terrace. Azrael landed on the stones, fury burning in his charcoal grey eyes as Jack and then Talia landed beside him.

"Those archangels are going to find their halos around their— ankles if they keep this up," Azrael said with a growl.

The archangel of death was fighting mad as he stormed into Eolowen, soot-colored wings folding tight against his shoulders. Leaving Jack and Talia standing on the terrace.

"What was that about?" Jack asked.

"Quite a few words were exchanged," said Talia, scanning the skies over Eolowen.

Like she expected trouble.

"Like what?"

"Threats. Fighting words," said Talia. "Those archangels threatened Azrael and the guard. And Berith. As well as you and me."

"These douchebags related to Raziel?" Jack asked. "Because they have all his pathetic moves down. Like disco. Or line dancing."

She shrugged. "I don't know if they have a connection to Raziel or not, but I can guarantee that they have a connection to Archangel Samael."

"That's worse," said Jack, making a sour face.

"Much worse. And now, we have to stay on alert, in case they attack Eolowen."

Jack sighed. "And with all of Heaven focused on Lucifer's trial, these asshalos can get away with murder."

A squad of death angels lifted off Eolowen's rooftop and flew low over the meadow, looking tense. And on high alert.

In the distance, a bright orange flash bloomed along the horizon. Like a flare had gone off.

When Jack turned toward Talia, she was looking in the other direction as another flare of orange light arced across the blue skies at the edge of Eolowen's long, grassy meadow.

"What was that?" he asked.

She glanced at him, a puzzled look on her face. "That flash?"

He nodded. "There was one over Eolowen. And another one toward the crossroads."

She frowned, chewing her bottom lip. "And a third one toward Celosia, Archangel Sidriel's grand hall."

"Couldn't be lightning, could it?" Jack asked.

"Heaven doesn't have thunderstorms," she said. "The only lightning I've seen has come from the forge. But that's high above the lower Heavens. Not low on the horizon like these flashes."

Her brow furrowed as she continued to watch the horizon, scanning the lower Heavens' skyline. But only puffy white clouds scuttled across a vivid blue sky.

When the sky and the horizon didn't light up, Talia turned back to Jack, smiling, like everything was okay again. But he felt uneasy.

"Tal," said Jack, beginning to pace, his dress shoes ticking against the stones as the skies over Eolowen filled with death angels returning from the spire. "Exactly how do these archangels plan to try and take these angel powers from me? When Heaven hasn't been able to extract them?"

"A very good question, Jack," she said as she leaned against the wall, her gaze still focused on the skies as another patrol passed low over the meadow. "From what Azrael said, they plan to take them after making sure you get thrown into the Lake of Fire."

Jack froze, every cell in his body screaming at once.

"Lake of Fire? Me?" His pacing intensified, ticking of his shoes like his heart tap-dancing against his rib cage. "Okay, I'm not exactly angel material and I've still got a lot of stuff to make amends for, but I don't think I've done enough to stand beside Luci on his swan dive into the Lake. At least I'm sorry for anything I've done."

Shaking her head, Talia moved toward him and wrapped her arms around his waist, holding him so close that he felt her heart racing against his.

"They think they can convince the Maker that you're too dangerous in this half-angel half-human state. Too unbalanced carrying around all these powers—like humans are too volatile to handle any sort of power. They intend to convince the tribunal that you're too unstable and need to be destroyed because the powers and the wings can't be removed."

"The only thing I've ever done with these powers was protect Heaven and my world," he said, scowling.

He tried not to let his anger color his words, but it painted the air in broad strokes now. And he couldn't rein it in.

Talia held him tighter, running her fingers through his hair in soothing strokes as he laid his head against her shoulder.

"Jack, most of Heaven knows that. And I think Seraphina would have much to say about that, too. She's trusted you with that power more than once."

He lifted his head and kissed her gently on the lips in a long, lingering kiss.

"And so have I," Talia added as she slid her arms around his neck.

She smelled like rain and jasmine, her soft, wavy black hair turning into ringlets around her face. She was still the most beautiful woman he had ever seen and even as their first wedding anniversary approached, she still made his blood boil.

"Mrs. Casey," he said as he brushed black curls away from her flushed cheeks, her winter pale skin so luminous against the vibrant blue sky. "Have I told you today how much I love you?"

He wanted to pick her up and carry her off to their Southern California beach house. And make love to her in their new bedroom. With décor that she had chosen. He'd loved watching her pick colors for the walls—a soft ice blue. And the joy that had burned on her face at selecting a comforter (that went from medium blue clouds to a starry midnight blue sky with a crescent moon on the pillow shams and cases).

She chose wood flooring the color of sand, thick white trim for the walls, and a soothing mint green for the living room, a sunny pastel orange for the kitchen. She had used omnificence to study an angelton of online images of beach cottages that had wide white wood trim and pastel colors. She'd also used his jar of beach glass for inspiration.

Every part of their new house reflected her tastes and his, something they'd never had before. Something that had delighted Talia and made him love her even more.

But he couldn't wait to present her with his first anniversary gift. He'd finally come up with the perfect gift. Even called his sisters in Santa Rosa and back in Indiana because he needed their help to make it happen. They had agreed on the condition that they got to be there when he gave it to her. All four of his sisters.

Of course, he agreed. He hadn't seen any of them in a few years. Meredith had been the closest thing to a mom he'd known growing up. He was thrilled that she and Whit wanted to see him again. They hadn't spoken since he got fired from *SanFran Confidential*. Even his two sisters who lived in Northern California wanted them all to get together. He couldn't wait.

"You haven't, Mr. Casey," she said and kissed him.

"Well then…I love you, Mrs. Casey."

He twirled her around and gently pressed her against the terrace wall, kissing her hard on the lips.

But Muriel landed on the terrace beside them, looking upset.

"Muriel?" said Talia, letting go of Jack.

Jack turned, Muriel's expression worrying him. "What's wrong, Muriel?"

"Kesien got in a fight with Archangel Uziel," she said, her mouth pinching. "It was ugly. Lots of Holy fire."

Talia gripped Muriel's shoulders.

"Is he hurt?" asked Talia.

"Douchebags," said Jack under his breath, making a sour face. "Tossing Holy fire at angels who can't return fire. Hope Kesien had his shield."

"He did," said Muriel. "But it was useless against three archangels."

"What?" Jack felt the fury bubble into his veins. "Those asshalos triple-teamed him?"

Muriel nodded, a tear sliding down her face. Furious, she swiped it away. "Kesien's really hurt." Muriel cast a strange look at Jack and switched to angel notes.

Dammit! Banished to the kiddie table again. They were hiding parts of the story from him as usual. To keep him from going after whoever did it.

"Spill it!" he shouted until Muriel glanced at him. "You're not hiding this from me. Not this time."

"I sent Deemah ahead to get Azrael," said Muriel. "But she hasn't come back."

"Muriel, where's Kesien?" Jack asked, gripping Muriel's arms.

Her face pinched. "Jack, they were so brutal. They cornered him behind one of those unfinished platforms in the square. We couldn't get to him…"

Muriel's voice trailed off. And again, a flurry of angel notes.

But this time, Jack didn't need to speak angel to understand what she'd told Talia. They'd attacked Kesien to try and draw him out alone. To the square and into some sort of fight or duel. Like Raziel had.

But this time, he'd make their wish come true. He'd face them. With seraphim powers in each hand.

"Don't bother," Jack said, top lip curling into a snarl. "I know why they attacked Kesien. Don't care if they're archangels. They're not getting away with this."

He blinked into the air.

"Jack, no—Jack!" Talia shouted.
"Jack, don't!" Muriel. "That's exactly what they want!"
Jack pointed his finger and blinked across the sky.
Toward the empty High House square.
To put three douchebag archangels in their place.

CHAPTER 11

TALIA TRIED TO BLINK AFTER JACK, BUT HE HAD THAT SERAPHIM BLINK. So, he just disappeared from the sky in a single blink before she could even follow him.

"Jack, wait!" Talia shouted.

Muriel grabbed her wings, holding her back from leaping into the sky after Jack.

"Talia, don't! Somebody…get Azrael! Now."

Talia shifted, intending to blink past Muriel into the grand hall and go after Jack, but Azrael and Berith appeared in the doorway of the round room.

"Get me for what?" Azrael asked.

"Wait, Deemah's not with you?" Muriel demanded.

Azrael shrugged. "Haven't seen her. Why?"

"Deemah, no." Muriel looked frightened as she glanced at the sky and then back at Azrael. "She must have gone back to the square. To protect Kesien."

Deemah went after those archangels—just like Jack. Talia was certain. Both of them could be in trouble. Talia had to find them before they found those archangels. And a storm of Holy fire.

Besides, Kesien was hurt and needed help.

"Azrael," said Talia, pointing toward the High House spire. "Those three archangels harassing you and Jack attacked Kesien to try and lure Jack into a fight. Kesien's badly hurt."

"Where is Kesien?" Berith asked, her grey eyes filled with fear as she turned to Azrael, a worried look in her eyes.

"Barricaded behind a ward in High House square," said Muriel. "The archangels demanded that we bring Jack to the square. I sent Deemah ahead to come get you, sir. And I left Anahera to watch out for Kesien."

Azrael's face turned pale. "We all know that Deemah and Jack went after those archangels. We need to catch up—fast."

Muriel shrugged, looking sick and frantic.

"Muriel, which way did Deemah and Jack fly?" Azrael demanded.

"Deemah was supposed to come get you and bring you back to the square," said Muriel, looking sick. "She flew toward Eolowen. I came to get Talia, trying not to involve Jack—but he figured it out and blinked toward the square. Now, they're both out there hunting those archangels and probably walking into a trap." Muriel covered her face with her hands. "What have I done?"

Azrael unfurled his wings, those charcoal grey eyes turning stormy. "We'll get to them in time. Were they both headed toward the square?"

Muriel nodded.

"Then let's go!"

Azrael leaped into the air and blinked across the sky toward High House. Talia followed right behind the archangel as Berith and Muriel followed.

Talia was only a short distance behind the archangel, but when she blinked across the rest of the distance to the square below High House, she found Azrael circling it.

She caught up to him, expecting to see Holy fire flashing like lightning across the square. But the place looked empty. Deserted.

Anahera soared up from the square. Alone. Looking worried.

Kesien and Deemah weren't there. And neither was Jack. Deemah had the longest head start. Did Kesien's ward fail? Had those archangels grabbed him? Where would they have taken him?

"Azrael! The archangels dragged Kesien off," she said with a moan. "I couldn't stop them. Or Deemah and Jack from blinking after them."

"You saw Deemah and Jack?" Azrael replied.

Anahera nodded.

"Let's go!" Azrael shouted, circling the square.

Muriel flew beside Anahera, reaching out to pat her shoulder. "It's okay. At least we have a trail to follow."

Talia nodded, staying close to Azrael as she scanned the square and the sky.

Not a single flash of Holy fire arced into the sky or crackled across the square. Not a sound emanated from the white stone streets or the square below. Everything was quiet and empty.

Where had they gone?

"There!" Azrael shouted, pointing toward a nearby park. "Holy fire!"

A pale white flash of light arced into the sky and went dim as a Watcher angel stumbled along the white stone streets a short distance from High House square. His blue-grey robes were singed and smoking, light brown hair disheveled as his wings hung at odd angles and dripped a pearly gold liquid in his wake.

Talia followed Azrael, landing in front of the dazed and confused Watcher. His robes were burned and scorched. His hair was covered in ash, velvety grey wings tattered and charred, most of the feathers blackened and still smoking. Both wings leaked gold light onto the white stones.

How had he even flown with wings so injured?

When the Watcher turned toward her, Talia saw the charcoal grey of his exhausted eyes.

He wasn't a Watcher at all. He was an angel of death!

And from the symbols on his right sleeve, he was part of Sidriel's guard.

"Death angel, what happened to you?" Azrael demanded.

When the death angel didn't respond, Azrael shook him.

"Death angel, report!" he shouted, shaking him again until his confused stare shifted toward Talia.

"Where are the couriers?" he asked, sounding dazed.

"What couriers?" said Azrael, squinting as he glanced around the quiet park.

"Lord Kushiel's couriers."

Talia felt a chill rush down her spine. Why did Lord Kushiel have couriers? And what were they bringing to the punishing angel?"

"Where are Kushiel's couriers?" Azrael asked.

When the death angel didn't respond, Azrael gripped his shoulder. "Please, we need to know," said Azrael in a soft voice. "What were Kushiel's couriers carrying?"

"The key," the death angel said with a hiss.

"What key?" Azrael asked, eyes narrowing as he cast a quick glance at Talia.

Talia felt like someone had punched her in the stomach. She knew exactly what key those couriers carried.

"Azrael…it's the key that opens the door into the Lake of Fire," she said with a gasp. "I'm certain of it."

The death angel nodded. "We had three squads from my guard, each guarding one of three couriers. We each took a separate path to the spire. We were so careful." He gripped the sleeves of Azrael's robes, leaving handprints of liquid gold light on the archangel's white dress robes. "But archangel, they knew." He winced. "They knew!"

"Knew what?" Azrael demanded. "And who is they?"

The angel of death hung his head, singed brown hair covered in ash, a cut leaking light along his left cheekbone.

"The archangels Raphael, Uziel, and Kotabiel. They knew our route. What we were carrying—everything."

Azrael nodded for him to continue.

"Each courier carried half the key and the third carried the reassembly chant. I don't know how the archangels knew all of that. Or that only cherubim could open the key cases. Regardless, they unleashed three simultaneous storms of Holy fire against us."

Azrael looked sick.

"Azrael!" Talia cried, laying her hand against the archangel's shoulder. "The flashes of light!"

He glanced at her, frowning. "What flashes of light?"

"Jack and I were standing on the terrace when he saw a white flash of light above Eolowen's rooftop. I saw one near Celosia Hall. Jack saw a third one near the crossroads. They were in three separate locations across the lower Heavens."

The injured angel of death reached out to her and she gripped his hand, gold light dripping down his wrist and fingers. She sent healing waves of white light through him, trying to heal his wounds. And his pain.

"Those flashes were the locations of the three couriers," said the angel of death. "And the squads protecting them."

"Easy now," she said in soothing soprano notes.

"The archangels who attacked us..." The angel of death shuddered as more light stained his charcoal robes. "They erased my whole squad." His eyes turned glassy. "And the courier we were escorting. Then they scorched all the stones until there was nothing left."

Fury burned through Talia's veins and shot to the tip of her wings. Burning those stones meant erasing any chance she had of bringing those murdered angels back with her resurrect power. Her eyes turned glassy, tears gathering.

Those angels of death were gone. Only the Maker could resurrect them now.

"How did you get away?" Talia asked, smoothing the death angel's burnt hair out of his haunted grey eyes where a half-moon scar encircled his right eye—an old battle wound from the looks of it. Scars were unusual to see on an angel.

"I—I fell out of the sky onto Celosia's rooftop. The archangels landed and started scorching the surrounding stones. I blinked off the roof and across the square where I hid in a public meditation room. I stayed there until I heard you and Archangel Azrael land."

"What's your name?" Talia asked in a soft alto melody.

"Caleal," he answered.

"You're safe now, Caleal," she said, getting to her feet as Azrael and Berith helped the angel of death sit up.

Call gritted his teeth. "I should have been safe then. This is Heaven."

Caleal was right. He should have been safe. They all should have been safe!

Those archangel monsters had unleashed storms of Holy fire on three separate squads of death angels. Within Heaven! Hadn't the Heavens seen enough violence on their home soil? Especially after so many angels died during the Sixth Flight's battle over Earth.

It would take a long time to recover from the loss of so many angels. But even after losing so many, monsters like Raphael, Uziel, and Kotabiel were killing more angels—including Lord Kushiel's couriers. Right under the Punishing Angel's nose. Did the archangel even know yet?

Lord Kushiel had a reputation for being the most monstrous avenging angel that Heaven had ever created. Many questioned his place in the light and likened his cruelty and lack of empathy to Lucifer, but unlike Lucifer, she wasn't sure if Kushiel was capable of empathy. She had always wondered if the Maker created him without it. To make him the best at what he did, but Talia knew that any creature without empathy had the increased capacity to fall.

Regardless, it took a lot of courage—or stupidity—to snatch the key to the Lake of Fire from Kushiel's couriers. And kill them. In plain sight of High House. In direct challenge to Lord Kushiel. Because he would come after them. Quickly and swiftly.

"I need to get to High House and inform Lord Kushiel," said Caleal, unfurling his injured wings.

"Can you fly?" Berith asked, a hand on his arm.

He nodded. "I'll get there. Kushiel has to know about this right away."

"Be safe," said Talia as the young angel of death rose with unsteady beats of his wings into the air and listed left as he headed toward High House.

It wasn't far. He'd make it.

Azrael began to pace the stones, his wings furling and unfurling, charcoal grey eyes flashing.

"They scorched all the stones where those angels fell!" He was livid, clenching his hands into fists, teeth grinding together as his halo burned brighter and spun wildly.

"They intended to leave no resurrectable witnesses," said Talia.

Azrael whirled around, his face taut with rage. "Here? In Heaven? Haven't we seen enough loss with the Sixth Flight and Hell's assaults? The Fall. This is Samael's doing, Talia. It's too coordinated."

"Do you think Lucifer ordered it?" she asked.

Azrael propped his hands on his hips, a tangle of emotions rushing across his eyes.

"To be honest, Talia, I'm not sure of anything." His gaze tracked off toward the crossroads. "We'll know who's involved when we locate the key to the Lake of Fire. Wherever it lands."

"Lands?" Talia asked.

"If the key ends up in Hell," said Azrael, folding his arms against his chest. "Then yes—I'd guess that Lucifer's trying to keep his life force from being obliterated in the Lake of Fire. But honestly Talia, I'm not so sure." The archangel sighed. "Lucifer seemed so resigned to his fate. But it could all be an act.

"He's a master of misdirection," said Talia.

Azrael nodded. "We need to check the Lake of Fire's chamber door. See if it's been opened. Only Lord Kushiel—and the Maker—are allowed to open that door, with Pravuil and a seraph as his witnesses."

Anahera, and Muriel landed in the street beside Berith as Azrael turned toward them.

"Anahera, go to High House and report these attacks to Sidriel and Pravuil. Let Pravuil report the news to Lord Kushiel, in case our injured angel of death fails to report this."

Talia glanced down at the scorched stones. Fails to report this? That was an odd reaction from Azrael.

"Of course, archangel," said Anahera. "I'll take care of it." She leaped into the air, short red hair fluttering in the wind, and blinked toward the spire.

"You don't trust Caleal," Talia said to the archangel. "Why?"

Azrael shrugged and fixed her with his piercing charcoal gaze. "Not entirely, no."

"Why?" Talia fired back.

"If those archangels were scorching stones to prevent us from resurrecting angels, they aren't leaving any witnesses. So why would they have left an angel of death alive? A survivor."

The archangel had a point. And that made her worry.

"To make sure someone told the story, so Jack knew where to go."

Azrael nodded. "Exactly. And walk right into their ambush. Which has to be near the Lake of Fire." He motioned Talia and the guard toward him. "Talia, Berith, Muriel, grab hold of my robes," said Azrael. "We've got to get to that door fast. Before something terrible happens to my angels." He sighed. "And Jack."

"You know where to find the door, sir?" Muriel asked.

He gave her a quick nod. "I do—and I shouldn't. Don't ask."

"Fair enough, sir," said Talia.

She grabbed hold of Azrael's sleeve as Berith wrapped her arms around the archangel's waist and curled her wings around Azrael's shoulders. Muriel gripped a handful of Azrael's billowing white robes and flexed her wings. Talia extended her wings, letting the wind roil through the dove grey feathers. Waiting for the archangel to blink.

Azrael closed his eyes, wings wrapping around them. And blinked. Across the spire. Past Eolowen.

Over the crossroads. Turning toward the stormy, hilly road to Hell.

Following the twisty road, Azrael blinked along it until a narrow, winding dirt path appeared on the right.

Azrael veered right and blinked again along the narrow trail that wound around black craggy rocks rising from the scraggly green grass. The air was cool and sharp, a hint of sulfur on the wind.

Boulders and yellow scrub grass quickly replaced the hard-packed dirt and green grass as Azrael followed the path down a hill and into a dark ashen valley. As the soil became black and volcanic, Azrael blinked into a sharp right turn, following an ashen path that snaked toward a craggy rock wall. And a massive, forbidding, rusty black door.

The towering, ornate door, carved with glowing Enochian symbols, was inset into the black lava rock. The letters blazed with eerie red and orange lava-like light. An array of locks lined the door's right edge.

To keep angels out, Talia wondered? Or something deadly inside, beyond this massive, sinister-looking door?

Azrael landed with a dull thump against the rocky ground, scattering plumes of ash, and rushed toward the door. Muriel, Berith, and Talia gathered around him, Berith looking unnerved. Probably because she'd been down this road before, exiled in Hell for millennia until Jack helped her escape when he'd been trapped in Hell.

The archangel looked ill as he stared at a huge lock in the center of the door.

Looking closer, Talia realized that the lock's mechanism had been turned. And released.

All the connections to each of the smaller locks had been tripped, allowing all the remaining latches to open. Every latch on the door hung open now. All around the door's edges, intense red and orange light guttered. With light and heat.

A chill raked her spine. It was too late. Because the door was already unlocked and ajar.

For a moment, Talia and the others stared at the door in shocked silence.

This door led to the Lake of Fire. The deadliest place that existed—for angels, demons, and humans.

And it was unlocked and thrown open like the door to an amusement park.

Right now, anyone or anything that wandered close enough could enter this cavern and find the Lake, its boiling waters eager to swallow anything and everything into its churning, incinerating depths.

That key had only been meant for the Punishing Angel's hands.

Not for greedy archangels trying to steal Jack's powers for themselves. Now, they had Kesien. Did they have Jack now, too? And Deemah.

Were they working for Samael? And Lucifer?

Talia's heart began to pound against her rib cage.

"Well, this open door tells the whole story," said Azrael.

Talia and Muriel moved closer.

"Azrael, I can assure you that Lucifer didn't do this," said Berith, arms crossed as she gazed around the landscape, looking frightened and apprehensive.

"Agreed, Berith," said Azrael in a quiet voice. "No, this is Samael's doing."

Then Talia understood. Uziel, Raphael, and Kotabiel were trying to collect Jack's seraphim powers for Samael who was too weak to fight Heaven without those powers. Or rule Hell.

Regardless of whether Lucifer was an archangel or a seraph, his position as firstborn granted him rare, unique powers. Powers that would have made him The Lightbringer in more than just name if he hadn't initiated The Rebellion and fallen from Heaven. If he had earned that title—and the powers it granted—he'd have been unstoppable.

"Samael can't control Hell without Jack's powers," said Talia.

Berith nodded and moved closer to Azrael. "Exactly. With Lord Abaddon guarding the Gates to Hell now and the Punishing Angel about to take Hell apart and restructure it, Samael would never last in a new fight to take over Heaven. Not without seraphim powers."

And an army.

"Until the Maker smited him out of existence," Muriel replied. "Seraph powers or not."

"Do you think they have Jack and Deemah?" Talia asked.

Azrael was silent a moment, eyes closed, lips moving silently. A prayer? A call to Pravuil?

She waited until he opened his eyes and met her gaze before she repeated her question.

"Archangel," she said, waiting until he fixed her with those intense charcoal grey eyes. "Do you think they have Jack and Deemah?"

"Let's find out."

Azrael opened the door wider and examined the entrance.

"Look at the ash pattern," he said, pointing at the cavern floor that stretched into the shadows toward the distant glow of lava. "They were dragging something. Kesien, most likely." He sighed. "They're setting a trap for Jack. Using Kesien as bait. I don't think they're even concerned with Deemah. Only Jack—and his powers."

"That's a mistake," Muriel replied. "Nobody messes with Kesien on Deemah's watch."

Talia knew how protective Deemah was of Kesien. Underestimating angels of death wasn't wise.

"They've made several mistakes so far," said Talia, flexing her wings. "Do they really think they can just take Jack's powers without any sort of retribution?"

"Talia, Heaven won't take back Jack's powers if it means harming him," Azrael corrected her. "But these archangels will kill him to take his powers. If they threw him into the Lake of Fire, those powers would be the only thing that survived."

"I've heard that celestial powers would float up from the Lake's depths and onto its surface," said Talia, barely able to say that out loud. "In theory, an archangel with strong enough wards, excellent armor, a powerful blink, and robust wings could fly across the Lake and scoop up those powers."

"That's the theory, Talia," said Azrael. "But no one's tried to test it until now."

Then it was true. It was possible. Her stomach twisted into a knot.

"They never intended to wait for this tribunal to end," said Talia. "They're using it as a diversion to throw Jack into the Lake of Fire right now and steal his powers while everyone is focused on Lord Kushiel and Lucifer."

Azrael nodded. "Because too many angels wouldn't stand for this theft. There are too many stories about Jack saving a battle or angels with his powers. And Lord Kushiel didn't seem convinced that Jack is dangerous. Regardless, this is such a huge, stupid risk."

"You mean throwing Jack into the Lake of Fire and taking what powers survive?" Muriel asked.

Azrael nodded. "There's also a big chance that those powers will burn up with him. And return to the Maker. Another chance that their wards will burn up before they get safely back to shore." He smiled. "And there's a reasonable chance that those powers would consume them when they tried to use them."

"Why are you smiling?" Talia asked him, feeling sick at her stomach.

She could lose Jack forever. Right here.

"Because," said Azrael, "There's also a chance that Jack's seraphim powers, sensing imminent destruction, would protect Jack and his powers from being thrown into the Lake. By incinerating every one of his enemies in one blast."

"A protective fail safe?" Talia asked, hoping that was true.

"Kind of like when the Nazis opened the Arc of the Covenant in Raiders of the Lost Ark?" Muriel asked, her charcoal grey eyes lighting up. "All the douchebags—to quote Jack—got erased. Just like those archangels erased three squads of death angels. Them burning up would be justice."

"Channeling Jack, are you, Muriel?" Azrael asked with the hint of smile on his face.

Muriel nodded. "A little Jackspeak to set the mood. All we need is his demon-splattering playlist and we're set." She frowned. "Hmmm, I wonder if he's got any good songs for splattering traitorous archangels?"

"Knowing Jack," said Berith. "He's got a song for everything."

Talia chuckled. "He does. Trust me. He's got a whole playlist dedicated to Archangel Raziel."

They all laughed, nodding.

"Good to know, Talia," said Azrael, motioning at her. "Now, we need you to use omnificence to locate these traitor angels' exact locations, Talia."

Nodding, Talia folded her hands together, bowed her head, and closed her eyes.

"Try to locate Kesien first," said Azrael. "And then Jack and Deemah."

Talia nodded, desperate to know where her husband was, but Kesien was hurt. They needed to find him first and treat his wounds. Then Deemah and Jack.

"Deemah is our wildcard," said Talia. "They won't expect her to come after Kesien. That's to our advantage."

"I hope so," said Azrael with a sigh. "I won't watch any more angels of death perish today."

"Azrael, do you think High House knows about the murder of Kushiel's couriers yet?" Berith asked as she moved closer to him.

The archangel nodded. "Anahera has probably just gotten the news to Sidriel and Pravuil. I tried to contact Pravuil directly, but he's not responding. Probably has his hands full protecting the Maker. And High House. And keeping Lord Kushiel in check—especially after he finds out that his couriers have all been erased and the Lake of Fire key stolen. I'm sure there's already quite an uproar in High House right now."

Talia focused her omnificence power down to the crossroads and then this path. And finally, down to the door and the cavern as she searched for Kesien.

Her senses flew through the darkness, flitting through the cavernous space, across the high ceiling and protruding stalactites. She rushed along the churning river of lava that meandered through the cavern and emptied into a roiling, bubbling Lake of Fire.

The acrid smell of sulfur stung her nose, but she knew it came from the lava and not demons. The smell of ozone rose above the sulfur, its clear, pungent scent crisp but watery. Like the chemicals in the swimming pools all over L.A.

As the cavern floor stretched closer to the bubbling red lava, Talia honed in on an Eternean metal dock that wrapped around the front edge of the Lake of Fire. Only coated Eternean metal blessed by Archangel Zephana's forge could withstand the Lake's destructive waters. The metal had been forged with a clear, sparkling celestial essence that deflected the massive amount of heat back into the Lake's murky red depths. Nothing survived in these waters that only existed for one purpose: the instantaneous destruction of celestials. A humane execution according to many angels. The Lake could also destroy human souls in a moment.

Talia questioned that. Of course, how would these angels know? None of them had ever felt these lava waters against their bodies. Not even for an instant.

She wondered how many angels had stood on that platform over the millennia, about to be thrown into the Lake of Fire. No human soul had ever touched these waters. Yet.

She had to make sure that Jack Casey wasn't the first.

Why hadn't the Maker already smited these evil angels out of existence? Including that traitor, Samael. Why had the Maker allowed them to keep causing such massive harm to innocents. And other angels who didn't deserve it.

If the Maker had more pressing issues, then why hadn't they sent Lord Kushiel to deal with Uziel, Raphael, and Kotabiel.

Allowing them to harm even one innocent human soul was unacceptable.

Samael's body count was growing. He'd destroyed nearly two dozen angels today. As soon as she got Jack back safely and they got through this tribunal, she would join the guard and go after Samael in Hell.

Returning to Hell would be a series of many intense fights and skirmishes through the caverns, but someone had to take Samael down before he became entrenched in Lucifer's former fortress. What was the point of punishing Lucifer when someone had already taken his place?

Through omnificence, Talia saw the Lake of Fire up close. Its bubbling surface roiled, the churning red waters thick and charged with celestial fire. Smoke rose from the surface in a thick haze, towering, writhing coils like snakes. Despite the distance, she felt the heat—through her omnificence. She felt it prickling across her skin and wing feathers.

Those terrifying lake waters burned things up the moment they hit its surface. There were no moments of suffering. No torture. Just an instantaneous destruction of essence and spirit.

Like Lucifer faced.

The archangels bringing Kesien here infuriated her. These waters were reserved for only the most dangerous and unrepentant angels, demons, and someday, humans. Those who refused to turn away from evil. Refused to obey the Maker. Refused to stop trying to tear down the fabric of the Creation and the Heavens.

Kesien didn't deserve this.

But these archangels deserved to be thrown in the lake. They became traitors the moment they offered their loyalty to Archangel Samael and went against Heaven. And now, they were playing God, crossing a line when they chose to throw a human into the Lake of Fire.

Only the Maker had the right to destroy living essence. Like Lucifer's celestial light—what remained of it.

Kushiel only recommended what should become of Lucifer, like the other judges. Only the Maker would condemn or spare the King of Hell from these lake waters.

Having the key to the Lake of Fire's cavern in traitorous hands like these three archangels was an affront to Heaven. And Talia would make sure they paid for their crimes.

Hopefully, Azrael and her squad had arrived in time to stop this twisted plan. The thought of Samael possessing seraphim powers terrified her as much as that monster seated on any throne. Were they working to unseat Samael somehow? Take it for themselves?

Regardless, when Pravuil and Lord Kushiel got hold of them, these archangels would be the next fallen angels on trial. If there was enough left of them to put on trial.

Talia intended to burn them all to the ground.

Before they could throw anyone into the Lake of Fire. The thought of them murdering three squads of death angels and three of Kushiel's couriers infuriated her. Did they think the Maker or Lord Kushiel wouldn't find out? That there wouldn't be any consequences?

At last, the cavern's outcrops and twisting paths rose out of the smoke and ash as she pushed her omnificence hard through the chamber. Desperate to locate Kesien and Jack.

Hot winds swept through the chamber, its dark projections of pocked volcanic rock, jagged stalactites, and spiked stalagmites everywhere. The path from the entrance threaded its way around the projections and split into two paths that edged around the rim of the glowing Lake.

One path jutted left behind a cluster of stalagmites, rock formations snaking around dark corners until it wound its way like a serpent around the ashen shores. The path on the right sloped downward where the chamber seemed flatter, the volcanic rock floor leveling out. Flames guttered along the lake's brittle volcanic shore, the water sputtering and bubbling, sizzling as it spattered glowing lava across the rocks.

The cavern seemed deserted, empty, making her heart shudder.

Had Uziel, Raphael, and Kotabiel already been here and gone? Had they already thrown Jack and Kesien into the Lake and retrieved Jack's powers? Was her beautiful husband already gone forever, his seraphim powers on their way to Archangel Samael in Hell?

No! She refused to believe that!

The archangels could be anywhere along these dark paths.

She sighed. And so could Jack and Deemah.

She pressed forward. Harder. Searching for the beat of Jack's heart. His essence.

Gritting her teeth, Talia dug deeper, forcing more power behind her omnificence. If Jack was out there, she would feel his presence. She would feel him! She had to…

All at once, his bold, bright essence fluttered at the edge of her omnificence power. Bumping up against it with a defiant strength that made her smile.

That was her Jack!

"I feel him!" she cried, her voice cracking. "I feel him out there, Azrael. Deemah, too."

Jack was a sharp, glowing presence in the darkness. Deemah's light was fierce and angry, scorching, wanting to directly attack. And like Jack, avenge Kesien.

Talia struggled to pinpoint where they were along the two paths. The Lake's presence made it difficult to separate its energy from Jack's and Deemah's. The Lake of Fire made her angel senses go a little haywire.

"Where is he, Talia?" Azrael asked, moving beside her, his eyes filled with relief. "And Kesien."

"Azrael," said Talia. "I sense Jack and Deemah deep in the cavern. Around the farthest edge of the Lake of Fire. That makes me think that the archangels haven't grabbed Jack or Deemah yet. But I still haven't located Kesien. Or the archangels."

Azrael sighed in relief. "Jack and Deemah are still alive. And still planning to fight. We just need to intercept them before they do anything brash or foolish."

She winced. Brash was Jack's middle name—especially when lives were at stake. And Deemah was blind with rage right now. Talia had to pinpoint their locations quickly. Intercept them before they acted.

"We move as soon as you locate Kesien and the positions of the archangels."

Honing her omnificence to a sharp point, Talia focused it deeper into the cavern. She traced along each path, searching for Kesien. And those traitorous archangels.

"Muriel, Berith," said Azrael, motioning them on the path into the cavern. "Get ready. As soon as Talia pinpoints Deemah, Kesien, and Jack, I want you two following the right-side path around the lake to the far dock. Get visuals on these traitors—and our people. But stay out of sight. Talia and I will follow the left path and we'll meet at the dock."

As Talia's senses moved through the sulfur, the ozone, and the heat, slipping along the left-hand path, she felt the prickly presence of three archangels. They tried to conceal their presence inside here, but her omnificence was too powerful. These archangels probably didn't even realize that she had this rare gift.

A rare gift that would be their downfall.

"Still searching for Kesien."

Again, Talia closed her eyes, centering omnificence throughout the cavern again. Searching for Kesien.

Her power crested the rise that stood on the Lake's left side. And slipped past it. Weaving down the path and the rocks to more level ground. The pocked black volcanic rock, splattered with glowing red lake waters, sizzled and hissed as her omnificence power slid past. Moving toward those tense, arrogant angel energies ahead. Toward the back of the cavern.

As her omnificence flowed around a large stalagmite, she felt Kesien's faint presence at the far end of the Lake of Fire. Where another Eternean dock, smaller than the first one, stood at the edge of the Lake waters. Coated by that same clear, sparkling celestial essence, the gold, forged metal deflected heat in swirling waves of smoke that flowed back into the Lake.

Around Kesien stood three other presences. Prickly. Sharp. Angry energies.

She gasped, stabbing pain radiating through her head, the cavern spinning. Weakness ached through her limbs. From Kesien.

He was hurt. Badly burned from Holy fire. He had a serious head injury and struggled to remain conscious.

Kesien couldn't get up from the ground and take on one attacker much less three of them. They would burn him out of existence with Holy fire. But he had to sense Deemah out there somewhere trying to rescue him. And Jack, too. Maybe Kesien was just trying to regain some balance and strength?

Even from this distance, she felt Deemah's rage pushing her to act, but she wasn't ignoring the fact that those archangels could burn her out of existence. Giving her just enough caution to plan her first shield bash.

Jack had no such tempering and that scared her. His seraph powers were enough to defeat all three archangels, but his human body made him much more vulnerable to Holy fire attacks.

She shuddered. And seraphim power overloads.

"Found Kesien," she said in a quiet voice. "And the archangels."

She let the images float away from her omnificence power and hang in the air in front of her.

"There's a smaller dock at the back of the cavern. That's where they're holding Kesien. And somewhere near there, along those paths, I sense Jack and Deemah hiding. Trying to figure out how to free Kesien."

Azrael's sigh of relief was palpable. "Thank Heaven Jack hasn't just thrown himself at those archangels. Or Deemah. She can be as hot-headed as Jack."

Talia nodded. "She can. She is fierce, Azrael, but shrewd enough to plan her assaults. Somewhere in the back of his head, Jack realizes that his human body makes him more vulnerable to those fiery lake waters."

"Key phrase being back of his head," said Muriel.

Berith nodded, looking worried.

Talia shifted her gaze toward the back of the cavern again. "That worries me, too. Deemah is trying to find a way to shield herself—and Kesien—from any more Holy Fire. While she shield-bashes them into oblivion. Jack is weighing a surprise attack, just enough to hammer them with his seraphim powers. And give Deemah time to free Kesien. Together, Jack and Deemah are a good match in a fight."

"Good," said Azrael. "Maybe they've found each other and are working together on their attack. We'll move toward that far dock from both sides and get into position to assist. Talia, maybe the three of us can create enough of a diversion for you and Jack to unleash your rare powers on these traitors?"

"Without obliterating Kesien," Muriel added.

"Yes, Muriel, thank you," said Azrael. "Protect Kesien." He sighed. "And Jack from himself."

Berith exchanged a worried look with Talia. "Okay, angels, same plan. Move along both paths until we meet in the shadows as close to the archangels—and that dock—as we can get."

"Berith, I can feel Kesien's injuries," said Talia. "He really needs your healing powers."

"I'll ward myself and head toward him the moment it's safe," said

Berith, folding her wings tightly against her back as she moved closer to the door.

"Berith, wait for my signal," said Azrael. "I don't want you getting in the crossfire."

She smiled, her rose gold halo brightening. "Always forgetting that I'm a soldier, aren't you, love?"

Azrael still had a worried, haunted look on his face, unfazed by her remark.

"No, still remembering how long you were away from me. So, please be careful, my love."

Berith's grey eyes got glassy as she flashed a brief smile at Azrael.

"Never again," she said. "Now that I am finally home, I will never again jeopardize having you by my side."

Azrael bowed his head a moment, overcome with emotion, a rare event for the archangel.

"Thanks to Talia and Jack," he said, his gaze drifting back to Talia. "Now, let's get Jack back to Talia. And Kesien and Deemah home."

Talia laid her hand against her heart and nodded at Azrael. "Thank you."

"And put these traitors in chains," Muriel said with a growl.

"Exactly what I was thinking," said Azrael as he reached for the door.

As quietly as he could, Azrael pushed open the door and held out his arm to keep Talia back. Did he sense her urgency to bolt into that cavern and blink across the Lake of Fire. To Jack?

Hinges began to squeak until Azrael used his archangel powers to muffle the sound.

When had this door had been opened last, she wondered? Before these idiot archangels had opened it? Where were the parts of the key kept? And the Enochian scroll that reassembled it? With Pravuil in the Archive? In Lord Abaddon's hands now that he'd been redeemed? Or did Lord Kushiel have complete jurisdiction over it?

"Wait for my signal," Azrael whispered in angel notes as soft as the wind.

Talia held position beside Muriel as Berith slipped behind Azrael.

Azrael spread his wings wide, deflecting a massive burst of heat that rolled out through the cavern's open door. The blast of heat surged on the wind and swirled through the dust when the cool air hit it, creating a dust devil that oscillated across the small, shadowy valley and disappeared into the scraggly trees and brush.

It took a few moments for the built-up heat to disperse. When the intense sulfur and ozone stench dissipated, Azrael let his arms fall to his side. Talia hoped those archangels got more than a face full of fiery heat when they first opened this door. She hoped it burned off their eyebrows.

"Okay, blackout your halos, wings out of sight," Azrael whispered in angel notes.

Talia took hold of her halo and dimmed the light until it went dark. Quickly, she folded her wings tightly against her back, the cavern darkening. When she looked up, the glow of their halos had vanished, wings out of sight. Jack was always surprised by how much light angels gave off. In this hazy darkness, the rocky paths barely visible now, she missed that angelic light.

"Dark wards," Azrael ordered in a quiet voice. "Cast them and keep them up, but don't let any light escape into the cavern."

Talia reached for her warding energies, funneling only her rare powers to fuel the white-gold shield. And then she extinguished its light. These archangels couldn't see their wards yet. To locate her—and any angelic wards—they would have to specifically search for the wards.

And her rare powers.

Dark angel wards thrummed around her, something she wasn't used to, but she worried that the hum, the resonance of the wards would reach the archangels long before they did.

"Azrael, I can feel all of these wards," she said with a sigh. "If I feel them, so will those archangels. Can you easily sense our wards?"

He held out his arms and closed his eyes, feeling for the wards until finally, he began to frown.

"You're right, Talia." Azrael said. "I thought my ward would shield the rest, but I still feel the others beneath mine. Even when they're dark. Except yours. I'd have to scan just for your rare powers to know your ward was present. But an angel of death ward shines like a beacon, even when its dark."

Talia considered her rare powers for a moment or two. If omnificence could bring all things together, all at once, maybe she could focus her ward-casting on all things and hide the energy flow through it. Concealing them from everyone in the cavern.

Everyone. Including Jack, Deemah, and Kesien. If it worked, she could protect her squad from these monsters.

Gingerly, she held out her hand and summoned the vibrating hum of the other wards, funneling the movements through her dark ward. Making them harder to detect, but they weren't invisible.

It would have to do.

"That's the best I can do, sir," said Talia. "The longer we're in this cavern, the easier it'll be to detect our wards." She smiled. "If they bother to scan for them."

"Fair enough," he said, motioning into the cavern. "Everyone, get in position. But wait for my signal."

"What kind of signal?" Muriel asked as she crept past him into the sweltering, dim-lit cavern.

"Oh, you'll know when," he said with a growl.

"I so hope it's a really big explosion of traitor archangels."

"Me, too, Muriel," said Talia.

Berith moved past Azrael, but paused. She reached out and brushed her fingers along the side of Azrael's face. He reached out, caressing her hand a moment, and then followed Muriel along the right side of the Lake of Fire.

In moments, they both disappeared into the dark shadows, headed down a rocky slope as the path ambled right and snaked around the red, bubbling waters. Bursts of steam shot up like geysers from the bright red waters as fiery sprays of lava lit the cavern for a moment or two. Like the surface of the sun. Mist roiled off the Lake in sheets, the water's steady boil rumbling throughout the cavern. Hopefully, those sounds would cover their movements.

Talia slipped into the cavern a few feet behind Berith, wings flat against her back. No light from the wards emanated even a soft glow as she followed the path down deeper into the cavern. Already the heat was prickly and oppressive against her skin, sitting heavy on her chest.

Azrael waited a few moments and then let the door slowly close against the rock wall behind him. It still hung open a little, barely ajar as steam gathered, hissing, slithering out around the door jamb. He was just a shadow against the door now, no halo and no glow of wards visible.

He moved close behind Talia as she stepped carefully over rocks and around holes in the rough, porous black rock softened by a gritty layer of ash and lake mist. The fine grey ash clung to everything and Talia was grateful she had a ward to keep it off her lips and out of her nose, eyes, and hair.

When the path split in two, Talia followed it as it curved left, upward on a gradual incline toward some tall, forbidding stalagmites protruding like knife blades from the volcanic rock. Above her, they hung like sharp, pointed teeth in the ceiling canopy shadowed with mist and gloom.

She wished for more of that gloom around her and the other angels right now. Shielding them from view. They just needed get close enough to launch an attack, then maybe they could save Kesien and Deemah. She, Jack, and Azrael were more than a match for three archangels. But she didn't want Kesien and Deemah to get extinguished in the process. Or Jack to do something dangerous.

The path rose again along a spiny, ridged hill, allowing her to get a good look at the far end of the long, cavernous chamber.

Archangel Raphael stepped out of the steam clouds rising off the bubbling lava waters as he moved across the smaller Eternean dock, its golden metal glowing red and white. Only Heaven-forged metal a thin veneer of clear, protective ethereal essence kept the Lake from consuming the dock.

Raphael was the tallest of the three traitors. His white shaggy hair dusted with blowing ash, hung at his shoulders. He was too arrogant to put up a ward. Didn't think anyone was capable of challenging him.

She chuckled. Wait until Raphael experienced her rare powers—and tasted seraphim energies.

Raphael's unfurled wings shifted every time the hot winds blew across them, their once-crisp white hue mottled grey with ash and smoke.

Great. If they fought in close quarters, the ash would make their wings look like angels of death. She had to be careful with her powers. She frowned. Precise.

Talia moved around the bubbling waters that hissed and spewed smoke and fire against the low, sloping banks. Toward the dock.

Following the curve of the lake, she saw Uziel's bushy mop of short white hair. To Raphael's right.

Uziel bent over something ashen.

Only when the path twisted and turned toward the dock did she see Kotabiel. Clutching Kesien by the shoulders. The archangel's long, wavy white hair blew in the dust and ash. He had the longest hair of the three.

Sharp, angry angel notes reverberated through the chamber, echoing in layers. But with the hiss and gurgle of the lake, they were too difficult to understand.

She crept closer, weaving around some massive stalagmites until she stopped about a hundred feet from the dock. She ducked behind some black rocks, assessing the situation.

Kesien lay curled in a ball on the dock. Uziel and Kotabiel dragged him away from the dock's edge. Like they'd threatened to toss him into the Lake. Kesien moaned, his breath ragged and uneven. Shuddering breaths becoming gasps.

Then she saw his wings.

Blackened and missing most of their feathers. Most were curled into slag and useless. Others were barely attached to his scapulas. The phalanxes that made his wings extend and fold, and housed all the feathers, hung at odd angles.

She bared her teeth, fighting the rage building through her like a hurricane. Her eyes burned and she fought not to unleash a barrage of

Holy fire at these three monsters. She wanted to take all three of them apart.

They'd broken his wings! And burned most of them off in the Lake of Fire.

The notes of their voices were grating discords and she fought to contain her fury as they clustered around poor Kesien who barely moved.

"You'd better hope that flying rat shows up soon, death angel."

The biting baritone notes were heavy and menacing, barely audible above the hiss and spew of lava and steam.

Raphael motioned toward the Lake.

"I'll give that flying meatsack one more minute before we toss this death angel into the Lake of Fire."

"You can't," Uziel replied, motioning across the Lake. "If that winged rat sees only us, he'll flee and we'll never get him near the dock."

"Looks like…y-y-ou s-still n-need me after all."

Kesien's voice was weak and shaking from pain. He was in no condition to fight these traitors.

But he didn't have to because she intended to take these archangels apart. Slowly. Deliberately. For what they did to him. Not very angelic, but that's how she felt.

"Jack!" Kesien shouted, holding his chest, every breath painful. "Get out of here! Now!"

Kotabiel struck Kesien, knocking him back against the dock again.

"Too late to warn him, death angel," said Raphael. "And you won't be here to see him take a swim."

Uziel's voice was an ugly harmony of tenor notes, "Because you'll be the very first swimmer in that Lake. You'll never see this stupid human hit the water."

Talia felt Azrael's proximity. He dropped down beside her, his fury and pain radiating at seeing Kesien so torn up.

Her focus on Kesien and Azrael almost made her miss the whisper of air that hissed along the trailing edge of the dock.

She turned toward the sound.

The three archangels looked up.

An Eternean shield cut across the mist and ash, knocking Kotabiel to his knees. The shield clattered against the Eternean dock, the sound like the Gates of Hell shattering.

Deemah slipped out of the darkness, a grim expression on her angry face, features taut and drawn, her grey eyes like cold steel as she brandished a flaming sword in each hand.

"The only thing hitting that Lake water today will be you, Kotabiel." Deemah's eyes narrowed, flashing with Holy fire as she pointed her sword at Uziel. "And then you." She pointed at Raphael with both swords, her face cold and shadowed. "And finally...you. Monster. You won't live to fear Lord Kushiel's Wrath."

Raphael looked smug, his expression sharpening. He had a cruel gleam in his gold eyes, his mouth twisting into a leering smile. Like she'd just offered herself up as a sacrifice to this traitor.

"Oh, Deemah," Azrael hissed. "What are you doing?"

"You think one lone angel of death can defeat three archangels?"

Deemah smiled, pointing at Raphael again with her swords. "Oh, I don't plan to defeat you," she said, shifting her position as she moved slowly around the edge of the dock to Raphael's left, smile widening into a grin.

Raphael looked smug. Like he'd already won.

"Oh, no," Deemah said, her wings unfurling at her shoulders, stretching wide. "I plan to make you disappear."

Uziel began laughing as he let go of Kesien and moved toward Raphael. Kotabiel turned toward Raphael, the glow of Holy fire beginning at the tips of his fingers. Uziel's began to glow with white fire as Raphael lifted his hands palms up. Coils of Holy fire quivered in his cupped hands.

"Last chance, angel of death," Raphael said in a condescending tone. "Don't give up your one chance at a quick death on the futile attempt to save your colleague."

Uziel moved between Kotabiel and Raphael. Leaving Kesien writhing on the dock.

The whine of gathering Holy fire grew louder.

Unaffected, Deemah stood her ground, her smile fading into a look of pain when she glanced at Kesien. And then Talia saw grim acceptance as she felt Deemah's resolve kick in. Felt her intentions as she bolstered her courage. Deemah was going to rush them. Knock all of them into the Lake of Fire. Knowing she would probably fall in with them.

"Deemah, get—out of h-here!" Kesien sputtered. "Now! You can't save me."

Kesien must have felt it, too. His voice was frantic above the pain.

"Better listen…Deemah," Raphael taunted, his hand glowing with Holy fire. "It's over. For both of you."

Something small and gold bounced across the dock and rolled past Kesien, stopping against Kotabiel's foot. Glowing gold.

Kotabiel glanced down, frowning, eyebrows pressed into a hard line against his dull gold eyes as two more small, round things rolled past him. Bumping against Uziel's robes. And then Raphael's.

Deemah couldn't contain her grin now. "Apparently, you've got all that backwards. Traitor," she said, backing away.

"Azrael!" Talia cried.

Azrael was grinning. "Murder marbles."

All three archangels lifted their hands, tangles of Holy fire writhing in their fingers, and pointed the deadly white flames at Deemah.

But the three oblivion spheres ignited. Exploding in a shower of gold fire, mist, and ash.

Three screams reverberated through the cavern. Two of them were silenced in an abrupt, fiery splash. The other scream got muffled by a hard slam against volcanic rock.

Jack shot out of the shadows, wings in motion as he blinked onto the dock. Deemah rushed toward him as he landed. They both dropped down beside Kesien.

"Damn, dude, you're going to need all of Berith's healing to fix this," said Jack in a pained voice. "Especially those wings."

"That was epic, Jack," said Deemah. "Thank you. I wasn't sure if you were even here."

"Had to look out for my squad mates," he said, gently rubbing Kesien's shoulder.

Deemah squeezed Jack's hand and motioned toward Raphael. The only archangel left after Jack's murder marbles knocked the other two off the pier.

Into the Lake of Fire.

With a blink, Jack shot across the cavern, landing with a thump in front of Raphael who struggled to his feet. The archangel tried to extend his wings, but Deemah shield-bashed him.

Raphael staggered, beginning to blink, but Jack tackled him to the floor of the cavern.

"Not so fast, douchebag," he said with a growl. "Got a nice warm seat ready for you at the defendant's table in High House. Right beside Luci. I'm sure Kushiel's got quite a few questions for you. Traitor. I'll give Samael your regards when I see him. In my sights."

Talia blinked down the path toward Jack, Azrael beside her.

"Oh, and this is for Kesien," said Jack, cocking his fist and slamming it into Raphael's smug face.

The archangel faceplanted against the volcanic rock surrounding the Lake.

"Jack!" Azrael cried. "We have to be better than these traitors."

Jack's eyes narrowed. "Did you see what he did to Kesien?"

Azrael nodded as a high-pitched whine thrummed through the cavern.

Jack's eyes widened, his gaze darting to the Holy fire gathering around Azrael's fist.

Azrael slammed Raphael with the burst of Holy fire. Raphael's eyes rolled into the back of his head a moment, teeth gritted as his wings caught fire, feathers burning as the archangel flopped on the ground like a fish out of water.

"Archangel?" Jack cried, shock gleaming in those pale green eyes as his gaze flicked from Azrael to Raphael. "Thought you said we had to be better?"

Azrael nodded. "I did, Jack," he said, hands behind his back. "My Holy fire's much stronger than this idiot's power."

Jack's laughter pealed through the chamber.

"Oh, please—let me help," said Talia as she slipped past Jack and secured the archangel with glowing ropes of Holy fire.

"Kesien!" Muriel's voice echoed across the dock as she blinked toward her squad mate.

Talia dragged the surviving archangel back down onto the dock and left him bound in Holy fire. Then, she and Jack moved back to Kesien as Berith appeared on his right side, gold healing light bathing her hands. Muriel knelt on Kesien's left. Deemah dropped down in front of him, laying her hand against his face.

"Hang in there, Kesien," she said in a soft voice.

"Berith, they tried to burn his wings off in the Lake of Fire," said Jack, his face a mask of pain and anger. "Almost succeeded, too."

Berith's gold healing light enveloped Kesien and the pain in his face softened a little.

"That should help with the pain," said Berith as she doused his wings with cooling white healing light. "Now, let's see what we can repair right now."

Talia put her arms around Jack, pulling him into a tight embrace.

"Jack Casey, I almost lost my mind when you blinked after those archangels."

He sighed, sliding his arms around her waist, and kissed her softly on the lips. "Sorry, Mrs. Casey," he said. "I had to go. They had Kesien."

She understood, but she was still angry.

"I didn't mean to knock those archangels into the Lake of Fire," he said, his voice falling. "I was just trying to get them away from Kesien."

"It's okay, Jack," said Azrael. "They brought this on themselves. You were just trying to save Kesien and Deemah."

He nodded, but she saw the remorse burning in his green eyes.

Suddenly, the cavern flooded with cherubim and angels of death as Lord Kushiel blinked onto the Eternean dock, fury shadowing his long, noble face. Eyes molten.

"Who has dared to kill my couriers!" Kushiel roared, his voice filled with celestial righteousness. "And who dared to assemble this key and enter this sacred and forbidden place!"

CHAPTER 12

JACK STARED AT THE FLOOD OF ANGELS LINING THE PATHS ALONG BOTH sides of the Lake of Fire as they flew toward the dock. They were everywhere. Like the cavern had been raided by an angel SWAT team. Or Heaven's army.

Too bad they weren't here a few moments ago.

Lord Kushiel looked totally unhinged, ranting and shouting at him, at Talia—even Azrael. Anybody still breathing in that cavern got the full verbal wrath of this dude's meltdown that made Chernobyl look like an overturned candle.

Kushiel pointed at the lead asshalo, Raphael, still tangled up with Talia's Holy fire ropes. All tied up in a neat angel of death bow.

"I want him in chains!"

Cherubim gathered up the idiot archangel and dragged him up from the cavern floor.

The smell of ash and sulfur made Jack cough and sputter as the cherubim stirred up tons more ash and dust from the volcanic rock as they blinked back and forth across the Lake. Out the only exit from the Maker's private sauna.

Kushiel wheeled around and grabbed Azrael by the shoulders.

"And where are the other two co-conspirators, Azrael!" he demanded.

Azrael frowned. "The archangels?"

"Of course, the archangels! I want all three of these traitors in my custody! Now!"

Azrael looked at a loss for words. He shook his head, hands splayed.

"Lord Kushiel...I'm sorry...they're..."

Azrael's voice trailed off.

Furious, still melting down, Kushiel whirled around, searching for anyone else to interrogate. And then his gaze settled on Jack.

Jack groaned. Just his luck he was the closest person to Lord Kushiel who was still amped up on some old school, biblical retribution. Like anybody he could torture would do right now.

"YOU!" Kushiel roared, pointing at Jack. "Where is Archangel Uziel and Archangel Kotabiel?"

Dude was gonna go nova when he found out there wasn't anyone else left to torture or to try in the Cloud Chamber. Just Raphael and Lucifer. Dude really needed to get a hobby other than torture and retribution. Wasn't healthy. Could use a keg of valium, too.

Jack glanced over at the dock, nodding at the glowing residue that floated in ringlets around the edges of the Eternean dock.

"Careful, Jack," Azrael said, his voice filled with apprehension and dread as he moved closer to Berith and Kesien.

"They uh, went for a swim," said Jack to Lord Kushiel in a quiet voice.

Azrael winced, biting his lip. "Jack!"

Guess that probably wasn't the best answer to give this now-murderous archangel of retribution, but it was true. Jack didn't know how else to break it to Kushiel.

Kushiel grabbed Jack by the throat and lifted him five feet into the air.

"They WHAT!"

"Swim," Jack croaked out. "Went. For a—swim."

Suddenly, Kushiel looked like someone had stabbed him in the heart with the Rod of Creation. He looked sick as his gaze snapped to the Lake of Fire.

"Sorry," said Jack. "Didn't mean to knock them into this lava pool of oblivion."

"Jack, don't," Azrael whispered.

"YOU?" Kushiel shouted. "YOU did this?"

"Was trying…to protect Kesien—and Deemah…from these—murdering bastards," said Jack, fighting for air. "Trying to—throw me into…deep end."

Kushiel's eyes flared with white flames, his hair turning to Holy fire as a crisp white light began glowing around him. Some sort of celestial fire that Jack hadn't seen before. It looked nothing like Holy Fire. It looked more like angelic napalm. And lava.

Time began to slow around him, the air seeping from his lungs.

Talia moved in slow motion toward him, but the air was thick and heavy, sounds muffled. She'd never get to him before this douchebag archangel of punishment killed him with Heavenly retribution.

Frantic, Talia inched forward, like she moved through sludge.

Azrael had his mouth open, shouting, reaching toward Jack.

Too far away to do anything. Moving in slow motion.

Damn, this dude was in total nuclear meltdown, his whole angel form igniting with wrath!

Jack groaned. He was about to go up in a fiery ball of Heavenly Wrath. And he couldn't stop it. Couldn't stop the tsunami of flaming celestial retribution about to explode all over him.

He fought against the building force, lifting his hand, fingers splayed, and called up a seraphim ward.

Before the ward sealed around him, he took a barrage of hits from this tsunami of angelic wrath.

It felt like being stung by a hundred box jellyfish, his body convulsing and shuddering, his tongue thick in his mouth, his muscles seizing.

His eyes rolled up into his head as he flailed like a fish out of water, Kushiel still holding him aloft.

But somehow, he held onto the ward. And called up another one over top of it.

"Kushiel! STOP!" Azrael's voice was panicked. Desperate. "You're killing him!"

Talia slammed into Kushiel full force, raining down bursts of white Holy fire.

An array of gold and blue and white torrents buffeted the Punishing Angel, driving him backward as she unleashed her rare angel powers. Omnificence? Resurrect? Oblivion spheres?

Or something else? Regardless, Jack's misfiring brain couldn't process it.

He was barely aware when his incredible wife knocked the Angel of Punishment and Wrath sideways. Breaking his deadly stranglehold. And the uninterrupted stream of Heavenly retribution raining down on Jack.

"Are you insane!" Azrael shouted, grabbing Kushiel by the shoulders, not a shred of fear remaining. "Jack's no angel—he's human, Kushiel! Human! Berith, need your healing power. Now."

In the swirl of darkness, sulfur, and ash, their voices sounded like they'd funneled up from a deep, dark well until Berith's frantic voice wound its way through his wards and the pain and growing darkness. Into his ear.

"Jack?" she cried. "Jack! Can you hear me?"

But he couldn't move. Couldn't speak. Couldn't even move his lips against the horrible pain shooting through every limb and every inch of skin. Couldn't let go of the wards either. If he did, this strange white fire would consume his body. He felt the danger in every pore and every sound.

But he couldn't respond to Talia or Azrael. It took a microdose of energy, but he just couldn't spare any right now. His entire body was focused on keeping out the rest of this incredible, killing force.

Trying to keep it from swallowing his essence whole. His soul.

Talia probably thought he was dead, but he couldn't respond. Had to keep all his seraphim powers up and blocking this tsunami of Heavenly punishment and wrath that Kushiel decided to unleash on him because two of his traitor angels burned up in the Lake of Fire. Leaving him no one to punish but Jack. And Archangel Raphael.

"My retribution and wrath…were meant for Uziel and Kotabiel," Kushiel choked out through the Holy fire haze burning in his eyes. "Not Jack Casey."

"Dammit, Kushiel! He's human! He can't survive this."

"How could you hurl those reckoning flames so carelessly?" Talia demanded, her voice breaking. "Berith, please—help him."

"It's Kushiel's punishing flame—meant for angels," Berith said with a moan as she called up healing light in her hands. "Lord Kushiel, why? Why would you unleash that on Jack?"

Kushiel was silent for several moments.

"Answer the question!" Talia demanded, fury in her voice.

"I…lost my temper," said Lord Kushiel, clenching his hands into fists.

Like that made it okay somehow? Jack was pissed, but too busy blocking this lifeforce-ending fire to do anything about it. And losing ground fast.

"Those traitors can't be questioned now because this fool knocked them into the Lake of Fire!" Kushiel.

Kushiel's eyes flashed white, his voice like thunder rumbling through the cavern as ash and smoke swirled around him. Dude was winding up again for an explosive fastball of wrath with his name on it. And he couldn't even close his eyes.

Could his wards block another one? Or was this it? End of the road.

He visualized another seraphim ward and twitched his fingers. Calling up another one. And another. Stacking them as the previous one fell. Until he had no seraphim mojo left.

That wouldn't take long.

Gone was any trace of remorse or regret as the anger enveloped Kushiel. He looked every bit the Avenging Angel. The terrifying Archangel of Punishment that Jack had never before witnessed in the Heavens until now. He'd rarely found archangels intimidating (except

Lucifer), but seeing Kushiel in all his dark, Angel of Wrath glory made Jack's skin crawl.

Besides Lucifer, this dude was the scariest angel he'd ever encountered since that night in his apartment when angels and demons first began appearing to him. And that look on Kushiel's dark, forbidding face had one goal.

To smite him from existence.

"This fool?" Talia shouted, fury burning in her eyes as they turned white and smiting fiery. "How dare *you!*"

Livid, Talia launched herself at Kushiel again, grabbing him by the collar of his smoky grey robes with both hands and slamming him against a stalagmite.

"Talia, don't!" Azrael shouted, his charcoal grey eyes bright with fear, a rare emotion in the archangel's eyes.

Her eyes were white fire as she glowed in her most terrifying form, a form that Jack had only seen once. And it scared the hell out of him.

She pinned Kushiel against the stalagmite.

"He was trying to save Kesien and Deemah, you fool!"

Jack was frantic—and powerless—as he watched his death angel wife take on one of Heaven's most powerful angels. If that bastard destroyed her, he'd hit Kushiel with all his seraphim powers. At once.

Kushiel's eyes darkened with deep-seeded fury as he struggled against Talia's powers, glaring past her at Jack, trying to rush at him again, right hand swirling with Heavenly retribution. Still aimed at him. Over and over, Kushiel rubbed the top of his left hand against his grey robes. Had Talia injured him with her rare angel powers?

Somehow, she held Lord Kushiel back in an unusual display of strength.

Jack never dreamed his wife's rare powers were a match for the Archangel of Punishment. Had she been holding these powers back all this time? Not letting the other angels (or him) know just how powerful she had become. Including Azrael and Berith who watched her with a sense of awe now.

"Oh, yes—two expendable angels of death saved! Praise the Maker!" Kushiel's sarcasm was razor sharp and venomous as he turned his dark, burning gaze on Jack again. "Oh, well done, you idiot human! At the expense of the two perpetrators who weren't working alone. And now, they're beyond questioning, their leader beyond reach! I should kill you right here, right now, human!"

Azrael blinked across the cavern, in Kushiel's face this time. He shoved Kushiel hard against the stalagmite, pinning him with a burst of archangel Holy fire that made Fourth of July fireworks look like an old incandescent lightbulb.

Again, Kushiel rubbed his hand against his grey robes. Like he'd injured it. With a glare, he faced Talia and Azrael. Unafraid. Undeterred.

Dude was still committed to ending him.

"Even if two of them are beyond questioning, Lord Kushiel!" Azrael shouted. "Archangel Raphael is not. What's the matter with you?"

Kushiel broke free of Azrael's and Talia's hold.

He shoved past Azrael, headed at Jack, but Talia blinked in front of him. She slammed both hands against Kushiel's chest. And shoved him backward with a burst of rare angel powers. Pinning him against the stalagmite again.

"You are incorrect, Lord Kushiel," she said in a fierce voice. "They aren't beyond questioning because I possess resurrect, a rare angel power." Fury still burned in her face and in those white fire-bright grey eyes as she pointed toward the dock.

Kushiel went silent for a moment, looking confused as his scary Old Testament Archangel of Punishment form began to dissipate.

"You have resurrect?" he replied, sounding surprised, calmer, left hand pressed against his robes.

Jack had no idea how long this sudden calm would last. Every time, it seemed like it was on a timer. Ever since Jack had encountered this Archangel of Wrath, Kushiel had been erratic. Quick to anger—mostly focused on him. Like someone had stabbed the archangel with sharp, pointy little sticks to keep him short-tempered and lashing out with his Heavenly retribution.

"Yes," said Talia with a nod, sounding calmer but still

exasperated. "Their ethereal essences still float on top of the Lake. Have your cherubim guard recover those glowing traces and I can resurrect the other archangels from that essence. For you to interrogate, Lord Kushiel." She shook her head, her face twisting with grief. "There was no need to slam Jack with all your punishing fire."

Finally, Kushiel's gaze shifted back to Jack and he stared for a moment. Deep in thought. Like he had just realized what he'd done.

Dude. About freakin' time!

"Truly, you have resurrect?" Kushiel asked with a strange, icy calm —like he hadn't understood her the first time. He held his left hand against his robes, like he was protecting an injury.

She nodded, tears rolling down her cheeks. Making Jack ache all over again.

"Cherubim!" Lord Kushiel called out, his gaze still fixed on Talia.

Wings fluttered around him, a squad of cherubim in eagle form landing as Talia let him go.

All four cherubim bowed their heads, forms shifting into angel forms.

"Yes, Lord Kushiel," they said in unison, awaiting his command.

Kushiel pointed toward the dock. "Recover the ethereal essences of archangels Uziel and Kotabiel that float on top of the Lake."

In an instant, two more cherubs materialized in front of Kushiel, their rippling white robes layered with Eternean plate armor, flowing white hair like lions' manes at their shoulders.

"How do we collect these essences, my lord, Kushiel?" one asked, face pinching in confusion.

Lord Kushiel turned back to Talia for clarification and motioned at his angelic squad.

"Ward a piece of Eternean armor and use it to collect the residue while flying low over the Lake," she said, her voice steady. "And hurry. The celestial essence will cling to the Eternean metal when it touches it, but you have to be fast and pull the metal out of the lake quickly because even Eternean metal will melt in seconds."

"You heard the angel of death," Kushiel snapped. "Go."

All of the cherubim blinked away as Lord Kushiel approached Jack.

Talia blinked beside Kushiel, putting her body between him and Jack.

Kushiel studied him a moment, remorse shining in his enigmatic eyes now as the Archangel of Punishment dropped down beside Jack, scattering a plume of dust in his wake.

"Forgive me," said Kushiel in a quiet but sincere voice, left hand cradled against his robes.

About time this dude felt bad for nuking him with Holy retribution.

Kushiel reached out his right hand, fingers splayed, and pressed all five against the side of Jack's face.

But the archangel jerked his hand back like he'd been shocked.

"Seraphim wards?" he said with a surprised look on his long, angled face.

Did this dude not remember that he'd just tried to kill him? Had he not noticed that something had kept Jack on his feet? And still breathing? Seriously?

Kushiel moved closer, leaning over Jack who still stared straight ahead, unable to move. Unable to risk letting a drop of all that retribution and flaming wrath slip through his wards and end him.

"Oh, Jack," Talia cried.

Jack didn't exactly know how he'd managed to trap all that punishing wrath, but he felt how brittle his wards were—and how lucky he'd been. He also knew that any slight disturbance, moving even an inch, even whispering an insult could break these wards. Releasing the rest of that retribution fire, letting it flow, unchecked, at him.

And then he'd ceased to exist.

Reaching out long, tapered fingers again, Kushiel's right hand hovered over Jack's face. His left hand was still pressed tightly against his robes. And Jack wanted to know why.

"Human. Listen carefully," said Lord Kushiel in that precise but mysterious voice.

Calm and collected. Like his previous meltdown had never happened.

Listen carefully? Dude, that was the only thing he could do right now. One muscle twitch and he'd cease to exist.

"Jack," Talia snapped, glaring at the Punishing Angel. "His name is Jack Casey and he didn't deserve your wrath. Not one splash of it."

Kushiel's gaze shifted to Talia, unblinking for several excruciating moments. Like he still didn't quite understand what he'd done, left hand still cradled against his grey robes.

Clock was ticking though. Why didn't this douchebag release him already?

Finally, the Archangel of Punishment returned his concentration back to Jack.

"I don't know if you can still hear me, Jack Casey," said Kushiel in a slow, deliberate cadence. "But I am going to attempt to pull back the flames. This fire is the most powerful instrument of punishment that exists—human or celestial. This fire consumes slowly or quickly, depending on my…will."

Jack would never know what Kushiel had intended because Jack had mostly stopped it at the door. Mostly. Stopped? Who was he kidding? It was distracted at best. Instant death or excruciatingly slow death, he'd trapped it between layers of seraphim wards, keeping it busy by continually attacking it with a seraph's dose of Holy fire from the wards. But his wards would come apart at any moment because he couldn't divert this retribution fire much longer.

Overpower? More like confuse it. In a moment, he'd have to start telling it jokes to keep it from obliterating him.

Guess if his wards fell, he'd know right away whether this douchebag had intended to kill him instantly or slowly.

Kushiel held his right hand above Jack's face and slowly brought that guarded left hand up and closed his eyes.

For only a moment, Jack got a good look at that left hand. The top of his thin, sculpted hand looked a little swollen and Jack saw three grey shadows, barely visible, floating beneath his angelic skin. What the hell were those? They almost looked like splinters.

The cavern began to quake as the shuddering, rolling flames trying to engulf Jack twisted back toward the archangel. Like Kushiel had called out to them and summoned them back to him. Like he'd sicked a couple of hellhounds on Jack and now, he was calling them home again. These writhing flames almost seemed alive. Sentient. And freakin' relentless.

Finally, Kushiel let his hands fall against his sides as he stood up straight. With a sharp inhale, he stretched out his arms, palms turned toward Jack.

Jack held his breath, his entire body trembling against this force that had almost chewed through the entirety of his seraphim wards. He couldn't hold onto them much longer.

Besides, he was out of wards.

Kushiel lamented a strange baritone melody, his angel notes dark and haunting as the notes wrapped around Jack's soul and quieted his growing panic.

As his wards began to flicker.

The cool, haunting darkness wrapped his soul with a soothing, protective chill that radiated through his bones, cooling the fire that roiled across his skin and tried to pierce his organs. Trying to get to his heart. And stop it. Like throwing the breaker and cutting all of his power.

The force was relentless. Icy. Unstoppable. Jack's failing seraphim wards were barely slowing it down now.

As Kushiel's melody invaded his head, shooting through his veins, the music flowed into his veins and lungs. Blocking the retribution fire's deadly wrath trying to march across his insides. Toward his heart. Leaving a trail of wreckage behind it.

"Return."

The single word flooded Jack's brain. His thoughts. His nerves. Filling his head. Softening his panic. Easing the pain strafing his body.

Inside, doors began to close. Barriers shifted across the fire's path until Jack felt the fire of retribution halt. And freeze. Filtering out the way it arrived.

Floating up and out of his body.

It lifted away from his skin and organs in waves. Layers. And slowly, the fire began to cool, the Lake of Fire's ash and smoke and shadows creeping toward him again. Across his body. Against his skin. Over his eyes. Until, at last, Jack felt the entirety of Lord Kushiel's retribution fire leave his body.

And retreat. Finally returning to its master.

The relief was intense. Overwhelming as his muscles knotted and his body began to ache. And like blowing out a candle, the seraphim wards he'd managed to call up (he hadn't counted them) went out in a ripple of white light.

He heaved a sigh of relief, his chest aching as air flooded his lungs. And darkness washed over him.

Somewhere inside his aching, smoldering brain, Jack thought that Kushiel had erased him from existence. But then he realized he still had consciousness. And he could feel. And remember what happened. That meant that somehow, he'd survived the Archangel of Wrath's best shot.

And they called *him* dangerous.

His body felt heavy. Sluggish and waterlogged. Like he'd drowned and his body sank to the bottom of the pool. Everything felt so dark and cold, but he couldn't find the energy to swim up and out of the dark. Much less open his eyes. He stayed curled up in the cold but safe darkness.

But his hearing was still sharp. The voices around him all talked at once. They had an edge, anger barely contained as they struggled to do something. He couldn't quite figure out what that something was—just that it was important. Their voices were a mix of angel notes and spoken words and he strained to focus on the words. Concentrate on what they meant.

"I know this wasn't supposed to happen, Pravuil!" Azrael.

Muffled sounds.

"Maybe there's a hint of remorse in his words, but what he did to Jack is inexcusable. And you know it!"

Something brushed across Jack's cheek. Through his hair. Gripped his hand.

Even from this distance, he felt Talia's energy connect with his, felt her love radiating around him in a warm surge of heat that pushed back the dark chill that hung at the edges of his consciousness.

She was beside him. He knew she hadn't left his side.

He tried to squeeze her hand, to move even one finger, but nothing responded. Like his brain had been completely disconnected from his body. Some people might claim that was his natural state, but now that he'd actually felt it, he knew better.

"Calm down, Azrael," said the gruff, scratchy voice. Pravuil. "Kushiel has shown remorse and he has offered to send over a cherubim healer for Jack."

"A little late for that, don't you think?"

"Calm down, Azrael."

"I will not calm down! That unhinged monster unleashed his full flames of wrath—on Jack! A human! Without a second thought! Lord Kushiel needs to be made accountable for this—this oversight as he puts it. This is Jack we're talking about here. Not some random soul."

A sigh. "Azrael, you know I agree."

"Then act like it, Pravuil." The archangel pulled in a heavy breath and footsteps ticked against stone, like he was pacing. "I've never seen Kushiel like this before."

"Neither have I," said Pravuil. "Think Lucifer has him spooked?"

"Maybe so, but I've worked with him before, Scribe," Azrael continued. "He has never attacked an angel with such little provocation before. Much less a human. And with the full fire of his Holy Wrath? Why?"

"Wish I knew." Pravuil. "He's under a lot of pressure to try Lucifer's crimes and that mouthy gallery of heckling archangels isn't helping."

"But Pravuil, he's not even called into situations like this. It's simply beneath his skillset to use his Wrath like this. On Raphael,

Uziel, and Kotabiel, yes. On internal issues like disobeying an order? Never!"

"Beneath his skillset?" Pravuil sounded annoyed now.

"Yes. He wasn't needed for a squad issue. Something that archangels could have handled. Especially not with the full force of his Holy Wrath!"

"All right, calm down," said Pravuil. "He's insisted that he didn't mean to harm Jack like that and I believe him."

"Don't tell me to calm down!" Azrael shouted. "I watched the Archangel of Punishment unleash his entire Heavenly retribution on a human being." Something hit the floor. "We're talking about Jack, here, Pravuil. And like it or not, he and Seraphina are the only two forces left in Heaven right now that can stop Lucifer in a firefight. Especially after so many angels fell in the apocalypse's Sixth Flight."

"And the Maker," Pravuil replied.

"Now, we both know that if it came right down to it," said Azrael. "The Maker would never harm Lucifer—that's why Lord Kushiel is here. To do what the Maker could never do to his firstborn angel."

"You're right," said Pravuil with a sigh.

"And with Seraphina still weak and recovering from the attack on High House, Jack Casey's seraphim powers are again, the only fully charged seraphim energies left in Heaven. At least they were. Especially with Samael trying to launch another Civil War across the Heavens."

Pravuil scoffed, wings fluttering. "Samael's trying for more than that. He's trying to take over Hell's crown. Flat out step into Lucifer's shoes."

"Fine." Azrael's voice was steely. "Let him try. Because there are plenty of seats around Kushiel's defendant table. About time the Archangel of Wrath starts using that Heavenly retribution on someone who deserves it."

More silence.

"Pravuil, you know Jack wasn't trying to obliterate Uziel and Kotabiel. He was just trying to protect Kesien and Deemah."

"Of course, I know that, you old fool," Pravuil snapped. "Just wish I understood why Kushiel turned his wrath on Jack instead of Raphael. He's the one who deserved it."

"And he calls Jack dangerous?"

Jack wanted to cheer. That was Azrael taking up for him. Maybe it was a good thing that Kushiel had taken his own powers too far? It showed Heaven that everyone had to be vigilant with these gifts. Especially an untrained human like him. But Jack had no idea if this incident would further fuel some of the archangel's—and Kushiel's—beliefs that Jack was dangerous. If it did, then he'd be the first to remind Kushiel that any and all power was dangerous.

Including the presiding archangel's Heavenly Wrath.

Pinpoints of light began to seep along the edges of Jack's vision.

He held his breath. Did that mean this strange state was beginning to dissipate?

"Where's Talia?" Pravuil asked.

Jack heard the Scribe's voice soften, sounding like he'd moved away from Azrael.

"At High House prison," said Azrael.

Jack's heart sank into his chest. In prison? No!

"Kushiel sent for her," Azrael continued, easing Jack's rush of emotions. "To try and resurrect Uziel and Kotabiel. Waste of angel powers, if you ask me."

"Couldn't agree more," said Pravuil. "Those two are a waste of angelic light. I wouldn't waste the time of putting them on the witness stand. Not when we still have Raphael. He's the one leading this little rebellion. For Samael."

"Exactly," said Azrael, his voice gaining distance. The two archangels must have moved across the room.

"I'll wager that Lucifer's enjoying every moment of this three-ring circus."

"Wager? Did you have to use that word, Scribe?"

"Sorry," said Pravuil. "Still a touchy subject. But yes, Lucifer is enjoying every moment, every chance to shove that blade in deeper. And twist it. He called Raphael an amateur and told him Samael was a pathetic poser whose time was coming."

"He's not wrong."

"Bet Talia didn't want to leave Jack to go help Kushiel." Pravuil. "She probably tried to smite him with her own powers."

"She did," said Azrael. "Had Kushiel against the cavern walls. Her power surprised me. I had to put myself between her and Kushiel until Berith assured her that Jack was getting better. Kushiel promised to assign a cherub healer to Jack if she brought back Uziel and Kotabiel. So, she'll be back soon with a cherub to further heal Jack."

More light leaked in around the strange shadows until Jack could see the hazy shapes of Pravuil and Azrael moving through Eolowen's round room.

From the ceiling portals, the gleam of a rose gold halo descending into the room washed across the white stone walls and floor.

It was Berith.

"Berith!" Pravuil cried as she landed beside Azrael. "You're back."

"How's Kesien?" Azrael asked.

The archangel turned toward her, hands gripping her forearms, pulling her close.

More light trickled in until Jack could see Pravuil's face. The worried creases shadowing his face. His gold eyes were owl sharp and eagle intense as he studied Berith, waiting for her prognosis. Like Jack. He felt the tension and uncertainty shudder between them as he opened his eyes a little wider.

Letting in more light.

"He's doing better after I did another healing session on him," said Berith. "Wings are recovering slowly. Feathers are starting to fill in. The guard will be without him for a little while, I'm afraid, but he'll recover."

Jack's eyes were wide open now as he watched Azrael and Berith standing in front of his bed in the round room.

"And before you ask," said Berith, holding up her hand. "Seraphina gave me some of her seraphim healing light infused into a stone. She was the only seraph we had that had healing abilities. I've been applying that healing energy several times a day to Kesien's wings. And to Jack."

Several times a day? Jack winced. How long had he been out?

Like a giant vise had released his soul and all of his limbs, Jack felt movement trickle back to him. Small but intentional movements at last. Did that mean Kushiel's Wrath was beginning to fade from his body?

"Azrael?" said Jack in a quiet, gravelly voice, unable to sit up yet. "Will Kesien's wings heal completely?"

"Jack!"

Azrael blinked around the bed to stand beside Jack, Berith hurrying around to his right side.

"We were afraid you wouldn't wake up again, Jack," said Berith as she laid her hand against his forehead.

"Just needed an extra nap to shake off Kushiel's...disapproval," he said as Pravuil flew over to the bed and sat down on the end.

Berith laid her hand against Jack's face, giving it a motherly caress. "How in Heaven did you survive Kushiel's full wrath? We were all terrified that your consciousness had been burned away. And your soul."

That thought made him shudder, but he couldn't gather enough strength to sit up. Or react. Could Kushiel really just reach in and shred his soul with that fiery wrath?

"I had a split second when I saw that white fire building in his hand," said Jack as he glanced from Berith to Azrael and finally, Pravuil. "So, I tossed up one seraphim ward after another. I got to about four when his wrath hit me. Full force. Kinda like the asteroid that killed the dinosaurs."

Azrael frowned and cast a glance at Pravuil.

"You had time to put up seraphim wards?" Azrael replied.

Jack nodded. "I just...started stacking them between me and the T-1000. Er, Kushiel."

Wings fluttered around the ceiling as Muriel dropped through one of the ceiling portals and landed at the foot of Jack's bed.

"Jack!" she cried, grinning as she moved closer, her wings folding against her shoulders. "You're awake!"

Azrael's brow furrowed. "T-1000?"

Muriel glanced at Azrael and then back at Jack

"Terminator, Azrael," she replied, looking amused. "Is that what you're calling Kushiel now, Jack?"

Jack nodded.

"What is a T-1000?" Azrael repeated, his tone sharp and insistent. Annoyed.

"It's this badass cyborg sent to kill Linda Hamilton, her kid, and Arnold Schwarzenegger in the movie, Terminator 2," said Jack.

"Sent to kill actors?" Azrael said, frowning.

"No, the characters they played."

"Great movie," said Muriel.

"T-1000 was unstoppable, they said," Jack continued. "Until he was stopped by a grenade and some molten steel," said Jack. "So, maybe I could have stopped Kushiel with a murder marble after he swam a few laps around the Lake of Fire?"

Muriel snickered.

Azrael's face turned bright red, his fury rising.

"It was a joke, dude!" Jack shouted, lifting his right hand from the bed—which took way more effort than he'd hoped. "Kushiel had me by the…oblivion spheres. Still don't know how I survived that brief introduction to Heavenly Wrath."

"Apparently, by stacking seraphim wards," said Pravuil.

The Scribe patted Jack's shoulder and stepped away from the bed.

"You stacked seraphim wards before Kushiel hit you with wrath, Jack?" Muriel replied in awe.

Jack nodded.

"Regardless," said Pravuil. "I'm glad to see that Jack and Kesien will be okay," said Pravuil. "But if I stay here any longer, Heaven will think I'm playing favorites. Azrael, I'll see you in a couple of days. When the trial resumes. After Kushiel's had time to interrogate Raphael, Uziel, and Kotabiel."

"Hope he doesn't have another meltdown," said Jack.

"Me, too, Jack. Thanks, Pravuil," said Azrael as the Scribe shot through a portal in the ceiling and with wings spread wide, he blinked across the Heavens. Back toward the spires.

"When will Talia be back?" Jack asked as Berith pressed her hands against his shoulders, transferring a warm burst of healing light to him.

"As soon as she resurrects Uziel and Kotabiel for Kushiel," Azrael replied. "To question."

"Kotabiel and Uziel won't talk," said Deemah as she landed in the round room from the ceiling.

More wings than a grade school Christmas pageant in here. Jack tried to shift his shoulders, stretch his wings, but they didn't respond.

"Berith, are my wings okay?" he asked.

She reached beneath his shoulders and he felt her warm gold light enveloping feathers and phalanxes until the light seeped into his shoulder blades.

"A little burnt still, but some healing light should fix those burns right up, Jack," said Berith. "Kesien's are going to need more work, but he'll be fine, too."

"Deemah, why do you say those traitors won't talk?" the archangel asked.

Deemah moved over to Jack's bed and then glanced up at the archangel.

"Because they're stupidly loyal to Samael. Willing to die for him and his self-righteous cause." Deemah made air quotes with both hands when she said self-righteous. "Believe me, Kesien and I have seen it before. Samael got rid of the angels who wouldn't blindly follow him. So, any more fighting we do against these archangels will be against fanatics."

"That sounds like fun," said Jack, trying to sit up. Couldn't. "As much fun as dodging Kushiel's Heavenly Wrath again."

Deemah sat down on the left side of Jack's bed. Smiling, she reached out and squeezed his shoulder.

"Just wanted to thank you for what you did in that cavern," she said in a quiet voice. "I knew you'd blinked after those monsters, but I was afraid that you would bow out of the fight when you saw the Lake of Fire."

Jack quirked up one corner of his mouth. "Me? Bow out of a fight where I can toss murder marbles at douchebags and asshalos? Never."

"I had to believe that you'd be there backing me up," she said, staring down at her hands. "But when the cavern got end-of-the-world quiet as I faced three archangels with only my flaming swords, I thought you weren't coming. I expected them to obliterate me right then and there. And then Kesien."

"Deemah…I'm so sorry. I couldn't give away my position because I was almost on top of those douchebags. So, I just waited for your diversion to spring my own."

She grinned. "And it was beautiful, Jack. Thank you. For Kesien, too. He asked me to come check on you."

"Tell him to get well quick," said Jack. "So he can help me, you, and the squad hunt Samael."

"Gladly," she said, the light at last radiating from her angel of death form, those grey wings velvety in the sunlight as she unfurled them again. "Take care, Jack."

And with a burst of warm air, light trailing like streamers from her wingtips, Deemah shot through the ceiling portal and disappeared into the cloud tops.

"Okay, Jack," said Berith as she and Azrael helped him sit up. "Let's apply some more healing to Kushiel's Wrath."

As soon as she hit him with her full healing light, Jack knew she'd see that his seraphim wards had blocked most of the damage. It hurt like the apocalypse, but Kushiel's Wrath hadn't done much permanent damage. Maybe a little cosmetic charring of his wings, but they were made from celestial light. They'd heal fast, too. All thanks to his seraphim wards.

The only thing that would take a long time to heal was his trust.

Jack dreaded being around Lord Kushiel again. And he worried that Kushiel would have another meltdown and try to fry him up like cheese sticks again. Regardless, he still needed to get in close and take a good look at Kushiel's left hand. Find out what those shadowy injuries were on top of his hand.

Or were they something else?

"Wonder how Talia's doing with Lord Kushiel?" said Jack, a little worried now.

He didn't want Kushiel melting down again—not with Talia in the crossfire. Even though she'd proven that she could handle the Archangel of Punishment. Regardless, that was the love of his life out there. His wife. Alone with this strange unstable archangel whose job was to punish angels and souls.

"I'm sure she's fine, Jack," said Azrael as he helped Jack extend his left wing. "Talia's rare powers held their own against Lord Kushiel. But just in case, I plan to blink up to High House if she's not back soon. Just in case."

Stable or not, Jack's money was still on his beautiful wife if Lord Kushiel started summoning that retribution fire without cause. And on her rare angel powers.

Honestly, he was worried about Lord Kushiel. Dude wouldn't know what hit him if he tried to use his powers on Talia.

CHAPTER 13

TALIA HOVERED, WINGS SPREAD, AT THE FRONT OF THE SMALL WHITE half-moon chamber, an interrogation room in the High House spire, and stared at Archangel Raphael. Raphael's gaze narrowed beneath his shaggy white hair that hung in his gold eyes as he paced his warded cell. The celestial holding cell was tucked two floors below the Cloud Chamber. One level below where Lucifer was being kept.

On this level, space was tight, the holding cells claustrophobic, but the white walls gave them an illusion of airiness—from a distance. The six small cells weren't meant to hold prisoners for the long term —just before and during a tribunal. Upstairs, with maximum warding and security—the block sealed with Holy fire—were two cells beside the courtroom. Reserved for those accused of the highest crimes against Heaven.

Like Lucifer. And Archangel Samael. The second cell had been prepared and sat waiting for that traitor.

Inside the lower-level block of holding cells, High House's vertical gallery was only visible through a narrow opening that wrapped around the half-moon space near its ceiling. Each of the six cells were warded and had no door. No way out.

Unless Lord Kushiel created one.

For angels used to soaring through wide open skies and warm updrafts, this block of tiny white boxes was the most devastating place to land—even for a short while. The cells made Talia feel like she was suffocating. The bare white walls carried a painful sense of nothingness without a view of blue skies or the feel of warm gold sunlight. Not even the cool, sweet scent of rain or fragrant jasmine penetrated the space. Those ubiquitous scents were of home and soothed the mind and spirit.

But, in this space, that was the only comfort.

Would days wrapped in this austerity make these archangels talk? Talia hoped it did because only Lord Kushiel could grant them release from the white emptiness.

Angels went crazy in places like this. It saddened her to see cells like this in the new High House spire, but she knew they were necessary.

And temporary.

How long these angels remained in these cells was up to them—and Heaven's master interrogator and only Archangel of Wrath. Lord Kushiel.

Blame it on Lucifer. Blame it on Archangel Raziel. On the Fallen and Archangel Samael. With all these self-serving traitors committing violence and openly professing their loyalty to either Lucifer or Samael, the need for these cells had grown.

And Talia despised it.

Archangel Raphael's gaze narrowed as he crossed his arms, shaggy white hair in disarray, white archangel robes covered in ash. He was angry and combative. Defiant. Saying nothing, his arrogance almost matching Lucifer's. She felt the darkness inside him smothering his angelic light. Anger radiated. And he blamed everyone but himself.

Raphael (and the other archangels) believed he had every right to Jack's powers. Even if it meant killing angels—and Jack—to get them.

She didn't want to hear anything this monster had to say. She just wanted to resurrect Uziel and Kotabiel into cells and leave these interrogations to the Archangel of Punishment. Otherwise, she might just take them all apart again.

"You call me a traitor," said Raphael, yellow eyes narrowing.

Talia glared, stepping closer to the cell until she stood inches from Raphael's face.

"You killed three angelic couriers. Several angels of death—even took one hostage. And then you tried to kill one of the Maker's chosen, knowing Lord Kushiel and the Maker would soon rule on the state of Jack's seraphim powers." Her gaze turned white and fiery. "There's nothing you can say to justify this. Any of it."

Getting one of these archangels to incriminate Samael was paramount. Heaven had to know whether or not they were still in league with that blatant traitor.

Or Lucifer.

"A human possessing some of the most powerful angelic abilities in existence!" Raphael's gaze was fierce. "Shameful. How can you be all right with that?"

"Because he didn't use them to murder anyone," she said in a cold, steely voice and leaned toward Raphael, her eyes still burning white. "You obliterated so many angels trying to grab those powers. How many more will die if you actually had them?"

With or without seraphim powers, Heaven would never allow Archangel Samael to rule Hell. Lord Kushiel would do whatever it took to remove Samael from existence—and that included any angels dumb enough to serve Samael. Heaven wouldn't tolerate another Rebellion—especially from a traitor like Samael.

Talia dreaded Kushiel's interrogations. They would expose even more traitors like Samael, and Raziel and their greedy narcissistic pursuit of power. Fighting over Lucifer's throne—like they belonged on one.

Samael and Raphael needed a good smiting. Right between their arrogant, self-important archangel eyes.

Raphael smiled, unshaken. "That depends on how many resist... and that includes Lucifer."

She shook her head. "Your arrogance knows no bounds. Lucifer was the Lightbringer. The most powerful angel in Heaven."

"If a human wielding those powers could use them to capture

Lucifer," his lips curled into a dangerous smirk. "Imagine what an archangel can do with them."

There was something tragic about Lucifer. Something wounded and painful that had intensified since Kushiel began questioning him. Granted, Lucifer was arrogant. Self-absorbed. Relentless. Saw himself as doing nothing wrong. That his cause was just.

Lucifer despised humans. Thought the Maker made a massive mistake creating them, so he planned to rid the universe of this embarrassment. In his own twisted reality, Lucifer truly believed that Heaven needed to be saved. That angels needed to be saved. That his father the Maker was the monster. And he was the only one who could save it all.

But Raphael, Uziel, and Kotabiel were only motivated by greed. Maybe the Archangel of Wrath knew something about these archangels that she didn't. That he hadn't shared yet. If that were true, she hoped Kushiel could uncover how they connected to Samael and Lucifer.

And how to make them talk.

A bright flash of light made her look away from Raphael.

She turned as Kushiel appeared in the room. He leaned against the white cell wall, his shadowy grey robes settling like smoke around him. He crossed his arms against his lanky frame, disheveled white hair hanging over one eye, enigmatic long face hiding as many secrets as those intense dark eyes.

Silent. Brooding. And dangerous with his kneejerk reactions as he focused his attention on Raphael.

Raphael's smug look quickly dissolved into fear.

Lord Kushiel's Holy fire—his Heavenly Wrath—was the most dangerous angelic fire in Heaven. She had to keep it as far away from Jack as possible.

"Where are the other archangels' remains?" Talia asked Kushiel.

"I have them," he said, patting his robe pocket.

Talia had all the shards needed to cast resurrect. She carried them in a small white pouch at her side, ready to return these shimmery smears of light back into Uziel and Kotabiel with resurrect. And try them for treason.

If she could bring them back.

Interrogating these archangels would keep Kushiel as far away from Jack as possible. Until the tribunal resumed. Like many angels, Lord Kushiel thought humans were stupid and inferior to angels. Something he had in common with these archangels.

And that made her sad.

How could angels be good shepherds to humans if they treated their flocks like mistakes. She sighed. She'd had to learn that once, too. And she knew now that humans were clever and brave and beautifully intense. Their capacity for love was their greatest strength. And the Creation would be a much dimmer place without them. Didn't these arrogant, ignorant angels realize humans were made in the Maker's image?

Like Lucifer, it would be their downfall.

But she worried that Lord Kushiel's attitude would condemn Jack and his seraphim powers, deeming them—and Jack—too dangerous for this world—which had been the archangels' plan all along. In Samael's name.

"If you're ready," said Talia. "I'll resurrect them."

Kushiel moved around the holding cells, stopping in front of Raphael. Staring. Kushiel's presence was intense. Intimidating.

Raphael shrank back from him, fear shining in his gold eyes.

"Patience, angel of death," said Kushiel, still staring at Raphael.

He seemed relaxed and focus. With all the time in the world to intimidate this archangel.

Talia just wanted to escape this holding cell. And Lord Kushiel.

"It isn't a lack of patience," she said, feeling the room shrinking around her, the walls sliding closer together. "I'm needed back at Eolowen."

Kushiel glanced at her, his gaze traveling up and down her angelic form. Judging? She couldn't tell.

"You will be back there soon enough," he said in his almost deadpan, matter of fact tone.

He didn't seem bothered by the small cell. To her, it felt like the walls were about to crush her between their narrowing spaces.

Her anxious gaze met Lord Kushiel's and she felt drawn to those intense dark pools of light that were bird of prey sharp. And in those enigmatic whirlpools fluttered shadows of the oldest powers in the Creation.

Wrath. Retribution.

She felt Lord Kushiel's strong sense of justice. It permeated him like the cloying, smoky musk incense Samael once burned in the dim-lit halls of Baladon.

"Lord Kushiel, these monsters are wasting our time," she said. "Lucifer's still the focus of this tribunal—not some greedy, scheming archangels with delusions of grandeur."

At last, Kushiel unfolded his thin arms and stood up straighter, the hint of a smile on his lips.

"All of that information gathered so quickly," he said in amusement. "Makes crossing them off my list of suspects useful. But time spent with monsters is never wasted, Talia."

She frowned. "Why is that?"

He paced around Raphael's cell with slow, deliberate steps, gesturing with his right hand. The close confines made her anxious, but not as anxious as Raphael who shrank back from Lord Kushiel, fear bright in that arrogant glare.

"Because the more time we spend with them, the more vulnerabilities they reveal."

"Like what?" she asked.

Her gaze narrowed as Kushiel whirled around to Raphael with a relaxed but deadly grace that showed his power. He was in control here. Not Raphael. His demeanor was practiced and deliberate. Calm. Nothing like his agitated, furious state back in the Lake of Fire cavern.

Kushiel's red-tipped wings were tightly folded against his shoulders, like he had nowhere to be anytime soon. That he had plenty of time to stay here interrogating his prisoners. Millennia.

The corners of his mouth lifted into the whisper of a smile, dark eyes brightening.

"When we learn to think like these monsters, we gain even more knowledge."

Think like these monsters? Her eyes sparked white with Holy fire for a moment. She wanted no part of their twisted thinking, but she understood that need. She and Lord Kushiel could learn what these archangels already knew about Samael.

And what he was after.

"Like Samael's plan," she offered, trying to distract herself from the suffocatingly small space. "His current location. His weaknesses. Who still supported him inside and outside of Heaven. Maybe even down on Earth. Making everyone believe Raphael cooperated with us."

Kushiel's smile unnerved Raphael.

"Wait, no," Raphael said with a gasp. "No!"

"Very good, Talia. That's it, exactly. But even more importantly." Kushiel pressed a long, tapered finger against the cell wall separating him from Raphael who tried to back away and couldn't.

"It lets us step inside their heads. Into their thoughts and desires. Think like they do. Long enough to know the truth—their truth. And what they might be planning."

He had a point. Learning everything she and Jack could about Lucifer had been critical. And with the King of Hell in custody, they still needed to capture Samael and stop him from digging into Hell.

His actions were much easier to predict than Lucifer's, but she considered him much more simple-minded by comparison.

Raphael took a step back, but the far wall kept him within an arm's length of Lord Kushiel—even through the Holy fire wards. He pointed a trembling finger at the Archangel of Wrath.

"You stay away from me! I've told you nothing. Nothing!"

"Samael is more arrogant that Lucifer," said Talia as she walked around the perimeter of Raphael's cage, her wings flat against her shoulder. "With no reason for such arrogance. He sees himself as something he'll never be."

Kushiel raised an eyebrow, those heavy white bangs sliding away from his left eye.

"And what is that?"

"A conqueror," she said. "A savior. A leader."

"And tell me, Talia…why is Samael not any of those things?"

Kushiel seemed intrigued. Or amused—like he might indulge a small child. She couldn't tell if he found her insights tiresome or valuable. He was so difficult to read. She feared setting him off, that he would explode with rage at any moment.

"Because Samael is a follower at best. A lemming at worst. He thinks he's smarter and shrewder than Lucifer." She folded her arms against her chest. "Basically, he's an idiot with delusions of grandeur. That's why he can never assume Hell's throne."

"Why?" Kushiel asked like she was his star pupil.

He seemed to hang on her answers. To see if she'd been paying attention to the archangels' claims and his line of questioning at the tribunal. And to him.

"Because that's a dangerous—and rare—combination. He'll lose control of the demons and cause so much collateral damage while we remove him from power."

Lord Kushiel paused a moment, staring at the floor. Finally, he looked up at Talia.

"You're right, of course," Kushiel said with a nod. "Samael's a follower who sees himself sitting on a throne. He will lose control of Hell and its demons, requiring Heaven to clean up a sizable mess. Unlike Lucifer. A natural leader who exudes power and confidence. As an experienced field commander, Lucifer is an extremely dangerous and cunning enemy. Samael is mundane and predictable. And insecure. But the cost of not removing him early on could be staggering. That is why I must put pressure on his minions. They will give away Samael's plans and lead me right to him."

Kushiel's expression shifted toward one of the cell walls.

"Cherubim!" he called out. "Prepare two more cells."

A cherub stepped through the wall of light, wings extended, lion's mane of white flowing hair windblown as she moved to a cell across from Raphael and opened it. She opened another one beside it and stood at attention, waiting for further orders.

Lord Kushiel reached into the pocket of his robe and pulled out a tarnished Eternean gauntlet. It sparkled with shimmery essence that clung to the Eternean metal like fabric. He let the gauntlet float between him and Talia.

Talia moved closer.

In the residue's oily sheen, sparks of angelic light still twinkled. As long as even one of those sparks remained, she could resurrect the angel attached to it.

Kushiel frowned as he motioned the gauntlet toward Talia. Like he didn't know what to do with it.

With thumb and forefinger, Talia picked up the gauntlet and set it on the floor of the first open cell, careful to keep the shimmery essence on top.

"Dismissed," Kushiel said to the cherub who blinked back through the wall, disappearing.

Lord Kushiel returned his intense, scrutinizing gaze to the gauntlet for a moment or two before his gaze shifted to Talia. Expectantly. Waiting for her to act.

He was a man of few words, expecting her to take the initiative in his infuriatingly silent way.

Still, the next step was clear. She claimed she could resurrect these archangels with her rare powers. He expected her to do exactly that.

Pulling in a deep breath, Talia reached into the pouch at her side of her Eternean breastplate and retrieved crystalline shards collected from the first Creation powers as she reviewed the steps of the ritual in her head.

She held up a blue shard the size of a sewing needle that came from the first drop of water from the Creation. It embodied the soul. And the heart.

She laid the blue shard on the floor beside the gauntlet as if laying out the shards on a supine body. She imagined that the gauntlet represented the body's left hand.

Kushiel watched her place the shards, looking intent and fascinated, a hand against his chin, eyes laser-focused on her arrangement on the floor. From his cell, Raphael looked over Kushiel's shoulder, looking confused.

"Where do these shards come from?" Lord Kushiel asked as she laid a small green shard below the blue one.

Where the stomach might have been located. The green shard symbolized the body of the world.

"We harvested some of these shards from the Garden and keep them in case resurrect is needed right away," said Talia. "I only had to gather a shard or two from the Creation's last grain of sand and its first spark."

She held the small yellow shard up to the harsh white light of the cell wards. This shard symbolized the mind and imagination. She laid it above the blue shard. Where someone's forehead might have been.

Finally, she removed a tiny red shard from the pouch at her side and laid it on top of the Eternean gauntlet. Against the shimmery residue gathered from the Lake of Fire. The red shard symbolized the lifeblood of Heaven, Hell, and Earth. If she'd had an angel body to resurrect, she would have placed this shard on the location of the mortal wound.

With only a tiny bit of essence remaining, and no wound to seed, she laid this shard directly on one of the two smears of celestial light that remained.

When all of the shards were in place around the gauntlet and on the celestial essence, Talia knelt on the floor in front of it. Taking a deep breath, she exhaled until a frosty white orb floated in the air above the gauntlet.

"What is that?" Kushiel asked, grimacing.

"This orb is the rare power of resurrect that I carry. The power of the air that changes all things."

She plucked the small white orb out of the air and held it above the red shard. And crushed the white orb between her fingers.

The frosty essence escaped, settling like powder across the gauntlet and the celestial essences. Clinging to the shards from Creation.

Red light trickled out of the red shard, a stream of blue light shooting from the blue shard into the red. And then the yellow shard's shimmery light. And finally, into the brilliant spring green shard. All four colors collided, mixing with the frosty white powder.

The lights twisted and danced until they exploded in a burst of light, strands of colors writhing against each other until all of the lights fused into a single burst of white fire.

The fire burned across the floor and exploded in a plume of brilliant white light.

When the smoke and clouds dissipated, Archangel Uziel and Archangel Kotabiel lay unmoving on the floor, eyes closed, the gauntlet lying between them.

"It worked!" Kushiel cried, looking surprised to see both archangels stretched out on the cell floor.

"Awaken," said Talia, pressing her fingers against each of their cold foreheads.

At her touch, a pale gold wash of light engulfed the two still figures. Until Uziel gasped for breath and sat up. Kotabiel pulled in a breath and wheezed as he looked around the cell, gold eyes lighting up with shock and confusion.

"Archangel Uziel," said Kushiel with a glare as the archangel got to his feet and glanced around the empty cell.

"No," said Uziel, a panicked look spreading across his face.

"No! Not like this." Kotabiel looked terrified.

"Surprised we brought you back?" Kushiel asked as he paced around the two resurrected archangels.

Kushiel grabbed Kotabiel and pulled him out of the cell. Into the one beside Uziel. With a wave of his arm, Lord Kushiel closed both cell doors and brought up the white wards of Holy fire, sealing the doors.

Uziel and Kotabiel looked at each other in confusion, fear shining in their gold eyes. Talia knew they had been ordered not to speak by Samael if caught, but Kushiel's interrogation would quickly break down their resolve to remain silent.

But something felt wrong. Like Uziel and Kotabiel had expected to be resurrected. Just not back here in Heaven.

Her stomach began to churn. Had they expected Samael to

resurrect them someplace else? Like down in Hell at Samael's side. But how? Resurrect was a rare angel power that few angels possessed. As far as Talia knew, only she and Berith possessed this power. So, who would have resurrected them?

"Now then, archangels," said Kushiel, hands behind his back, a dark smile spreading across his face, that enigmatic look briefly revealing his emotions. "You are going to tell me all about Archangel Samael and his plans."

"What are you talking about?" Uziel said with a growl. "What plans?"

Talia blinked toward him. She held up her hand and slammed Uziel against the far wall with her rare angel powers. Through the ward.

"Taking the seraphim powers, you miserable traitors!" Talia said, brow furrowing. "You *are* going to tell us what Samael intended to do with Jack's seraphim powers."

"Obviously, he will ascend to Hell's throne with them," said Uziel.

"Shut up, Uziel," Raphael snapped.

Kushiel got in Uziel's face, those deadly shadows across his eyes making him look so dangerous.

Even behind the Holy fire ward, Uziel looked afraid.

"You're lying," Lord Kushiel snapped. "The throne is empty. Seraphim powers weren't needed to claim it. But I thank you for acknowledging there was a plan."

"Even a fool could see that those powers would be needed to keep that throne," said Kotabiel with a smarmy smile. "I've heard."

"From Samael?" Talia asked with a growl, wanting to obliterate these archangels again. "Only a strong leader can control those demons. It'll take much more than seraphim powers to control Hell. Qualities that Archangel Samael will never have."

"That's what Raphael said," Uziel muttered.

"What?" Raphael's eyes narrowed, brow furrowing. "Shut your mouth, Uziel."

"Continue, Uziel," said Kushiel, nodding for him to continue.

"Raphael said Heaven would try and take the powers away from Samael," Uziel continued. "So, we have to be stronger."

"I'll obliterate you myself!" Raphael shouted.

Kushiel slammed Kotabiel against the wall through the ward. "You idiots. All you're doing is putting incredible power into Archangel Samael's hands. Powers that he'll never be able to control."

Uziel's gold eyes narrowed. "How dare you! If that flying meatsack can master seraphim powers, then so can an archangel. Especially Archangel Samael."

Tali shook her head, arms crossed against her chest. "Now that you've all incriminated yourselves, understand this. If Samael gets those powers, you two will be the first ones he smites. Along with Raphael here. He doesn't need you for anything else now."

The two archangels stared at each other and then Raphael, looking unnerved.

"Of course, he needs us!" Uziel insisted.

"He said we'd be royalty," said Kotabiel.

"Shut. Up." Raphael snarled.

Talia smiled. "More like roadkill. But thanks for leaving no doubt that Samael's behind this."

Kushiel's expression brightened as he approached Kotabiel. The Archangel of Wrath's right hand began to glow with white fire.

A burst of retribution was coming the archangels' way.

Talia stepped back out of the line of fire as Kushiel unleashed the first pain of interrogation. Retribution. As the Archangel of Wrath. They were drowning in guilt. It would be up to Lord Kushiel whether they were returned to the Lake of Fire.

To oblivion. For eternity.

Kushiel's Heavenly retribution would be their last, painful reminder that they had one chance to continue their existence. By telling Lord Kushiel everything he needed to know about Archangel Samael. To give up Samael's confidence and his secrets.

Or face the Lake of Fire again.

Lifting both glowing hands into the air, Kushiel flung his roiling fires of retribution at the three archangels. His wrath penetrated the wards, striking the archangels in the chest.

All three archangels screeched, teeth gritted as they collapsed in the floor, convulsing against the ravenous white fire rolling over them.

"Let that burst of wrath wash over you a moment," said Kushiel as he stood over the writhing archangels. "It's only a sample of the level of harm you've caused by turning traitors."

Talia leaned against the wall and watched Kushiel interrogate the archangels. The Punishing Angel's eyes brightened, like he enjoyed his work. As the Archangel of Wrath, he was in his element. A master of interrogation, skillfully questioning his subjects until they gave up every last drop of information that he sought. He seemed to enjoy exercising his Holy Wrath as much as he enjoyed observing its aftermath.

When the archangels refused to speak, they quickly changed their minds after Kushiel's Heavenly Wrath burned through their traitorous hearts.

Lord Kushiel was a master of his craft. Talia didn't know whether to be impressed or terrified of this enigmatic archangel, so different from every other archangel she'd ever encountered.

But his volatile nature unnerved her. And she worried that he might easily turn his wrath on her, demanding answers about her and Jack's relationship. Or worse, turning powers meant to punish angels on her human husband again. She had no idea how powerful Kushiel's Wrath was against Jack's seraphim powers. And she never wanted to find out.

She'd already witnessed that wrath chewing through seraphim wards like they were smoke. Kushiel had power over every angel in Heaven because of his station as the Archangel of Punishment. That power was lethal to angels. To humans, that power was total annihilation. And she would keep reminding Kushiel of that until these uncontrolled outbursts of rage stopped. Or the trial ended— whichever came first.

"Now then, archangels," said Lord Kushiel as he slowly paced around them. "Let's try this again, shall we? Archangel Raphael, tell me about your role in all of this." He leaned against Raphael's cell and reached through the ward, laying his hand on Raphael's shoulder. "And Samael's plan."

Kotabiel started to speak, but Uziel slapped his hand against the translucent cell wall between them.

"Keep quiet," Uziel said with growl. "You know what Samael will do to us."

Talia leaned toward them. "Lord Kushiel's Wrath is infinitely worse than anything Archangel Samael can dish out. Better keep that in mind before you decide to keep quiet. Lord Kushiel will tear it from your angelic light—piece by piece."

Were they that dense? Fearing an archangel of death over the Archangel of Punishing Wrath? Raphael, Uziel, and Kotabiel couldn't be that ignorant. Could they? What did Samael have on them?

Kushiel turned toward Uziel's cell. He reached through the ward and laid his hand on the back of Uziel's neck. Squeezing. Hard.

"Samael will fail. And when he does, you will all share in his fate. Make sure you understand that. Because Samael is headed for the Lake of Fire. And the three of you will follow him. Supporting a losing side isn't smart, angels. Just ask Lucifer about that."

All three archangels skittered back from Lord Kushiel's reach, fear shining in their gold eyes. But Talia saw that they feared something else more. Something beyond Raphael. Or Samael. Or even Kushiel.

Was it Lucifer?

"Or you can just stay quiet," said Talia, arms crossed. "Kushiel will interrogate you all until there's nothing left. And if anything remains, it'll be obliterated in the Lake of Fire. Either way, you're done."

Then Talia had an idea. Raphael had given her a way to get these fools to talk. To spill everything they knew to Kushiel.

"So, be smart like Raphael," she said in a quiet voice, her grey eyes widening as she strutted around them. "Admit you're working for Lucifer."

"Wait," Raphael snapped, looking confused. "Admit what?"

Uziel snapped toward the cell door. "What are you talking about?"

He glared at Raphael. "You've been playing us this whole time, Raphael?"

Raphael frowned, shaking his head. "Playing you? I'm not working for Lucifer. I'm not! I swear it!"

"The longer you two keep quiet," Talia continued. "The more Lord Kushiel will erase with his Heavenly Wrath. Slowly. Painfully. Or you can come clean—like Raphael did."

"What do you mean?" Kotabiel said, exchanging a frightened look with Uziel. Then he glared at Raphael. "You've been lying to us this whole time?"

"No!" Raphael insisted. "I swear! I work for Samael, not Lucifer!"

"That's not what you confessed before I resurrected Uziel and Kotabiel," said Talia, giving them a mock look of surprise. "You said you'd been working for Lucifer this whole time."

"Lucifer?" Raphael looked terrified now. "Wait a minute! I never even spoke to Lucifer!"

It was against her nature to lie, but for this interrogation, she had to trap them into revealing their truth. Now, Uziel and Kotabiel wouldn't believe that Raphael hadn't spilled everything while they were still in oblivion. And they wouldn't think to study her long enough to see that she was lying either.

"Collusion with Lucifer?" Uziel looked scared. "Raphael, you traitor! It's true. You sold us out."

"Sounds like Lucifer will have company when he's thrown into the Lake of Fire," said Kushiel.

Raphael banged his fists against the ward. "I confessed nothing! And I'm not in league with Lucifer! You can't throw me into the Lake of Fire. You can't!"

"Traitors end up in the Lake of Fire," said Talia, trying to look smug. "That's the way it works in Heaven. And Uziel, you and Kotabiel will follow you into the Lake. Again. Unless you talk."

Uziel's eyes widened.

"Not the Lake of Fire again," said Kotabiel, looking sick.

Talia knew that the memory of being obliterated was still fresh and raw in their memories.

Raphael escaped that fate in the cavern, but he was currently standing on the dock. Along with these two. Talia didn't think there had ever been a case of angels being thrown into the Lake of Fire twice. Pravuil would love writing up this story.

"No!" Raphael shouted. "No, you can't do this!"

"Don't forfeit your chance at a quick death!" Kushiel shouted, getting in the other two archangels' faces. "Confess what Samael's planning like Raphael did and maybe, I will spare you that final death."

"I'm not saying a word," Uziel said.

"Of course, I can also recommend that you two burn for eternity," said Lord Kushiel. "Instead of burning up."

Kotabiel gasped, a hand to his mouth. "Eternity?"

"Eternity, Kotabiel," said Talia, clicking her tongue. "That's the price you pay for treason. Protect Samael and you will burn for eternity."

She was enjoying this little drama she and Kushiel were playing. It was all angel theatre. No one burned in the Lake for eternity. The whole point of its existence was a quick end. She only hoped they'd get the information they needed to shut down Samael's treachery. And finish this trial. So she could return to her life with Jack.

Most likely, if they told Kushiel everything, these three archangels would end up in High House, being reeducated, banished to the Middling, or made fallen angels and sent to Hell. Not to rule it.

Kushiel stepped back from the archangels. "If you three had just given up Samael, your sentences would have been…mitigated. Instead, you'll burn forever."

"Forever," said Talia, emphasizing Kushiel's fake verdict as she turned her gaze to Lord Kushiel. "Exactly how long is that, Lord Kushiel?"

"Millennia," said Kushiel, playing off her questions like a master. "For as long as time exists. For as long as the Creation lasts. And the Maker. The amount of time is incalculable."

That should hammer the point home to these hard-headed archangels.

Talia leaned toward Uziel. "To burn. Forever." She made a show out of shuddering and stepped back again.

"Okay!" Uziel shouted, scrambling to his feet. "I'll tell you everything."

"Shut your mouth, Uziel," Kotabiel shouted, slamming his fists against the cell wall as Uziel spread his wings and blinked back from Kotabiel.

"Don't, Uziel!" Raphael shouted. "Keep your mouth shut."

"I'm not burning for eternity for that arrogant, vain bastard!" Uziel turned his anxious gaze to Lord Kushiel. "Look, Samael and his guard have been plotting to take over Hell ever since Lucifer hatched his Phoenix Shift plan."

Uziel pressed his back against the wall, terror burning in his gold eyes as he glanced from Talia to Lord Kushiel. And finally, Kotabiel who was scowling.

Kushiel reached through the ward and grabbed the front of Uziel's robes, shaking him. "When? I said when!"

Uziel's voice began to tremble. "During the chaos of the apocalypse! But when the payloads didn't go off, Samael used the Sixth Flight to cover his tracks. Then he waited to see if Lucifer would return to Heaven in chains or to Hell as Heaven's conqueror."

"Playing both sides?" Kushiel replied, raising an eyebrow. "Samael's dumber than he looks. The moment Lucifer suspected that turncoat was playing him to get at his throne, Lucifer would have fed him to his demons."

"That's why he needed that human's seraphim powers," said Uziel. "To protect him from Lucifer until…"

Talia stood in front of Uziel, the realization becoming clear.

"Until he could lead Heaven right to Lucifer," said Talia. "And the moment Lucifer was in Heaven's custody, Hell's throne would be empty. And Samael would claim it. Samael sold Lucifer out. Didn't he?"

She grabbed Uziel through the ward and shook him.

"Didn't he!"

"Yes," Uziel said with a moan. "He sold out Lucifer."

"Shut your mouth, Uziel," Kotabiel said with a snarl. "Samael will crush you."

"How did Samael sell out Lucifer?" Talia demanded.

"By moving the Rod of Creation."

How did that sell out Lucifer?

"You're not making sense," said Talia.

"Uziel, stop!" Kotabiel's voice was trembling. "Samael has ears everywhere. You're sentencing all three of us to obliteration! Not even Heaven can protect us now."

Talia frowned. Samael didn't have that kind of power. But the cold chill sweeping along her wing feathers made her question that.

Samael never did anything directly. He didn't have the power–or the army–for a direct assault. Lucifer was the king of misdirection. He hid things in plain sight. Relying on deceit and hidden enemies, but he led those battles himself.

Samael just ran.

Lucifer had been so focused on Jack and Heaven, he hadn't thought to look for the enemy at his back. Because that was the only way Samael could have setup Lucifer. And only if he was certain that Lucifer couldn't retaliate.

In chains, Lucifer couldn't strike back at Samael. Leaving that monster to entrench himself in Hell and take control.

"Uziel!" Lord Kushiel snapped, sounding weary now. Tired of this runaround from traitors. "Explain about the Rod of Creation."

"Samael sent some of his guard out to move the Rod of Creation," said Uziel. "That delay bought Heaven more time. Enough to get more angels into the Throne room to oppose Lucifer. To alert them of Lucifer's target."

Talia thought back to the old, sprawling east coast graveyard at the edge of the sea. Where she and Jack had rushed off to try and beat Lucifer to the Rod. But when she and Jack got there, the Rod had been dug up already.

So, Lucifer hadn't gotten to the Rod of Creation first. Samael had.

But he hadn't given it to Heaven. He'd only displaced it long enough for her and Jack to get to the Throne room first. Ahead of Lucifer.

Samael wanted them to clash.

He'd been waiting for the Maker to smite Lucifer, so he could feign support for the winner. Long enough to take control of Hell. And if, by some chance, Lucifer survived the Throne room assault, Samael and his squad would have testified against Lucifer archangels to testify against Lucifer. Covering Samael's tracks and indirectly supporting Heaven's decision to throw Lucifer into the Lake of Fire. Either way, he'd have control of Hell without having to fight Lucifer for it.

A fight that Samael would have lost.

So, Jack's seraphim powers became the new distraction in court. Another diversion. But now, those powers were the only fail safe against the hordes of demons that Samael was losing control over. Samael needed Lucifer to burn. And he needed Jack's seraphim powers to maintain control. No, to defend it.

But the most terrifying aspect of this terrible plan was Samael's arrogant incompetence. He wasn't powerful enough to take control. Abaddon was still trying to manage the half-open Gates of Hell. But even he couldn't stop a red tide of demons from rushing those gates.

For the first time in its existence, Hell's demons could walk the Earth. And Lucifer's fallen angels would be freed, too. If that happened, it would make the apocalypse look like a traveling circus. Heaven would embark on a never-ending war with demons. With humanity caught in the middle. Something the Maker never intended.

Something Samael should have foreseen.

Now, Heaven had to find a way to reclaim Hell's throne before Samael created a hellscape that couldn't be undone. Abaddon could be the first casualty, forced to take Hell's throne.

But even he couldn't be in two places at once.

No, those gates had to be closed and the throne had to be occupied. But not by someone incapable of controlling it. Someone like Samael who wanted to watch the Creation burn.

"Uziel!" Talia shook him. "What have you done?"

Kushiel slammed Uziel with another bolt of Heavenly Wrath.

Uziel screamed, trembling as he slid down the wall.

"Everyone knows Samael can't handle that throne! Even you know that!"

Uziel thrust his arm over his face, bracing for another burst of Holy Wrath.

"He can with that human's seraphim powers."

"Idiots!" Kushiel ground his teeth together, eyes burning white. "For a task that large and celestial powers that strong, they need a steady source of energy to maintain them. Like a seraph's body. Seraphim powers alone were never designed to control Hell."

Talia began to pace, the walls closing in as everything felt like it was spiraling out of control.

"Lord Kushiel, Samael can't handle that throne!" she shouted. "Much less that many demons. And that many souls. If Samael's incompetence allows those demons to escape Hell, they'll overrun Earth and Heaven. That power-hungry lunatic will thrust us into permanent war with demons!"

Kotabiel leaned against the wall, looking unnerved. "Couldn't Lucifer just take back the throne?"

Kushiel whirled around, slamming the floor with a wild burst of Wrath.

"It's much too late for that!" he shouted. "Hell's throne has been vacant for too long now. And no one in Heaven is willing to unchain Lucifer on the chance that he would actually take control again. He would escape and destroy Creation. Besides, those demons have probably already begun to tear Hell apart. Inevitably, it will lead to Armageddon."

Armageddon? Talia slumped against the wall, feeling sick.

She never dreamed that things could get worse with Lucifer in chains. Or that Archangel Samael was capable of bringing about Armageddon by himself. That had been his goal all along.

Annihilate all the players and take control of what survived.

The Creation was quickly headed that way unless Heaven took control of those demons. And closed Hell's Gates. Fast. Before demons invaded every town and street on Earth.

And triggered Armageddon, the final battle between light and darkness.

CHAPTER 14

Jack distracted himself by visiting Kesien in Eolowen's inner sanctum, getting there with slow, careful movements. And thanks to Kushiel's Wrath, that was all he was capable of making.

Kesien's condition was still serious after those loser archangels tried to deep fry him in the Lake of Fire. Using Kesien as bait to ambush Jack and steal his powers. Somehow, Kesien survived, but the veteran angel of death wasn't healing as fast as everyone hoped.

Jack worried that this incident would scar Kesien, knock the fight out of him. Before this, Kesien had been obsessed with bringing his old squad—including that douchebag Samael—to justice. Jack hoped this hadn't changed the patient and calm angel of death who had always been an angelic voice of reason—and a force for good.

In a small, quiet room far from the terrace, Berith made a bed for Kesien, a good distance from where the guard trained. In case Kesien was tempted to slip out and go after his old squad, using the drills as a diversion.

The bed was arrayed with soft white pillows, crisp white sheets, and a warm white quilt draped across Kesien's six-foot-sixish frame.

His black curly hair was short, now, most of the length burned off. It would grow out, but the wings were another story.

Jack winced at the stink of cold ash and stale charcoal that had overpowered Heaven's soft jasmine and honeysuckle scent, a stench that took Jack back to the Lake of Fire. Especially when he saw Kesien.

Kesien's dove grey wings were slag. Almost burned off his back. Berith was busy wrapping what remained in thick, glowing gold bandages. The angel of death was asleep beneath those soft covers, something angels didn't do—unless badly injured. His wings would take a while to regenerate—if they healed at all. And that terrified Jack.

"Didn't think angels slept," said Jack, an ache in his chest as he watched Kesien's deep, labored breathing.

That was scaring the hell out of him.

"They don't usually, Jack," said Berith as she laid her hand on Jack's shoulder and gave it a motherly squeeze. "But that sleep is the only thing that will heal his wings." She sighed. "That and time."

Berith moved back to the bed and pulled the covers up underneath Kesien's strong chin. He'd never seen Kesien incapacitated like this before and it unnerved him. Why didn't he get to that cavern sooner? Tossed murder marbles sooner—faster. Knocked all those asshalos into the Lake of Fire. Before they hurt Kesien.

When he looked up, Berith was standing in front of him. Arms crossed. A worried expression on her face.

"Jack…" She wagged a finger at him. "I see that look. This isn't your fault."

He sighed. "I know. I just wish I'd gotten there sooner. Acted sooner."

She gripped his arm. "You got there in time to save him from obliteration, Jack. That's what matters."

He nodded, staring at his Vans. He knew it wasn't his fault. But why did he feel so guilty? If he hadn't played those archangels' stupid game, maybe Kesien wouldn't have gotten so badly hurt?

"Jack. The wings can be fixed."

"Berith, they almost burned him up in the Lake of Fire. If I'd tossed those murder marbles a few seconds later—"

"But you didn't," said Berith, her voice rising. "I know how close he came to oblivion. And there was no guarantee that Talia and I could have even recovered his celestial essence from that lava lake. Much less brought him back. But Jack...he will recover."

Jack nodded. He knew she was right, but it still hurt seeing Kesien like this. Kesien was one of the strongest, most courageous angels he knew. And he couldn't help but feel a little responsible. Those archangels took Kesien to get to him. And his seraphim powers.

"Until then," said Berith, letting go of Jack's arm. "I will keep him in this sleep-like state and concentrate all of my rare healing powers on those wings." She cast a scrutinizing look at him. "And after you tangoed with Kushiel's Holy Wrath, you need your rest, too, Jack. Kushiel almost killed you."

"Tango? No, I was slow-dancing with death, Berith. Wasn't sure I'd live through that slo-mo sway with Kushiel."

Dude wanted to kill him. Jack wasn't sure why Kushiel didn't throw a second burst of Wrath at him. Probably too many angels present. He couldn't have gotten away with killing Jack with so many witnesses.

"As soon as Talia's back from High House, I'll get some sleep," he replied. "I want to make sure Kushiel didn't dance with my wife, too."

Berith took him by the shoulders and led him out of Kesien's healing chamber. Into the hallway. Blinking him to the end of the long, airy nave. Into the round room.

"Now, Jack Casey," said Berith with an impatient smile. "Talia knows where to find you and I assure you, she's fine."

Berith nudged him into the round room and blinked back into the hallway. He paced the room, way too tense to sleep right now. And worried about Talia.

As he moved around the foot of the round, white bed for lap sixteen, an angel shadow crossed the floor. He glanced up as Talia flew across the roof and landed on the terrace. Her soprano voice rose above the clash of swords and thump of shields.

"Azrael! I need to talk to you. Now!"

Jack's heart began a drum solo against is rib cage as the archangel blinked across the round room's rooftop and landed on the terrace beside her. Jack watched them both through the billowing white curtains in the doorway, listening, his gut tying new knots.

He gritted his teeth. If Kushiel hurt her, he'd be dropping by High House with a murder marbles gift bag for the Archangel of Wrath.

The terrace was mostly empty. Azrael's guard had been stationed around the spire, finishing up the placement of the last remaining viewing platforms for Luci's trial. They were also providing extra security now that Uziel, Raphael, and Kotabiel had been taken into custody.

Everyone feared a surprise demon jailbreak, orchestrated by Lucifer. Or Samael trying to break Lucifer and these archangels free.

This trial wasn't going well.

"Azrael!" Talia again.

"What's the matter, Talia?" said Azrael, beside her now, his soot-grey wings folding against his shoulders.

"Sir, we've got a big problem," she said, panic burning in her luminous grey eyes.

"Tal, what's happened?" Jack asked as he stiffly slipped out between the billowing curtains on her right, trying not to startle her into a smite reflex.

He'd already seen Kushiel's and wasn't too keen on seeing a replay.

"Sir, we finally got confessions out of Uziel, Raphael, and Kotabiel." She sighed, propping her hands on her hips, but Jack knew that look. Things were bad. "And some details about Samael's plan."

Azrael's charcoal gaze darkened as his wings twitched against his shoulders. Jack knew that look, too. The archangel of death looked worried. Took a lot for him to crack that marble poker face he'd perfected over millennia.

"About time we knew what that traitor's been planning." Azrael sounded energized, ready to act.

Talia shook her head.

"He played both sides during the apocalypse," said Talia.

Azrael's eyes darkened. "How?"

Talia hesitated a moment, the anger churning in her gaze. Jack already knew this story was gonna suck.

"He moved the Rod of Creation from its resting place."

"What!" Azrael roared. "That monster had possession of the weapon that could kill the Maker and he let Lucifer get hold of it?"

Azrael's face flushed, his eyes wide and beginning to burn with Holy fire, wings unfurling again. He was moments away from a full archangel meltdown, courtesy of Archangel Samael.

"Afraid so, sir," said Talia, sounding flustered. "He intentionally delayed Lucifer from getting to it. Buying us time to reach the Throne room before Lucifer."

Azrael frowned, looking puzzled. "Helping Heaven? For his own gain, no doubt. Still, why would he gamble with the Maker's existence like that? Why?"

"First time he's helped Heaven with anything," said Talia.

"We both know it was to help himself." Azrael again.

Talia nodded. "Exactly. He did it to help himself to Lucifer's throne in Hell. While we were all busy in the Throne room."

"That megalomaniac can't control Lucifer's throne," said Azrael. "Not even on his very best day."

If Samael wasn't powerful enough, what happened to the throne when he failed?

Suddenly, Jack felt uneasy. That was a problem he'd never even considered. Until now.

"Didn't stop Samael from taking it though," said Talia. "And now, he's losing control of the demons."

Jack watched the archangel's expression shift from fury to trepidation, his face turning pale. This wasn't going to be good news, was it?

"The Gates of Hell!" Azrael cried. "They're still partially open. And now, he's losing control of the demons. This is bad, Talia. Very bad."

"Exactly, sir," she said. "Without someone powerful enough to maintain control, those demons will force their way out. And flood the Earth."

"And we'll be locked in an eternal war with them." Azrael said, getting quiet as a bazillion thoughts raced across his charcoal grey eyes.

"Then somehow, we need to close those gates," said Jack. "Can't the Maker close them?"

"They can," said Azrael. "*Will they* is always the question. They avoid intervening in the Creation's timelines."

"Why?" Jack frowned. "Why wouldn't the Maker close the gates? And save Creation? That makes no sense."

Azrael folded his arms against his chest. "One word, Jack."

"One word?" Jack frowned, feeling confused.

"Armageddon," said Talia.

"Armageddon?" Jack shook his head. "That the Maker's garage band or something?" Jack asked. "Hope they're not gonna do a cover of Final Countdown. Even the eighties are tired of hearing it."

Azrael raised an eyebrow. "Garage band? And what countdown are you referring to?"

Jack chuckled. "Heaven has the most epic garage band ever crossed over. John Bonham and Neil Peart on drums. Jimi Hendrix and Eddie Van Halen on guitars. Aretha Franklin and Janis Joplin on vocals. The Maker could drop an epic new song, Save the Earth. Making Samael and the Demons look like some crappy sixties cover band out of Reseda."

"You're not making sense, Jack," said Azrael, shaking his head.

Frowning, Talia crossed her arms and glanced from Jack to the archangel. "He is, sir," she said. "If you've ever heard Jack's demon-splattering playlists."

"The Maker's epic garage band could play all of us out of Armageddon," said Jack. "Besides, no one, anywhere, wants to hear Samael and his demon cover band play. Even in Hell."

He sighed. Guess Azrael wasn't a music fan.

"Uh, Talia," said Azrael, looking confused. "Please translate."

"Why doesn't the Maker handle this instead of leaving it for us to solve?" Jack said. "They're much better equipped to solve it than we are. And every delay will cause needless injuries and deaths on

Earth. And no one wants Samael to win. That make more sense, archangel?"

"Jack," said Talia, her voice shaky as she tried to pull in her panic. And probably keep her boss from smiting him. "Armageddon is the final battle between angels and demons. Light and dark. Good and evil. Once certain forces have been set in motion—it can't be stopped or solved. Not even by the Maker. One side will win and one side will lose. It's that binary. So, the Maker can't just handle it. And the apocalypse with its Seven Travelers and their payloads was just the opening act."

Azrael sighed. "She's right, Jack. The Maker's epic band as you call it can't just play all of us out of Armageddon in some battle of the bands with Samael. Especially now that the apocalypse has played the stage."

"Very good band analogy, Azrael–I'm impressed," said Jack with a smirk. "But getting real here…didn't we stop the apocalypse?"

"No," said the archangel in a dire voice. "We stopped the payloads from activating, but the apocalypse still happened. All but the Seventh Flight of angels took flight. That Seventh Flight must still take place before the battle of Armageddon begins."

Jack felt a cold chill roll across his skin. "What? But that's the worst of the plagues. It means death for my world."

"No, Jack," said Talia. "Remember? We stopped the Seventh Flight's payload, too. But the Seventh Flight will take to the skies because they are the herald of Armageddon."

"And now, Samael's found a way to hurry it into the air," Azrael continued. "And when the Seventh Flight does take to the skies, the Gates of Hell will stay open. Releasing all of those demons on the Earth. Triggering Armageddon, the final battle between Heaven and Hell. The Maker's army versus Hell's army—and whoever sits on Hell's throne."

Jack winced. "So, there's no stopping any of this?"

"Afraid not, Jack," said Azrael. "I wish there was a way. But Samael, in his arrogance and stupidity, forced these events into high gear again."

Talia slid her arms around Jack, laying her head against his shoulder. He held her tight, his chest in knots now.

"The only thing we can control, Jack," said Azrael, his voice softening, "is whether we battle Hell's demons here in the Heavens or down on Earth."

"Well, then that's something, right?" said Jack, feeling a flicker of hope ignite inside him, easing the tightness in his gut and chest. "We find a way to detour these demon douchebags at Hell's Gates and then splatter their asses all over the crossroads. Keep the fight up here. Away from Earth."

"It's the best we've got Jack," said Azrael. "But somehow, we've got to help Abaddon hold those gates. And we've got to control Hell's throne somehow. If it stays in Heaven's hands, then Hell's champion won't have the power to defeat Heaven, pausing Armageddon. I'll confer with Seraphina and Kushiel. And Pravuil."

"Why?" Talia asked.

"We need to speed up this trial. Before all Hell literally breaks loose," said Azrael. "Samael's probably going to try and interrupt it with Armageddon and the Seventh Flight."

"Can't argue with that," said Jack. "Hope it doesn't send ol' Kushiel into another meltdown though."

Talia nodded.

"Has he had any others—besides the Lake of Fire?" Azrael asked in a wary tone.

"I don't know," said Jack, motioning toward the High House spire. "But I'd lay money on it."

Talia was nodding. "He has, archangel. Smaller incident, but still a meltdown."

"Then I'll confer with Pravuil and Seraphina first." Azrael looked distracted again. "Discuss the situation before bringing Lord Kushiel into the conversation."

But the loud trumpet blast that echoed across the Heavens made them turn toward the High House Spire.

Green and white smoke coiled up from High House' golden dome, fluttering around the dove finial, making it almost look like it was in flight.

"Green and white smoke? Never seen that before. What's it mean?" Jack asked.

"Green means the trial is resuming," said Talia, her gaze on the spire.

"And white means that the defendant will take the stand tomorrow." Azrael's wings tensed against his shoulders as he turned toward Jack and Talia. "That means Lucifer will take the stand. And it will be Lord Kushiel against Lucifer until Kushiel calls for a verdict."

Talia slid her arms around Jack's waist and pulled him closer.

"That also means that, for now," said Talia with a relieved sigh, "they won't be asking us questions about our relationship, Jack. It will all be focused on Lucifer."

It looked like Luci was about to come to terms with his denial and daddy issues. Whether he was ready or not. And that included Lord Kushiel—and whatever ate away at the Archangel of Punishment. Jack wasn't sure which one would crack first—Kushiel or Lucifer.

Or would it be the Maker? He and Talia were about to find out.

CHAPTER 15

THE RETURN TO THE HIGH HOUSE SPIRE FOR LUCIFER'S TRIAL HAPPENED sooner than Talia expected.

She barely had a chance to process the archangels' interrogations and Samael's growing threat. But now, the trial was back in session and she and Jack were back in the courtroom, seated at the witness stand beside Azrael as Watchers lit the braziers throughout the sprawling chamber. Firelight crackled in each of the angel statues' golden bowls, illuminating the Enochian words on each bowl. Fragrant but husky hints of dried jasmine and honeysuckle blooms warmed the chamber, the air currents cool and smelling like new fallen rain.

As she watched each Enochian word catch the light and reflect it throughout the space, she wondered if Lord Kushiel had considered any other tenet besides truth and justice.

Kushiel's very name had always sent tremors of fear through most angels. No one wanted to encounter the Archangel of Wrath. Much less be interrogated by him. Even his celestial form made him look half-demonic, his face long and shadowed, his tall, lean body draped in flowing charcoal grey robes. He had that grim reaper look that most humans thought of when they thought about death. Or when they imagined an angel of death. In other ways though, Kushiel seemed more the mad scientist seeking justice with his shadowed, hooded face, his silent approach as he relentlessly pursued justice. And truth.

He was the stuff of nightmares to all of the Creation. But in the archangel's presence, Kushiel was usually calm and patient. Soft-spoken. Careful. Meticulous.

Until suddenly he wasn't.

His behavior in the Lake of Fire cavern had been unhinged and out of control. Talia had never heard stories of the Archangel of Wrath losing control and throwing his Heavenly Wrath at a human before. She had seen smaller instances here, in the court proceedings. And during the Archangel of Punishment's interrogations.

Something seemed off about Lord Kushiel, something even he didn't sense. Had he been somehow...comprised? By choice like Raziel? Or by deception like Samael's latest pet archangels: Uziel, Kotabiel, and Raphael? Had they somehow...done something to Kushiel?

Compromised him in some way? To influence the tribunal's outcome? Or distract him from something else?

Either Samael's disciples were trying to kill Jack and take his seraphim powers or...they were trying to force a quick conviction of Lucifer. She shuddered. To take Lucifer's powers.

Even in chains, Lucifer was still the most powerful angel in Heaven. Even though he had never come into his Lightbringer powers because of his Rebellion and the Fall, those powers were still inside him. Waiting for him to awaken a celestial angel's highest power.

The Maker's dream for their firstborn.

Had Samael infiltrated the Heavens with his agents, trying to manipulate the trial into a quick convict? And then seize Lucifer's powers from the Lake of Fire? Gather them from those boiling, sulfury waters.

But at the moment, Talia didn't know where else to look for more traitors. There were too many shadows to check.

At least the key to the Lake of Fire's cavern had been recovered and was back in Kushiel's hands now, the cavern resealed. Nevertheless, Kushiel was still acting strangely. She barely knew this archangel. How was she qualified to judge whether he was himself or not?

But she, Jack, and Azrael agreed that Kushiel's meltdowns were out of character. They would not only have to prove that to the judgment dais, but they would also have to prove that to Kushiel.

With some hard evidence.

Off to the right of the courtroom, the chamber angled toward the new pyre that tapered away, emptying into the vast blue skies and white clouds of the Cloud Chamber that allowed powerful seraphim angels to preside over the trial while also being at a safe distance from their searing Holy fire. Seraphina remained the only surviving seraph. She looked lonely out there, turning gracefully, like a dancer in the air currents as she floated on the updrafts, searching for a dance partner. Talia didn't remember a time when Heaven only had one seraph.

She wondered if the Maker would resurrect some of the lost, higher-ranking angels. Especially after losing so many angels during the Sixth Flight. The Enochian Apocalypse.

She gazed up at the judgment dais. Empty.

Behind her, the gallery was beginning to fill. From Watchers to archangels, they crowded into the long, narrow gallery behind the courtroom. Waiting to catch a glimpse of the Maker or Lord Kushiel in the lower Heavens. Or Lucifer, the Fallen One.

Besides the apocalypse, this was the biggest event that the lower Heavens had seen in a very long time. Since Lucifer's assault on the Throne room. Or the time when Jack Casey appeared in Eolowen's meadow after escaping Hell. Beside Lucifer. With all of Heaven ready to smite him because they thought he'd been turned.

Across the sprawling, airy courtroom, the defendant's table stood empty. The cherubim hadn't brought Lucifer in yet.

Talia wondered how the new information about Samael's treachery would color Kushiel's approach to Lucifer. Unlike Samael,

Lucifer hadn't hidden his involvement or even lied about it. He'd always acted unaffected.

Right on cue, the sharp, staccato jangle of chains rose from the back of the gallery, growing sharper and louder until four cherubim in angelic form appeared in the chamber—with Lucifer between them. He wore the same torn and burned black general's coat, gold buttons missing, gold braids and flourishes unraveling and blackened. His sunlit blond curls were bright against his dusty black boots and trousers, clear glass-blue eyes a mystery as he held his head high and approached the table.

Talia tried to read the emotions that churned in his stormy eyes. Today, they were a maelstrom of emotions. Strong. Defiant. Willful. But beneath that façade, for the first time, she felt his pain. His feelings of betrayal. Of abandonment. So powerful that she had to look away. He'd made no effort to try and hide any of it this time.

Lucifer had never seemed troubled before today. Much less vulnerable. But she felt those emotions roiling in him now. He was about to face his father again, a being he had not seen for millennia, not since the Rebellion. And the Fall.

Eons had passed since the Fall, but on this day, Talia felt Lucifer's raw emotions. Like he had just fallen from the Heavens. Like he had just been cast out. And been forgotten.

She understood how that felt. She'd felt that sharp pain ache through her body when Azrael took her wings and threw her from the Heavens. That horrible splintering rejection. Feeling no longer worthy. And that steep, crushing free fall through the clouds. Accelerating. Twisting and tumbling through the airstreams she had once soared along.

Even now, she remembered her own terror and the memory of that painful shunning a jagged tear across her heart. Followed by that aching loneliness and churning anger at being treated so badly. Yet knowing, right or wrong, the choice she made led her to fall.

She wondered if Lucifer, deep down, knew that, too.

She related to Lucifer's pain in a way that made her

uncomfortable. She didn't want to empathize with the King of Hell. The Prince of Darkness. This monster, who delighted in turning humans, stealing their souls, and torturing them for eternity. This beast who only wanted to watch the Heavens and the Creation burn.

But the part of her that had plunged from the Heavens understood him in a way she'd never expected. If Jack hadn't caught her—and loved her—would she have followed in Lucifer's footsteps? Demanding vindication. Craving vengeance for pain that never went away. For the isolation and demeaning treatment that made her feel like she was nothing. Like she no longer mattered. To anyone.

But that night in south L.A., Jack Casey saved her again. His love almost made her forget her Fall. When Lucifer fell, he only had demons and Fallen Angels for company. Creatures as hungry for vengeance—and making others pay for hurting him and tossing him aside—as he was. Eager to follow him anywhere to get it.

Maybe if Lucifer had had just one angel, one soul to love him despite what he'd done, then maybe he wouldn't be standing in the Cloud Chamber on trial?

That realization made her feel queasy. And sad. Knowing that Heaven's mantra, its tenets which were written across these chamber walls and stamped on statues around this room weren't all equal.

Maybe Heaven just needed to be reminded of those words again? Like Jack had already told them. But they'd dismissed him. What did he know? He was just a stupid human. Arrogant for thinking he understood angelic ways. But Jack understood them better than they realized. He understood both sides. And that included Lucifer, too. That's why he'd warned them about walking their talk. The very thing that Heaven had damned humans to Hell for—and sometimes, Heaven was as guilty as her human charges at missing what mattered most.

She looked away, toward Azrael who hovered behind the witness table, beat of his wings a whisper against the dull thrum of noise rumbling through the chamber. But when she glanced at Jack, who sat in a chair behind the table where she floated, he was staring across the aisle.

At Lucifer.

"Look at him," said Jack, his gaze unblinking. "Dude looks wrecked."

Intrigued, she said nothing.

"Wrecked?" she asked.

"Yeah," said Jack with a sigh as he leaned his elbow on the table, watching as the cherubim steered Lucifer into the only other chair in the room. They'd made Lucifer stand through the last session.

"He already looks defeated. Like all the fight's knocked out of him. Like he's on death row. Mr. Nothing-Can-Touch-Me. Like he's made of tungsten."

Lucifer's black wings were bound against his shoulders, his wrists and ankles bound in Eternean shackles and chains. His blood-red halo spun in a furious wobble above his head.

Agitation? Anger? Or trying to sort the flood of emotions washing over him right now?

Maybe he was plotting to destroy every angel in the room? Or maybe he felt powerless against the weight of his destiny dragging his celestial form ever closer to the Lake of Fire? And after everything that had happened, maybe he just didn't care anymore what happened as long as it all ended?

"Death row?" Talia asked, still studying Lucifer.

Maybe Jack was right? Lucifer seemed resigned to his fate, but without all that fire and indignation that he'd exhibited the last time at this tribunal.

"Yeah, like he's about to walk that last green mile to a barbecue. And he's the pulled pork."

An obvious observation. But did Jack sense more than that?

"He has to know what he faces," said Talia. "Now that he's been chained and brought before the Maker. And Lord Kushiel."

Jack was quiet, chewing his bottom lip. "But it's more than that, Tal," he said in a soft voice, forcing her to lean closer. Like he didn't want anyone else to hear him. "It's like he's looking back on all of it. Seeing his own real face for the first time. Feeling the pain of what he's done for the first time."

So, she and Jack saw similar emotions in Lucifer. Was it all an act? She really didn't know.

Jack looked up, a melancholy, conflicted look turning those pale green eyes glassy.

"It's like it's the first time he's really understood that he caused a shit-ton of pain and suffering for a lot humans, angels—even demons. That he inflicted a lot of damage to Earth and Heaven, too. I don't think it's something he's ever felt before. Not sure what made him see it, but now, he can't unsee it."

Jack's comments unnerved her. Did his seraphim powers allow him to feel what Lucifer was feeling? Allow him to see the tide of truth and clarity that Lucifer had always refused to see before.

But she felt it too, through her own rare angel powers. Through omnificence. That was pure, stark epiphany in Lucifer's eyes. The first glow of remorse. The first realization of responsibility for everything that had happened since he proposed that very first wager to Azrael. A wager that set in motion his dark, devious plan to get his wings and halo back.

His power and his revenge.

All this time, Lucifer saw himself as the injured party in all of this. But she and Jack both saw that realization flickering and slipping somewhere beneath Lucifer's contempt. That he knew he was guilty of attempting to destroy Creation and trying to kill the Maker—his father.

"It's like a deep, open wound," said Jack. "One that wasn't there last time. Two kinds of pain. A deep, age-old hurt that he's carried forever. And a new one that's deepening every time he realizes he's at fault. It's guilt. Something I'm betting he's never felt until now."

Jack also felt Lucifer's unrepentant defiance. The impenetrable armor Lucifer had worn into Heaven was showing tiny, feather-like cracks of remorse. Would it crumble?

"Does he even know what's causing that pain in his eyes?" Jack asked, the corners of his mouth quirking into that sexy smirk. "Does he even know what remorse feels like? I doubt it."

"He knows what it feels like," said Talia. "It's flickering in his eyes. But I don't think he knows that it has a name."

Jack nodded. "Probably the first time that Luci's ever felt guilt and remorse before."

"He also knows that it won't change his fate," Talia added, realizing that was the origin of that hint of sadness in his face.

"Too little too late, I guess," said Jack in almost a whisper.

Talia nodded. Like a wounded great dragon holding his head high as he awaited the golden knight's killing blow. But she heard the quiver of uncertainty in Jack's voice. Jack had a unique perspective on Lucifer. Jack had witnessed Lucifer unhinged with an insatiable thirst for vengeance in Hell. Later, the King of Hell had honed a cold, emotionless shell as he carried out the last vestiges of his plan to make Heaven pay.

Jack sighed, running his hands through his hair as he leaned in close, his voice a whisper this time.

"But Tal, I can't help feeling like he's just an angry child, acting out in every way possible. And all he really wants is his father's attention, but he doesn't know how to get it without tearing apart half of Creation. Does that make any sense?"

Jack's voice had hints of pain in it. And a strange sense of empathy, despite everything that Lucifer had done to him. Talia knew it came from Jack's painful—and similar—relationship with his mother. Even with his father who would disappear on binges for days at a time until he died of cancer when Jack was seventeen. Jack hadn't gotten what he needed from either parent. He'd internalized it, but Lucifer's had fueled his sense of outrage for millennia.

And it led to the apocalypse.

Even so, she saw that, on a certain level, Jack understood Lucifer better than almost anyone in Heaven. But she couldn't deny the pain that the Maker felt toward Lucifer on the first day of the trial.

Jack glanced over at Lucifer again and then back at her, his voice still a whisper. "Sorry, babe. Guess I'm still a little conflicted. I could have acted out like that. And it would have changed my whole life, too. Not on that scale, but you know what I mean."

Talia slid her arms around his neck and kissed him.

"Instead, you turned it inward," she said against his ear. "Lucifer blamed the world. You blamed yourself. And it did change your whole life."

He nodded. "Guess I just feel like that could be me in so many ways. In those chains, facing the consequences of my actions."

She held him tighter. "Jack, that *was* you. You were addicted to cocaine. Broke. In massive debt to the wrong people. You'd lost everything. You'd given up. And you were a breath away from ceasing to exist when I landed in the middle of that stupid reality TV show. You were daring me to save you from yourself. And me from my own bitterness toward humans."

His face turned pale and he snapped up straight in his chair, a haunted look on his face. Almost like he'd forgotten that his Book of Life and Death had already written the very last line of his story—until Lucifer's wager. But it wrote in that book that he'd overdosed in the wee hours of a long, dark night. Alone. Forgotten. Broken. With no one around to save him.

Yes, Lucifer had meddled in Jack's life. In his parents' lives. All to engineer a Phoenix Shift that would bring back Lucifer's powers, his halo, and his wings. But that wager still saved two souls. Hers. And Jack's. And between them, they'd saved so many others. Even a fallen angel. An archdemoness. And more than a few lost human souls.

Lucifer's wagers hadn't destroyed the Creation. They'd strengthened it. Whether he'd intended it or not.

Jack had a funny look on his face and he stared at Lucifer again. "Tal...I know you saved me. But we both know it was only because of that first wager."

She nodded. "I can't deny that."

"Neither can I."

He looked shaken. Conflicted as he kept his gaze fixed on Lucifer. Talia couldn't read the emotions rolling fast and furious across those pale green eyes. But Jack seemed to be having an epiphany of his own. One that he wasn't entirely comfortable with—and she felt the same way.

Someone tugged on her sleeve.

She turned to see Azrael studying her with bright charcoal grey eyes. He looked concerned as his gaze flicked from Jack to Lucifer and back again.

"Something wrong?" he asked.

"Maybe," she said, not really wanting to put what she was feeling into words yet. But she already knew Jack was struggling with it. "I think Jack's had another view of this tribunal rise up and hit him in the chest."

Azrael frowned. "Another view? What does that mean?"

"I think he's just now realizing some things he hadn't understood until now." She shrugged. "Like me."

"Still not sure what that means," he said. "But you both look a little worried. Has something changed?"

"Maybe," she said. "Maybe not. We'll just have to wait for the tribunal to tell the rest of the story."

Azrael nodded, but Talia knew he didn't understand a word she'd said. Maybe she didn't understand the words either, but like Jack, she understood the emotions. They didn't lie. She'd have to trust Lord Kushiel to bring all of it to light. And Lucifer when he testified.

Maybe it was nothing. But maybe it was everything.

A hush fell over the chamber as Pravuil blinked through the gallery and ascended to the judgment dais in the front of the courtroom. He took his place left of center and looked out on the gallery, his face taut, his gold eyes intense.

The tribunal was about to begin again.

Seraphina's bright fiery light gleamed at the edge of the platform as she took her place as close to the judgment dais as she could reside.

Talia wondered if the Maker would take their place in the center of the dais again today. But her thoughts shifted as Archangel Sidriel blinked through the gallery and floated up to the judgment dais, her long white hair hanging in bouncy waves, velvety grey wings majestic against her white robes and ebony skin. Her charcoal grey angel of death eyes glittered against the brazier's warm gold light as she took her place beside Pravuil.

Archangel Sarathiel was a breath behind her, blinking through the gallery and blinking over the tables. He took his place to Pravuil's right, his bushy white hair soft around his angular, dark face, gold eyes lemon-bright.

But the whispers that hissed through the chamber made her uneasy. And she knew without looking up that Lord Kushiel had entered the chamber. His shadowy form, windblown white hair, and those enigmatic hawkish dark eyes gave him an intensity that unsettled her. Like he could see through her words, right into her heart. Into her most private thoughts where he could find guilt. Shame. Wrongdoing. Like he could twist even the purest light into a shadowy, questionable thing.

She wondered if Kushiel saw the good in anything. By his actions, the Archangel of Wrath only saw the need for retribution. She hoped his slanted perspective hadn't poisoned the Maker's views on angels and humanity. Or the outcome of this tribunal. An Archangel of Wrath was needed, but the Creation needed more light not punishment.

And she wanted truth not wrath. Change not retribution.

Kushiel's dramatic movements through the space, his long, red-tipped wings spread over the gallery like a bird of prey, filled the suddenly quiet chamber with trepidation as he slowly made his way up to the judgment dais. Where he took his place to the right of center.

Leaving the only unoccupied position on the dais in the center. The Maker's place.

Would the Maker attend this time? Or would they leave this decision up to their Punishing Angel? Their Archangel of Wrath? A being of pure judgment who saw only wrongdoing and used only punishment to fix it.

If ever the Maker's light was needed, the Maker's love, it was here. Now. At this tribunal. But she feared that light had been lost beneath the angels' thirst for reckoning and righteousness. Angels were soldiers after all, but even soldiers needed distance from each battle in order to see the objectives more clearly.

Lord Kushiel stood with wings extended, hands folded against his shadowy grey robes, those dark eyes ruddy today like brazier flames as he watched the room. Judging it? Ready to punish all of Heaven with the entire might of his Wrath. Like the force he'd unleashed on Jack at the Lake of Fire.

He rubbed the top of his left hand with his right thumb, a hint of shadows beneath the skin. She'd seen him do that before.

Was it a nervous habit? Or something else.

He made no move to converse with Pravuil or Sidriel. Sarathiel wasn't even on his radar. He seemed lost in thought. Poring over evidence already given? Gathering his thoughts into a line of brutal questions he would wield like weapons until his anger bloomed. Or would he use his cold, calculating Eternean shell to evaluate everything in binary terms, isolating everything out of context as he pronounced sentence?

Maybe because it was Lucifer, the most formidable adversary that Heaven had ever fought? So, he was always on guard because of Lucifer's masterful manipulations. She understood that well.

And she knew that Kushiel could not pass sentence alone. There were three other voices on that dais, from three very different worlds of experience. And the fifth voice—the Maker's—carried the most weight. Together, she hoped they would all judge fairly.

Even Lucifer deserved a fair judgment.

As Kushiel stood statue-still, whispers grew louder in the gallery. Growing restless. Impatient. The angel notes degraded from harmonies and major chords to discords until it just became noise. Calling for Lucifer's execution.

"Think the Maker's gonna call in sick? Use some PTO today?" Jack asked, leaning against Talia.

"The Maker has to be here," she said. "Their voice is essential to the tribunal's outcome."

"Yeah," said Jack, gazing around the chamber. "Because I doubt Kushiel's going to give a fair judgment to anyone. Just suggestions on how to execute Lucifer."

Talia bristled. She understood why Jack would say that, but it still made her uncomfortable that her husband felt the same thing.

"Kushiel is only one voice up there."

"Yeah, Tal," he said, lowering his voice. "But it's loud and angry and stoked to chop off heads. All amped to obliterate angels and yeet Lucifer into the Lake of Fire. It may come to that, but I just hope it's because all five voices were heard. Because it's the right thing to do. Not because the Archangel of Wrath's shouts were extra."

She stared at him a moment. "Extra what?"

He sighed. "Louder than everybody else. Extra."

"You're not wrong, Jack," she said finally, understanding after he explained his Jackspeak. "But Sidriel and Sarathiel are both voices of reason. They would never support a careless order—even from the Archangel of Wrath. And Pravuil is all about evidence and proof. As the Maker's Scribe, he'd never allow anything that subjective into his decision."

Jack nodded, his gaze fixed on Lord Kushiel whose presence was oppressive and dark despite all the angelic light in the chamber. It wasn't evil. It was heavy. Burdened. And narrow. Without the Maker's brilliant white light, she worried about the damage Kushiel might do here. Damage that couldn't be repaired.

"I mean, Luci and I aren't even frenemies," said Jack, glancing from Kushiel to the defendant's table. At Lucifer. "But I'm seeing some changes in him that are making me…" He sighed. "Dammit, Tal—they're making me feel bad. Is he playing this card deliberately? Playing all of us. Again?"

Kushiel's statue-like stance continued until at last, a sudden, radiant beacon appeared at the edges of the courtroom. Near the Cloud Chamber.

The gallery grew quiet, the angel notes softening into intense melodies and harmonies as the glow grew brighter. Until finally, a pure white fiery column of light descended through the top of the spire. Through the gold dome. And into the courtroom.

Talia reached out and covered Jack's eyes with her hands as the brightest flash of light she'd ever witnessed in Heaven exploded through the room. Erasing every trace of shadow and darkness in the space as the light moved with fiery brilliance between Pravuil and Kushiel. Into the center spot on the judgment dais.

The Maker. In all their ethereal brilliance. Too bright this time for human eyes. Had the Maker forgotten there was a human present? That meant they were distracted. Emotional? Talia couldn't help but wonder.

She kept her hands over Jack's eyes until the light's intensity began to soften, allowing all the shadows and outlines and shades of grey to return to the chamber. Only then did she lift her hands from his eyes.

"Thanks, Mrs. Casey," he said with a smile, but it quickly faded into that brooding look he got when something bothered him.

Those sexy pale green eyes were watery as he tried to adjust to the light. He rubbed his eyes a moment and then stared at the dais. Overcome by the sight of the Maker and the feel of their presence in the chamber.

But slowly, the light began to change. Flowing and swirling as the radiance began to coalesce into a form. A body. Angelic in form until human features began to emerge. Golden hair that hung in waves around their face and at their shoulders. Oval face. Aquiline nose. Glass-clear eyes that sparkled like gems. And a perfectly sculpted mouth. Their form was beautiful. Pleasing. Androgynous in gentle genderless features. Ageless. Tall and lean.

This was one of the Maker's many forms. Humans had been created in the Maker's image after all. And so had angels. Talia saw both human and angelic features in the Maker's form today. They were trying to make everyone in the room feel comfortable. To let them see a little of themselves in the Maker's appearance.

She glanced over at Lucifer. He looked conflicted. A mixture of awe and dread and pain as he looked upon the ethereal light of his father. With the face that Lucifer probably recognized—and hadn't seen in millennia. The only parent Lucifer had ever known. Back in the days when angels spoke directly to the Maker and saw them more as a parent than the supreme being over all. Back before there were hierarchies of angels.

Talia understood. Azrael was the closest thing to a parent that she had ever known.

Lucifer's expression quickly became all pain. Like he remembered the Maker's form. Like he'd seen it many times before. Had some painful memories attached to it.

"This tribunal will now come to order," Pravuil announced, his gruff, gravelly voice filling the chamber.

The whispers in the gallery dissipated as attention shifted to the front of the chamber. To the Maker.

"Bow before your Maker," Kushiel commanded, hands still folded in front of him, thumb still rubbing the top of his left hand, mouth a tight flat line, white eyebrows furrowed over those hawkish dark and rusty eyes.

Angels throughout the chamber bowed their heads or dropped to one knee with heads bowed. Even Seraphina's light had shifted into a bow.

Jack dropped down on one knee and bowed his head as Azrael folded his frame into a bow on one knee.

Talia bent her head downward and floated to the floor on one knee as she turned toward the Maker. And glanced past Jack. At Lucifer.

He sat in his chair, chains clinking. But to her surprise, Lucifer pulled in a deep breath and struggled down onto one knee beside his chair. The cherubim shifted as one, ready to defend, but she saw the surprise burning in their eagle-like eyes as they watched Lucifer bow before the Maker.

He bent his head downward, eyes closed, shackled wrists in his lap as the chains hung down on both sides. A sight that Talia had never expected to see.

She poked Jack and nodded toward Lucifer.

Jack's eyes got wide, his mouth open as he stared at Lucifer. Talia wondered why Lucifer had chosen today to bow to his father, the Maker. After everything that had happened. After trying to end them in the Throne room.

"Wonder what brought that on?" Jack asked, his gaze flicking to Lucifer and back to her.

"I'd love to know," Talia whispered.

"Lord Kushiel will oversee today's proceedings," Pravuil announced as Jack lifted his head and got to his feet. "Witnesses will be called, so if you're in the gallery, keep that overhead aisle clear. And keep your opinions to yourself unless you hold a position on this judgment dais. Any disturbances will be met with cherubim and expulsion from the chamber. Or worse. So, mind your manners."

Today's tribunal hadn't even started and already Pravuil was cranky. That didn't bode well.

"And remember, your Maker still presides over this tribunal," Pravuil continued. "Their smite reflexes are in rare form today, so don't tempt fate and end up a sparkly smear in High House square. Because eternity's a very long time to spend staining cobblestones."

Jack chuckled along with a few other voices in the gallery.

Then a bushy-haired angel with ashen blond hair and ivory robes, dull white wings in motion, flitted through the gallery. He soared over the tables and landed beside Kushiel who had floated down below the dais. The young, lanky, sable-haired angel leaned against Kushiel's ear, whispering, a hand on the Archangel of Wrath's left sleeve.

One of Kushiel's assistants? She wondered if the angel carried some last-minute information from Raphael. Giving up more of Samael's secrets. And maybe even the traitor's battle plans.

The angel gripped Kushiel's left sleeve above the wrist, fabric bunched tightly in his long fingers. Shadows roiled around his fingers for only a moment. If she'd turned her head, she would have missed it.

A chill danced along her wings. What were those shadows?

Almost immediately, Kushiel began clenching that left hand into a fist.

For a third time, the angel leaned in and whispered something in Kushiel's ear. Kushiel paused a moment and whispered something back to the angel, still clenching and unclenching his left fist.

And then the angel let go, launching across the marble floor past the witness stand. The angel folded his wings against his back and strode away toward the gallery. Odd. Angels always preferred flying. Walking was slow and made any journey longer than required. But here was this angel walking. She frowned. Like he'd been born to it. That made Talia uncomfortable...and very curious.

As the angel passed her table, Talia's gaze snapped up. To the half-moon scar around his right eye. Eyes that had been charcoal grey, not the soft teal green of a Watcher when she'd first met him. Almost everything about his appearance had subtly changed since she met him.

She thought back to High House square. And the injured angel of death they'd found. When she first met this angel. Called Caleal. This critically injured angel who'd survived the archangels' attacks when they took Kesien as bait. Telling just the right story to get hers and Azrael's sympathy. He had the right color eyes and the right color hair. Even his wing color had been spot on...for an angel of death.

But now, he was presenting as a Watcher. She shook her head. Who preferred walking to flying.

A cold chill ruffled her wings.

All three of Kushiel's couriers died in those attacks along with their angel of death escorts. Uziel, Raphael, and Kotabiel wouldn't have left one lone angel of death alive. Not unless he'd been in on it, meant to pass on that story. Exactly like he'd told it—to get her and Azrael into the Lake of Fire chasm.

Or more bait to lure Jack? They had been after her rare powers, too.

"Caleal?" she called out.

The angel stopped and turned toward her. For a moment, she and Kushiel's Watcher stared at each other, his soft teal eyes looking so young and innocent against those bright white wings.

"Sorry, no. I'm Raum, Lord Kushiel's courier."

All of Kushiel's couriers had been killed.

And in the square, Caleal claimed that he'd been one of Sidriel's guard. The only survivor of that attack. This angel looked nothing like Caleal that day in the square. Nothing like an angel of death. But his light did. It had the same subtle blue and gold hues and a gentle blush of sunset beneath an angel's long, flowing shadow. A shadow? Her omnificence power allowed her to see the colors of angelic light—and their arrangement. Angelic light was like the pattern of a tiger's stripes. Each big cat's pattern was different. Like the colors and radiance of angel light.

And Raum's light exactly matched Calael's. Except that his carried more shadows. A lot more shadows.

What was happening here?

She didn't know every angel in Heaven, but she knew that only cherubim could change their faces. Angels could shift into any form when they appeared to humans. But not to other angels who could see through any shift in angelic light to change their appearance.

Her omnificence picked up every color and its degree of radiance. This angel was Caleal. She'd healed him. She'd felt his angelic light mix with hers as she tried to heal him. If he'd somehow been hiding his appearance beneath shadows—or something else—her healing light and her omnificence power would have detected it.

He now had Watcher-like eyes and that same half-moon scar that was apparently inflicted against his angelic light during that attack in the streets. Like Lucifer's halo burn on his forehead. Every form he took would reflect that celestial scar.

"Kushiel's couriers are all dead," said Talia, watching for any change in this angel's light.

Watching for any shadows in those chameleon eyes that she'd never seen on any angel before. How was he doing this? What exactly was he?

Raum bowed his head. "Yes, I'm afraid they were all killed. I was brought from mid-Heaven to take over courier duties for Lord Kushiel."

"You mean the Middling?" she asked, pretending like she was trying to correct him as she laid her first trap.

The Middling was one of the Maker's failed experiments. And a place where angels exiled from Heaven were sent and some early, primitive humans who refused to leave it. She also knew there was no such place as mid-Heaven. There were only lower and upper Heavens. Every angel in Heaven knew that.

Except for this Caleal or Raum or whatever his name was.

He wasn't a Watcher and he certainly wasn't an angel of death. And he wasn't part of Sidriel's guard any more than he was a courier to Kushiel.

He smiled, his face flushing with embarrassment and innocence— again, out of character for an angel. "Yes, the Middling, forgive me," he said. "I'm a Watcher who's been assigned to courier duties while Lord Kushiel's here."

Just vague and confusing enough that most angels would just let it go. Except she wasn't most angels.

Talia hid her shock, offering him her best sympathetic smile. "I understand, Raum. The Seventh Flight changed a lot of our duties, didn't it?"

"So many losses," he said, his expression pinching. "But I consider it an honor to serve as Lord Kushiel's courier."

"Thanks for taking on extra duties, Raum," she said, smiling sweetly at him.

Not letting on that he'd failed all three of her checks. Stepped into all three of her traps. He wasn't a Watcher. Or a courier. And now, she doubted that he'd spent any time at all in Heaven. She needed to figure out who he was. Fast. Because he had direct access to the Archangel of Wrath. Who floated right beside the Maker.

"Of course," he said and Talia felt his tension begin to dissipate. "Happy to serve where I'm needed. And if you'll excuse me, I'm needed outside the tribunal."

Raum/Caleal scurried away from the table. On foot.

Jack waited until Raum disappeared into the gallery.

"What was that about?" he asked. "Nice acting, by the way, my beautiful angel of death wife."

She laid her forehead against his for a moment. "I learned from the best."

His luscious mouth quirked into that sexy smirk as she gave him a quick kiss.

"Something's not right about that angel," she said against his ear. "I'll tell you later."

He frowned. "Tal, that wasn't an angel."

She held her breath a moment, studying the surprised look on his scorching hot face.

"What do you mean, Jack?"

He cast a quick look over his shoulder at the gallery, as if making sure Raum/Caleal was gone, and then fixed her with his intense, sexy gaze.

"I spent enough time in Hell being tortured by Luci's finest to recognize a demon when I see one. Not the little red minion demons. It's like this one's only partly demonic—according to my seraphim powers."

Her breath caught in her chest as she thought back through the imprints that Raum's light had left on her angelic form. Every angel saw a demon's true face. Her rare angel powers—omnificence—gave her a deeper more precise look at them. But Jack's seraphim power had the most granularity, allowing him to see nuances.

She shuddered. Like Raum only being part angel. Why hadn't she seen that? Wait—the shadows! Raum *was* part demon. And not a minion demon, like Jack said. But his humanity limited his sight of angels—despite his seraphim powers.

That's when she saw what Jack couldn't. Something horrifying that even she was afraid to voice.

She reached out and gripped Jack's hand. "Oh, Jack—I know what Raum is."

"Quiet in the courtroom!" Pravuil shouted.

Jack leaned against her, whispering. "What do you see?" he asked. "What is that thing?"

"A Nephion," she whispered.

"Half human half angel?" he asked, eyebrow raised.

"No, Jack…half demon half angel."

"Still killable with murder marbles," he said with a smirk.

She shook her head. "Jack, no—not this time. I recognized parts of his ethereal light patterns. Because they were familiar."

He frowned, nodding for her to continue.

"Jack, he's no ordinary half demon half angel."

Jack glanced up at the judgment dais and then leaned closer to her. "Then what exactly is he?"

"Lord Kushiel, please begin," said Pravuil.

Kushiel's wings extended around his shoulders as his withering gaze swept across Azrael, Talia, and finally, Jack. And then it shot across to Lucifer.

"Heaven calls Lucifer to the stand."

"Tal?" he whispered, his gaze shifting from Lord Kushiel to Lucifer.

"Jack, he's the Beast."

"The what?" he whispered. "Like the fairy tale? Beauty and the Beast?"

Talia vehemently shook her head no. "No, Jack…he's THE beast," she said with a hiss. "The beast of prophecy."

Hiding among angels. That meant Samael's plan was as dire as she'd feared. He *was* triggering the Seventh Flight of angels. And Armageddon. But she recognized both the demonic shadows and the angelic light within Raum. Wound so tight that she couldn't assess the strength of either.

Samael's archangel light coursed through this Nephion. Alongside the archdemoness' shadows.

Zanth.

"What does that mean?" Jack demanded, eyes wide.

"It means that we need to take Raum into custody. Immediately." She stared at Jack who looked stricken. "Jack, he's influencing Kushiel."

"Silence in the courtroom!" Pravuil shouted. "Don't make me come down there. Cherubim, bring the defendant before the dais."

"Pravuil," she called out in a piercing angel note that only the Scribe would hear. "You need to hear me. Now!"

The four cherubim forced Lucifer up and out of his chair. With those chains clanging, he hobbled between the four cherubim guard to the table below the judgment dais. He walked up the three or four steps and stood behind the table, staring up at the Maker for several long moments. Until his arrogant stare shifted to Lord Kushiel. For several unblinking moments.

"Talia? What is important enough for me to interrupt Lucifer's testimony?" Pravuil's baritone angel notes filled her head. Sounding incredulous.

"Armageddon," she sang out.

"Sorry, Talia," Pravuil's voice filled her head again. "Can't halt these proceedings. Not even for Armageddon."

"How about for the Beast?"

CHAPTER 16

Pravuil went deathly silent, looking surly, distracted, and tense as Kushiel spoke, beginning the trial as Talia waited for God's Scribe to respond.

"Let the record show that, based on previous witnesses and testimonies," said Kushiel in a matter-of-fact tone from the judgment dais above the courtroom. "Lucifer initiated a premeditated plan to destroy the Earth and then Heaven."

"Objection."

Lucifer's gaze was steely. Sharp. Those glass-blue eyes were piercing. He looked annoyed. And he gave no ground to Lord Kushiel.

"Objection?" Lord Kushiel said, sounding incredulous as he glared at Lucifer.

"Yes, Archangel of Wrath," said Lucifer, still staring through Kushiel as he shifted his legs in front of him, chains rattling. "I object. Yes, it's true. I premeditated a Phoenix Shift, attempted two takeovers of Heaven, and attempted to murder my father. But not to destroy Earth and Heaven." He looked indignant. "Heaven, despite what you might believe, is still my home. And those wingless…children below are necessary. They've taught me a lot during my exile—in spite of my resistance and my…attitude."

Jack turned to Talia, looking shocked as he mouthed the words, *wingless children.*

Talia shrugged. She'd never heard Lucifer speak this way before. Ever.

"When has he ever had that attitude toward humans?" Jack whispered, eyes wide. "It's always been flying rats."

Talia shook her head. "Never, Jack."

She focused her omnificence power on Lucifer, studying the color and radiance of his angelic light. Was he lying to the room, using his immense powers to cover it? As the colors and patterns emerged, she compared them to Raum's angelic light.

Raum's angelic light looked familiar, the colors, the brightness, but from memory, only two angels' core lights were a close match to what she had seen and felt. Were they a match to Lucifer's light? Was he the father of this Nephion?

Had he slept with Zanth to create his last and deadliest attack on humanity and the Maker? Creating the beast who would lead the dark armies at Armageddon? Lucifer's last little surprise attack?

He'd begun the apocalypse. Why not Armageddon, too? But no, that had been Samael's doing, not Lucifer's.

Using omnificence, Talia peered closer at Lucifer's light as she forced the rest of the overwhelming angel lights in the room to dim. She focused on Lucifer's light until the colors stood out.

To her surprise, they had changed. And so had their radiance. Softer but richer burgundies. Pale deep golds became buttery yellows. Charcoals became silvery streaks, like trout scales in a sunny lake. Damp, muted midnight blues became denim, cyan, and chambray. Lighter. More fragile. Brighter. Colors she'd never seen in his angel light before.

"Yes, I know," said Lucifer, his gaze shifting to the Maker. "That's never been my attitude toward humans. But some of them have actually taught me their value. That angels have as much to learn from them as they have to learn from us." His gaze shot back to Kushiel. "And yes, I know, too little too late. But you will detect no malice or untruth in my words. Not only have I begun to see their value, but I've also begun to actually like some of them."

A cacophony of surprised whispers reverberated through the gallery.

Lucifer sighed, looking bored at the surprised responses as he turned and faced the gallery.

"Oh, stop. If any of you self-righteous drones were honest with yourselves, you'd admit that most of you despise humans. And see yourselves as better somehow." His look of deadly disdain frightened the gallery into silence. "Here's a newsflash, featherbrains…you're not."

He held up a shackled hand, pointing toward the Maker. "Want proof? Look upon your Maker who appears to you this day in human form. Do you think it's because my father felt like wearing a meatsuit today instead of all his celestial light? Because it looked better with the blue robes than the red ones?"

Slowly, the ripples of voices and angel notes began again in the gallery.

"Clue that into you swollen, pretentious airheads and let that settle a moment. Father created those humans in his own image. They are his children and his love for them is infinite. He suffers their heartbreaks with much more patience than he ever did ours and do you know why?"

Lucifer's silence grew and so did the volume of the murmurs drifting through the gallery, clogged full of angels, archangels, and Watchers now, all pushing toward the front to get a good luck at the King of Hell. To hear him speak.

"No…of course you don't."

He held out his arms, chains rattling.

"Because we know better!"

The murmurs grew into nervous protests.

"Yes, that's right my winged neanderthals. We. Know. Better. We carry knowledge from the Beginning. From the Word. The Light. And from millennia as soldiers. Their lives are like fireworks. A short trail of light, a burst of sparks, and then a spindly afterglow of colors that quickly goes dark. And then, if they weren't absolute knobs about it, their souls ascend. To learn from us. Their teachers. Not their servants. Because we, too were created in the Maker's image. It's time that every single angel got this through their thick, stupid heads. Mine especially."

Voices grew louder until shouting erupted from the gallery.

"Order!" Pravuil shouted.

But the gallery seemed in an angry panic.

"Blast it, I said order! Shut your prayer holes and listen before *your* turn in front of this dais comes up." He pointed. "And if you keep that up, it's going to be soon."

The room went quiet.

"Well said, Scribe," said Lucifer, smiling. "Yes. This is me, Lucifer, the King of Hell. The Fallen. The Prince of Darkness. Saying these things. Learn from my destructive ways. My arrogance. My insolence. Before you, too, face the end of your existence. Your last spindly little trail of afterglow. Maybe, if you'd just bloody listen, you'll recognize their worth before it's too late to turn back?"

Then he turned back toward the dais.

Lord Kushiel looked stunned silent.

And the Maker's face glimmered with a dozen emotions as they stared down at Lucifer.

Lucifer's eyes turned glassy, his mouth twitching as he finally looked away.

Talia saw the journey he'd taken to understand and then mean those words that he'd just shouted at the gallery, silencing the entire tribunal with them.

Jack looked stunned as he stared at Lucifer. Like the Maker, a dozen emotions tracked across his face, flickered in those pale green eyes.

"So, Lord Kushiel, back to your original statement," said Lucifer, his glass blue gaze razor sharp. "Yes, I object. And let your record show that I never premeditated a plan to destroy the Creation or Heaven. Only myself when I chose to try and kill my father. Let the record show that yes, I did my absolute bloody best to try and drag every last human soul down to Hell to share in my own exile and misery. Because I wanted to show my father that he was wrong about these children that he'd chosen over his firstborn. I never dreamed that they would show me my own true face."

Lord Kushiel seemed at a loss. Lucifer had completely taken charge of the tribunal. And the Archangel of Wrath made no move to take back control.

"There," said Lucifer with a quick bow his head. "You have my confession. Can we end this thing? Get this Wrath bit over with. I tire of the wait. End it already." He bowed his head. "I know what I've done and what I've earned," he said in a quiet, humble voice. "Just...be merciful," he said, the slightest quiver in his voice. "Even though I don't deserve a quick end, end it."

Lord Kushiel stared at Lucifer for several unnerving moments until finally, he turned toward Pravuil.

"Scribe," he said, sounding uncertain about how to proceed.

Like he'd expected to rain down Heavenly Wrath on Lucifer until he'd forced a confession out of the Prince of Darkness. But Lucifer had just cut right through the whole spectacle. And laid out his confession. After first warning the other angels about their own arrogance and condescension.

Talia was still as stunned as Jack at Lucifer's testimony.

Pravuil's gaze narrowed as he studied Lucifer with a pensive expression. Like he was trying to detect any malice or lies. Or any tricks. Things that Lucifer was famous for.

Finally, his gaze fell onto the Maker. Slowly, the Maker's human form slipped away, becoming the column of celestial light that they had displayed on the first day of the tribunal. The lights shifted and changed as Pravuil's gruff baritone angel notes echoed at the front of the chamber.

Several long moments dragged by until Pravuil turned back to the chamber.

"The Maker has requested that testimony still be presented."

Lucifer winced as the cherubim led him away from the judgment dais and back to his seat.

Lord Kushiel seemed to recover in the face of the tribunal returning to its natural structure.

"Lord Kushiel," said Pravuil. "The Maker asks that you assemble your witnesses and call them before the dais. After these witnesses have appeared, a vote will be taken and judgment made."

"Yes, Scribe," said the Archangel of Wrath. "I request a brief recess to gather the witnesses."

"Granted. All right, angels. Clear the chamber."

"Pravuil!" Talia called out in the sharpest angel note she could summon as the cherubim escorted Lucifer from the chamber. "Did you hear me? I said the beast."

Jack rose from his chair as Azrael closed ranks, shuffling him in close to her.

"Stay close," Azrael whispered. "Something's not right. I feel it."

Talia wondered if Azrael was sensing Raum's presence. Or did he feel her shock over discovering the Nephion's presence here in Heaven? Knowing that Raum was much more than a hybrid angel and demon.

And she had to get word to Pravuil. Quickly. Before something terrible happened.

She was certain that Raum was the beast. And she was certain that he was controlling Kushiel. She also knew that his demon half had been birthed by Zanth. But she had no evidence to put with these chilling facts.

"That's only the surface, Azrael," she whispered.

Finally, Pravuil appeared in front of her.

"Talia, beast or not, this is really not a good time," Pravuil said in an anxious voice as he glanced from Azrael to Jack and then Talia.

"Pravuil, you need to hear me. Now."

"Grab hold of my robes," he said.

She grabbed his crystalline white sleeve with both hands. Pravuil reached out and grabbed Jack and Azrael by the arm and in a flash of light, they blinked out of the courtroom.

Another blink.

Out the Cloud Chamber portal.

Another blink.

Into the Archive spire. Into Pravuil's private, well-warded workroom that had no windows. Only a warded portal inside the white-walled white stone room at the top of the Archive spire. It smelled clean like rain and electric like ozone. Only a rectangular white table stood in the center of the empty room.

"Uh, Tal…" Jack said, looking confused as Azrael frowned and spread his wings until he hovered in the space. "What's going on?"

"Yes, Talia," said Azrael. "Something's wrong. I feel it."

She laid her hand against Jack's face and gave it a quick caress as she turned to Pravuil.

"Your feeling is correct, Azrael," she said and turned her gaze to Pravuil. "I know we don't have much time, so listen carefully."

Jack just shrugged. "This is about the Nephion, right?"

Azrael's mouth gaped. "What Nephion, Jack?"

Jack just gestured at Talia.

"Remember the angel of death in the square, Azrael," she began.

Already, Pravuil looked impatient.

"The lone survivor of those attacks on the couriers?" said Azrael, charcoal grey eyes flashing with unease. "When the key to the Lake of Fire was stolen."

Travail's face turned ward-white. "The key to that cavern…was stolen?"

Talia nodded. "That angel was in the courtroom today. As Kushiel's courier."

Azrael frowned. "Wait. I saw that angel. But that was Watcher. This surviving angel was an angel of death. Caleal, right?"

She nodded. "This courier angel was called Raum, but his light signature is identical to Caleal's light signature. Their eyes are different colors, Azrael. And in the courtroom, he grabbed hold of Lord Kushiel's wrist, releasing shadows that seeped into the archangel's left hand."

Pravuil's eyes got wide. "Shadows?"

"He's been rubbing that hand since he got here," said Jack.

"Especially right before he has a meltdown. Like when he launched all his Heavenly Wrath at me in the Lake of Fire cavern."

"Lake of Fire? Heavenly Wrath!" Pravuil's face turned pale. "Why wasn't I informed that key had gone missing?"

Talia shook her head. "Kushiel knew it had been stolen and his three couriers who each carried a piece, were murdered. He should have told you, Pravuil. I sent word to you, too."

"Well, I never got these messages." Pravuil stared past her now at the white wards surrounding the room. "Since Kushiel's chosen to keep these details to himself, that can only mean that Kushiel's been compromised by this strange angel and he's being controlled somehow."

"Gotta be a Linda Blair move," said Jack.

Pravuil glared at him. "Jack, I don't have time to decipher your strange code!"

"Possession, Scribe," Jack said quickly. "Don't you people study human culture? This Raum dude is half demon half angel, remember?"

For a moment, Jack's response broke the Scribe as he rubbed his face, looking unnerved now.

"And you believe this thing is the beast, Talia?" Pravuil replied in a subdued tone.

Azrael whirled around, nearly falling out of the air. "What? THE beast? From prophecy? Now?" He gripped Pravuil's sleeve. "Scribe, how? The Seventh Flight hasn't even flown from Heaven yet. How can we be at Armageddon's door without that Seventh Flight taking to Earth's skies?"

"Wait a damned minute!" Jack shouted. "Are you sure that flight's not going to drop the worst payload of all on Earth? Death? Worse than the other six combined?"

"Yes, Jack," said Talia. "We interrupted the apocalypse's progression, but we disarmed all seven payloads. So, that last event— the Seventh Flight—was…paused. Waiting for the beast of prophecy to rise and set the Seventh Flight in motion. Starting Armageddon."

Jack frowned. "Paused it…I think I'm gonna hurl. How can we just jump from apocalypse to Armageddon? Aren't there any other events that fall between these two catastrophes? Another *a* word? Oh, yeah… there is." He sighed. "Antichrist. Dude, I'm cooked. And Armageddon was not on this year's bingo card."

"Only the beast can bring on Armageddon, Jack," said Azrael, his gaze dire as he fixed Pravuil with an uneasy stare.

"Great!" said Jack, slapping his hands against his sides. "Somebody's been dragging us around by the leash, pushing this tribunal into motion, pushing Kushiel to a quick execution for Lucifer. Obliterating Talia and me to get our rare angel powers after getting Luci out of the way."

Talia nodded as she moved beside Jack and slid her arm around his waist.

"Paving the way for the beast to trigger Armageddon," said Talia. "With Abaddon trapped at the Gates of Hell, trying to close them, hordes of demons are now free and roaming the Earth. Heaven is still down two seraph, two sets of rare angel powers, and the Lightbringer. With those odds, it's an easy win for the beast because Heaven already lost so many angels during the Sixth Flight."

Azrael's eyes narrowed. "And the only coward I know who would do his best to eliminate anyone more powerful and then trigger Armageddon…is Archangel Samael."

"It's the only way that asshalo can win, Azrael," said Jack. "Gotta clear the board of anyone even remotely strong enough to shut down his pathetic army."

"Coward," Azrael said with a growl.

"That's why he's possessed Kushiel," said Jack. "That's his last resort if things don't go his way in the Cloud Chamber."

"Exactly, Jack," said Talia. "Somehow, Kushiel let that demon in. Probably doesn't even realize it yet."

Pravuil looked stricken as he spread his wings and blinked around the room.

"That archangel for pacing, Scribe?" Jack asked.

"Fraid so, Jack," said the Scribe, a hand to his chin, wings shifting as he moved back and forth behind the table. "But I'm afraid Samael's had Lord Kushiel commandeered to smite you and Talia, Jack. If Samael can't get to your power, he means to destroy it. Maybe that's through Kushiel and maybe it's through that courier angel? This beast. Either way, we've got to be on watch for any moves toward you and Talia."

"I'll cast wards at the counsel and witness tables and keep them up until the tribunal recesses again," said Talia.

"So, you don't think Samael's trying to spring Lucifer?" Jack asked.

"Definitely not," said Pravuil, blinking back across the room to face Jack. "Not after hearing Lucifer's objection. It's obvious that Lucifer would never help Samael now. So, Samael just needs him to be obliterated and out of his way. So he can try and harvest his powers."

"But who birthed the Nephion?" Azrael demanded, anger flushing his face, his red-gold halo beginning to spin faster.

Talia smashed her eyes closed as Jack gripped her hand.

"About that…" said Jack.

Azrael whirled around, grabbing Jack's arm. "Jack, what do you know? I feel it. Tell me."

He sighed. "From my seraphim powers, I can see dark and shadows that the demons possess. Like angels see angelic light signatures." He winced and Talia saw a flash of guilt in those green eyes.

Pravuil gritted his teeth, blinking in front of Jack.

"Blast it, Jack! Talk!" Pravuil demanded. "We're running out of time here."

"Zanth gave birth to this Nephion," he said. "The archdemoness. I'm certain of it."

Azrael's eyes filled with rage as he pointed a finger at Jack. "The archdemon you let go from purgatory!"

"Yeah, Azrael," he said in a defeated voice. "Raum's demonic half belongs to Zanth, but I'd bet my life that she didn't do so willingly."

"You have bet your life on this, Jack," said Azrael, his tone dark. "Kushiel may hold you responsible when he learns that you let an archdemoness escape."

"Stop it!" Talia shouted, sliding in front of Jack. "No one in this tribunal is going to touch my husband." She glared at Pravuil. "And that includes Lord Kushiel."

Pravuil's hands were on his hips, his gold eyes looking stern.

"I can't hide this, Talia," said Pravuil. "Not from Kushiel and not from the Maker."

"We weren't trying to hide it," she snapped. "And we will talk to Zanth. After the tribunal. But right now, we don't have any answers."

Talia needed to know Zanth's side of this story.

"Talia's right," Azrael said with a sigh, wings unfurling around his shoulders. "We'll deal with this Nephion, this beast, but it won't be now and it won't be at this tribunal."

"For now, I will forget that I know any of this," said Pravuil as he folded his arms against his chest. "For now, we get through the witnesses and then deal with the Nephion."

"Do you know who Kushiel's calling?" Azrael asked, staring at Pravuil.

"First witness is Rachel Daniels. Then Berith. And then you and then Jack. Better be thinking about how you're going to answer Kushiel's questions." Pravuil held up his hands. "And don't mention a word about Zanth or this Nephion!"

"To the Archangel of Wrath? Are you kidding me, Pravuil? I don't even want to mention my grocery list to this dude."

At last, Pravuil's intense, the-sky-is-falling mood lightened along with his expression at Jack's response.

"Casey! Explain to me why you bought brand name puffed rice cereal!" Jack said, mimicking Kushiel's speech pattern. "And the expensive cheese from Ralph's? Where *is* the spray cheese, Casey?"

For a moment, Jack had Pravuil and Azrael laughing. Until the call from High House rippled across the lower Heavens. A melodic series of five notes, calling the tribunal back in session. Notes too high for Jack to hear.

"Okay, who's singing the angel notes I can't hear?" he asked, crossing his arms. "You're all talking about me, aren't you? Making fun of the human, aren't you?"

Azrael patted him on the back. "The signal calling the tribunal back into session just went out across Heaven. Too high for you to hear. Sorry, Jack."

"Jack," said Pravuil, taking Jack by the shoulders. "Just promise me not to agitate Kushiel on the stand. I'm going to consult with Seraphina and the Maker about Kushiel being compromised. It probably won't change the outcome of the tribunal, but we have to be ready to stop him from using his Heavenly Wrath outside this trial. Only Seraphina and the Maker can do that. Or order him to use his Wrath."

"I can hold it back," said Jack, "but not long."

"Good to know, Jack," said Pravuil. "For now, don't bring up this Nephion until I've consulted with Seraphina and the Maker."

"You have my word," said Jack.

"And mine, Pravuil," Talia replied.

Jack pulled her into a tight hug and kissed her in a slow, hot kiss that made her weak in the knees.

"No matter what happens, Mrs. Casey," he said in a subdued voice. "I love you. Now until forever."

She stroked his hair and then pressed another quick kiss to his lips. "I love you, Jack. Forever my Prince Charming. Let's go fight for our happily ever after. Again."

Azrael hurried out of the warded portal with Pravuil.

Jack entwined his fingers in Talia's and together, she and Jack blinked through the Archive spire wards. Into the warm afternoon air. Blinking across the sky toward the High House spire.

Just ahead, two glittering white lights shimmered in the Parrish blue sky. The lights belonged to Azrael and Pravuil who flew along the warm air currents ahead of them. Turning in a graceful arc upward toward the gold dome, they blinked to it and slipped through the warded portal into the Cloud Chamber.

Arm in arm, Talia and Jack followed.

CHAPTER 17

BY THE TIME TALIA AND JACK RETURNED TO THE LONG CLOUD Chamber gallery, more and more angels had crowded into both sides, wings in motion, halos bright, and the angel notes deafening.

Watchers, archivists, angels of death, archangels, and even angels from the Heavenly forge, faces smudged with ash, halos gleaming like embers, filled both sides of the gallery. Others spilled into the aisle that led from the portal all the way to the witness stand where the judgment dais floated above it.

Already, the air felt charged. Electric. Ready to ignite, the smell of ozone rising above the soothing honeysuckle and jasmine scents warmed by the seven lit braziers.

Wings in motion, a tangle of white robes that faded across the crowd to dark charcoal, the angels packed close, hovering, floating, bobbing in the soft air currents that circled through the huge room, halos a haze of soft white light. The crush of the crowd pushed toward the front of the gallery, rising, sinking, maneuvering for a glimpse of Lucifer versus Lord Kushiel, two of Heaven's most intimidating angels.

Most of these angels in the gallery had never been in the same room with the enigmatic Archangel of Wrath. And they had only heard stories about Lucifer until the night he showed up in the meadows behind Eolowen, testing out his new army. A push for control that ended with Lucifer in chains, facing the end of his existence. For every angel in Heaven, this was the trial of the millennia.

They pushed and shoved, trying to get a glimpse of the dark angel of wrath with his lean, shadowy features, windblown white hair, calm and sometimes explosive manner, and those long, red-tipped wings.

But most wanted to push past Kushiel, to say that they had glimpsed the infamous fallen angel, Creation's first angel, in all his dark lord glory. Full, shiny black wings and blood red halo. Charm and deadly manipulation wrapped into the façade of the most beautiful angel the Maker had ever created. One possessing all the powers of a firstborn angel. Archangel? Seraph? No one was really sure except that there was only one. Lucifer Morning Star. The King of Hell. The Lightbringer.

The melodies and harmonies had become noise as angels sang out in loud conversations about watching Lord Kushiel face off with Lucifer one last time. And they were eager to hear witnesses tell more stories, things they had only heard about in whispers. Or read about in the Archive.

Talia kept a tight grip on Jack as she flew up and over the crowd, blinking with him across the gallery to the witness table in front of the courtroom. Azrael hovered above the table's side, one hand pressed against his chin, his distant charcoal eyes lost in thought.

He barely responded when she and Jack landed beside him. Jack glanced across the chamber. Where Lucifer sat, angry, distant, resigned. He looked as lost in thought as Azrael and Talia couldn't help but wonder what was going through his head. His gaze was on the dais. On the Maker, she realized.

His expression was wistful, far, far away from this chamber. Like he was lost in the magic of those early days of the Creation. Before humans. Before the Garden. Before those first feelings of abandonment had begun to fester. Before he'd fallen and come close to deceiving all of the Maker's Chosen. And usurping Heaven.

All of the judges were present on the dais, including Kushiel who kept referring to some texts that floated around him in a slow-moving circle. As he looked from book to book, his shaggy white hair bunched around the shoulders of his grey robes, he rubbed the top of his left hand as it occasionally twitched. Like he was trying to lift his arm.

Talia wanted to rush up and grab hold of Kushiel's hand, pull up his robe sleeve, and examine the top of his hand. And where Raum had gripped the archangel's wrist.

Had the beast truly possessed the Archangel of Wrath?

She knew very little about Kushiel's Wrath powers—much less this beast or its powers. This Nephion...what powers did it possess? Did Raum have any sort of rare angel powers? Like Vassago had, the formerly blind fallen but redeemed angel with a rare gift of forced possession. Did the beast have archdemoness dark powers, too—like Zanth? The most formidable combination of dark and light powers in Heaven?

Only Vassago could take over someone's body without their consent, but Talia knew almost nothing about the beast. She hoped that Pravuil did, so they could figure out how to free Kushiel from whatever had compromised him.

And she had to be prepared to stop any sudden action inside this courtroom. One was coming. She felt it in the core of her angelic light. Why else would someone possess the Archangel of Wrath while he was prosecuting the deadliest angel in Creation?

She knew how unstoppable Zanth had been. And depending on the father of this Nephion, this beast's angel powers could be equally as strong. Strong enough to control the Archangel of Wrath and force him to do his bidding inside this courtroom.

But what?

As she glanced from Lucifer to Kushiel, she couldn't help but feel a chill against her heart.

Was Lucifer deceiving them all with his sudden humility and resignation to his fate, knowing that his offspring, this Nephion, was his last gift to Creation and the Maker. An unstoppable beast from prophecy who possessed rare demonic powers and those of the most powerful angel in Creation.

About to free his father and lay waste to humanity and Heaven?

The thought terrified her.

Somehow, she had to figure out who had fathered Raum—or whatever his true name was. And whether Heaven had enough power to stop him before Armageddon. But even her omnificence hadn't been able to identify the light signatures in Raum's angelic heritage. They were too similar. But she knew the signatures either belonged to Lucifer or Samael.

Had that been part of the plan? Anticipating hers and Jack's rare powers and finding ways to circumvent them?

"Gallery, come to order!" Pravuil's gruff voice filled the chamber and managed to capture the attention of the massive crowd of angelic gawkers pressed into the space so tight that none of them could fully extend their wings.

Their halos were like a thousand flashlights dancing through the chamber, the braziers' flickers making them almost strobe. The scents of fragrant jasmine and honeysuckle that emanated through the space, warmed by the braziers, drifted in a soft calming haze.

But it wasn't enough to calm the electric tension as the scent of ozone began to rise.

"I said shut up back there or you'll be sent outside to the platforms to watch the rest of this trial!"

Pravuil's demeanor had gotten even surlier than it had been in the Archive. And Kushiel seemed even more hyper-focused and overstrung. She worried that the smallest thing would set him off. She expected another meltdown, but she worried that he would fling Heavenly Wrath at a witness. She sighed. Like Jack.

Was that by Raum's design? Or whoever stood in the shadows behind him? But she felt it in her heart that a much deadlier action was coming.

And she didn't know what—or how to stop it.

Sidriel seemed uneasy, her gaze darting expectantly around the chamber. Sarathiel looked impatient, ready to end this tribunal.

Heaven didn't let such events drag on like they did on Earth. They moved quickly and came to a vote and verdict at lightning speed. And Lucifer's tribunal would be no different.

Today, the Maker was back in human form, in that same androgynous human appearance that Lucifer seemed to recognize. Seated in the center of the judgment dais, the Maker looked peaceful, but their features looked drawn. Almost melancholy.

Even across the courtroom, Talia felt the Maker's apprehension hanging over the entire proceeding. She had no idea what emotions the Maker was experiencing and did not presume to know, but Lucifer's emotions hung on the ragged black sleeves of his general's coat. Remorse was heavy in his face and hints of grief gleamed in his glassy blue eyes.

"All right, order in the gallery! In the courtroom! Lord Kushiel, please call your first witness," Pravuil's gruff baritone voice filled the chamber. "And gallery...keep it civil or I'll boot the lot of you out that portal into blue skies. Don't try me today."

Seraphina hovered at the edge of the platform, her brilliant seraphim light burning at a comfortable distance. Talia felt her anxiousness as the seraph hung close.

Lord Kushiel approached the edge of the dais, red-tipped wings in a slow, regular motion as he hovered there, looking out on the gallery. And the courtroom.

"I call human and former damned soul, Rachel Daniels to the stand."

Jack bristled, his eyes narrowing. "Great. Speaking of meltdowns."

Talia frowned. She'd missed a lot on the set of the show, things Jack hadn't talked about. Like meltdowns.

"What sort of meltdowns?" Talia asked as the sharp, anxious tick of high heels echoed through the chamber.

"Not quite Kushiel level," said Jack. "But close."

Murmurs thrummed through the gallery as two cherubim led Rachel through the gallery to the witness table below the judgment dais. Her auburn hair hung in ringlets at her shoulders as she walked up the steps. She wore that heavy palette of smoky grey eyeshadow around her bright blue eyes. Her milk-pale skin was freckled, a deep red lipstick covering her full lips.

To Talia's surprise, she wore a white double-breasted blazer dress cut just above the knee. Not at her upper thighs. It looked stylish but a little frumpy for Rachel Daniels.

She wore a pair of sensible white pumps, reasonable height. With those red soles that Jack hated. But for Rachel Daniels, this was a conservative outfit. She carried a flat white purse in her hand and she held it against her stomach as she paused at the witness table. A chair stood behind the table and Rachel pulled it out and sat down as Lord Kushiel slowly descended from the dais and landed beside her.

Talia had to remind herself that Rachel and Jack had finally made their peace and that she wasn't out to get him anymore. Talia also had to remind herself that Rachel had been in Hell after her contract with Lucifer was up. But Jack's forgiveness had been a loophole in that contract that got it rescinded. And released her from Hell.

Rachel knew Lucifer well. She'd been doing his bidding for a long time—she and Lare Dumont—at Lucifer's Malibu beach house. Talia had been there with Jack as he began to remember some horrible, broken memories. She had never heard the full story, mostly because Jack didn't know it and it wasn't even clear in his Book of Life and Death. But she shuddered, knowing some of that might come out now. And blindside Jack.

"Rachel Daniels," said Lord Kushiel, hands behind his back as he paced in front of the witness table. "I am Lord Kushiel, Archangel of Wrath. Please tell us about your unique relationship with Lucifer. And I don't have to remind you that you are among angels. Who know when you're lying."

Rachel's blue eyes darkened, her red, glistening mouth pursing as she studied Kushiel beneath long lashes and hooded, shadowed eyelids. Talia didn't know if Rachel had ever met Lord Kushiel, but she acted unaffected by his forbidding demeanor.

Why did humans always think they were invincible?

"When I'm lying?" said Rachel.

"Yes," said Kushiel.

"I will be sure to alert you before I begin any lie. Lord Kushiel."

One corner of Jack's mouth lifted in a smirk. He liked her response and that made Talia feel uncomfortable. Rachel was still Jack's ex-girlfriend and even now, Talia couldn't help but feel a little jealous at times.

Even though he'd been her husband for almost a year now.

"Tell me, Miss Daniels," said Kushiel, his dark, rusty hawkish gaze intense, darkening at Rachel's statement. "Are all humans so flippant and facetious?"

Rachel smiled like a camera had moved in for a closeup. "Only the ones accused of lying by angels they've just met. I resent that you assume I'm lying."

Jack was smiling. And Talia had to admit…she didn't like it.

Lord Kushiel nodded. "Point taken, Miss Daniels. Forgive me for assuming that you are lying. Now, could you please tell us about your relationship and business arrangement with Lucifer."

Rachel nodded and in that smoky alto voice, she began her performance. With Rachel Daniels, reciting a grocery list was a performance.

"I came to Hollywood when I was nineteen," she began. "Breaking in as an actress is difficult. And I quickly learned that only certain types got certain parts. So, I set out to gain that look. Which required plastic surgery. Hair weaves. Color. Highlights. Acrylic nails. Pilates. Diets—acting classes." She sighed. "I was working two jobs, going to every casting call I could get. But I just couldn't get a chance at even one of those big roles. That's when I heard about this British influencer out in Malibu. Who made actors into stars. At a steep cost. His name was Lucifer. At the time, I thought it was a stage name."

Lord Kushiel rubbed the top of his left hand with his thumb as he continued to pace around Rachel. Talia didn't know if Rachel was anxious or nervous because she gave nothing away seated at that table. But Talia felt queasy every time Kushiel rubbed the top of his hand, arm twitching a little, and she feared that a demon was taking charge of him—and his Heavenly Wrath. Or someone in Hell was controlling his movements. His questions. Or outright possessing him.

"So, you went to see this influencer called Lucifer? Out in Malibu, was it? A beach house?"

A smile brightened Rachel's face, her nose scrunching a little. "Well, calling it a beach house is an understatement. It was a compound. Isolated. Right on the beach. With several bedrooms that were suites. Like a hotel. He was polite, charming, and magnetic and I found myself drawn to him as he told me exactly what he could do for me. After he'd explained how he worked and what would be expected of me, he laid out the contract."

"An actual contract?" Kushiel asked, eyebrow raised.

"Yes, a long, complex contract that made my head spin. Then he looked me in the eye and told me exactly who he was."

"And who was that, Miss Daniels?"

"His eyes began to glow red and he told me he was the King of Hell. He said right up front that if I signed his contract, my soul would belong to him after ten years. In Hell."

Kushiel looked surprised and intrigued.

"And you signed it?"

She nodded. "That was the price for fame and money in Hollywood, Lord Kushiel. I would have sold my soul for far worse if I'd signed with another agent. Who was far less honest than Lucifer. He made no bones about what I was signing. He even told me that after ten years, he would give me the opportunity to bring him souls in exchange for contract extensions." Sighing, she bowed her head. "And that's where Lare Dumont and I began our little…side hustle."

Talia felt Jack stiffen beside her.

Kushiel didn't look affected, only surprised as he continued his slow but rhythmic pacing around the table.

"So, every year, you had to bring Lucifer one soul or end up in Hell?"

She shook her head, her voice softening. "Four souls a year for each of us. And after Lare and I became huge Hollywood stars, gathering them became child's play. A private, exclusive Malibu party, little promises of help, a little coke, some sex, and some success—and bingo! Kept Lare and I out of Hell for a very long time."

Murmurs began in the gallery.

Talia glanced over at Lucifer. He looked bored. Uninterested. Distracted. Jack, however, white-knuckled the arms of his chair, his eyes a little haunted, his lips dry as he swallowed a breath and listened to Rachel's testimony like he had never heard these stories before.

And maybe he hadn't heard all of it in such objective, distant terms. She'd literally drugged Jack's soft drinks at these parties. He hadn't drunk back then much less done drugs after watching his father binge on both since he was a small child.

"So, you collected souls for Lucifer," Kushiel stated the fact.

"For years. Lare Dumont and I both did."

Kushiel looked up from his pacing, across the room at Jack, and then turned back to Rachel.

"Tell me about Jack Casey, Miss Daniels. Did Lucifer order you to take his soul?"

Rachel frowned. "Jack? No. I'm the one who brought him to his first party."

"Was he a struggling actor?"

"Jack?" Rachel's laugh was big. "No. Jack was Hollywood's darling. Fresh-faced, scorching hot knockout who walked in barefoot to an open call for the hottest show on television. Wearing torn, faded Levi's and an old grey Purdue T-shirt. Casting director took one look at him and lost her mind. Hired him on the spot."

Kushiel leaned against the table, his gaze piercing. "I feel quite a bit of jealousy and anger in your voice, Miss Daniels. Please explain."

"Nineteen-year-old kid. Lands the hottest job in Hollywood. Every television actor in L.A. wanted that role. And unknown, lucky-as-hell Jack Casey just walks in and gets it." Rachel glared at Kushiel. "And you bet that was unfair! I was twenty-five years old by then. You name it and I had to do it to make it in Hollywood. To get the lead on that show. And that included lots of plastic surgery and selling my soul. But not Jack Casey. No! He just walks in the door, smirks for the cameras, and women and casting directors just fall at his feet."

Jack sighed. "It wasn't like that," he whispered.

Talia knew how hard he'd worked before that. She'd read his Book of Life and Death. He'd worked three jobs for over a year to make rent every month. He ate rice and ramen for most of his meals. He took any acting job offered to him, starting in commercials, guest spots, and one-off characters. She rubbed his shoulders.

"Any angel can see your Book and know how hard you worked. She isn't lying. That's what she believes is the truth, Jack, and that will never change."

Jack grumbled, folding his arms against his chest.

"So, Jack was yours and this Lare Dumont's costar?" Kushiel asked, still polite and still driving his questions toward something that Talia couldn't anticipate yet.

"Yep. Our brand-new costar. Who was hogging all the attention. And the spotlight."

Jack bit his lip, those green eyes sizzling with anger. "I hogged nothing. I showed up and did my job. Did everything they asked me to do."

Talia kept rubbing his shoulders until she felt his muscles relax a little.

"So, what happened next, Miss Daniels?"

"Jack became the next soul on our harvest list," said Rachel. "But that's where things got complicated. Because I wanted him. Like I'd never wanted anyone."

Kushiel raised an eyebrow. "You were in love with him?"

She nodded, bowing her head. "But I belonged to Lare who hated Jack. And no matter what I did, I knew I could never have Jack. Because of Lare and those contracts I'd signed. So, he became our next soul to take for Lucifer."

For several moments, Kushiel leaned against the table, deep in thought. Until finally, he returned to pacing, his expression focused and distant.

"So, what did you do, Miss Daniels?"

"We invited him to Malibu. To the party. Where I tried to get him hooked on coke. But he didn't drink. He didn't smoke. And he definitely didn't snort. Lucifer told me to leave him alone, but I was determined. So, I kept at Jack. He just wouldn't take the bait. Lucifer even ordered me to stop again, but I knew I could bring him around. I just needed more time."

Kushiel whirled around, grimacing. "Wait a moment. Lucifer told you twice to stop tempting Jack Casey, but you continued?"

She nodded. "Several times. I wanted Jack and I knew the only way I could get him was through the drugs. After months of failure, I finally drugged his Coke Zero one night. When he passed out, I took him to one of the suites."

Murmurs grew louder in the gallery.

Lucifer shook his head, running his fingers through his sunlit blond hair. He looked uncomfortable.

"And tell me, Miss Daniels," said Kushiel as he leaned his palms on the table in front of her. "What happened next?"

"Well, I had my way with him, of course."

Jack stiffened.

"You what?"

"Had my way with him. Look, I'm telling you what happened. I'm not proud of what I did and I'm still trying to atone for what I did to poor Jack. You didn't ask any of that. You wanted the story, the facts. Here they are."

Kushiel sighed. "Proceed, Miss Daniels."

"Jack was out cold. So, I undressed him and had my way with him. One of Lucifer's demons joined me. But Lucifer interrupted before... well, before it had its way with Jack."

"Wait—Lucifer interrupted?" Kushiel clarified.

Rachel nodded. "He popped into the room, scolded me about consent—and demons in the bed—and he scooped Jack up and left."

Jack's head snapped up and he stared across the courtroom at Lucifer.

Kushiel blinked across the courtroom to stand in front of Lucifer.

"Lucifer, what happened when you took Jack Casey from that room."

Lucifer's eyes narrowed. "Jack Casey was unconscious. He had not consented to any of that. Much less a bloody demon assaulting him. I picked him up and took him to another suite where he could sleep off whatever she'd roofied him with. Without being molested."

"You rescued him?" Kushiel said.

"Okay, fine. I rescued him. A typical Saturday night in Malibu. Can we get on with this, please?"

Kushiel was insistent. "You rescued Jack Casey from being assaulted. More than once?"

Lucifer rolled his eyes. "Every Saturday like clockwork. Until finally, Jack gave into the cocaine. Not by my doing. But as you can see, Rachel Daniels can be quite…persuasive."

Jack looked confused. "Tal, I never consented. After she forced it down me, I had cravings that I couldn't control. That's when I gave in."

Suddenly, Kushiel was standing in front of Jack.

"Do you object, Jack Casey?"

Jack rubbed his forehead. "For the record, I never consented to the drugs. They got forced into my system enough that I started craving them. And then, I couldn't control the cravings. That's when I gave in."

Kushiel turned toward the judgment dais. "Let the record reflect that Lucifer did not manipulate this human into doing drugs. And apparently, rescued him from some rather…uncomfortable situations on more than one occasion."

Talia appreciated that entry being added into the record, but Jack seemed a little shell-shocked.

"But Lucifer, you said that you—" said Jack as he stood up and faced Lucifer.

Lucifer sighed. "That I had my way with you. More than once. I lied, Jack. Because I knew you had no memory of those nights, only flashes of that demon in the bed, so I wanted you to think I was an asshat. The evil devil who takes advantage of every human he encounters. It put you off center. Made you easier to control. Made you fear me."

Jack wasn't buying that. "No," he said, shaking his head. "That's what you want everyone in this room to believe and I'm not sure why. But that's not why you did it. You did it because it wasn't right."

"All right, fine," said Lucifer in a clipped tone. "It wasn't right. And I didn't like it happening in my beach house. Not even to you, Jack Casey."

Stunned, Jack sat back hard in his chair and stared at Talia, looking more confused than ever.

"Jack, what is it?" Talia asked, laying her hand against his pale face.

"He protected me, Talia?" Jack said, sounding incredulous. "All those months at the beach house. When I'd drink Coke Zeros in the kitchen and wake up naked in the back of someone's Bentley. Or in the Breckenridge suite with flashes of demons hanging over me, the hazy memories of Rachel all over me and I couldn't move. And that whole time, he was keeping Rachel from assaulting me. Until she finally managed to get drugs down me." He looked up at her, almost sad. "Why, Talia? Why would Lucifer bother to protect me like that? I was his target."

"Because, Jack," said Lucifer from across the room. "All's fair in love and war and taking souls. And I only wanted your soul taken fairly. It's like cheating at cards. There's no fun or challenge in that."

Jack looked at Lucifer, studying him for several long moments.

"Bullshit," he said finally.

Lucifer's smile didn't waver. Was Jack right, Talia wondered? Had he done a good deed or two? The King of Hell?

Talia tried to see past Lucifer's expression, but couldn't. Lucifer was a master at keeping people out.

"So, then what happened, Miss Daniels," Kushiel asked, returning to the witness table.

"It took me almost two years of gaslighting, drugs, and setup until I finally brought down Jack Casey." Rachel's voice got shaky. "And he was fired from the show. Leading to his downward spiral that landed him on Heaven's short list for souls to save. And that was the beginning of Lucifer's Phoenix Shift." A tear slipped down her cheek and she hurriedly swiped it away. "And despite everything I did to him, when it really mattered, he forgave me. And that broke my contract with Lucifer. Got me out of Hell. I'll never forget what he did for me. And because of him, I'll teach my own children about the quality of mercy."

"Do you have children, Miss Daniels?"

Jack began to squirm. "Please say no."

Rachel smiled as she turned around toward the table where Jack slouched in the chair, terrified of her answer.

"Not yet," she said. "But come October…"

Jack shot up in his chair, terror burning in his green eyes.

Rachel laughed. "Relax, Jack. It's Eric's. We're getting married in June."

"That's why she's been melting down on set, Jack," said Talia. "She's pregnant."

Glancing up, Jack smirked at Talia. "So, are you saying Kushiel could be preggers, too, Tal? That he put a Nephion bun in the oven?"

Talia couldn't hold back her laugh. She hid it behind her hand and forced it into a congratulatory angel note, even though Rachel couldn't understand it. She shushed Jack and tried not to smile, but couldn't when that sexy smirk lifted one corner of his mouth.

"Do you have anything else to add, Miss Daniels?" Kushiel asked.

She looked past Kushiel. At Lucifer and a distant look touched her blue eyes.

"Just that he was always fair. Never tried to twist those contracts. I can't really speak to any of the things at this trial, but Lucifer's worst moments came from painful memories. And I can't help but wonder what he would have become if he hadn't fallen. If someone had just listened. Everyone needs someone to listen—even the King of Hell."

"Thank you, Miss Daniels," said Kushiel who motioned two cherubim to the table.

Two cherubim escorted Rachel out of the courtroom.

For several long minutes, Kushiel kept his back to the room, scribbling something down on some papers that he spread out across the witness table. When he was done, he put away the quill pen in a pocket in his grey robes, and rolled up the papers, sliding them into a deep robe pocket.

He nodded at Pravuil who leaned against the judgment dais, addressing the room.

"This tribunal now calls Berith the Redeemed to the stand."

More murmurs filled the gallery, much louder this time as two cherubim flew over top of the gallery, into the chamber with Berith between them, her rose gold halo bright and soft against her dove grey wings. She landed behind the witness table and sat down in the chair facing Kushiel.

"Berith, you have known Lucifer from the Beginning, have you not?" Kushiel stated as he turned his intense, hawkish gaze on Berith who looked anxious and a little afraid.

After she'd fallen with Lucifer and after millennia, she had been redeemed and got her halo and wings back, Talia knew that a proceeding like this would be terrifying for her.

Berith, thick white hair pulled back from her face, turned to glance back at Azrael for support. Azrael and Berith were in love, and Talia was grateful that Jack had brought her out of Hell with him when he escaped.

"Yes, Lord Kushiel. Back then, the creation of humans had been a frightening event to many angels."

Kushiel frowned. "Explain."

"Back then, we had direct access to the Maker. There weren't as many angels needed like there are today, so we were a tight group. And Lucifer was the most magnificent angel in Creation. Magnetic. Persuasive. Angry. He hated the attention shown to them—the humans. The favoritism. And how angels were increasingly being shoved into the background in favor of these backward, inept humans."

Jack looked sad.

"Jack," said Talia, leaning against his ear. "She's talking about how she felt in the early days. Not now."

He nodded, but Talia could tell that her words hurt. Because she was like a mother to him. His own mother's love had been conditional and most of the time, she'd used it like a weapon against him.

Kushiel gazed over at Lucifer who looked up through a thick fringe of dark lashes, his sunlit hair tangling in curls around his face. Still the most beautiful angel in Creation. Who hid a dark heart and painful wounds for millennia. He listened to Berith's story with disinterest and no emotion.

"Lord Kushiel, we felt rejected by our Maker, too. Thrown over for these wingless humans that looked more like our Maker than we did. And these humans had captured the Maker's heart and attention, relegating us to duties befitting servants."

Murmurs rumbled through the gallery.

"So, you joined Lucifer's Rebellion," said Kushiel as he turned and faced the gallery. "And you fought a war on Heavenly soil with Lucifer as your commander." He snapped back around and slammed his hands against the tabletop, startling Berith. "And what did any of you hope to gain? The Maker's favor? The destruction of all of humanity? An apology?"

"Justice. A place beside the Maker, not one beneath humanity."

Noise erupted in the gallery, discordant angel notes as arguments broke out.

Berith looked past Kushiel. Up at the judgment dais. At the Maker.

"But Lord Kushiel, it took millennia for some of us to understand just how wrong we had been."

Kushiel turned back toward her. "So, you admit you were wrong?"

Berith nodded. "Of course, we were wrong. Most of us get that now. But most of us saw ourselves as beyond redemption by then. And with no path back home again, we kept…doing what we were doing. Dealing with damned souls." She brushed a strand of white hair out of her eyes. "And dreaming of former glory was our only comfort. That and planning an assault on Heaven."

Kushiel's eyebrows raised.

"So, you admit, that even now, the Fallen still plot against Heaven. Like Lucifer."

She shook her head. "No, I'm telling you how we coped, Lord Kushiel. Because none of us had ever let go of the fact that we were still right. That we had been wronged. And that only vengeance would vindicate us. And it wasn't until Jack Casey got dragged down to Hell that I had thought of anything else. That I had dreamed that anything else was possible."

Frowning, Kushiel's gaze flicked toward Jack and then back to Berith.

"What did Jack Casey do that changed your thinking, Berith?"

"I was still spouting my hurt and anger, that me and the others had been wronged. That we were exiled and lost. And Jack looked me right in the eye and asked me if I'd tried asking for forgiveness. And meaning it."

"How did you react to this human's arrogance?" Kushiel asked.

Berith smiled. "At first, I was outraged. This…this child who knew nothing about angels or Heaven, who survived on a dim hope and a blind faith, living a short life that taught them nothing about anything. This child was telling me, who had lived millennia, the simplest of solutions to fix a problem he couldn't even fathom."

She turned her head and glanced back at Jack with a bright smile that put him at ease.

"Lord Kushiel, that's when I got it. This child needed my wisdom, my guidance—my protection. I wasn't subservient to some spoiled, petulant monster favored by the Maker. I was his protector. His guardian. His teacher. Walking beside him, not bowing to his superiority. His was a simpler side of a very complex coin that none of us angels could decipher. It took that childlike point of view to see the answer."

"So, you are saying that you understood that the Rebellion had been wrong?"

Berith nodded. "Yes. But we didn't know how to make amends. We thought our Maker wanted us banished forever. That they didn't love us anymore."

The Maker bowed their head.

"But Lord Kushiel, they were just waiting for us to ask! Waiting for us to ask to come home. And we had never even tried to ask forgiveness. To ask to come home. And that's when I began to change. Because I was sorry for what happened. For the harm I had caused. I was ready to atone for it all. And I never dreamed I would get my wings and halo back."

Talia glanced over at Lucifer who looked disgusted.

"Did you share this knowledge with the other Fallen, Berith?"

She shook her head. "No, I did not. At the time, it was only a dim hope. A human hope. But Lucifer had placed me and one of his succubae in charge of protecting Jack while he was in Hell, so I decided to take Jack's advice. For the first time since the Fall, I asked for forgiveness. And I kept asking."

Kushiel frowned and bent toward Berith. "Wait, Lucifer assigned you and a succubus to protect Jack Casey in Hell?"

Lucifer rolled his eyes and looked away.

"Yes, Lord Kushiel," said Berith. "Jack wasn't a soul. He was a living human who needed food and water daily. And protection from Hell's citizens. So, I stuck close to Jack while Lucifer's succubus brought him food and water. When she couldn't, Lucifer brought it."

Kushiel's eyes darkened, anger tightening his features as his gaze snapped across the aisle to Lucifer and then back to Berith.

"And Lucifer brought food and water? The King of Hell? To a human?"

"Yes, Kushiel," Lucifer snapped as he rose from his chair. "I brought the little meatsack food and water to keep him alive. What a shocking revelation. Humans feed cattle before they slaughter them. What's your point?"

Talia chuckled at Lucifer's outrage. He was embarrassed.

"Luci even brought me a burger and fries once," said Jack. "They were delicious. But I had to pass on the apples. Too Biblical."

The gallery broke into laughter.

Even Lucifer offered a faint smile that didn't quite reach his eyes. "In hindsight, the apples were a bad choice, I'll admit."

Kushiel's gaze fixed on Lucifer as he spoke to Berith. "So, Lucifer also took care of the human he dragged off to Hell."

"Yes, Lord Kushiel."

"Any torture?"

"Yes," Jack replied. "There was."

Berith nodded. "Mostly as scare tactics. But Lucifer had me heal Jack on those occasions."

A rare smile rose on Kushiel's long, shadowy face, those rusty hawkish eyes bright with amusement.

"Minimal torture. Healed afterward. Strange behavior for the King of Hell, wouldn't you say, Berith?"

"I needed him," Lucifer shouted. "It was as simple as that, so perhaps even your stunted angel brain can grasp that hostages have to be kept alive. Lord Kushiel."

It was like Lucifer was trying to paint himself a bigger monster than he was. Was it guilt? Some strange sense of justice requiring his execution?

"So, how did Jack Casey escape from Hell?" Kushiel asked.

Berith stretched her wings and leaned against the table. "It's quite a long story, but Jack played a role."

"Called First Betrayer," Lucifer snapped. "The little meatsack betrayed me to Heaven."

"Jack pretended that Talia had gotten him captured because she'd *dumped him* as the humans say. He had all of Heaven believing he'd turned. Including Lucifer."

"How, Berith?" Kushiel asked.

"Jack convinced Lucifer that he wanted the angels dead. So, Lucifer brought Jack with him, after Jack proved his loyalty in the cage fights. Once in Heaven, Jack led Lucifer and the angels into chasing him. Into the abandoned Garden." She bowed her head. "Where he fused the lock on the gates and trapped himself and Lucifer inside."

"And I killed him for it, too!" Lucifer raged.

"Lord Kushiel," said Talia, floating above the table. "Lucifer sought to drag me off to Hell because he wanted my rare resurrect power. When Jack sacrificed himself to save me, Lucifer took him instead because he also had the resurrect power."

Kushiel blinked over to the table and stared at Talia for several moments.

"Lord Kushiel, he needed that resurrect power to resurrect fallen angels in his army. And he had to know that in the Maker's abandoned first experiment, there were all the pieces present to cast that complex ritual."

Already, Lord Kushiel was shaking his head.

"Please explain, Talia," he said. "I'm not following you."

"Lord Kushiel, he knew that I had the tools to cast resurrect—and other rare powers—that would bring Jack back to life."

Lucifer sighed and stared up at the ceiling. "Why are you angels all such marshmallows at your cores. That never even occurred to me. I wanted Jack Casey dead."

Talia pointed at him. "But you still needed him."

Lucifer rolled his eyes, holding out his shackled arms. "All right, point taken."

"Then what happened, Berith?" Kushiel continued.

"After a little seraphim magic, Talia brought Jack back. We brought Jack to Eolowen to heal and left Lucifer locked in the Garden. But Lucifer's Phoenix Shift had popped. When it completed, his wings and halo would grow back. And with his powers back, he could break the wards binding him inside the Garden."

"So, I take it that Lucifer wasn't trapped there long?" Kushiel asked.

Berith shook her head. "Not long. A couple of months or so. And then he broke out, preparing to march on Heaven."

"And in the meantime," said Kushiel. "You began working on a path to redemption."

Excited, Berith smiled as she stretched her wings wide. "Yes, through the seraphim and Azrael's guard, I atoned for my mistakes. And was granted forgiveness. And my wings and halo back."

She rose from her chair and got down on one knee.

"Thank you," she said. "For giving me a path back home again, my Maker."

The Maker's light form brightened, radiating warmth that made Berith's smile widen.

"And you were in Heaven when Lucifer marched on it with his full army?"

Berith nodded as she rose to her feet and sat back in the chair. "When he had Talia in his control. But working together, we sent Lucifer back to Hell. Interrupting his assault."

Lucifer had his head bowed, looking disgusted.

"And later, he kidnapped you, taunting Jack and Talia to come after you in Hell," said Kushiel.

Berith nodded. "I was never in danger. He just wanted Jack."

Kushiel leaned toward her, his gaze intense. "To destroy him?"

Berith shook her head. "To get him close enough to the Book of Secrets to trigger a rare angel power that opened the Gates of Hell and set the apocalypse in motion."

Talia remembered that it took Jack a while to stop blaming himself after Lucifer escaped Hell and started the apocalypse.

"Do you have anything else to add, Berith?" Lord Kushiel asked as he floated back from the table.

"Just that for some angels, we don't think that mercy applies to us," said Berith as she rose from the chair, wings in motion, and cast a long look around the courtroom—at Lucifer. "Some only know dark and exile. And their pain and self-loathing prevent them from asking for mercy—or even seeing that there is a path home."

Lucifer scoffed, the corners of his mouth briefly lifting.

"And for some, dear Berith, that moment has long passed." He gazed up at her. "Even after you have finally come home."

Berith's grey eyes grew watery. "All you have to do is ask," she said, her voice barely above a whisper. "And mean it."

"And therein lies the problem." Lucifer's voice was quiet and a little rough.

Berith cast a forlorn look at Lucifer and then turned to Lord Kushiel.

"Cherubim," he said in a soft voice, left hand motioning toward them.

They blinked beside Berith and led her from the courtroom as Pravuil leaned over the edge of the dais.

"Lord Kushiel," he called. "The Maker requests a word."

Nodding, Lord Kushiel flew to the judgment dais and knelt beside the Maker, head bowed, thumb rigorously rubbing the top of his left hand.

"What do you suppose that was about?" Jack asked, leaning close enough that Talia smelled a sultry breath of Jack's woodsmoke and cedary cologne.

Talia watched Berith disappear out the portal with the cherubim and finally, shook her head.

"I'm not sure, but I think Berith was pleading with Lucifer one last time to come home." She reached out and pulled Jack close, feeling suddenly sad. "But I think Lucifer just told her goodbye."

Jack wrapped her in his arms and held her tight.

She felt his turmoil. Things that would take him time to put into words, but she knew he felt the same rush of emotions that she did.

Lord Kushiel nodded at the Maker and stood up. He stretched his wings wide and drifted back down to the witness table where he stood at attention, hands behind his back, red-tipped wings folded against his shoulders as a Watcher angel placed a second chair at the table.

Talia stiffened and let go of Jack.

Kushiel cast a quick nod at Pravuil.

"Talia and Jack Casey, please take your place at the witness table."

Their second time in that hot seat.

Jack swallowed a breath and unfurled his wings. Reaching out, he took her hand, and together, they flew to the witness table as the gallery began a roar of angel notes.

She was grateful that Jack couldn't hear those notes. That spared him from hearing some of the hateful things hurled at them. About flaunting their forbidden relationship. Calling Jack a Nephilim. Her a human. And more.

Lucifer smiled and shook his head, the disdain burning in his eyes.

"Lord Kushiel, please control your insects in back," Lucifer said with growl. "Their narrow-minded, uninformed, and shortsighted views about the hive have no bearing here. Their pointless banter is just noise. And it's insulting."

Jack glanced back at the noise chirring from the gallery as he settled into his chair, wings folding.

"Shut your prayer holes!" Pravuil shouted. "If I don't get silence… now… I'm closing down the gallery and the perches and sending all of you outside. Last chance."

The gallery went quiet.

"That's better," Pravuil called out. "Now, check your arrogance at the door and know your place. Or I'll find a new one for you. A lot farther south than you'd like."

Lucifer's chuckle was the only sound in the room.

"Proceed, Kushiel."

Kushiel walked around the table, looking stern.

"Talia, Jack," he began, standing between them at the front of the table. "Tell me, when was the first time that you openly broke Heaven's rules with your illicit relationship."

Furious, Jack leaped to his feet, glaring at Kushiel.

"Object!"

CHAPTER 18

THIS DUDE WAS GETTING ON HIS LAST NERVE AND JACK HAD TO FIGHT down his desire to punch Kushiel in his smug, Archangel of Wrath face.

"Jack, don't!" Talia shouted.

Behind him, Lucifer's peal of laughter filled the chamber.

"You object?" Lord Kushiel shouted back at him. "You? A human?"

Jack's eyes narrowed as he stared up at Kushiel's nearly seven-foot-tall frame.

"Yes, I do," he fired back at this judgmental douchebag. "I object to your attitude and I object to you insinuating that we were sneaking around everyone's backs like a couple of sex-crazed teenagers."

A curious smile rose on Kushiel's lips. "Weren't you?"

"Since everyone in this chamber has known about my relationship with Talia from Lucifer's first wager, what do you think the answer to that question is? Lord Kushiel."

He felt Talia's hands on his arm, pulling him back toward the table. And into his chair.

But he refused. It was time that everyone in this tribunal stopped trying his and Talia's relationship. He'd had enough.

"Tough day at the office, Kushiel, ol' boy?" Lucifer replied. "Even the bloody humans are rebelling. Your Heavenly Wrath seems to be slipping."

Kushiel's eyes began glowing red, his fingers glowing white as his chest began to heave with rage.

Well, we went from *take the stand* to *smite* faster than a Maserati changing lanes on the 405 during rush hour.

Jack stood his ground, gathering every last bit of his seraphim wards into his hands, ready to throw down when Kushiel decided to take his best shot.

He'd had enough.

Suddenly Pravuil was between them. Pushing Kushiel back.

"Enough!" Pravuil shouted. "Kushiel, another word with the Maker please."

After throwing one last fiery glare at Jack, Kushiel blinked up to the judgment dais.

Pravuil turned to Jack, grabbing him by the dress shirt. "Jack Casey, do you have a death wish?" the Scribe whispered.

"I'm tired of his accusations, Pravuil," said Jack in angry whisper. "That dude doesn't want the truth. He just wants to smite something. A human. Because he's too scared of Luci to challenge him."

Pravuil pulled in a calmer breath and walked Jack back to his chair.

"Just stick to the truth, Jack," said Pravuil. "Step around his accusations and his leading questions. And tell the truth."

"I have!" Jack insisted. "This went up the chain to the Maker who was fine with it at the time. I don't answer to that gallery of insults back there and I couldn't care less what they think. Talia and I never hid our relationship. And we asked permission to wed."

Pravuil leaned in. "Let the Maker handle it."

"I was until Kushiel broke his leash."

"Wait for it," said Pravuil, patting Jack's shoulder.

He nodded and Pravuil blinked back up to the judgment dais. Where again, Kushiel knelt beside the Maker. His eyes were still a little red and a little fiery, but slowly, the fire fled.

"Jack Casey," Talia said against his ear. "If you get smited by the Archangel of Wrath, I'll kill you myself."

Jack couldn't halt a smirk from rising on his lips. He reached out and gripped her hand.

"Noted, Mrs. Casey."

In a few moments, Kushiel blinked off the judgment dais. And returned to the witness table.

There was an uneasy calm in his eyes as he rubbed his left hand with his thumb. Jack squinted,

A shadowy patch, like a deep bruise stretched across the top of his hand. Dark. And a little sinister. His thumb rasped back and forth in a nervous rhythm that made Jack uncomfortable.

"The Maker has informed me that some of my facts are..." His gaze narrowed. "Incorrect."

Jack wanted to respond, but he took Pravuil's advice and kept quiet. He gave the archangel a sharp nod for him to continue.

"The Maker acknowledges that you and Talia made several good faith efforts to...inform Heaven. And to obtain permission for your— forbidden relationship."

Jack bristled. Poking him again. He bit his tongue to keep his mouth shut.

"Continue," said Jack finally, letting the insult go.

"In addition, the Maker acknowledges that in the face of so many...concerns and questions, it has become necessary to rule on the state of this...illicit union."

Jack felt his seraphim powers roil at his fingertips and he clenched his hands into fists to try and hold back his anger. And those powers.

If he didn't, they'd label him dangerous.

He glanced at the darkening blotch on Kushiel's hand. Somebody was working Kushiel's strings. Poking the bear. Trying to get him to react.

He closed his eyes and pulled in a deep breath. Holding it. And then he exhaled, letting his anger dissipate. Smirking, he looked up at Kushiel.

"Please...continue," said Jack as Talia's hand clamped tighter on his.

Kushiel's expression darkened as he stared at Jack. Trying to agitate him, Jack knew. But he wasn't rising to this douchebag's occasion. Not today. Finally, with lips pressed into an angry line, eyes narrowing, Kushiel's gaze shot back to Pravuil as he stepped back from the table.

"All right, angels," Pravuil began. "This is a statement from your Maker because they want it spoken in this chamber and if you heard the Maker's voice, all your eardrums would explode."

Jack glanced at Talia and squeezed her hand. She nodded, biting her lip.

"Your Maker says that due to the extremely unusual circumstances surrounding angel of death Talia having a human soul and human Jack Casey's apparently ambiguous position between mortality and immortality. As well as rare powers mirrored through a bond that no one in Heaven understands—except our Maker. Because of these circumstances, Talia and Jack have the Maker's official blessing to remain together and remain married."

"Yes!" Jack shouted and threw his arms around Talia, kissing her hard on the lips.

Her face was wet with tears as she kissed him back with enough fire to blast his dress shoes into the Cloud Chamber.

"Let all of Heaven know that this relationship is sanctioned and celebrated. And anyone who feels otherwise can purchase a one-way ticket to—"

Pravuil.

The Maker's voice whispered through the chamber, but it was inside Jack's head, in his ears, and thrumming its way through every cell in his body. A full sentence might have shaken his body completely apart.

"To somewhere else," Pravuil replied, sounding annoyed. "Furthermore, Jack and Talia will gain special clearance to pass through the portal to where the risen souls reside. Because the Maker wants Jack not to be separated from loved ones who pass away. We still don't know whether Jack will live out a mortal life or an angelic eternity. If his life turns out to be a mortal one, then a mortal eternity with the risen will await him. Talia could still pass through the portal for short visits."

Short visits? Jack's stomach dropped and he cast a nervous glance at Talia. "Tal, what does that mortal eternity and short visits mean?"

She looked confused, her big, luminous grey eyes fixing him with an unblinking stare. "I don't know, Jack. I will take that up with Pravuil first chance I get. In the meantime, be careful."

Pravuil's body trembled and he turned his head toward Talia. "Talia, the Maker says you can work with Archangel Azrael to determine how much time you may spend on Earth. Mortal or immortal, Jack will not be barred from Heaven. He can work with Archangel Azrael and the guard on any necessary parameters whenever he is in Heaven."

Murmurs were shrill and loud in the gallery.

"Your Maker has spoken. This matter is now an ex-matter. And any angel who decides to try and reopen the case of Jack and Talia's relationship will be turned away from High House and the Archive. And the Maker will have…words with said angel. So, their marriage is officially sanctioned. And closed. Says your Maker."

Talia threw herself into his arms and he held her against his chest, shaking.

It was over. It was finally over. He and Talia could be together for the rest of their days. But that part about a mortal eternity and short visits nagged at him. After this trial ended, he'd bring it up with Pravuil, too.

"Kushiel, do you have any more questions for these witnesses?" Pravuil asked.

Kushiel cast his withering gaze around the courtroom as the gallery went suddenly silent. His gaze stopped on Lucifer who looked through him, that devilish smile unnerving.

And Jack worried that Lucifer still had one last plan in motion.

"No, Scribe."

"You may return to your seats, Jack and Talia. That concludes witness testimony."

Hand in hand, Jack and Talia blinked back to the table with Azrael who hugged Talia and shook Jack's hand.

"The defense rests, Lord Kushiel," said Lucifer. "Do your worst."

Lord Kushiel straightened his lean body to his full seven-foot height and blinked onto the dais where he huddled with Sarathiel, Sidriel, and Pravuil. The Maker remained in their place.

The conference took only moments. Finally, Kushiel blinked down from the dais and moved slowly across the aisle. Stopping in front of Lucifer.

Lucifer's gaze flicked upward. Sullen. Distant. Steady.

"Lucifer Morning Star," said Kushiel, hands behind his back. "The Fallen One. The Lightbringer. The King of Hell."

Lucifer's glare sharpened, his mouth flattening into a tense line.

"Heaven and the Maker find you guilty on all charges."

As the verdict traveled through the courtroom and echoed through the gallery, the intense silence became unnerving.

"Judges," Pravuil called from the dais. "It is time to cast your vote for sentencing."

Two cherubim blinked into the courtroom carrying a small brazier with a shimmering gold basin. On one side of the basin, five white flames guttered. One the other side were five curled white feathers.

"One by one," said Pravuil. "I ask you to choose Lucifer's punishment by tossing either a mote of white flame for the Lake of Fire or a feather to spare him."

The low, rhythmic thrum of angel notes began in the back of the gallery.

"Tal," Jack said, leaning against Talia. "What are they chanting?"

She looked at him with a dark expression. "Flame."

Jack nodded. It's what he'd expected. His gaze traveled around the room, at the seven angel statues each bearing a word.

"Tal, what are those words on the statues and the wall again?"

"Archangel Sarathiel," said Pravuil. "Approach the brazier and cast your vote."

Sarathiel floated down from the judgment dais and hovered in front of the brazier. He seemed resigned as he cast one last look at Lucifer and then turned back to the brazier. He swept up a mote of white flame.

And tossed it into the basin. It flared, guttering, and then settled against the fragrant dried jasmine and honeysuckle lining the bottom of the bowl.

"The words are: penance, communion, faith, truth, freedom, justice, and love. And the words on the wall say, For All."

Again, these were the tenets that Heaven lived by. But seeing the word love there still made him squirm. It didn't seem to have a place in this chamber. Or in Heaven. And that bothered him. A lot. Everything good came out of that word and here it was just an Enochian symbol decorating the room. Almost an afterthought.

"Archangel Sidriel," said Pravuil. "Cast your vote."

Archangel Sidriel blinked down from the dais and approached the brazier. She stared at it for a long time, her gaze flicking from flame to feather. Until finally, with hand shaking, she lifted a mote of white flame and dropped it into the bowl.

It flared with a burst of white light and settled against the soft crackle of dried jasmine and honeysuckle.

"Lord Kushiel," said Pravuil as he descended the dais.

Lord Kushiel stood in front of the brazier only a moment. He cast a look up at the Maker as he pulled a mote of flame from its holder and tossed it into the basin. It roiled with white flames and dimmed.

"I will now cast my vote," said Pravuil.

The Scribe looked a little sad and remorseful as he approached the brazier. Finally, he turned toward Lucifer, as if he were looking for one reason, no matter how small, to pluck one of the feathers from its holder and toss it into the bowl.

Lucifer's gaze was like granite until finally he gave Pravuil a slight nod.

The Scribe's mouth twisted as he turned back to the brazier. And took a white mote of flame and dropped it into the bowl.

Then he froze a moment, his head snapping upward, eyes closing.

He shuddered for a moment or two and then opened his eyes. He cast an uncertain look at the Maker who nodded.

Only then did Pravuil turn back to face the courtroom.

"The Maker has asked to abstain from voting," he announced to a whole lot of buzzing angel notes throughout the gallery.

Jack gave Talia a confused look but she just shrugged, shaking her head.

"The Maker has instead asked that a proxy vote in their place."

"A proxy?" Jack whispered.

"Why wouldn't the Maker cast their vote?" Talia replied. "It's just prolonging the outcome."

Yeah. Talia had a point. Was it a needlessly cruel delay—even for the King of Hell—or was there a really good reason to have someone vote in their place?

Pravuil pointed at Jack. "Jack Casey, the Maker has asked that you vote in their stead."

Lucifer looked horrified. "Jack Casey?" He smashed his eyes closed.

"Come on, Jack," said Pravuil with a shrug. "Approach the brazier."

Jack rose from the chair and moved toward the aisle where the judges still clustered and stopped in front of Pravuil.

"Dude, you sure about this?" he said in a quiet voice. "I'm just a human."

Pravuil shrugged. "The Maker said that's why they wanted you to vote in their stead. It was only fair that humanity have a vote as well."

Jake nodded, feeling uncomfortable as he stood in front of the brazier. He looked up at Pravuil.

"Focus on the tenets around the room and do them justice, Jack," said Pravuil. "That's all you can do."

Jack looked up, his gaze settling on each angel statue and its Enochian symbol as Talia's voice filled his head with the words. She was projecting them back to him from her chair. He turned and looked at each one.

Lucifer had his face in his hands.

After Jack looked at the last one, he turned his gaze to the wall.

For all.

He turned his gaze toward the brazier. Four motes cast into the bowl. Five feathers in their holders.

"Guess it's pretty clear how Heaven feels," he said, motioning at the flames churning in the basin.

Again, he looked over at the statues.

"I keep looking at your tenets. Penance. Communion. Faith. Truth. Freedom. Justice. Love. And I've seen all of them in action in Heaven. All of them but one. Love."

Buzzing began in the gallery.

"Heaven, time and again, was ready—and eager—to call the love I felt for Talia wrong. Impure. Unnatural. At every turn, they told Talia it was forbidden. Illicit. Against everything that Heaven stands for. And yet, I see love on this wall. Just the word love. No conditions. No rules. No constraints. Well, one actually." He pointed up at the wall with the words For All. "That one. It says for all."

He turned toward Pravuil and the judges.

"But throughout this tribunal, Heaven wanted us punished for this relationship. So, if love isn't for all in Heaven, or just for all full stop, then who's it for? I love Talia more than my own life. I'd fight for her to my last breath. And I never want to live even an hour without her. She is the love of lifetimes. She's a piece of my soul. She's a part of my heart that will never beat again without her. And yet, Heaven was all set to tear us apart over the letter of some law. Some tenet. I didn't even know Talia was an angel until I was so in love with her that I never wanted to be without her."

Pravuil patted Jack's shoulder. "And the Maker has officially sanctioned your relationship, Jack."

Jack frowned. "What about everyone else, Scribe? Other relationships that angels and humans may feel they have to hide because of that lame rule about love being forbidden."

Pravuil glanced up at the Maker and then back at Jack, shaking his head. He didn't have answer or a response. Not that Jack had even expected one.

"See, that's the problem, Pravuil. The whole time I've fought for Heaven, fought beside Talia and her guard, one message has resonated across the lower Heavens. Even with the seraphim. Love frees all. And this room says *for all*."

A burst of red and gold light filled the edge of the platform as Seraphina's plume of seraph power roiled through the space. Jack smiled. She was casting her agreement. He felt it.

Again, he faced the brazier. "And here we are, determining Lucifer's fate as all these words burn through this room. Love doesn't free all in Heaven. It only frees some."

The voices in the gallery grew louder.

"Maker," said Jack, turning his gaze up toward the judgment dais. "Hope you don't smite me for this, but you chose me to vote in your place. So, I have to say this. Love only frees some. Because if it really, truly freed everyone, you would see that you made Lucifer who he is. You made him do what he did."

"Jack!" Pravuil gasped.

"I'm not excusing a single thing Lucifer's done or asking anyone to forget any of it. Because it's a lot. But you made humans in your image and the difference between your angels and humans is love. You taught us humans to love, but you never taught your angels how to love. You forgot that step when you told them about their new little brothers and sisters. That you doted on while kind of pushing them aside."

Pravuil stepped in front of Jack and turned to face the Maker.

"Please, forgive his humanity," said Pravuil. "He doesn't mean to—"

Pravuil shuddered like he'd been shocked and then he stepped back.

"They said for you to continue," said Pravuil, a little surprised.

Jack cast a humble look up at the Maker. "I don't mean to criticize or insult the Creator of the entire universe. I'm just saying that maybe if you'd shown that love to your angels, starting with Lucifer, he'd have championed humans instead of loathing us. All the dude really wanted was his father's love. And he responded by trying to take everything you loved more than him apart."

The noise in the gallery was growing in volume and pitch. Jack ignored it.

"All I'm saying is that if Love Frees All is the tenet that Heaven lives by, then it's gotta free all. Not some. And if you throw Luci here into the Lake of Fire, then you're saying Love Frees Some."

He glanced at the brazier and cast one last look at the Maker. And then he plucked a white feather from the other side. And tossed it into the basin. Where it floated above the fire, turning gently in the warm updraft of the four fire motes below."

Pandemonium erupted through the gallery, forcing the cherubim guard to rush in and subdue the chamber.

When he sat down beside Talia, he expected her to be furious. She wrapped him in her arms.

"Jack, that was beautiful," she whispered in his ear.

"I'm sorry, Talia," he said. "I may get smited, but I had to be honest."

"You did great, Jack," she said, kissing him.

Kushiel looked unfazed. "Four flames and one feather," he announced. "The decision has been made."

But the room dimmed as Pravuil's body began to shudder and shake, a white light emanating from every pore.

The Maker! Speaking through Pravuil.

"As much as I struggle against your words, Jack Casey, I cannot deny that there are certain truths in your direct if not limited world view. In the Beginning, with a capital, I made mistakes. And one of those mistakes was how I introduced angels to humans. And I inadvertently led my angels to think that my love stopped with my human creations. So, with a heavy heart, I must take some responsibility for what Lucifer became. And the other angels who fell with him that day that broke my heart. It was a very long time before my anger cooled."

Jack nodded. "I could never even begin to understand how any of this must have felt. And I apologize for my oversimplification. But if you throw Lucifer into that Lake of Fire, then you're saying that Love Frees Some. If it truly frees all, then it has to free Lucifer, too. You have to give him that chance at redemption. You have to extend that love to him or take these words down from your walls because these tenets mean nothing."

Murmurs and whispers exploded through the gallery, a chorus of angelic harmonies and melodies filling the space.

Kushiel knelt in front of Pravuil. "But Maker, the decision is made. Four votes to one. His fate is oblivion. The Lake of Fire."

"In all of the Heavens today," the Maker continued through Pravuil. "Only one of you was willing to speak for Lucifer—yes, I hear the views of the angels in the gallery, too. But only one of you was willing to grant forgiveness to the most loved once of my angels. To my firstborn. Who became the most feared angel in Creation. Who sought to destroy it all. Only one of you was willing to risk mercy to the worst of us. Love Frees All is Heaven's most fought for tenet and I will not sacrifice that tenet for the others. Nor will I risk all of Heaven and Creation to a heart unwilling and unworthy to embrace that tenet."

Pravuil paused as a heaviness descended on the courtroom, intensifying Jack's anxiousness. He glanced at Talia whose gaze was fixed on Pravuil, eyes wide with shock, her beautiful mouth pursed.

"But...little moments of hope and worthiness emerged in this trial," Pravuil continued and Jack pulled in a breath. "Small kindnesses, care and protection of the weak, and respect for souls and immortals. For consent and free will. Flickers of remorse and regrets. Glimmers of light in a dark heart, dark from millennia of pain and grief like so many of the Fallen who gave up hope for redemption. For forgiveness. Those glimmers of light deserve a chance at redemption. Jack Casey's white feather will stand. Because on this day, it weighs more than all four flame motes combined."

"What?" Kushiel rose to his feet. "Maker, what are you saying?"

"I command that Lucifer be given one chance at mercy. At redemption. Lucifer, I am placing you under the authority of Archangel Azrael and I command that you spend time shepherding humans in their most difficult time by crossing them over from human to spirit. And if you can truly be saved, it will be reflected there. In Eolowen. With my angels of death. Azrael, do you accept this arrangement?"

Jack glanced over at Lucifer. He looked shocked. Stunned. His eyes were glassy as he stared up at the Maker. At his father.

"Yes, Maker," Azrael called out. "Lucifer will have a place in Eolowen and we will work out a plan to integrate him within the guard."

"Lucifer," said the Maker. "You and I have many things to discuss. Show me, my firstborn, that my mercy has been justified. That you can be redeemed. That Love Frees All."

Lucifer nodded, but Jack saw that he was too overwhelmed to speak.

With a burst of white light, the Maker left Pravuil. He looked a little dizzy and confused, but he recovered quickly.

"You heard the Maker!" Pravuil shouted to the courtroom. "The verdict has been cast. Cherubim, Azrael, Lucifer, we have things to discuss."

Kushiel looked furious. Probably because he didn't get to body slam anyone else with his Heavenly Wrath.

Cherubim began ushering out the shocked silent gallery of angels through the portal.

But Kushiel's scream tore through the courtroom, making everyone freeze. As a black shadowy shape burst out through his left hand.

Cherubim rushed forward, surrounding the shadow that began to take solid form. Another force of eight cherubim encircled the judgment dais—and the Maker.

Until Jack saw Raum standing at the front of the gallery, black wings extended, red halo spinning like it was on overload. A red haze undulated around him. Some sort of demonic ward…like Jack had seen Zanth summon before. That worried him. Did this arrogant hell spawn carry the powers of an archdemoness—and an archangel or seraphim? He had been controlling Kushiel all along. Possessing him. And now, Jack wondered how much had been Kushiel and how much had been Raum.

"I come bearing a gift and a message from the new King of Hell."

Raum looked amused with himself, his condescending gaze

washing over the crowd as cherubim moved in closer. He held up both hands, cupping an eerie black flame in each palm.

"Archangel Samael sends his regrets that you've chosen not to execute Lucifer. But no matter. Lucifer's time is over. Samael wants you to know that he's putting things back on track."

Lucifer was on his feet, fury white hot in his steel blue eyes, a murderous look darkening his features as his chains rattled.

"That half-witted, battery-powered windup angel who changes his mind like his loyalties?" Lucifer was furious. "He's a simpleton who lacks the capacity for original thought and can't function without the adoration of idiots. You're mad. I'll crush him. That's a promise."

Raum lifted his hands toward the ceiling. "And here is the gift I've brought you. On deck and ready to launch."

A horrible, otherworldly soprano chant echoed as it passed over the High House dome. Every angel in the courtroom looked toward the ceiling, horror shining in their eyes.

Jack glanced at Talia who had turned ghostly white, her intense grey eyes filling with fear as she stared up at the ceiling.

"Talia, what is that?"

"No," she whispered. "Not yet. Not now."

Horrified expressions rose on the judges' faces as Azrael moved in closer to Jack and Talia. He looked unnerved, too.

More cherubim blinked into the courtroom. Surrounding Raum.

"Archangel?" said Jack, hoping someone had an answer for him.

Azrael's face paled. "Jack…it's the Seventh Flight. The arrival of Samael's Nephion has launched the halted Seventh Flight. Twenty-four hours after they take flight from Heaven, they will empty the seventh bowl upon the Earth."

Jack frowned. But they'd disarmed all of the Seven Travelers' payloads, stopping the Seventh Flight from taking to the air. Halting the apocalypse. Stopping all seven plagues!

"But Azrael," he replied, his gaze flitting from the ceiling and back to Azrael. "There is no seventh bowl. We disarmed all the payloads. All of you keep telling me that paused the apocalypse."

Raum burst into a fit of laughter.

Azrael shook his head, his gaze locked on Raum who looked so smug, like he controlled all of this. Like he was untouchable.

"All true, Jack."

Jack grabbed hold of Azrael's sleeve. "So, are you saying that this last flight of angels is still gonna drop a shit-ton of death onto my world after all? That we failed to stop the last payload?"

"No, it's worse than that, Jack," said Azrael.

Talia wrapped her arm in Jack's and pulled him close as she turned to Azrael. "Azrael, explain. You're not making sense. We don't understand."

Raum laughed. "Of course, you don't. You weren't expecting Archangel Samael to outsmart you." He fixed Jack with his condescending dark gaze, eyes beginning to glow red.

"And you weren't expecting Lucifer to give two weeks' notice while you were planning a surprise weekend getaway to Armageddon, did you, Watcher?" Jack fired back at him.

"Watcher?" Raum smiled. "That's stupidly charming."

"Jack's right," said Talia, glaring at Raum. "That's why you're doing this. Because we interrupted your Armageddon timetable. Now, you're forcing it back on schedule by recalling the Seventh Flight. I think the Maker will have something to say about that."

"Clever, angel," said Raum as he fixed Talia with his piercing gaze. "The Seventh Flight has returned at my command, ready to take flight. And their payload is setting Armageddon in motion. The final battle between Heaven and Hell will still go on as planned...the fight between Light and Darkness. Good and Evil. Where I will lead evil to victory."

Talia stood her ground. "We'll never let you get that far. The Maker decides when the world ends, not you."

Raum motioned toward the empty judgment dais. "The Seventh Flight has already risen—it's too late to stop it. In three angel days, the Seventh Flight *will* take that flight from Heaven and fly over the Creation. Signaling the assembly of armies for the final battle that will lay waste to the Creation. Victor takes the spoils." Raum chuckled. "Loser is put to the sword as the world ends."

Surely the Maker had a big red abort button to push. Didn't they?

"Who are you?" Azrael demanded, soot-colored wings stretched wide, fury igniting in those charcoal grey eyes.

Raum couldn't contain his grin, those dark flames still roiling in his palms. "You already know who I am, archangel."

Dude had been controlling the Archangel of Punishment like a cheap dollar store hand puppet. And now, he faced off with the Maker and all of Heaven like it was just another Thursday night in L.A. This dude wasn't even an archangel. Jack had no clue where Raum fit into the hierarchy of angels and how he compared to Kushiel, Abaddon, or even Lucifer. But if Samael was Hell's new king, then there was only one way to stop this…

Heaven had to neuter this Nephion—and Samael—fast.

Or get the Maker to nuke them from orbit.

"The beast," Talia whispered.

"Why would you fight for a pathetic douchebag like Samael who isn't even strong enough to control Hell's demons?" Jack demanded. "He's lost more battles than any angel in Heaven. But he's got that retreat maneuver down to a science. Why bat for the losing side?"

Raum's face darkened as he glared at Jack, hatred burning in his red eyes.

"Because he's my father."

Lucifer gritted his teeth and pointed at Raum, shackles rattling. "And you tell that inferior little traitor that I'm coming for him. Once and for all."

A squad of cherubim in angel form emerged from the vertical gallery and blinked toward Raum, swords raised.

Raum threw the black flames in his palms at the floor and released waves of smoke, vanishing in the dark, choking plumes. Just before the cherubim guard reached him.

Jack pulled Talia close as cherubim stomped out the fire and the smoke cleared. Samael had been busy while Heaven tried to save the world. While everyone was trying to stop Lucifer from killing the Maker, that backstabbing coward, Samael pulled out the jumper cables and found a way to jumpstart Armageddon. After he'd fathered this Nephion beast.

Armageddon was the big fight. The all-out final, pay-per-view battle between good and evil, gloves off, pleasantries tossed, and weapons drawn. Where Luci was supposed to run around and do his worst. But the bad guys didn't expect him to end up in chains. In Heaven's custody.

And win or lose, Armageddon ended the world.

Jack sighed. Apparently, his world couldn't exist without both good and evil. His whole life, he always thought that these things were symbolic and figurative at best and well beyond his lifetime at worst. Regardless, this war was against the totality of evil. And it would make the apocalypse look like a bad day at the office.

Somehow, they had to take down Samael and his evil beast spawn before they took the field and triggered the end of all things. Maybe if Heaven took down Samael and Raum, they could end this thing before it began? Preempting Armageddon.

But they'd come after his powers for a reason. Maybe it wasn't Samael who needed his rare powers? Maybe it was Raum? Maybe Hell's intern needed Jack's seraphim powers to win this battle?

Had to be…why else would they try to deep fry him and Lucifer both in the Lake of Fire. Because Lucifer could crush Samael. So could Talia's rare powers and Jack's seraphim powers. The bad guys needed those powers. And Jack was betting the farm that without stronger abilities, Raum could be defeated like his pops. Before this final battle began.

But they had to take them down before the Seventh Flight flew over Earth.

That's why Samael and Raum were throwing gears and running stoplights, trying to get this race on the track and to the checkered flag before Heaven responded. Sort of like winning the match on a technicality.

None of it felt real and all Jack could think about was his life on Earth that had just shattered into pieces. He longed to move into that newly renovated beach house with his wife. The love of his life. Talia.

He also needed to start auditioning for his next role—after *The Cinderella Hour*. And he needed to coordinate with his sisters to give Talia the perfect first anniversary gift.

Dammit, he still had things to do! And he wasn't finished with this world yet! Stupid Armageddon.

"We have to take the fight to Samael and Raum," said Talia, looking pale and frightened as she stared at Jack and Azrael. "Now. Before the Seventh Flight touches Earth."

"And before Samael fast-tracks the end of the world," Jack added.

That meant returning to Hell. But this time, they would empty the place like a celebrity estate sale.

The End of THE ANGELIC ANNIVERSARY SHOW: A Game of Lost Souls, Book Twelve

The series concludes in the explosive last book...

THE PERDITION PICTURE SHOW: A Game of Lost Souls, Book 13 (Series End)

AWARD-WINNING BESTSELLING AUTHOR
LISA SILVERTHORNE
THE PERDITION PICTURE SHOW
A GAME OF 13 LOST SOULS

Novels by Lisa Silverthorne

Standalones:
ISABEL'S TEARS
LANDFALL
PACIFIC BLUE TATTOO

A Game of Lost Souls series:
THE CINDERELLA HOUR
THE PRINCE CHARMING HOUR
THE EVER AFTER HOUR
THE FALLEN HEARTS SEASON
THE RISING SPIRITS SEASON
THE ETERNAL SOULS SEASON
THE ROYAL WEDDING HOUR
THE HEAVENLY HONEYMOON HOUR
THE DIVINE NEWLYWEDS SHOW
THE CELESTIAL COUPLES SHOW
THE ENOCHIAN APOCALYPSE SHOW
THE ANGELIC ANNIVERSARY SHOW

Curse and Crown series:
THORN & BLADE
STORM & STEEL

The Spiral series:

BETWEEN

REPRISE

AVENGE

The Resurrectionist Papers

GRAVE RECKONING

Short Story Collections

THE SOUND OF ANGELS

THE MAGIC OF ORDINARY THINGS

TIMELESS

Science Fiction Writing as L.S. Silverthorne

Standalones:

REDISCOVERY

Experiencing True Purple series:

RECOMBINANT, Book 1

HELIX, Book 2

SPLICE, Book 3

FORTHCOMING!

A Game of Lost Souls series:

The Perdition Picture Show, Book Thirteen (Series End)

Curse and Crown series:

Flame & Dagger, Book Three

Frost & Foil, Book Four

Curse & Crown, Book Five (Series End)

The Spiral series:

Ruin, Book 4

Descent, Book 5 (Series End)

The Resurrectionist Papers:

Corpses Delicti

Stiffed Again

Cease and Deceased

SCIENCE FICTION WRITING AS **L.S. SILVERTHORNE**

Experiencing True Purple series:

Cipher, Book 4

Renascence, Book 5 (Series End)

ABOUT THE AUTHOR

LISA SILVERTHORNE, an award-winning bestselling author, has published over 25 novels and 150 short stories and novelettes in many genres. She is the author of *A Game of Lost Souls* series, *Experiencing True Purple* series, *The Spiral*, *The Resurrectionist Papers*, and a new series, *Curse and Crown*. She lives in Las Vegas, Nevada.

Before you go, you are invited to please leave a **review of this book**!

Reviews are a wonderful way to help an author. They are also an exciting opportunity to share your honest thoughts with other readers, so **please post yours,** in as many places as possible!

Thanks for reading! We appreciate your support!

facebook.com/lisa.silverthorne.author
bookbub.com/profile/lisa-silverthorne
amazon.com/author/lisasilverthorne
tiktok.com/@lisasilverthorne
bsky.app/profile/lisasilverthorne

www.ingramcontent.com/pod-product-compliance
Lightning Source LLC
Chambersburg PA
CBHW060648190726
48289CB00002B/319